HOWELL GRANGE

HOWELL GRANGE

THE HOWELL FAMILY SAGA

BRUCE HARRIS

The Book Guild Ltd

First published in Great Britain in 2019 by
The Book Guild Ltd
9 Priory Business Park
Wistow Road, Kibworth
Leicestershire, LE8 0RX
Freephone: 0800 999 2982
www.bookguild.co.uk
Email: info@bookguild.co.uk
Twitter: @bookguild

Typeset in Adobe Garamond Pro

Printed and bound in the UK by TJ International, Padstow, Cornwall

ISBN 978 1912881 918

British Library Cataloguing in Publication Data.
A catalogue record for this book is available from the British Library.

Bruce Harris grew up in the north-east of England and started writing after a career in teaching and educational research which included some journalism. He has published three collections of award-winning short stories, *First Flame* (2013), *Odds Against* (2017) and *The Guy Thing* (2018), and three poetry collections, *Raised Voices* (2014), *Kaleidoscope* (2017) and *The Huntington Hydra* (2019). For details, see www.bruceleonardharris.com

CONTENTS

PREFACE

Howell Grange, the long-standing seat of the Northumbrian Howell family, was extensively developed from a farmhouse belonging to the adjacent Harrington estate, which explains why certain parts of the inner house rightly appear to pre-date the rest of it. The three triangular arches are all presented in Tudor-like black beams against a white background, rather incongruous against the grey slate of the roof and the grey stone which serves as a background to the middle storey and its three large square windows. Three semi-circular arches form a portico-like structure in front of the main door and a terrace in front of the house overlooks the spreading acres of countryside which still form the Howell estate.

George Howell was the eldest son of Matthew, who was until 1822 the Howell representative on the board of the company which owned extensive colliery property in the area and beyond. Matthew Howell became ill to the point where he was forced to hand control over to George. Some of his letters betray his anxieties about this; he describes George as 'headstrong' and 'too willing to ignore or circumvent existing conventions and procedures". In 1822, George was only twenty-six; profits pushed on considerably in the four years before he married, making the Howells very well off indeed, but there was already evidence, reflected here and there in the Howell papers, that George was ruthless and corner-cutting and had come to dominate the company board. When the couple married in 1826, George was thirty and Elizabeth only twenty-two. The five of their children who survived to maturity included a soldier maimed in the Crimean; a campaigner for mine safety who became a Member of Parliament and was widely reputed to have been involved in an assassination plot; an initially frail girl who was to be one of the very first female doctors in the country; a daughter who succeeded in establishing a new dynasty of her own; and another whose desperation to have children was to have tragic consequences. They and the generations who followed them were destined to travel, fight, campaign, pioneer, write, educate, develop the family's industrial base and, of course, find their own loves and fight their own battles, spreading the family connections across Britain and beyond, including the other side of the Atlantic, by the end of the nineteenth century. Not all of the Howells were virtuous and law-abiding, nor were the choices they made always wise or purposeful. These chronicles visit the family at historical intervals, choosing momentous or significant days to reflect the point reached in the family's history.

1

DESPERATION – 1844

SATURDAY 20 JULY 1844, 11.25AM

George Howell and his family are waiting for the arrival of Elizabeth Howell's parents, Sir John and Lady Charlotte Harrington. George is standing, and in front of him, sitting down, is his wife Elizabeth. Only one of the Howell children, the eldest, Charles, aged fifteen, known to everyone except his parents as Charlie, has been allowed to join the welcoming committee.

Elizabeth Howell looks tense and shaken, and her left shoulder, where George is resting his hand, is slightly dropped, as much of a disgusted withdrawal from her husband's hand as she dares exhibit. She is pale and unsettled, and has uncharacteristically chosen to sit while waiting for her parents.

Charles Howell's gaze seems at first the conventional filial devotion of a young boy for a rich and successful father, but at closer quarters, there is a hardness in the eyes which could be fear, hardly surprising if George conforms to the uncompromisingly harsh ideas of fatherhood common at the time, which he does, but could just as easily be contempt, as if the boy is afraid for others apart from, or perhaps as well as, himself. His physical separation from his parents suggests a reluctance to be too close to them.

George himself, bareheaded and moustachioed without an accompanying beard, is a fiercely handsome man whose staring eyes and slightly turned head are indicating a growing impatience. If he is at all aware of his wife's disgust and tension, he shows no sign of it. He stands with one hand on his wife's shoulder and the other grasping his lapel as if conscious of being essentially the owner of the scene and everyone in it.

The forthcoming meeting he anticipates with Sir John might, he knows, involve some dissension and dispute, but George does not let a proper respect for an older and more eminent man mutate into fear. Elizabeth's eyes are also straying occasionally in the direction of her eldest son; he has presented himself on time and in the decent clothes required of him, but she knows how very easily the relationship between father and son can turn to antagonism, and she feels that her day has already had more unhappiness than she can easily assimilate.

Standing only just inside the portico, ready to help and greet when called upon to do so, is the Howells' second son, Francis, a pale, green-eyed, ascetic-looking boy of thirteen, who is watching his elders with some anxiety; he also knows how easily his brother and his father can arrive at confrontation, and he is aware enough that something has upset his mother, though it is not for the reason he thinks it is; such is being thirteen.

Discreetly watching a little way back from the library windows which overlook the front entrance are the eldest two Howell daughters, twelve-year-old Charlotte and ten-year-old Anne, both neatly and carefully, but not ostentatiously, dressed; their grandmother Lady Charlotte particularly abhors ostentation in young girls. Anne is more mobile and more anxious than her sister; her darting little eyes and quick, nervous hands reflect her impatience with waiting. Charlotte's hands are folded and immobile in front of her, and her eyes, with the same irate darkness of her father's, are focused firmly on the drive approaching the Grange, except for the odd irritated dart at her sister.

The third Howell daughter, five-year-old Alice, is where she almost invariably is and has been since birth – in bed. Like three other Howell offspring who did not get as far as their third birthday, in one case as far as his first, it has been universally believed of her that she will not linger long in the world to which she has so recently arrived, but, to everyone's amazement, her wasted, waif-like figure is still with them, and her habitual defiance may well see her appear at her bedroom window, on the right of the library windows and well towards the eastern extremity of the Grange, to wave to her arriving grandparents, regardless of what her nurse might think about it. From where he stands, Francis can see her window and his eyes are flickering up towards it from time to time. He cannot acknowledge it to himself without a certain puzzlement, but it is most certainly little Alice who has become the easiest sister for him to talk to, strange as it seems, and his relentless ache of anxiety about her health is almost as persistent as his mother's. Charlotte, he knows, will do well enough; Anne doesn't inhabit any world that he knows anything about, and Charlie – Francis sighs, as quietly as he can manage, which is what he almost invariably does every time he thinks about Charlie.

Charlie begins to move towards the approaching coach and is immediately ordered to stay where he is by his father. Charlie shoots a look in his father's direction which, happily, George doesn't see, concentrating as he is on a properly dignified greeting; not only is his father-in-law immensely important in his life, he is, as ever, adamantly determined that the distinguished Harringtons will always see his family in their best possible light. Charlie pulls as ugly a face as he dares behind his father's back. In the library, Anne sees it and giggles; Charlotte sees it and purses her lips. Inside the portico, Francis shakes his head and sighs to himself again. Between his brother and his father, the day is once again developing in the way that most days do, and it might again be the rest of the family who have to pick up the pieces.

SATURDAY 20 JULY 1844, 8.46AM

Elizabeth made her way gratefully back to the suite which was the very personal domain of herself and George alone, apart from the inevitable servants. The morning so far had been tiring and demanding. Mrs Granger, the cook, showing her usual tendency towards near panic on the big occasions, had allowed preparations to lag way behind schedule and it had now become necessary for every available hand, including two of the children, to lend a hand in food and table preparations, mainly under the capable supervision of Armstrong, though the butler's disdain for having to stray into the actual kitchen area was plain enough. Elizabeth had discovered early in her marriage that being mistress of a fine house, while replete, of course, with generous compensations, was nevertheless a full-time and arduous business requiring a broad range of skills from diplomacy to organisation, and as the looming cloud of the quite astonishing age of forty edged closer and closer, her tiredness was becoming more frequent and more debilitating.

This room, with its adjoining bathroom and dressing room, was increasingly her refuge and her own personal territory. The years of child bearing were over. Two healthy sons and three daughters remained from her eight pregnancies, although one of the daughters, Alice, now aged five, had been fragile since birth and might not survive for much longer. Elizabeth considered her duty fully concluded, and the fact that George spent more and more time in the dark wooden severity of his study and its small adjoining, very simple bedroom, suggested that he thought so too. The marriage had never been particularly affectionate. George, eldest son of a well-established mine-owning family, had come wooing in the relentless, determined fashion she was later to become all too wearily familiar with, protesting that he loved her for her beauty, grace and style, and the fact that she was the greatest catch of the neighbourhood was entirely subordinate. She saw George's single-mindedness in the way he wooed her parents almost as assiduously as herself, arranging elaborate hunts and banquets and making endless direct references to the growing profitability of 'his' group of collieries, as if he was the sole partner in the business. Sir John, still essentially a gentle man and a farmer by professional inclination, came to her one night with a troubled face, his eyes with the slightly abstracted cloud of pain which was later to become ever-present.

'He is, in many ways, a loud and tiresome young man, my dear, which wouldn't be of any concern to either of us, but for the fact that he is clearly about to make a proposal to you. If you find him entirely unbearable, you know I would not, could not insist on plunging you into personal unhappiness. But he and his family are wealthy and well connected, and he is the kind of man, to give him his dues, who will work hard to keep you and the ensuing family comfortable, with every advantage accruing to your children in due course. The decision is, and will remain, yours. For the moment, I ask only that you consider it.'

Elizabeth had considered it. The only real opposition at the time was a pale, ethereal curate who seemed to appear and disappear in her life with bewildering variations of intensity and enthusiasm. Her supposedly prim manner, which her brother was all too eager to taunt her with, might well continue to shrink her possible suitors, and she was twenty-two with a younger sister already married. Feeling a little like a citadel forlornly raising a white flag, she accepted George's proposal, typically carried through with a veritable hurricane of flowers and promises of timeless devotion, theatrically on his knees next to the grand French fountain in the middle of the Harrington gardens.

Elizabeth sighed and moved through the beautiful room, mostly in careful light blues and whites, towards the windows leading on to the terrace outside. Behind a gigantic plant pot on the terrace, a dark, crouched figure shifted further round the pot away from the doors. Dan Robson had been desperately suppressing a sneeze for some minutes and his haunches, used enough to squatting in the fetid damp of the pit, nevertheless were making protests in twitches and aches. Beside him, the long, sharp and well-honed knife he'd lifted from the Robson kitchen caught a beam of sun and glistened dangerously. He caught it with his foot and edged it under his body. His heart accelerated at the approach of light footsteps. The worst, the most intense, howling madness, had subsided somewhat with the chill of the morning and he was aware enough of the realities – the stink of the clothes unchanged for a week, the agony of the foot sores under what was left of his boots – to be able to qualify this against the insane dream it had seemed to be only the day before. But he would have his dues, and if his resolve had ever ebbed in the black country night, travelling remorselessly with only vague notions of how close he was to his destination, the vision of pale, emaciated Meg stiff and arched back as if racked, the tiny stillborn child by her side, ironed his will all over again. It was enough, more than enough, of itself, without the extrication of her father and brother from that pit, a death trap even by the standards of the local collieries, her brother coming out in three pieces. That had finally broken the redoubtable will of his Meg, standing there in the pale light as the men were carted away like waste earth, causing her miscarriage and death and leaving him with five children and not a soul to take care of them while he sweated his shifts away in that wet, subterranean hell and waited his own turn. He would have his revenge on the beast Howell, the worst of the whole group of them, contemptuous of safety and determined on profit at whatever cost. Howell had taken his woman; he would take Howell's. Even in his present insanity of fury, his instinct allowed him to keep the cunning of a life-long poacher, uncaught since boyhood, when a sequence of brutal beatings taught him care. He waited, concealed in the woodland facing the front of Howell Grange, prepared to remain for as long as he needed and live on the woodland creatures. For the moment, his children were split between the houses of his brother, sister and mother, as if each of them weren't burdened enough, and if he never went back, they would have as good a chance as he could ever give them alone. He knew the layout of the Grange from the summer fairs Howell put on as a sop to the men who were spilling their blood and breaking their bones for him for the rest of the year. Even then, Howell charged them for it, with hardly a single stall which didn't need payment. Howell would make his annual speech, his brood around him, to a low murmur from the surrounding acres, but few had the guts not to clap at the end of it.

In the early morning, he saw Howell and two of his men set off in the handsome green coach he'd acquired, no doubt with some new inventive twist of bribery or extortion. Elizabeth Howell had not accompanied them. The terrace where Howell made his summer speech was connected to the Howells' private quarters, on the third floor of the house at least thirty feet from the ground. Dan reached the bottom of the wall after taking time and elaborate care to ensure that he wouldn't be seen, and he was now so dirty and encrusted in the consequences of moving and sleeping in the open that camouflage was no great problem. He looked dubiously at the ivy creepers and tested them with a few strong pulls, deciding if he could move quickly enough and find footsteps on the rough stone, he could reach the terrace. At shortly after nine, he did, immediately concealing himself, once again silent and waiting, the patient predator.

With her hand actually on the door handles of the splendid full-length French affairs which gave her almost as much pleasure as the spreading terrace itself, Elizabeth was struck by a thought, yet another troubling thought, and she turned back towards the main door into her quarters. The key was still in the lock and she turned it. She must, absolutely must, take ten entirely private minutes to herself to think and plan. She left the key in the lock to allow for the unlikely contingency that Armstrong would find something he couldn't handle and come knocking at her door. George had gone to bring her mother and father over in his usual handsome fashion and that would take at least two to three hours, depending on the state of the roads and the time they would need to wait for Lady Charlotte, who was not constitutionally capable of simply being ready to go even if she'd had three weeks' notice instead of a paltry one.

She returned to the doors leading on to the terrace and swung them open, breathing in the mingled odours of the late spring countryside even as she shuddered slightly at the cool breeze playing on her face. As she walked out on to the terrace, Dan Robson took his chance and moved in to the house, relishing the warmth and trying not to freeze and betray himself with his amazement at the luxury and beauty of the room. Checking back, he saw the woman sitting on one of the comfortable built-in benches looking down over the estate. He moved to the door leading out to the rest of the house and saw the key in it. He checked it was locked and put the key in his pocket, then scurried behind one of the stupendously and unfeasibly large armchairs. Poacher patient, totally still, he waited again.

Elizabeth was trying, yet again, to ponder rather than sorrow on her eldest son, now aged fifteen, known to his siblings and almost everyone else as Charlie, but to his father and to herself, as she could not permit herself disloyalty, as Charles. Stubborn, wilful and with an apparently unshakeable determination not to act in accordance with his class and situation, Charles continued to be a problem in spite of all attempts to deal both firmly and kindly with him. He would run with the local boys, poaching, swimming, making a nuisance of himself, fighting, smoking and drinking. The thought that had given her pause with her hands on the door to the terrace was that she hadn't yet seen Charlie – Charles – this morning, and the boy was habitually up and about early on. Beatings, admonitions, even occasional more gentle persuasions – nothing seemed to deter Charles from doing just exactly what he wanted to do. Sending him away to school had only moved the problem elsewhere. He had been at his present school for almost three years and his credit had almost run out. Both at school and at home, he was beaten ritually, mechanistically, and when he was home, however far away she managed to take herself, that endless gasping and swishing rhythm penetrated her mind. Every time he returned from school for the holidays, he seemed taller, stronger and more defiant, and it was becoming very clear that only a few more years would be needed for him to be big enough to wrestle the cane from whoever was administering punishment, even his father, if that form of discipline continued.

His sister Anne, now aged nine, had a few weeks before been bursting with something she'd seen and wanted to ask about but hadn't yet dared. Elizabeth prised it out of her gently. She and a friend, attracted by a commotion of voices on the outskirts of the village, had seen a group of boys in a clearing on the edge of the woodland surrounding the Howell estate. Crouched behind trees, they had watched, terrified, as Charlie settled a score with some local lad who'd crossed him and an unfeasibly large group watched and cheered.

'Kicking, scratching, punching, anything, Mama. And blood, especially on the other boy. Even after you could see his blood, Charlie went on hitting him, Mama. And some boys on the edge looked like they were all going to turn on Charlie. We were so worried and frightened we didn't dare move.

'Then some men got out of a farm cart, watched for a minute, then chased the boys off. They separated Charlie and the other one, Abe Slater I think it was, farmer's boy. Then Abe and Charlie wandered off with their arms round each other,

Mama. Why do they want to fight, if they finish up being friends like that?'

True enough, Charlie had all sorts of mitigating characteristics: cheerful, brave, athletic and an easy – too easy – mixer with people of all classes. He reminded her very much of what people in the family had said about her Uncle William in his boyhood, but she doubted that even William was so frequently as casually and wantonly defiant as Charles. A greater contrast between him and his dour, single-minded father could not be imagined. He had been home for the holidays for three days and had already defied his father's instructions twice; only George's busy schedule had prevented yet another beating, but it would come. And this morning, Elizabeth knew only too well, the boy had already gone off to fish, swim, fight or generally transgress with whichever of the village scruffs was available on a weekend morning. If he wasn't here when George got back, on hand and decently presented to greet his grandparents respectfully, George would hit the roof and the ensuing violence would cast a shadow over the whole day.

How much easier it would be for Charles to be in the same mould as his brother Francis, now thirteen, whose scientific leanings, gentler nature and fascination with his father's mining activities was already clear enough. The fact that neither of them were replicas of their father was a mercy in itself, though she kept the thought very much to herself. Charlotte, eleven years old, named after her grandmother and shaping up to be as pretty as Lady Charlotte had been as a girl, was, oddly enough, George's closest heir, carrying his imperial air around with her and already irritating the servants on a regular basis. She even had George's fierce dark eyes, always looking as if a storm was in prospect or just receding. Anne was bright, alert and more inquisitive than it behove a girl to be; her reckless proximity to one of those wild boy fights being a case in point. And Alice. Elizabeth's grip tightened on the cloth of her dress at the thought of Alice, now in bed again, tiny, brave, uncomplaining, a weird, pallid little saint apparently destined to return from wherever she seemed to have been unnaturally wrenched before she reached her sixth birthday. Elizabeth gazed at the handsome, verdant country spread for miles before her and tried to remember the last time she had been able to simply sit and contemplate it. However, inactivity, as ever, solved nothing; she would have to send someone to track Charlie – Charles – down, even at a time when hardly anyone could be spared, and it really wouldn't do for her to skulk away here like this and leave Armstrong to take the entire burden on himself. She headed back into the bedroom, carefully closing the door on to the terrace behind her.

As she moved back to her usual chair in the bedroom, something dark reared up directly in her line of vision like a long shadow suddenly and grotesquely appearing in an indoor room. Elizabeth Howell did not flinch easily, having been bloodied at the hunt as a child and witnessed untold bloodshed since, including her own, and she did not screech; Harrington ladies simply did not. She gasped and moved back a pace or two, her mind finally registering that the spectacle was an intruder, a very dirty man in his late thirties or forties, with the squat, powerful build of the miner and carrying a large kitchen knife. The heavy aroma of sweat and unwashed clothes which she had detected with incredulity on re-entering the bedroom was now explained, and in truth the man was only half-clothed, with gaps and tears in his ragged shirt and trousers, one or two of them verging on the indecent, and boots which were clearly in the process of disintegrating.

'Who are you and what on earth do you mean by intruding into my private quarters in this way? Explain yourself or I shall ring a bell and have you arrested immediately.'

For a moment, the lady's easy assertion of control took the man aback, and Elizabeth was contemplating how to follow up immediately when he sprung like a panicked creature from behind the chair and seized the back of her hair with one hand, pulling her head back and laying his knife across her throat with the other. She almost retched at the pain and the stink of him.

'Such a grand lady to be married to a murdering, ruthless bastard like George Howell. Keep a civil tongue with me, lady, or so help me I'll cut it right out of your throat as I stand here. Put both your hands behind your back.'

She did so, calculating that struggling might unnerve him into a conclusive act, and she felt two strands of rope tie her wrists together, immobilising them and cutting into the flesh.

'Sit down,' he said.

She obeyed and he produced a filthy rag from his pocket.

'If you make any noise other than speech, I will gag you down to the back of your throat.'

He spoke in the staccato north-eastern way, sentences consisting of no more than two or three compound words run together and the long Scandinavian 'a' vowel sounds double-syllabled, but Elizabeth had been listening to this accent since birth and had no trouble understanding him. They sat facing each other.

Dan looked at the knife, long and ridiculous in his right hand, and back to her. The woman was forbidding, perfectly still, her chin erect as she sat up stoically in her chair, her long black hair tied back quite severely. Her green eyes searched and examined, and only a few tiny hints of red in her cheeks gave any sign of the recent violence. He saw, to his wonder, that she really was not afraid and thought of what proud spirit needed to be preserved for anyone partnering such a man as George Howell. For a moment, he felt foolish and on the edge of desperation, but the vision of broken Anne rose immediately and the blind, inner madness returned as predictably as ever.

'My wife died three days ago. Just after giving birth to a stillborn child. Pale and broken like a tortured prisoner.'

'I'm sorry to hear it,' she said quietly. He grimaced.

'Are you now? But she was no fine lady such as yourself. A Blackwell pitman's daughter who had just seen both her father and her brother hauled out of a pit, no more than bits of blood, flesh and bone, one of the pits belonging to your murderous brute of a husband.'

'What was her maiden name?' He looked up to see the green eyes watching him carefully.

'What?'

'What was her maiden name?' Still, the green eyes panned over him, cool, detached.

'Field,' he snapped, his grip on the knife handle tightening in his struggle to remain dominant and a vague suspicion that this woman might be trying to make game of him. 'What of it?'

'The Fields who once had the shop, in Blackwell village?'

'Yes, right enough, though not enough of your sort ever came his way, and he wasn't good enough at crawling to the likes of you on his knees, so he finished where every man in this place finishes up unless he wants himself and his family to starve, down the pit. And the loss of him and her brother Jed was bad enough to break my Annie's heart and allow her sixth child to kill her.'

'There might have been other reasons. Some women are able to continue the interminable business year after year. Some are not. It may not have been sorrow which killed your poor wife. I used to see Annie Field playing around that shop in Blackwell occasionally. Engaging child, but a will-o'-the-wisp. For some of us, the strength just runs out.'

'What the hell do you know about it?' He was up on his feet and she saw the knife edged towards her face. 'When was the last time you saw one of your menfolk hauled out from underground in a bloody mess?'

She was suddenly up on her feet and putting her face right into his knife, her eyes flashing.

'I saw my uncle come back from Waterloo with an arm missing. I saw three of my own children die at birth, and twice I've been not much more than minutes away from the same fate as your wife. You think you are unique in suffering, you foolish man?'

Footsteps, sedate and male, were heading for the door. He forced her to sit down and stood behind her, one hand on her shoulder and the other holding the knife blade half an inch from her throat.

A discreet knock and Armstrong's deep, magisterial tone.

'Are you well, madam? I trust you are not indisposed?'

She cleared her throat and he marvelled at the clarity and evenness of her voice.

'I am just resting a little, Armstrong, before what will inevitably be a long and demanding day. Is Mrs Granger coping?'

'With a good deal of assistance, madam. I think we have restored the essential timing of the provisions and will be ready for Sir John and Lady Charlotte at the appointed time.'

'Is Charlie – Charles – in the house?'

'No, madam.'

'Well, Armstrong, can you send someone, ideally his brother if he's available, if not at least one of your more resolute underlings, to tell him that he will incur my severe displeasure if he does not present himself, suitably washed and dressed, at the arrival of my parents?'

'I will attend to the matter, madam. Will you feel able—'

'Twenty minutes at most, then I shall go to Mrs Granger personally. Thank you, Armstrong.'

'Thank you, madam.' The footsteps receded in stately, meditative fashion. Dan's grip tightened on the woman's shoulder.

'So much in charge. Such a fine matron in the service of Howell, all your luxury paid for by the blood of me and my kind. Every year, every pit, hundreds of men and boys butchered because Howell and his friends will not attend to proper safety, drying the places out, providing proper equipment, testing for gases that will explode. Year after year. Slaughter after slaughter. The worst Wrekenton pit, last April, twenty-seven men and boys blown to pieces. This January, Whitehaven, eleven more carried out in bags. Countless others, single men, mates, groups, before and since, everywhere. Did you ever look at the Wrekenton names and ages, my lady? David Kidman, aged fourteen. John Kidman, aged ten. Abraham Field, aged twelve. How about that, my good lady Howell? How would that suit, as an end for your own fine young sons?'

'We regret, of course—' she started.

'Be quiet!' he hissed and pressed the knife closer into her flesh. 'Be quiet, you Howell bitch, or I'll slit you like a young deer, so help me God!'

'Well, do it, then, damn you,' she said, clearly and defiantly. 'Five more motherless children when you hang. And the deed will make you so much superior to my husband, won't it? What was the term you used, murderous brute?'

'Hold your tongue while you still have it—'

The knife pressed ever closer into her neck. She gasped as he forced her head back, and experienced a bizarre moment of total recall.

'Dan Robson. I remember. Betty the maid reported the whole Blackwell wedding to me.'

The hand holding the knife began to shake, almost imperceptibly.

'And little as I know of Annie Field, Mr Robson, I remember one or two details, and if I am about to meet up with her again, what opinion will she have to express, I wonder, at the knowledge that her bereaved husband has just butchered a woman in cold blood?'

The knife shook very visibly now; it drew away from her throat and a great gasping sigh broke from him. She braced herself to jump from the chair to the floor and reach the door before she could stop him, or at least deflect his lunge from her head. From the corner of her eye, she felt the ropes around her hands being cut away and then the knife descend to the floor in front of her, seeming as if its pace slowed to a sedate fall in the air and taking an inexplicably long time before it flopped absurdly and silently into the carpet. She looked wildly around for him and saw that he had simply taken his place again in the chair facing her. His whole torso looked sunk in defeat as if burst. She carefully edged the knife under her chair and kept her foot on it. His eyes were fixed to the floor, like a resentful child.

He reached into his pocket and took out the room key, laying it on the small table beside her chair like a surrendered trophy.

'There. Call your lackeys. Their dogs would have me before I could be clear of your land in any case. Let's have it done. I don't care what anyone does to me now.'

Something stirred in her memory again and relief from immediate danger enabled her to make connections; she felt sure that the collapse of Field's little Blackwell shop had not been so long ago.

'How old are you, Mr Robson?' she said.

For a moment, he didn't seem to hear, then his eyes turned wearily towards her and, pained, red-rimmed as they were, she could see she was right.

'What does it matter? Twenty-seven, if it please your ladyship. Call your men. I'll dangle on a rope and be done with it.'

She turned her face away and allowed something else as strong as relief to sweep over her. The price of Howell prosperity: young women stretched on slabs, young men's smashed bodies hauled out of the dark and dirt they worked in, one young man so insane with grief as to have what she suspected was a very different nature warped out of all recognition.

She started to talk, and again, the evenness and control of her voice surprised him, though now he stared across and struggled to make any sense of her words, spent and exhausted to the point of collapse as he was.

'Both my father and I have spoken to Mr Howell about the safety of the mines, on more than one occasion. My husband, I might say, is not quite the indifferent monster you think him. He talks of negligence, proper precautions not being taken, the fact that, should the cost of maintaining the mines become too burdensome, their lack of profitability would close them and send the entire workforce to the workhouse. And the rate of death and injury is slowing, Mr Robson.'

Dan saw that he was expected to say something, and marvelled at how quickly and easily their relationship had resumed its usual class pattern.

'Yes, my lady. Whatever you say.'

Her voice continued, now sounding to him like a kind of echo in a dream, far away and more about vague sounds than words, until the actual meaning of what she was saying finally managed to communicate to him.

'You know well enough that my family have widespread interests and influence in this part of the world, quite independently of Mr Howell or any of his partners. My father, Sir John, is basically a farmer by trade and inclination and the Harringtons have vast landed interests given over to agriculture. If you wish it, I will secure you farm employment and a cottage of some description somewhere on the Harrington estates; parts of it are my sole property, I should add. I will ensure that the community in which you settle is one where your children can be put to school, and once the healthy countryside has made you more presentable, Mr Robson, I dare say you will find someone who might at least make you a dutiful wife, even if she cannot replace your dear Annie.'

He was crying now, softly, the sorrow finally breaking through the wild anger, and she hurried on.

'I am not offering you a sinecure. Farm work means long hours and hard toil. Neither will I acknowledge, at any time, my role in securing you employment; my appointed agent will come to you and execute my wishes without my direct involvement. What has happened here will never be spoken of again. If you ever return to these premises, on any pretext whatever, I will ensure that you are arrested and prosecuted, and if you ever speak to anyone at any time about my role in your new employment, a similar result will ensue.'

She saw that he had quietened, and was looking across at her with an entirely different expression on his face, a mixture of wonder and a kind of disbelieving awe.

'Children are the innocents in this, Mr Robson. Always. How right you were to refer to those poor boys who died at Wrekenton. This is another matter where progress will be made; I know well enough what Sir John thinks of it. It would be monstrous for your children to lose both of their parents in such dreadful circumstances within days of each other. No child deserves such a fate, though I don't doubt it happens too.'

The footsteps were approaching again. She sat forward, her voice dropping.

'Go now. Go the way you came, Robson, it is the only way. Things will happen as I have promised they will. Go!'

He jumped up as if struck, but paused beside her chair. He bent towards her and her foot closed in the knife, but his hand momentarily held her neck again in a very different way, which made her wonder at the contrast between the touches he was capable of. Then he was gone, and before the knock at the door sounded, Elizabeth lifted the knife from below her chair and found a very obscure niche for it in her personal dressing room. Where, she decided, it would stay, in case any other Robsons should nourish similar ideas at any time in the future. The removal of the ivy creepers, in her view unsightly and threatening to the building in any case, would also be urgently attended to. She picked the key from the table and emerged from the room almost at the very moment that Armstrong arrived outside the door. Such a pallor, Armstrong thought; she had been right to take a rest before the demands of the day.

*

On the edge of the Grange grounds, Francis and Charlie Howell were approaching the house in a bad-tempered procession of two, the younger boy urging his brother on.

'For heaven's sake, Charlie, will you get a move on? Father could be back just about any minute, and you'll be in the cart again.'

Francis was smaller and paler than his brother, with a pinched look of perpetual anxiety entirely missing from Charlie's open if slightly sardonic features, the head lifted and the chin jutting forward in reply to anything said to him in even a slightly aggressive way. The fact that this was accompanied by a broad grin suggested a certain fondness for the younger brother, even if accompanied by a determination not to take his strictures too seriously.

'So he'll thrash me, Frank. So what? My backside is tenderised, like beaten beef. One more session with his stick won't make a lot of difference one way or the other. I won't be blubbing and whimpering like some people I could mention, on the rare occasions they dare do anything they will get beaten for. In any case,' he said, moving up to the fence where Francis had stopped impatiently, 'he won't be bigger than me for much longer. Another year and I'll be taking his cane from him and snapping it in front of his eyes.'

His brother's head flounced away from him, the face turning to look towards the house, the eyes not far from tears. Charlie paused; this was a touchy reaction even by Frank's standards. Frank, he said once more to himself as he had a hundred times before, just worries too much.

'Why, whatever's the matter now, Frank?'

'You know well enough the grans are coming today—'

'Are they?' Charlie's eyes spread wide in an entirely convincing demonstration.

'Charlie, you great oaf, do you seriously mean to tell me...? Everyone's been talking about it for days...'

He noticed Charlie's even wider grin and stopped. He muttered to himself a couple of words which stretched Charlie's eyes for a different reason, as he hadn't believed they were words Francis knew.

'It pleases you to make game of me, I don't doubt.'

Charlie's big arm swung round his brother's skinny shoulders.

'Frank, old lad, you're a bit too easy to make game of, that's the trouble...'

Francis turned full on to his brother as the two of them leaned on the fence. Charlie saw an unusual colour in the other's cheeks and an equally rare flash in the clever little eyes; he smiled ingratiatingly. But Francis would not be mollified. Charlie found himself backing away a pace as the words were spat at him. 'If you know well enough that they're coming and the arrangements made, why are you deliberately late and not even dressed yet? Why do you always do this to Mother?'

Charlie looked genuinely surprised. 'Mother? What's anything here got to do with Mother? And is it so strange, Frank, that I want to keep out of the way of a father who is so endlessly brutal to me?'

Francis raised his voice and allowed himself a rare outlet of fury.

'Don't you even realise how painful Mother finds it to see the conflict, the intensity of dislike, between you and Father? You don't see her face when you are off somewhere being thrashed by him yet again. She doesn't even have to be anywhere close, Charlie, or even hear it. She feels it well enough. Next time you're sure that he's not really hurting you, perhaps you could remember that he *is* really hurting her—'

Francis saw that Charlie's eyes had drifted away from him and tutted loudly, but he couldn't stop himself from following the glance and both boys stared open-mouthed at the sight of a very dirty man in rags, far too disreputable to be a Howell servant, running out from behind the east side of the house where their parents had their private quarters.

'What the devil—'

Charlie jumped the fence and made to start chasing the man, but Francis called to him.

'He'll be in the woodland before you get anywhere near him, Charlie. Let's get inside and tell Armstrong – he can get a dog team together from the hound pack.'

The two boys ran to the house, but found themselves getting short shrift from Armstrong, who had known them both since birth and was in no sense about to be distracted from the main business of the day. A gypsy, a pedlar, fancying his chances of a berth for the night or some stolen food and thinking better of it when he saw the activity of the house and the number of people coming and going; nothing of sufficient importance to take precedence over preparing for Sir John and Lady Harrington. Armstrong repeated the words, looking very pointedly at Charlie's scruffy clothes and dishevelled appearance.

'Sir John and Lady Harrington, sir. Your grandparents. Soon to be here; very soon, sir.'

As usual, the brothers' reactions were very different. Francis accepted Armstrong's position and went to the front of the house to look out for his approaching grandparents. Charlie frowned deeply at Armstrong, a man he normally got on with effortlessly well, and immediately stormed up to his mother's room, shedding bits of mud and river from his boots on the thick carpet of the staircase.

He almost burst straight in, but a modicum of common sense intervened and he knocked energetically on the door, his hand already turning the handle. He fancied he heard a gasp of breath and a rustling noise, as if she was placing herself to receive visitors.

'Very well, Armstrong. What problem have we now?'

'It's Charlie, Ma. Sorry. Charles.' He pushed the door open and she was in the familiar chair, but the handkerchief twisting in her hand, the pale complexion and the eyes either near to or just beyond tears stalled him for a moment where he stood. This was not familiar territory at all. He paused uncertainly, his hand still holding the door jamb.

'An unknown intruder in the grounds, Mother, and Armstrong seems unwilling to do anything about it. I think perhaps I should insist, on your authority.'

The little jump he fancied she gave on the word 'intruder' was so nearly imperceptible that he let it pass immediately. When her face turned fully to him, he could see that she really was genuinely upset about something, Mother who was always so easily, loftily in charge of everything, and a sudden spasm of childish panic went through him.

'You will do no such thing. My goodness, Charles, do you presume so much? Armstrong has been valiantly mustering this entire household for the visit of my parents – your grandparents – for some hours now, weathering one crisis after another, including your own inexplicable absence, and you expect him to drop everything to have people chasing after some gypsy or tinker trying his luck from the shelter of the woods? And look at the state of you, treading filth all over the house, and their arrival now so imminent—'

She broke off, and the cracking voice, the now wildly twisting handkerchief, the gleam of her distraught eyes, scared him even further and he dropped to his knees like a suitor before her, reaching a hand out to touch her arm.

She looked down at him. As always, he was the very picture of rude health, the flush of the outdoors on his cheeks and the astonishingly alert wide eyes. As usual, he carried an aroma of the outdoors about him, fresh air and greenery with a touch of the less salubrious ingredients of the bank and the river itself. But she could see that she had, for once, penetrated the armour of his masculine bravado. The opportunity presented itself, and she took it.

'I really did hope against hope that today would be about harmony, that your grandparents could visit in peace and amity, and now, no doubt, the whole day will be sacrificed to the usual acrimonious atmosphere between you and your father. Why do you provoke him so, when you know very well what the outcome will be?'

Charlie's eyes fell to the ground and a slur of resentment reddened his face.

'I suffer his beatings and indignities, Mother, I don't seek them. But perhaps this state of affairs will not continue for so much longer. I am already not far away from his equal in size and strength, and soon we will see an end to his persecution. Soon only Francis will be small enough to feel the sting of his cane.'

She looked at the broad set of his square shoulders. She knew he was right, and for some reason it touched off a now genuine fury in her. She sat bolt upright and threw the handkerchief from her.

'And then where will you be, pray? Free to drag the Howell name in the mud in every town and village in the county? Free to drink, whore and despoil your way around our countryside with your village ragamuffin friends? I don't wonder your father is still trying to beat some sense into you, my boy, before it's too late. And let me tell you, Charles, that if he ever finds himself unable to do so, I will take the cane to you myself rather than see you finish as a disgrace to your family.'

His scarlet face rose to her and she saw, with an odd mixture of gratification and regret, that she had almost drawn tears. An empty little cough sounded from the door, and they both looked in the direction of Francis, almost as red-faced as his brother, standing hesitantly in the door space.

'The grans are sighted, on the road out of the village. They could even see me waving, because they waved back.'

Elizabeth stood up and heaved Charlie to his feet in front of her.

'Remove those boots now, and carry them with you. Go and make yourself not only presentable but impressive, with the use of the particular clothes which I know full well Armstrong will have put out for you. Francis, help him, if you please.'

She watched them disappear down the corridor, Charlie already tearing off his rag of a shirt with the frenzy of enthusiasm which a hefty push in the right direction could touch off in him and Francis following resignedly behind, shaking his head slowly and philosophically at his brother's bizarre antics, not for the first or even the hundredth time. The ghostly smile on her face lasted only as long as it took her to close the door behind them, and then a flood of tears so copious and unleashed as to be beyond her control forced her all the way through the bedroom and the dressing room and into the dark blue and white luxury of the bathroom which she now had entirely to herself for almost all of the time. She locked the door and sat on the side of the bath, sobbing silently and shaking an extraordinary amount of unwanted moisture from her eyes and face.

Two hours later, the older members of the family assembled in front of the portico to welcome the Harringtons. Francis, relieved if a little disappointed to learn that he was not to be a member of the main welcoming committee, took up a strategic position where he could actually see everyone in the family at the same time, acting, once more, as his father's fixing assistant.

George Howell, surprised and gratified to find his wild boy of a son and heir clean and even looking quite handsome in a bottle green coat specially provided for him for such occasions as this during the holidays, has relented even to the point of promising the boy that he will stay with his father and grandfather when the ladies and children retire after dinner.

'We will see, Charles,' the deep voice announced, while Charlie wondered how the dark eyes managed to look threatening even when they seemed to be smiling, 'whether you have any head for brandy. There now, such a test for a man as was ever devised!'

Charlie kept to himself the actual number of occasions, both at home and at school, when his head for brandy had already been amply tested and established and made a mental resolve at a suitable play act. His amazement at his father's mellowness had given birth, for the moment at least, to a tiny seed of real belief that he might actually be capable of being what his father wanted him to be, when he'd finally managed to discern what that might be, beyond certain rather prosaic levels of cleanliness and presentability. His fairly simple soul did not attach the weight it should to his father's essentially snobbish desire not to allow Sir John and Lady Charlotte to see any overt disharmony in the domestic Howell idyll.

Elizabeth flinched at the touch of a man on her shoulder, even her husband. Charlie watched his father with narrowed eyes and a growing awareness that his time would come and was doing so with every passing day.

From a narrow upstairs window, the tiny face of Alice Howell, aged five, appeared as she stood between the knees of her gratifyingly large and solid nanny. Being out of bed was a treat in itself; being allowed to stand and watch the grans' arrival below was a rare delight indeed, and the visual memory of the little waiting group below is one which remains with her for the rest of her life, which proved to be rather longer than most people imagined it would be. Her brother Francis pulled an affectionate face at her. She chuckled and waved, and that is another image which lasts a lifetime, though this time for her brother.

2

PERISHED BY
THE SWORD – 1852

WEDNESDAY 17 MARCH 1852, 3.15P.M.

Six men are standing in the middle of featureless grassland, with village buildings in the background and the stream flowing a few hundred yards away on their right. Francis Howell is next to a large wooden cross in the ground; Richard Burridge, the Howell company's mining manager at the time, is standing about twelve yards behind him on his right. Four other men are in a bunched group behind and between the two main figures. Francis is standing close to a disused mine shaft, the entrance to which is marked by the cross.

Francis Howell in 1852 is a slightly built twenty-year-old with normally a rather baffled air, used as he is to trailing around in his father's impressive wake; however, he looks at this moment much older than his years, and the narrowed mouth, unnaturally gleaming eyes and odd stooping posture clearly show the immense emotional strain he is suffering.

Six men are in the group, but the appearance of the two men in the foreground is most striking, largely because of the considerable contrast between them. Francis Howell seems to exhibit a gaping chasm between his youth and the cares he has heaped on him. Richard Burridge, heavily moustachioed, an older, stouter man, indicates by the rigidity of his torso and the suspicious stare he is directing towards nowhere in particular that he clearly regards the whole proceeding as inappropriate. There is also a suggestion, in the slight angling of his body to his right and the forward placing of one foot, that he is eager to leave the place as soon as possible. The other four men are colliery managers or deputy managers, all in their late thirties or early forties and all looking as shocked and concerned as if they had only recently left a bloody battleground.

The overwhelming mood is of crises, both recently past and newly approaching, and loaded largely on to the youngest and most vulnerable-looking member of the group, who looks too young and frail to cope with the burden he has had to take on.

TUESDAY 16 MARCH 1852, 9.36 A.M.

Francis did what he always did on mornings when he'd been left alone in his father's big office. He headed for the four shelves of books in the corner of the room, each about three feet wide; probably almost a hundred books and papers in all. Most of them he had introduced to the office himself to his father's indifference, if not hostility. George Howell distrusted books, identifying them entirely with the schoolroom and boyhood, but even he conceded that some of the volumes Francis managed to get his hands on had interesting bearings on the whole business of mining, its history, techniques and methods. Francis had long since accepted that his father would never willingly hand him any real executive power, but as it seemed to be increasingly clear that he would inherit the family's mining business simply by default, Charlie being quite determined not to involve himself, he wanted to be sure he didn't come to it entirely ignorant and unprepared. George Howell's tepid approval of one son's actions and attitudes clashed dramatically with his vehement disgust at the other's. Charlie wanted to join a regiment and get away, 'to see the world, make my fortune or die in the attempt, anything but rot in this place living off the proceeds of sending men and boys to choke and die in dark holes', a description definitely for the ears of his brother Francis only. The latest episode in the long, loud battle of wills which continued to exhaust and intimidate the rest of the family was Charlie's current trip to Newcastle to meet some men who had intimated they may be able to provide him with a commission at what his father had defined as a 'reasonable price' without specifying any amounts. Charlie was only being allowed to take the trip at all because his mother had unexpectedly and with great misgivings changed sides, at least to the extent of persuading George to let the 'boy' look properly into the possibilities. 'Boy' had become a wildly inapt description of the twenty-three-year-old Charlie, a good two inches taller than his father, huge in the shoulders and chest and immensely popular with the whole Howell workforce even as they grinned behind their hands at his impenetrable boredom with the business of mining and his disconsolate trailing round after his father when compelled to do so. All and sundry were well aware by now that George would very soon be unable to compel Charlie to do anything; as the son had ultimately secured total victory in the long-standing Charles v. Charlie battle, so the issue of him inheriting his father's mining mantle had only one possible victor in the long run when one of the disputing parties would no longer be alive. With his father now fifty-six years old, Charlie had time on his side, and Charlie knew it.

Francis settled himself to read a chapter on the development of coal over unimaginable periods of time. At the moment, he minded the shop and did little else. He had resigned himself to what he saw as the multiple, even wilful, misinterpretation of his motives by other people; Charlie read his brother's interest in mining as simple fear, an unsubtle form of kowtowing to the tyrant George, who in his turn saw Francis as inadequate and attempting to compensate with pointless book knowledge for his lack of presence and authority. Even his mother seemed to regard Francis as a little desperate in his attempts to define some function for himself. Francis, who had a self-will and determination which no one had yet recognised properly, forced himself to indifference and carried on the course he had chosen for himself regardlessly, unaware that it was this withdrawn, defensive side to his nature which created the blank spaces people filled with their own answers.

Francis was good-looking, though he himself would never have credited such a description, in a rather pallid, ascetic way which contrasted unfortunately with his brother's robust, ruddy features, his brother being the person with whom he seemed doomed to be compared in almost every conceivable way. In actual fact, at close quarters their facial similarities were much more pronounced and obvious, and Francis's quizzical green eyes, directly inherited from his mother, made more of an impact in proximity than did his brother's expansive, vague good nature.

Richard Burridge approached the office door and caught sight of the long lonely figure in the corner of the room, entirely engrossed and self-contained. Burridge was a seasoned, middle-aged industrial operator, diplomatic as he needed to be, ruthless as he occasionally had to be, a survivor in a world which allowed few. Understanding the Howells was part of his business; liking them was something different again, and he had no illusions about George even as he'd conceived of a grudging admiration for his effectiveness. But this young Howell was something of an enigma. Burridge had somehow managed to retain the ability to be honest with himself, and a couple of years of having this youth in his daily working world was leading him dangerously close to liking the boy, an emotion he viewed with suspicion. Many had fallen for the superficial charms of his brother, but to Richard Burridge, Charlie was a nuisance and little else, an encumbrance fooling about on the periphery of his world with very little apparent function but to make his already difficult role more so. Francis had already, on a few isolated occasions, actually proved to be useful and was undoubtedly making a serious attempt to learn about the business. A recent incident had caused Burridge's alarmingly sympathetic inclinations towards the youth to strengthen, but as they'd come about from a clandestine act of defiance of both father and mining manager, some kind of confrontation with Francis had to be brought about. Burridge looked at the peaceful reading figure and wondered whether his father's temper was in there somewhere, just waiting for a suitable opportunity.

He clashed open the office door with deliberate emphasis. Francis looked up.

'Good day to you, Mr Burridge,' he said, and returned to his reading.

'Good day indeed, Mr Francis,' Burridge said, and occupied his own desk on the other side of the office. For five minutes, he consulted the reports and figures he needed to look at, then he faced facts, a habit he'd come to be good at, and entered casually into the subject matter he knew had to be broached.

'Interesting incident at Stangate the other day, Mr Francis. Very much discussed since.'

He saw the other's body stiffen, though the eyes remained firmly on the book.

'Young man turns up at the pithead, dirty, not more than a few rags on him. Accent difficult to identify. Begs, actually begs, the pit manager Thubron to take him on. John Thubron doesn't think he's got enough strength in him to do even a single shift, but he agrees on just that, a one-shift trial. The youth, who says his name is Tom Carlisle, or some such, does just that, one shift, then disappears. Not been seen since.'

A long pause, filled with nothing but a scrape of a chair and a book being placed on a surface. The onus is on Francis to say something; Burridge decides that is the way it will be and holds his own peace.

'Is that so remarkable, Mr Burridge? There are always occasional itinerants, pedlars, gypsies, needing a little money, aren't there?'

'Right enough, Mr Francis. But what is remarkable, I feel, is Thubron's observations on the youth's appearance. He said he dismissed it because it was just not possible. Not that he'd ever seen this youth at Stangate, right enough. But he believed he might have seen him at a certain annual fete, and maybe even hanging around this office. Dirt and rags don't change the young as much as they might an older man.' Francis turned in his chair and Burridge got the full strength of the narrowed green eyes.

'What are you saying? Are you going to tell my father?'

Burridge put his papers down and pushed back his chair. He let a few seconds pass, so the boy didn't have it too easy.

'No, sir, I'm not. Many people have accused me of many things, but informing and sneaking haven't been among them. But I'll say this, Mr Francis,' he said, raising his voice – Howell or no Howell, there was dangerous ground here – 'I've been in this room and heard your father state absolutely plainly that you must not, in any event, go underground yourself, whatever you may think you know of the theory and experience of it. If he hears of it, it won't just be your hide, think of that.'

'What do you mean? You're not answerable for my actions, Burridge.'

Burridge, nettled by the absence of the Mr, got to his feet and for a moment the two men stared across the desk at each other, already nervous about where this was going.

'Mr Howell receives a report to say that you have illicitly made a trip underground at Stangate. It may or may not have been with approval, tacit or otherwise, from Mr Thubron or myself, but if Mr Howell is to decide responsibility between his employees who have been working for him for eleven and twenty-two years respectively and his son who has been here for two, what choice do you think is most probable, Mr Francis? Knowing your father as you do, no doubt much better than Thubron or I?'

The youth's face looked more pale and pinched than ever.

'Oh, Lord, Mr Burridge, I didn't think.'

'No, sir.' Burridge sat down again, the confrontation diffused. 'Young men seldom do.'

He looked up again and saw Francis was staring out of the window, his face creased in anxiety while his hands rubbed together in front of him. Once again, against his instincts and better judgment, Burridge was touched.

'But nobody will tell him. Firstly, because people suspect but they don't know, and you don't go to a man like your father with suspicions, only certainties. Secondly, because none of the men would want to get you into trouble, Mr Francis.'

Burridge saw the genuine surprise in the boy's face and felt pleased by it, for some reason.

'Wouldn't they?'

'No, sir, of course not. Everyone knows that sooner or later, you will be the Howell partner in the company, and there is widespread goodwill towards your willingness to teach yourself something about the business. Many of the men also feel, though I have to say I do not share such sentiments, that if the pits are as safe as Mr Howell maintains they are, he and anyone else in his family should not hesitate to visit the coal face.'

'You don't agree with them?'

'No, I don't. One miner is more dispensable than a member of the owner's family, and that is the reality of it. Such is the way of the world, Mr Francis, like it or not.'

'But they're not safe, Mr Burridge, are they? They're nothing like safe.' He was leaning forward over Burridge's desk in his eagerness, and Burridge sighed inwardly while avoiding those eyes. He'd always known this question and this source would come together sooner or later, but he had a position to think of and a family to keep, and the evangelism of the young was not a road he was prepared to be led down.

'The props need better wood in their construction, and more time spent on embedding them safely. The whole mining areas, especially the face, need to be better lit. The machinery which works the cage needs to be better and more regularly maintained. More stringent tests for gas levels need to be introduced—'

'Mr Francis,' Burridge stood glowering over his desk, though he felt as if he'd been backed into a corner and made to intervene to stop such a heretical flow. 'This business is about making money. If we don't make money, we don't make profit, and if we don't make profit, we don't have a business, I don't have a job, and neither do any of the men. If we spend more on the provisions you describe than our competitors, our profits will drop, we will be forced to raise our prices accordingly, and we will be squeezed out of business. That too is the way of the world, Mr Francis. And the eventuality of accidents, I feel bound to say, is often a consequence of human stupidity and nothing more; men cutting corners, men not doing what they know they ought to do, that is the stuff of most mishaps underground. Human stupidity, which stoutly resists all regulation.'

'Men and boys, I think, Mr Burridge. Children, in some cases.'

Burridge sat down and looked at the paperwork on his desk a little forlornly.

'The Government in its wisdom banned females and children under ten in 1842, and probably rightly so, in view of the heat and the state of undress it often causes, but these restrictions have made both recruitment and labour costs even more difficult than they were before. At least, the consequence is that the body of our employees is dominated by fully grown men, part of whose job it is to see that the boys do what they should do. This, too, will inevitably help the accident rate to lessen. And now, Mr Francis, if you will forgive me, I must attend to my work. I mean no impertinence when I say that your father is an exacting employer; he will be arriving very soon and he will expect me to be familiar with whatever production or purchase figures he wishes to examine today. And may I be allowed one more remark, Mr Francis, with a hope that my presumption may be forgiven?'

Francis already understood the physical vocabulary of Burridge, and when the man's hands came together over his papers and his hefty torso inclined slightly forward over the desk, he knew Burridge was drawing his line in the sand. Even his father had sometimes, albeit rarely, been faced down by Burridge in this way.

'Any further expeditions underground, sir, without the knowledge and permission of myself or my staff, will force me to take all necessary actions short of discussions with Mr Howell to prevent any repetition, including a circulation of a physical description if necessary. I would be grateful if you could indicate that you understand me, Mr Francis.'

Francis opened his mouth to speak, but thought better of it and simply nodded. He knew Burridge well enough to be selective about which matters ought to be fought to the limit over, and this wasn't one of them. He also knew, for the moment at least, he had Burridge's goodwill concerning dealings between father and son, and that was worth preserving.

Burridge turned back to the papers on his desk and clearly considered the matter closed. Francis returned to his corner and his book, but what had represented a coherent geological account now seemed no more than confusing black squiggles. He found himself re-living again the dreadful experience of that shift – the enormous physical effort required to hack away at the hard coal and heave it away in cumbersome wagons on uncertain tracks, the stench of the place, men's sweat the least of it and gas a clear ever-present, the ominous creaking of props around them, the immense difficulty of maintaining regular breathing while wondering what vileness was entering eyes, nose and mouth, the degradation of having to work almost completely naked in the oppressive heat, the filth, moisture and scurrying rats underfoot, the presence of boys, supposedly eleven or twelve, who were little more than walking, dwarfish skeletons.

He had conspired with a young lawyer friend, Peter Alston, who lived near Stangate and was an old school friend, over the whole shift plan. Alston, earnest and mostly serious of purpose from early schooldays onwards, sympathised with the idea of experiencing an underground shift and pledged himself to secrecy, though he declined to join Francis, declaring it a risk he was not prepared to take because of the enormous difficulties any drastic mishaps would create for his father's firm, this accompanied with a very significant look, Peter's father being a gentle and lenient man compared with George Howell, a sentiment Alston could hint at but not openly express.

Peter had his own quarters in the Alston home, of about the same comfortable size and sprawling comfort as the nearby Vicarage, and met Francis at a pre-arranged spot. He was clearly shaken at the filthy and exhausted state of his friend and smuggled Francis into the house through his own door. As soon as the back door was shut and curtains drawn, Francis stripped naked and Peter immediately disappeared with the clothes to dispose of them while Francis went straight to the bathroom. Years of showers and school changing rooms had made the business of nakedness between them inconsequential, and Peter soon wandered back and sat on a stool on the other side of the bathroom.

'My God, Francis, look at the state of you.'

Francis glanced down at the miscellany of cuts, scrapes and bruises which covered his body. His ignorance and clumsiness, largely unaided by suspicious miners, had caused him to catch against objects, blunder into obstacles and at one point, almost have his ankle dissected by an accelerating wagon. He had, on more than one occasion, lost his footing and found himself sprawling about amongst the filth on the ground. The water of the bath had already turned a deep brown/black.

'The incidental cuts and scars are of no great consequence. What I cannot begin to imagine, even though I know it to be a fact, is that the men and boys I worked alongside would be required to do all of that again tomorrow, and tomorrow, and every day of the week except Sunday. I'm twenty, Peter, probably as fit as I shall ever be, but I think such a job would kill me in a relatively short while. I had to force myself to realise that all the middle-aged and decrepit figures around me were probably in their early thirties at most.'

But, curiously enough, it hadn't ultimately been Peter Alston, sympathetic good friend as he was, to whom Francis had fully opened his heart. Not for the first time in recent years, it was his sister Alice, still only thirteen and still a tiny girl only slightly over four feet tall. Francis had been moving awkwardly for some days, still suffering from muscle aches and bruises everywhere, and typically, Alice noticed, though nobody else appeared to. Alice knocked on his bedroom door – he had had to insist on this from all of his siblings, especially the sisters, but Alice was the only one who always remembered – and when he told her to come in, she stood there, the way she did, the big hazel eyes wide, her little arms folded in front of her as if she was about to start a recitation.

'You don't have to tell me, Francis' – 'Frank' was now Charlie's alone – 'except to say that it's none of my business, but you are moving as if you are in pain for much of the time and I really needed to be reassured that there is no illness taking a sinister hold on you.'

Typical, so typical, of Alice, such a defined, decided person compared with the discontented fierceness of Charlotte, at constant odds with all servants, and the fleeting, perpetual trivia of Anne, darting from one local imaginary scandal to another and constantly attempting to replenish or enlarge on her supposedly eternally inadequate wardrobe.

He looked at her fragile but so tough little figure, a girl who already should have been dead a hundred times, and realised how much he needed to tell someone how he actually felt, how he really felt, about his mining experience, without the bluff bravado school front he needed to put on with contemporaries, even with Peter.

Striding between bed and window like some caged beast, he told her the whole story, while she sat, immobile, saying nothing, her tiny hands folded demurely into her lap on his bedside chair. Only the wide eyes sometimes widening even more and occasional gasps and sighs emanated from her until he'd finished. When they started to talk about it, he found, once again, she was entirely unshocked and her questions showed quite clearly that she'd assimilated every word he'd said.

'Certainly, you must try to change these things, Francis, as soon as the opportunity presents itself openly and in the meantime, by guile if necessary,' she said, with that odd certainty and authority her little presence seemed to exude.

Francis attempted to force his mind back to the book in front of him. Ever since the experience of the shift, he had clung on to the hope that the thorough study of coal might produce answers, clues, directions, some feasible definition of a different, more humane and easier way of obtaining coal in large quantities. Profit without slaughter, a properly constituted viable business without the enormous toll of human misery, should surely not be unattainable. He marvelled at his own arrogance and probably naivety, knowing that what was happening now had evolved from hundreds of years of experience. But the only established exponent of the process he knew well was his father, widely acknowledged to be successful in production and profit if nothing else. His father was usually dismissive of theory, deeply suspicious of innovation and apparently quite persuaded that the human cost of mining was affordable for people who had no other working opportunities except to slave away on agricultural land for capricious and unpredictable yields. 'What else are they going to do?' was a frequent refrain from George Howell whenever anyone even began to question the conditions his workers endured. Yet Francis still found it difficult to think of his father as a cruel man; on the occasions when he had been beaten by him, he had probably deserved it and the beatings, while painful and temporarily humiliating, were not excessive by comparison with schools and other boys' experiences. He also knew well enough that, suspicious of books as he may be, his father was not a stupid man. If he could only devise ways of modernising production while also making it safer, his father would listen to authoritative and well-researched answers. And, ultimately, the time would come when he would be in a position to put them into practice anyway.

A faint but unmistakable noise registered in his mind. Francis put his book down and stood up. His air of expectancy distracted Burridge from his papers.

'Is anything the matter, Mr Francis?'

'My father's coming.'

Burridge stood himself and listened, but he heard nothing. He gazed quizzically at the younger man; was this some bizarre kind of sixth sense?

'Do you hear something?'

'I can detect that clack in the surface of the back wheel, the one that Thomas still hasn't got round to mending properly. But his coach is not alone; another is following him. It's a procession that I can hear.'

Burridge continued to wonder for some seconds until he picked up the faint noises himself, clear enough against the occasional voices in the yard outside the office. A few minutes later, George Howell's private hansom cab clattered into the yard, followed rapidly by a simple gig whose passenger wore an expression of barely contained fury.

Howell nodded at Burridge and Francis and all three headed for the office. Burridge glanced behind him at the door and saw that the man emerging from the gig was Edward Lowtham, one of Sir John Harrington's more substantial tenants, with a considerable holding which he rented and worked on the Harrington estates near Camwell. Lowtham was a long beanpole of a man in his early forties, weathered from long hours in the open air and generally a courteous, competent fellow on the rare occasions when the Howell company had had any dealings with that part of the Harrington land. But today, he seemed almost beside himself with rage, his face almost scarlet and his arms waving agitatedly before him.

The Howells had disappeared into the office. In circumstances such as these, Burridge's job was about diffusing whatever situation had arisen, and he knew it. He stood in front of the office door and faced the approaching man. Lowtham stopped just a yard in front of him, waving his riding crop as if it was a weapon.

'Out of the way, Mr Burridge, I beg you! I am going to whip that man in there until his blood flows as freely as he has caused others to flow! Please, Burridge, let me pass!'

The man was as close to tears as he could be without letting them run down his cheeks. Burridge looked him up and down, a skinny, overworked shrinkage of a man, and drew him quietly away from the office and to one side some ten yards away. He could feel in the man's quivering arm that the anger was simply masking a tumult of sudden grief.

'Mr Lowtham,' Burridge said, confidentially, 'I really would most earnestly advise you not to offer violence to Mr Howell, whatever you feel the provocation may be. He may be an older man than yourself, but he is very strong and quick to take offence. Please have a care for your own well-being, sir.'

Now the tears were coming, and Lowtham was scarcely coherent.

'My boy, Mr Burridge! My dear young Daniel, our great family hope and beacon!'

Burridge, who knew the fourteen-year-old Daniel Lowtham from a couple of previous cases of trespass on company property, had a different view of him, but he kept his peace.

'What of him, sir?'

'Dead, sir! That's what of him, sir! Every bone in his body broken, his neck snapped like a twig! A tumble down one of Howell's disused mine shafts, left to pockmark the countryside, left unmarked for innocent children to fall to their deaths!'

Burridge sighed long and hard. It was widely known in the area that Lowtham exercised little control over his unruly battery of sons, and Lowtham's land bordered the area of the current and former Camwell shafts and tunnels. Such an incident had been in the offing now for some time. His own warnings to Howell that a single relatively small notice board on the edge of the company's land would not deter the local youths, who had regarded much of that land as their legitimate rousting-about territory for years, and that dismissal of the issue as the responsibility of parents would not help if some well-connected youth met with an accident. Lowtham alone was not a man with any great local influence, but Lowtham's landlord was Sir John Harrington, Howell's father-in-law, and Burridge knew that Sir John had expressed some disquiet at the lack of proper marking of disused shafts, so far only in private. Burridge could remember his own very precise words:

'A fatality, sir, could place the company in a difficult local situation, whatever the legal rights and wrongs may be.'

In the case of the Camwell shafts, there had already been one, but he'd only been an old itinerant pedlar and tramp.

However, there had been several near misses and one where a boy had fallen but managed to break his fall by grabbing on to a piece of overhanging metal twenty feet from the surface, where he'd held on long enough for a rope to be sent down to him. Howell's threat to institute trespass proceedings had suppressed the family's protests, but also inflamed the already volatile local opinions.

'Something will need to be done, Mr Burridge, and quickly,' Lowtham continued, managing to collect himself and breathe a little more regularly. 'A number of Camwell people have already gathered at the spot, the mood is ugly, and I intend to remove my poor boy's broken and twisted body for burial only after I have ensured that every member of the local populace has seen the consequences of Mr Howell's criminal indifference.'

George Howell, of course, was not the man to skulk indoors when such a hubbub as this was going on in his vicinity, and Burridge's heart sunk even further when he saw his employer framed in the open door, his chin in the air and one large fist opening and closing with great deliberation. Francis Howell's pale features appeared over his father's shoulder.

'What the devil is going on here, Burridge?'

'Going on!' screamed Lowtham. 'I'll tell you, sir, what's going on!'

'The crop, please, Lowtham, I entreat you,' Burridge muttered, and Lowtham reluctantly gave it up, but there was no reticence in the way he stormed almost up to George Howell's face and virtually spat his words at him.

'I have lost a precious son, because of you, sir! Because of you and your company's negligence and incompetence, my son's broken body has just been heaved out of a shaft sunk long ago by your company and left to plague the poor Camwell people ever since!'

Howell looked past Lowtham and his eyes settled on Burridge, those deep-set dark spaces already beginning to flash with anger.

Burridge found himself wondering about the over-preponderance of Howell eyes in his life.

'His son?'

'Yes, sir,' Burridge said. 'Daniel, fourteen.'

'I see. Daniel Lowtham. Yes, I recognise the name.'

Francis listened to the rumbling authority of the voice, which had so completely dominated his home life, and saw that these men, adult and accomplished professional men as they were, seemed to be almost as susceptible to it. The active and mobile scene had momentarily frozen to a tableau, and even Lowtham had subsided, standing with his arms at his sides, his chest heaving.

'Mr Burridge will correct me if my facts are wrong, but this is, is it not, the same Daniel Lowtham who has twice been warned for trespass on the company's Camwell land? I regret such a drastic fate befalling one so young, but I think perhaps this negligence cannot all be laid at my door, Mr Lowtham?'

Lowtham made a vague, unco-ordinated physical lunge in George Howell's direction and the dark eyes narrowed even more; Lowtham drew his body back and compensated for it by screeching even more loudly.

'We shall see, sir, where the negligence will lie! We will see at whose door the properly constituted authorities lay it! We will see to it in court, sir!'

'No, we won't,' Howell said quietly, and began to move towards his Hansom cab. 'We will see to it now. I have enough business and enough expense of lawyers not to need anything additional; we will face this now and understand the exact reality of it. We must all examine the scene and the situation for ourselves before all the lawyers have our time and, God knows, our money.'

'I would not advise it, sir, not now. A number of local people are there; some time needs to elapse before matters can be discussed in a level-headed atmosphere.'

'Oh, fiddlesticks, Burridge. You know as well as I do that we cannot afford further time and money; we will nip this in the bud. Come with me, and if my manners are too rude, you can ease my way to them. We will see this for ourselves. Get in your gig and go, Lowtham; we will follow, you have my word.'

Lowtham's mouth set and his hands lifted in another peculiarly awkward gesture of grief and distraction, but at last he turned back towards his gig, shouting to its driver as he climbed in.

'Let me do this, Father,' Francis said, touching his father lightly on the arm. 'I know many of the Camwell people; it is work I can take off your hands. Let me go with Mr Burridge.'

For the rest of his life, Francis never forgot the expression on his father's face as it turned to him at that moment. For once, the hard features softened, the clenched temples relaxed, and for once, his father was looking into his eyes, directly at him, rather than at some spot past his shoulder or at someone more worth his while listening to.

'Thank you, Francis. But I need you to stay here.'

Francis grimaced and sighed, probably more loudly than he'd intended, because in a moment the eyes were back again, initially with a flash of anger and then that strange calm, which even at the time Francis felt had a terrifying valedictory feeling about it.

'Staying here is not a disgrace, Francis. I do not leave anyone in charge of this office, the company's central Howell office, on their own unless I trust them implicitly. You have arrived at that stage in two years, Francis. I very much doubt whether your brother ever will.'

George Howell moved off, and Burridge prepared to accompany him. Even the ill-natured dig at Charlie couldn't stop the singing feeling all over Francis's heart region. And then George stopped again, turning round completely to face his son.

'You are a good man, Francis. Take care of everything for me.'

The good feeling inside the young man was suddenly usurped by a wild panic; he wanted to race after his father and beg him not to go, at whatever cost to his dignity and credibility, because a deep-seated premonition of something namelessly dreadful had taken hold of him. But he recognised the futility of chasing his father immediately, and even at the cost of allowing whatever was going to happen to happen, he couldn't face George Howell's bleak disappointment and embarrassment as Burridge turned his face away to avoid the scene.

As the coaches faded into the distance, Francis stood watching them for a long time, the larger cloud of his father's Hansom pursuing the smaller of the gig as if both condemned to an eternal chase which neither could win and neither could lose. Only when the clouds had disappeared over the horizon and he could not hear so much as a hint or an echo of the rhythmic clack of the faulty wheel did he turn back to the office, feeling, ridiculously and illogically, that what he'd just watched vanish in an ever-decreasing mass of dust and earth was his own youth.

Almost three hours passed and a few routine matters were dealt with, apparently to everyone's satisfaction. The thick streak of common sense and distrust of anything not logical or demonstrable to him had retaken Francis Howell, and he refused to allow that the time being spent on this matter was any more than it needed to be – the journey to Camwell alone would take the best part of an hour. He waited, with slowly mounting impatience, for his father to return and allow the two of them to go home, perhaps to find Charlie forlorn or exhilarated according to his fortune; typically, Charlie hadn't even specified just how long he thought his expedition would take.

When Francis eventually heard the Hansom on its way back, the wheel clack was resounding at such a speed that he had concluded long before the cab's arrival that an emergency had arisen. He doubted such a speed could be reached unless it was only carrying the driver's weight, and all the weird, undefined suspicions of earlier had returned by the time the cab came storming into the yard.

Thomas didn't even bother to descend.

'There's been an accident, sir, a dreadful accident! Your father, sir! You must come!'

His entire insides turning over until he was almost sick on the spot, Francis climbed into the cab and it headed off at the same breakneck speed, the clacking now banging away in his ears like a drum beat of battle.

As they passed through Camwell village with the pit buildings looming over all slightly to the west, they felt the heavy oppressive silence and glimpsed an occasional spitting child following the cab to grab an opportunity when it slowed. Francis could see no sign anywhere of a warning notice, yet it was well known that this whole area on the east of the village was infested with shafts, some of them well over a hundred feet deep, from the original mine workings. The long stretches of scrubby grassland which lay between Camwell and the distant hills was a bleak landscape at the best of times, and the scene, to Francis's tortured mind, had many of the characteristics of a bizarre nightmare. A keen northern wind was blowing into his face and the words of others, even when shouted, had an eerie broken quality; banks of blackened cloud were scudding across the sky at an improbable speed and people seemed to be moving slowly, deliberately, as if their environment overwhelmed and intimidated them. A hundred yards away from the concealed mineshaft entrance, something in the region of fifty or sixty of the local people, most of them women, were watching sullenly. A body of men were standing firmly between them and the group of company officials gathered round the entrance; occasionally, one or more of the local people would shout something abusive and the majority of them would immediately try to shush them. Camwell had few enough employers and the Howell company were far and away the biggest of them.

Burridge was moving away from the group of men around the shaft entrance as soon as the Hansom cab appeared; Francis had only just stepped down from the cab when Burridge took his arm, an almost unprecedented act of physical contact between them, and edged him to one side, holding out a hand to prevent any of the company men approaching them.

At this moment, Francis noticed a long, low cart like an unroofed hearse, with one man in the process of latching its rear gate while the other moved towards the driving seat.

Burridge was clearly in a state of shock, his usual dour equilibrium vanished into quick, gasping speech and a scarlet face. His eyes seemed to have become so deep set that the heavy eyebrows almost extinguished them. Francis took this in with one glance, and then his own glance turned irresistibly across to the low cart. He set off towards it in blind anger and panic, and Burridge touched him again, this time actually trying to grab roughly at his arm. He turned, only just restraining himself from an answering blow, and Burridge swore afterwards that the light in the green eyes was so intense, so gleamingly hostile, as to verge on the demonic.

'Mr Francis, please!'

Francis broke into a run just as the man on the driving seat was taking up his whip.

'Stay exactly where you are! If you know what's good for you, my man, you'll stay still until I give the word!'

The driver looked wildly between Burridge and Francis and Francis saw Burridge nod at him, which served to intensify his anger, until he looked over the side of the cart, and then all anger became suddenly futile. His father lay there at a curious angle, his head arched backwards and one leg bent crookedly across the other; his clothes were torn and soaked in blood, especially around the front of his throat and down one side of the straight-lying leg. He was tied to a crude litter, which seemed little more than some old discarded door. Francis edged slowly to the front of the cart where he could see the whole face, another nightmare image in its unnerving rigidity and impossible combination of peace and agony, the eyes wide and staring madly backwards while the mouth had closed to a strangely tranquil line.

Burridge, Francis realised after a few seconds of listening to the wind and stray voices floating in and out of it like wandering spirits, was talking to him.

'… and he'd positioned himself near the very edge of the shaft entrance to look for himself at the supposedly extremely dangerous depths and sharp protruding rock from the sides and at the base, both of which contributed to killing the boy, so the locals said, but Mr Howell is the kind of man who will only believe what he sees for himself. One of the local men – the whole place was thick with villagers at the time, many more of them men than are here now – spoke to me and I turned to answer him, and there was a sudden great shout, and when I turned back Mr Howell had disappeared. One man started a stuttering explanation about the ground at the neck of the entrance suddenly collapsing under Mr Howell, but I was too occupied at the time with gathering rope and men to mount a rescue as quickly as possible after the dreadful long thud we'd just heard.'

Francis breathed deeply and looked at the diminishing crowd of local people.

'This is murder, Burridge.'

Burridge saw the cart driver look down with mad anger in his eyes at the words and once again edged Francis away.

'Please, Mr Howell' – Francis reeled at the thought that this was the first time Burridge had ever addressed him in that way – 'there will be time to investigate and many people to talk to, but it is not to be advised, sir, very much not to be advised, to make accusations of that sort here and now. I've had to get some Camwell officials to fetch some non-Camwell men who work at that pit to get here for a protection force as it is. We must get your father's body, God rest his soul, out of here, and ourselves too; transport is on its way. That will be the time for questions.'

'Very well, Mr Burridge, but I want the Camwell officials to mark the precise spot and arrange for it to be watched and guarded permanently until further notice. Do you understand me? Guarded permanently, with as many men as necessary, and armed if necessary, until further notice.'

Burridge nodded, and even in his distress, the ease with which this young man took control, even at such a time, had a quality about it which impressed him. The noise of clattering horses distracted them, and they turned to see four fully armed and mounted troopers, their sabres ready at their sides, riding across the grassland. At the sight of them, the remaining local people begin to drift away.

'At last,' Burridge breathed. 'At least an hour too late, but at last.'

From this time until meeting with his mother, the day blurred in Francis's mind. He realised, on reflection, that he and Burridge must have successfully arranged for the troopers and some of the Howell men to accompany his father's body back to Howell Grange, making the perilous part of the return journey through the deserted streets of Camwell much safer than it would have otherwise been. He could remember mentioning to Burridge at some point that no warning notices were in evidence anywhere in the whole area, and Burridge replying that every time a notice was put up, some locals would chop it to pieces for firewood, and George Howell had decided, on the third theft, not to persist. He would always shudder, even years after the event, at the race back to the Grange in the cab, not knowing whether or not the hubbub had been so widespread that his mother already knew, turning over in his mind again and again ways in which he might make the telling somehow more bearable and reflecting that, appalled as he normally was at the idea of physical pain and the excruciating experience of that seemingly interminable shift, he would rather repeat the whole thing again and again than have to tell her at all.

As he stepped down from the cab, he saw his mother and all three of his sisters gathered at the huge window of the central drawing room upstairs, overlooking the portico entrance. They were all staring into the distance, and every look showed a difference of character and attitude. His mother was pale but very calm, holding her head up, as she always did when she wanted to assert herself or show defiance; she looked down at him and her eyes warmed a little. Something between a smile and a grimace appeared briefly on her face, before she resumed her watching vigil. Charlotte's angry, flashing eyes glanced down at him for no more than a split second before she resumed glowering into the distance, a study in frozen, hardly contained rage. Anne, bemused and near tears, blinked down, her face contorted with pain. Alice turned her whole face towards him, and in the same spirit of slow motion unreality which had characterised so much of the day, her expression broke slowly into a great smile of affection and sympathy, her head tilting slightly to one side and her torso moving towards him.

Francis walked up a few steps of the entrance staircase and turned to look at what they were all seeing. That long, low cart again, moving in that same gradual, deliberated parody of life, with a mounted trooper at each corner, and the clinking of sabres and spurs, the occasional laboured breaths of the horses, the creak of the cart's wooden joints, all clearly audible to him even at such a distance. Francis sat down on a step, put his head down between his knees and closed his eyes; an enormous and urgent return to a childish mentality made him wish, fervently and with every last ounce of sincerity he could summon, that this whole thing was somehow a mad, fatigue-inspired dream, some grotesque residue of his mining shift, a mind momentarily twisted out of shape. But the noises and smells would not be denied, and when he opened his eyes again, they filled the entire world, Howell men arriving from all sides, troopers dismounting, and, when he glanced at the drawing room window, all of the Howell women already coming down to complete the scene to such an extent that he could no longer pretend to any other reality than the one surrounding him, overwhelming him, on all sides.

But if that day had a sense of unreality, the next two days were reality enhanced, so vivid and pronounced as to be seared in his mind forever afterwards. On the following morning, he rode first to the office to speak to Burridge, insisting that he and the main Camwell officials meet him that afternoon at the scene of the 'accident' – he had already taken to uttering the word ironically – and arrange for the precise position of the shaft to be recorded and the area around it to be cordoned off and guarded, with the local press notified and their men recording the scene and the place. Burridge made to protest, rumbling on in his reasoned, ponderous way that there were more immediately important matters to attend to, but Francis surprised both himself and Burridge by his eloquent and resolute outlining of his position and his absolute determination to be obeyed.

'Attempts may be made to disguise the place; to doctor it, or to somehow make the accident explanation more plausible. In due course, when the shaft has been filled – which it is going to be, Mr Burridge, cost or no cost – there may even be local attempts to make the events into a myth, a story, all invented by the Howells to camouflage some violence or outrage on my father's part. I expect there is already some local mythology, some attitudes being taken, is there not, Mr Burridge?'

'This is hardly the time, sir—'

'No, Burridge, please. These coming weeks will be hard enough without burying my head in the sand. I need you, more than ever, to be honest with me; I have to know what people are saying if I can have any chance of countering it.'

'Perished by the sword, then, sir, if you'll forgive me, is what they're saying. Because of his long-standing neglect of safety in existing pits and old pits. He lived by the sword of recklessness and a fanatic concern with profit and production; he perished by it. That, sir, is what they're saying, accompanied by an absolute and impenetrable blanket of silence to shelter the person or persons responsible.'

In the office, next to where he had sat only the day before innocently reading, some distracted boy from a far-distant planet, Francis shook his head in disbelief.

'A sword which provided them all with a living for so many years. Work, Mr Burridge, hard work and resolution, that's the only sword my father died by.'

So they stood, on that same afternoon, on the windy Camwell grassland, as Francis hammered into the ground the wooden cross which had been fashioned overnight at Howell Grange. Burridge stood to one side, and even his careful veneer of attention and respect could not disguise his feelings of the futility of the whole business. The main Camwell men, gathered in a little group behind them, were more bemused and embarrassed than hostile.

After Francis had placed the cross, they all had to remain still for a sufficiently long period for the two gentlemen of the press who were accompanied by photographers to complete their pictures, with clear enough vistas, Francis had insisted, to make abundantly clear that the place could always be identified. Francis struggled to keep his mind and attention on doing everything as he would wish it to be; his stomach had rebelled at a lack of proper food for two days and he was close to vomiting. Eventually, the photographers announced that what needed to be done had been done, and men were beginning to move away when they realised Francis was about to speak.

Controlling his heaving insides with an effort, Francis determined to speak loudly and slowly enough for everyone to understand his meaning without any possibility of ambiguity.

'Gentlemen, it is my intention that the company will protect this spot with a surrounding brick-built building and some company workers will be employed in completely filling this dangerous shaft as well as protecting the building and the area at all times. When the process is completed, a permanent memorial will remain in the building and it will be part of one employee's duties to take care of it. I will have my father properly commemorated and we have now ensured, thanks to the gentlemen here today, that exactly where yesterday's events took place will be remembered forever afterwards. If my father perished by any sword, it was the unkind stab of ingratitude on the part of those who were provided with a livelihood by him for so many years. Because I remain unconvinced, gentlemen, that my father's fall was an accident, or that it was entirely unconnected with the unhappy earlier death of Daniel Lowtham, and you should also know that no effort will be spared to uncover the truth, however unsavoury that truth may be. In this enterprise, your help and diligence will be sought and appreciated. Thank you, gentlemen.'

On his journey home, Francis did have to stop the cab and his sickness seemed almost therapeutic, expelling some of the horrors and impositions of the recent hours.

On the morning of the following day, when he had finally had some food, if still very little sleep, he stood on the exact spot in the grand drawing room where his mother and sisters had watched the body approaching, and he was the first to spot a lone rider on the far horizon. This was no dream-like wraith procession, this was a young man riding with all his might, and even at such a distance, Francis recognised the big shoulders and the powerful pump of the legs. The rider was heading for the Grange, and aiming to get there as soon as it was humanly possible for him to do so, and perhaps even a little sooner than that.

Francis ran downstairs and charged across to the stables.

'Thomas, have we a horse ready?'

'Of course, sir,' the coachman said, incredulity in his voice. 'Always got at least one ready.'

Francis was through the yard and out of the Grange front gates in a matter of seconds. A ridiculous and inconvenient mask of moisture had spread its way across his face, but it didn't matter very much; he simply shook off the drops, dug his heels in tighter and rode off to meet his brother.

3

THE QUESTION OF MEN - 1855

As George Howell had died intestate, the decisions regarding the inheritances of the two brothers became the province of Elizabeth Howell, who determined different legacies after consultations with Charlie, Francis and her parents. Her diary is quite scanty on this period, though the terseness of the language is an indication in itself of the pressures on her at a time when grief alone would be enough of a burden. 'Further conversations with my sons, both separately and together. We are all of us in individual turmoil and the need for decisions weighs heavily upon us.'

Charlie's pressing wish to join the military and the tentative arrangements he'd already made to buy a commission in the 55th Westmorland Foot, with the help of Howell and Harrington money and after his uncle's service at Waterloo, albeit not in the same regiment, made his direction virtually inevitable. Contemporary accounts suggest, without being categorical, that he had refused to take on his father's role, or any other role, in the mining company and would head abroad if he was unable to buy his commission. Francis already had a considerable knowledge of the mining industry. Four months after George's death, the family's decision to name him as his father's business heir was generally welcomed.

The volume of Howell correspondence sent to and kept by Charlie in the Crimea, though probably not all of the originals, has enabled the fiction elements of the following story to be firmly based.

TUESDAY 24 JULY 1855

Outside a tent on the outskirts of Sevastopol, an officer sits looking into the distance. His dress has a hint of informality; the uniform jacket is unbuttoned and opened. Even so, he is warm and looks it.

Lieutenant Charles Howell is an entirely convincing infantry officer. He is moderately side-whiskered and moustachioed by the standards of the time; he is steady-eyed and firm-jawed with his same unruly boyish mop of lightish hair. However, at twenty-six, most signs of youth have already vanished; there is no reticence, no gaucheness, either obvious or implied in his position or his carriage. But there is a stiffness, a certain self-consciousness, in the way he is holding back the shoulders and thrusting the chin a little forward, which may be partly due to his discomfort at being a lone subject for a photograph, but is also suggesting an element of pain, a determination not to allow disillusion and disenchantment to show, as if a facade for the sake of the picture is being carefully maintained.

The photograph is rumoured to have been the work of Roger Fenton, the 'official' war photographer sent out to the Crimea with the publicly expressed approval of Prince Albert, but rumour is the strongest word possible. It has never featured in any public Fenton exhibitions or been acknowledged by the Fenton estate, and came into the family's possession from Colonel Sir Stephen Travers, who did not identify the photographer and who Charlie served as an adjutant during the Crimean War. Colonel Travers' circumstances and opinions, relevant as they are to the Howell story at this point, have been researched through his correspondence and military records. While inevitably battered about and stained by its existence in a war zone, it has remained a precious possession of the Howell family and is still kept in the library at Howell Grange.

The library also keeps the Crimea medal presented to Charles Howell. With the uniquely ornate oaks and acorns of the clasps, it is one of the relatively few with all of the four clasps which could be awarded to soldiers: 'Alma' (20 Sept. 1854), 'Inkerman' (5 Nov. 1854), 'Balaklava' (25 Oct. 1854) and 'Sebastopol' (1854-55) – Sebastopol spelt in the English way with a 'b'. The obverse bears the diademed head of Queen Victoria with the inscription 'VICTORIA REGINA' and the date 1854. The reverse shows a winged figure of Victory crowning a Roman soldier, who is holding a shield in his left hand and a sword in his right, with a laurel wreath. The word 'CRIMEA' can be seen to the left while the designer's name of Wyon is visible in tiny letters to the lower right.

The medal is kept in its own small safe, because of its enormous value, both as a family heirloom and a highly sought-after collection piece.

MONDAY 23 JULY 1855
ON THE PLAINS OUTSIDE SEVASTOPOL, 5 A.M.

Dawn was already well established, and through the semi-opened flap of his officer's tent, Colonel Stephen Travers could see a beautiful half-light, yellow and silver, poised over the sunken whites of the city's buildings, undisturbed beyond a few lightly drifting clouds, and incongruously harmonious with the walls and batteries where such carnage had taken place just five weeks ago.

The Colonel was already up and mostly dressed, though his heavy uniform jacket remained in the wardrobe for the moment. Unusually at this hour of the morning, there was little sea breeze disturbing the morning warmth, and he particularly wanted to be able to think clearly on this day. The tent was basic enough, in comparison with the Colonel's well-appointed Travers House in his spiritual home, the Lake District; no more than a few bits of wooden furniture, a wardrobe, a circular table with three somewhat precarious and rickety wooden armchairs, a cupboard with a few books, but mostly piles of charts and diagrams of the dispositions of the various Allied armies and navies around Sevastopol, as well as the latest and best-informed opinion of where Russian force was most obstructively assembled. At the other end of the tent from the bed was a long, low, nebulous piece of furniture with a flat top, where the Colonel's personal drinks provisions were kept, such as they were, mainly some brandies and whiskies of a rather more edifying quality than the rotgut which constituted regimental supplies. This enabled him to offer some sort of hospitality to fellow officers and even occasionally visiting civilians. In the adjacent corner stood a washstand with a mirror above it attached to a tent pole. It vaguely equated to a gentleman's bedroom with canvas walls, in which the Colonel was expected to have more or less his entire being, but he knew well enough that compared to the dog-tents, bivouacs and holes in the ground used by most of his men, it could only be described as palatial. He felt a certain duty on him to do the military thinking which his easier circumstances allowed, knowing as he did that his men's daily occupations were usually and inevitably centred entirely on simple survival.

The Colonel put down the papers he had been reading and sighed heavily. Never a man inclined to fat, the exigencies of this campaign had reduced his frame to something like slenderness, to which his height and narrow features added a vaguely scarecrow-like identity. 'He looms there like an anxious ostrich,' he once overheard one lyrical colleague say. He would have liked a better adaptability, an easier way about him to camouflage his ever-present anxieties and give the men greater confidence in his calm control, especially as now, at the age of fifty-seven, he was so much older than most of them. Something like the massive presence of Lord Raglan, he supposed, and sighed again. His Lordship had died on Thursday 28 June, ironically enough, in his bed, given his famous penchant for standing everywhere and anywhere that the Russians could shoot at him. Dysentery was medically attributed as mostly the cause, a common enough condition in this hellish place, though many believe the death of his old friend General Estcourt on the 24th and the brave failure of the attempt to take Sevastopol on the 18th were the real nails in the coffin. Raglan had taken on himself everything the caustic British press, especially *The Times*, had thrown at him, however monstrously unjust it was at times. Even before that assault on the 18th, he had, rarely and untypically, allowed the French commander Pelissier to convince him that a commencement in darkness at 3 a.m. was better than a three-hour bombardment and assault at 6 a.m., with the consequence that various blunderings about and misunderstandings in the dark had doomed the attack from the start. Once again, Raglan took the blame without deserving it, just as he had some months before when idiotic and some said wilful misunderstandings on an advance order had caused the Light Brigade to launch themselves at a target which, admittedly, was no more than a few hundred yards away from the intended destination, but which any sane cavalry officer could have discerned was suicidally unobtainable. Lord Raglan faced the press in contemptuous silence in the same way as his insouciance challenged the Russians to kill him, while the politicians and their administrator lackeys, with their endless catalogue of ineptitude, bungling movements of troops, horses and supplies, hid safely behind their London parapets.

But his Lordship was dead and could take the blame no longer. Once again, as so many times before in this wretched war, Travers thought, the pieces had to be somehow reassembled and the whole futile business driven on, the whole being a grotesque, bloody translation of the ridiculous public schoolboyish idea of little third-form boy Turkey being disgracefully held to the fire until his breeches burned by the big bullying Flashman, Russia. Thousands of men had to die of cholera, grape shot, artillery shells, heat in the summer and cold in the winter, to appease the Westminster public school boys and their Eton playing fields notions of honour and world affairs. Travers was a public school boy himself, of sorts, but by far the happiest boyhood memories for him were centred on the family's glorious 3,000 acres of Cumberland and Westmorland – farm, woodland, lake and fell, hard farming, glorious hunting, and still with spots proving a delightful magnet to well-heeled tenants. Being a second son, the military had been his initial fate, until his brother Jack had been on one binge too many and died childless at the age of thirty, leaving Stephen and his bride of two years, Polly, supposedly so far beneath him, in charge of the whole estate at the age of twenty-seven. For his sins and his exaggerated sense of duty, he had stayed with the Army for another six years, leaving the estate largely to Polly, who proved remarkably good at it, perhaps because her lack of noble birth had better acquainted her with daily economic realities. In 1833, he had finally wrenched himself out of the Army and into a near-blissful country life, including three surviving children of five conceived, only to be talked back into service by a government minister and northern neighbour on the death of the previous commanding officer. He could still see the dark, haunted Silas eyes peering across at him over the port.

'If we don't take a stand, Stephen, there'll be Russian armies in Austria, then Italy, then France. This Tsar's ambitions know no bounds. Rhythmic lines of Russian boots pounding up the road from Manchester, eh, Stephen? Where will the democracy stool pigeons be then, I wonder? Raped maids, butchered plough boys, Windermere running red.'

And so on and so forth, and nonsense as Travers knew so much of it was, he'd been convinced, like so many other honest but impressionable men, that Something Had To Be Done and it was no use leaving it to everyone else. And, finally, in amongst the lurid scenarios and fanciful horrors, Silas Fletcher had sat his clincher, at first almost unnoticed.

'And I will tell you, directly if confidentially, Stephen, that with the additional arguments of your previous service, your considerable assistance with the regiment even when technically a civilian, and your intelligent and productive stewardship of such a hefty chunk of this part of the country, that the Minister would consider a knighthood an entirely justified recompense for your help with the Crimean campaign. A royal sword on the shoulder, eh, Stephen? Not to be lightly dismissed, I think.'

Which, of course, it wasn't, even for a man whose vanity and dignity were so lightly worn as to allow him to play at farm animals on the floor with his children and not so long ago, his grandchildren. He told himself it was mostly for Polly's sake, Polly who had taken herself up from a maid to a schoolteacher and listened with such interest and patience to all his doubts and insecurities when he took his leave and they strolled along the side of one beautiful lake or another. She could and did hold herself proudly against all the great ladies, but he dearly liked the prospect of her being one of them. Even so, he admitted, in his most mercilessly self-analytical moments, still frequent enough even in his late fifties, that it was also about the country boy making good, the skinny fell-running woodland imp going to see the Queen.

He could not but relish the idea of a northern boy's coat of finery to dignify his coming old age, if cholera, dysentery, grape shot or a bayonet didn't do for him first.

He forced his mind back to the charts and papers spread on the table. This afternoon would be yet another long and detailed discussion on how to finally get hold of what was left of Sevastopol. Deserters in their droves had been telling the Allies how close they came to actually taking the city on the 18th – accounts which, again, would not have improved Lord Raglan's state of mind. Many of them made very clear that another hour or so of general bombardment to add to the literal piles of Russian soldiers and the Allies could have walked their armies in with flags flying. But the Russians had and were strengthening their defences again, they still had their bridge to the north bringing in whatever supplies and troop reinforcements they might need, and the end of it seemed no nearer in sight than it had ever been. The following issue, of what they would then do when Sevastopol was taken and they had to contemplate marching on to mainland Russia with their diminished and disease-ridden armies facing freshly gathered and supplied Russian armies of hundreds of thousands, Travers didn't even allow himself to think about.

The opening at the front of the tent still produced no breeze, and now promised a hot, interminable Crimean summer day which one had no feasible option but to endure. He endured. Indignation, the use of subordinates for the bad-tempered relief of accumulated frustrations, pointless wandering about finding work for idle hands; he knew these were all his foibles from time to time and he had long since ceased to see himself as any kind of model commanding officer, but this place, and this war, were enough to test the patience and temper of the saints themselves, and he had no illusions about himself in that quarter. Everyone had been waiting for the mail to arrive for two days, and when that which was supposed to happen didn't happen in the Crimea, the explanations could be several and various, but probably not good. A Russian sortie out of Sevastopol could have destroyed both the cart and its couriers; a false horse move could have sent the whole ensemble plunging into a ravine, and they featured emphatically in the terrain on the entire route from here to Balaklava. Travers himself regarded the mail as a mixed blessing; his sons Richard and William, resolutely kept out of the military, made a generally good fist of looking after the estate and maintaining good relations with neighbouring landowners. In fact, Travers thought wearily, they were passably gifted at getting on with just about everyone in the world except each other. Polly did her best as an umpire, but occasionally things had to be put up to Father, the Solomon in the Crimea, to resolve, and Father had quite enough on his plate, especially in the Solomon line.

The mail's arrival would also mean further acerbic press editorials, no doubt, papers which lower ranks were largely kept away from but which senior officers felt obliged to read in case additional slanders and inaccuracies made their appearance. But many of the men, and especially the junior officers, had little else but letters from home and the lamentable local liquor to sustain them, and the lack of one could exacerbate indulgence in the other.

At the same moment as this discomforting thought crossed his mind, one of his adjutants appeared in front of a smaller tent about fifty yards away and sat himself down right in the Colonel's eyeline. Charlie Howell, shirt half on and no boots yet, chewing his lip and bouncing his ankles like some caged beast, which in Charlie's case wasn't so fanciful an analogy. Travers knew his soft spot for Charlie was mostly about seeing a kind of mirror of his younger self. Like him, Charlie had entered military service as a generally plain and straightforward northern boy; like him, he strongly suspected, Charlie had started with a wildly idealised and romantic view of what serving one's country was all about and a pathetic belief that those in political and military authority knew what they were doing. Galloping up to some equally gloriously uniformed opponent with a hearty 'Have at you, sir!', followed by a noble and skilled sword duel, while the men carried all before them with their sheer pluck and fighting spirit. All the not so glorious stuff, men literally blown to pieces in front of your eyes, body parts randomly spread across the landscape as far as the eye could see, corpses in the last frozen spasms of agony after a bayonet had pierced their guts, men dying in their own mess in field hospitals, screams and streams of blood as piles of severed limbs grew like gruesome plants; these didn't figure in the young man's imagination. Nor did the fact that the nation who had been our sworn enemy and with whom we had been at war for over twenty years not so long ago, the nation which had almost fatally wounded Charlie's uncle at Waterloo, was now our ally and fighting companion. The world as ordered by statesmen and politicians was almost too much for Charlie, as it had been all those years ago for Travers himself. And when Travers had discovered that Charlie had begun his commission just after the death of an authoritarian father, his fellow feeling had ratcheted up again; such a brutal disillusion, so unarguably mortifying, to discover that the worst a father could do in boyhood was as nothing compared with what authority could accomplish in manhood. Travers saw again his own sad-eyed, fatalistic father, something of a beanpole as he was himself, picking up his cane in pained silence and realised that the expression he had so unkindly interpreted as something like enjoyment, some perverse appreciation of the humiliation he was about to witness, really had actually been pain. The first time young Richard had backed him into a similar corner, when, to his utter and gut-wrenching astonishment, the boy had been conclusively exposed as a thief, Travers had actually found himself weeping afterwards.

But now he sometimes found himself questioning, dangerously if silently, as he suspected Charlie Howell did, what all that supposedly dutiful and devoted discipline had actually led them to – what nature of man resulted from the brutalities of a conventional upbringing? Was it so virtuous to have men so afraid of the authority placed over them that they were prepared to stand and be shot to pieces rather than disobey orders? Was the Army actually best served by officers who, even in a clearly hopeless situation, would place themselves at the front of their men and urge them on at all costs, simply to be shot down or blown apart right in front of the men they were supposed to be inspiring, as had happened in this war time and time again? The most urgent question in the minds of men – were they really men? Was any price, up to and including death itself, worth paying to be what other men defined as a man? And what were such definitions worth, when the outcome was entirely about gore, waste and fields of violently disarranged bodies, men reduced to bits of men? In the dark, small hours, when every night guns and yells could still be heard over the whole Sevastopol theatre, Travers would sometimes wake in sweat and shame, seeing that regimental flag at his feet, his men unsure and dying behind him and a firmly entrenched battery of Russian guns ahead, his duty demanding that he either pick up the flag and go forward until the grape shot tears his flesh open or face an eternity of cold-eyed stares, whispered conversations, groups of impertinent, leering men treating an officer known to 'lack conduct' in the traditional manner. War suited no one but maniacs and profiteers, but it was an even more unfathomable puzzle for simple souls like Charlie Howell and himself.

Not that Lieutenant Howell was stupid – far from it. Paternal instincts would not have been enough for the Colonel to take him on to his staff if he wasn't suitable. The regular daily difficulties did not need the aggravation of enduring the vacuous, arrogant sons of the aristocracy foisted on to some officers, who didn't understand anything more than monosyllabic instructions and were perfectly capable of delivering entirely the wrong messages to entirely the wrong people – witness the Light Brigade catastrophe. Because Travers' regiment was the less glamorous infantry, he could pick adjutants on the basis of skill and ability, the aristos not wishing to serve in such a humble outfit. Charlie was attentive, intelligent, a superb horseman – not something to be taken for granted, by any means, and essential for a message-carrying adjutant – and possessed of the kind of courage which Travers personally preferred, courage tempered by common sense. If a message needed to get through, Charlie would get it through, one way or the other, but if it needed to take another five minutes to get there rather than not get there at all, Charlie could make a judicious pause or a strategic detour. A few oblique references had indicated that Charlie had a girl back home and Travers suspected that, medals or not, she would take a dim view of him getting his fool head shot off before their nuptials became possible.

Travers looked up from a depressing reading of the number of defensive guns the Russians supposedly still had in Sevastopol. Charlie was talking now, chatting earnestly to a fellow adjutant, Robert Hartley, a thin, studious young man, very different in both appearance and temperament from the ruddy, outgoing, broad-shouldered Charlie, but the two of them seemed to get on well enough, which was also useful. Hartley was an adjutant by inclination as well as order, though Charlie probably wasn't; happy as he professed to be in the role, Travers suspected he would prefer to be in the field leading men. Travers remained sympathetic but largely indifferent; he would prefer to be boating gently across Windermere for a picnic on the other side, he and Polly, sons and daughters-in-law, grandchildren who still were children. What had to be had to be, in war if not in peace.

A pleasant, if slightly controversial, idea suddenly appeared in his mind from nowhere in particular. Tomorrow would bring a potentially irritating mid-morning appointment with Mr Roger Fenton, the war photographer, publicly approved of by Prince Albert and reputedly sent on his way with the injunction 'no dead bodies'. As far as Travers was concerned, Fenton was an irrelevance and a nuisance. The regiment was supposedly being done a favour, a gesture which showed that it wasn't just the cavalry who were to be favoured with his work, but today Travers still had a lot of material he wanted to examine in detail before the afternoon's strategy meeting, literally a matter of life and death, and tomorrow would be concerned with examining the proposed strategy's feasibility. However, he conceded to himself that Fenton had gathered a little more kudos and a little less notoriety since arriving in the Crimea. He was, without doubt, good at what he did, and he had occasionally proved useful in countering press stories rather than supporting them. As for the dead bodies story, Fenton had always made it clear that even transporting, let alone setting up, his heavy, cumbersome equipment on or near a battlefield would be an impossible task at short notice and the Russian artillery might neither realise nor respect his peaceful intentions.

Travers decided that, since he had to deal with the inconvenience of such a visit at such a time, he would arrange for photographs to be taken of himself and his adjutants, at his own expense if necessary. Even if Fenton considered himself unable to oblige and did not have such portraits in mind, rumour had it that he was not averse to his assistant – he always had at least one with him – doing a little business on his own account. Travers felt that he was entitled to take the opportunity of retaining the image of some brave men he had fought alongside, so that, if he were spared and allowed some remaining life in the Lakes, the nightmarish memories of the Crimea could at least be partly assuaged by a remembrance that there were decent, personable officers alongside him at the time. And if either Hartley or Howell did not themselves survive, their own families would undoubtedly appreciate such an immediate and personal record.

The whole idea pleased him to such an extent that he determined to act on it immediately. He walked to the tent entrance.

'Lieutenant Howell! Lieutenant Hartley!'

They both jumped to attention and Charlie began rapidly doing up his uniform jacket.

'Never mind about that for the moment, Howell,' Travers said, and he sat down again as the two younger men walked in. Their manner towards him was respectful, but not forced; the stiff, apprehensive formality which some junior officers were unable to conceal in the presence of their seniors was missing. In an organisation of hierarchies and unquestionable superior ranks, a fair-minded and fallible CO like Travers was a mercy, and the lieutenants knew and appreciated it.

'We will have a visitor tomorrow morning, gentlemen. Mr Roger Fenton, war photographer, personally approved by His Royal Highness Prince Albert. Our orders are to offer him every assistance which our duties will allow. I have decided to request that, whatever else Mr Fenton chooses to portray, either he or his assistant take a number of private photographs of certain individual regimental officers, to include myself and both of you and at my own expense if necessary. It seems perfectly reasonable to me that our respective families should have some visual representation of what we are doing here and why, especially if, unhappy as it is to contemplate such possibilities, we do not survive the campaign. I would also like some personal record of some of the men with whom I have had the privilege to serve in this extraordinary war. Have you been photographed before?' he added, to cover the faint flushes of embarrassment appearing on their cheeks.

'No, sir,' said Hartley, with an odd little rueful grin, as if the idea of someone wanting to was ridiculous in itself.

'Yes, sir,' said Howell, equally unsurprisingly, Travers thought. 'By men from the press. At my father's funeral in 1852. Scrubbed and wearing my best coat in one final attempt to do as my father would wish, which regrettably had never been easy for me.'

A long speech by Charlie's standards, Travers noted, and saw the lieutenant's face turn away, as if he'd made some kind of confession which had surprised even himself.

'In that case, you at least will know what to expect. It is a tedious and rather awkward experience, keeping quite still for long periods of time for the dubious consequence of being recorded, warts and all, for posterity. However, I suspect our duty will make considerably more formidable demands on us before this business is over, gentlemen. And speaking of this business, I think perhaps it is time we got down to it. Further proposals for raising the siege will be discussed by senior officers this afternoon and I want to be able to make a coherent and well-argued contribution, should the opportunity arise. Towards that end, there are a number of technical questions concerning the coming assault on which I wish to canvas your views. Please sit down.'

During their discussions, the mail finally arrived, and Travers found his temper pressurised again through the elaborate and time-consuming process of dividing and distributing it. A few supply and disciplinary issues had also arisen during the previous night and the morning. The Colonel would generally only be accompanied by a single adjutant to a conference of senior officers, and Charlie found himself wishing, for once, that it would be Hartley, as did Hartley himself. Hartley had no girl back home; he had two aged and querulous parents who seemed quite persuaded that he was spending most of his time drinking and roistering like soldiers do, in spite of all the publicity coming to them from the Crimean, and whose correspondence was usually a litany of the deprivations and inconveniences his absence was causing them. His married sister wrote quite rarely and sparsely. For him, mail arrivals were occasions to be glossed over and seen through with mercifully more pressing duties.

For Charlie, the experience was very different. Post from the family meant a kind of temporary escape from this hellish place, sometimes for hours on end. It could also, on occasions, reduce him to paroxysms of homesickness which made the necessary return to ghastly reality all the more difficult, but even so, he would not choose to forego the letters from home, and especially, the letters from Mary Prentice. There had been one special occasion when he'd met Mary while paying a visit with his mother to the Prentices, one of the more affluent Harrington tenants, Henry Prentice's farming methods being heartily approved of by Sir John, in terms of demonstrating to one and all how to increase yields without major additional expense or the sacrifice of quality. He'd met Mary on several previous occasions; Elizabeth Howell's rounds of the major Harrington tenants were intermittent, dutiful expeditions, and she always insisted on being accompanied by at least one of her offspring; she regarded it as essential for their social training. But the special occasion was the first time he'd really noticed Mary. She was almost exactly his age and her charms seemed to have accumulated in proportion to his ability to notice them. In June 1853, when Charlie was still raw from the death of his father, they began by talking inconsequentially in and around the conversations of their mothers, but they both felt something entirely different had been ignited which would not easily peter out, and when Charlie went back for a solo return visit, on the spurious excuse of lending Mary something about mining which she had improbably requested, the talk accompanying a stroll round the Prentice land had become a good deal more personal.

'I almost wish I hadn't joined up now, Mary,' he'd admitted, as they sat on a dubiously moist river bank, both splendidly indifferent to what the ground might be doing to their seats. After all the rigours he'd been through to get the commission and even allowing for the seemingly interminable Carlisle-based training, Charlie could hardly believe he was hearing his own words.

'Will you really have to go abroad?' she said, and there was a catch in her voice, and a sudden red flush in the middle of her cheeks, which penetrated more deeply through to Charlie's heart than anything he'd known before. Her face then, still quite pale even in the sun, turned so closely to him that he could see the dilation in her dark eyes and the contradictory luscious red of her otherwise rather prim little lips, had returned to him again and again as he'd tried to reconcile an idealised past with a calamitous present.

As it transpired, Hartley was the man chosen – Travers was no fool. Charlie's afternoon was about routine officer supervision in this strange hiatus of the war, and by mid-afternoon he had arranged matters so that he could retire to his own tent with a collection of letters burning holes in his hands.

He began with the family, knowing that it would be Mary who would drive him to the greatest extremities of his feelings and if he started with her, the simple concentration required to absorb everything else would be too dissipated.

Dealing with them one at a time like this was an odd experience. In the daily hubbub of life at the Grange, when many other people were constantly about in addition to his family, one-to-one conversations with any of them were relatively rare. Charlie had also conceded to himself ever since the start of his life away from home that he'd probably never been the world's best listener, always with his own affairs prominent in his mind. Reading their letters like this was something like being sat down in a room with them arranged in a semi-circle in front of him, told to hold his peace and listen to each of them in turn talk about their lives without his own impinging, for the moment, in any way. His guilty awareness grew that he had probably at least doubled his real knowledge of each one of them, with the possible exception of Francis, since he had left home.

They were collected together in a heavy, cloth-wrapped bundle, intended to survive the worst rigours of naval transport. An earlier package, to Charlie's intense, almost teary, frustration, had arrived as a filthy heap of hopelessly saturated paper and his reply, speaking anger in every syllable, had ensured that any repetition would not be the family's fault.

He unwrapped the bundle, not without effort and scissors, and separated the letters. Even the paper used, from Anne's slightly scented pinks and blues to Francis's ripped out office notepaper, was a badge of identity, before he even began to distinguish the handwriting.

With a brief, impatient spasm of guilt at effectively ranking her last by reading her first, instantly suppressed in comparison with the weightier pursuits of the Crimea, he reached for Anne's coloured paper and neat, slanting writing, which he sometimes found difficult to decipher. She'd written double-sided and the whole amounted to almost twelve pages. As the little pile of sheets fell away, he picked up what was marked as page 4 and read an extract from the middle of the page. Anne had not long since celebrated her twentieth birthday; what she seemed to want more than anything else was to have children and she grew increasingly impatient that the apparently necessary preliminary marriage did not appear to be happening. At present, her only suitor was a clerk called Thomas Henderson, who worked at the Howell offices and would occasionally go for walks and picnics with her, but Elizabeth Howell didn't think poor Thomas any kind of a match. Their tentative expeditions were usually chaperoned by one of the other Howell children and occasionally even Elizabeth herself, which could drive Anne to distraction. Anne was a sweet, good-natured creature, Charlie thought, though over-sensitive to even the most gentle teasing. It wasn't a brother's place to decide on her prettiness or otherwise, but, unhappily, no one seemed to say it of Anne; she had the same lugubrious, narrow-boned rather pinched Harrington features as Francis and, for that matter, Sir John himself, but neither Francis nor Sir John needed to be pretty. Anne, unfortunately, probably did.

'Of course, it is the Howell staff summer picnic and it would be outrageous for Mama not to be there,' Anne wrote. 'And of course one has no wish to flaunt one's wealth in front of the family employees. But Mama's strictures against the dress which I, a grown woman, feel it is appropriate for me to wear are rather out of place, I feel. Thomas will doubtless be in the best – perhaps the only – suit he possesses, and it would be insulting to him and the company generally for me to be wearing no more than a humdrum day-to-day summer ensemble. Mama seems unable to see the basis of my annoyance. The others are, as ever, quite hopeless; Francis simply looks dreamy and vacant if I ever mention the subject to him, and Charlotte will dismiss the whole matter with her customary contemptuous snort—'

Charlie put down the paper and closed his eyes momentarily; sleep had become problematic, even in the relative torpor of present affairs, perhaps because the images of the past months repeated themselves again and again in ever more grotesque nightmarish interpretations. Last night, the images of Russian soldiers bayoneting wounded British infantrymen on the field of Inkerman came back, at a stage of the battle when rescue was impossible, and even at a distance, he could see men's eyes turned towards him in dumb supplication as the steel point of the bayonet loosened their entrails. He would listen to Anne's dress problems for a million years, he thought, for the sake of being there to hear them and not here to read them.

Most of the remaining pages were in the same vein, but near the end, she suddenly managed to wring his heart.

'Alice steadfastly refuses to tell me what she appears to have discovered about this cholera business, but I read the papers too and I know whatever it is must be horrid in the extreme as it seems to be killing as many men as the battles. Dear Charlie, do take care and watch what water you drink; please take whatever precautions you can. It's hateful to think of you ill and suffering, even with Miss Nightingale to take care of you.'

He paused at some nearby commotion, which proved to be men arguing over cards. Charlie made his opinions clear in the blunt soldier language they used themselves, and Charlie's tendency not to make idle threats was well known. The game subsided into surly peace and Charlie went back to his letters.

Charlotte next, on correct unlined white paper. Charlotte remained unmarried at the age of twenty-two, but not for much longer. In her case, her suitor had been there since childhood; a boy and now man called Eustace Thirwell, whose land bordered the Howell estate and who was the very suitable heir of Nathaniel Thirwell, a partner in the mining company. Thirwell had proved capable of defusing the worst excesses of George Howell's temper and keeping the lines of communication open between Howell and his other partners. Charlie had always liked Eustace, almost an exact contemporary with whom he'd spent a lot of time as a boy in the summer holidays from school. Eustace was a good sort, if not very good at pushing himself forward and rather in the shadow of his overpowering father. Whether or not anyone would see him as good-looking was, again, not Charlie's to say, but even though Charlotte tended to be generally considered as pretty at the least, with her flashing Howell eyes and healthy complexion, Charlie nevertheless suspected that Eustace was more or less being bullied into a match. Charlotte, like Mother, liked to be involved with the land and saw the prospect of effectively being heir to the Thirwell estate as a way of finding a dominion entirely uncluttered with Howells and Harringtons. Charlotte was similar to her father in many ways, often ill-tempered and thoroughly self-willed, but she also possessed a caustic wit and mischievous humour which he had never had, though Charlie wondered sometimes whether he did have and had just never let Charlie see it.

'Eustace is to be land manager for the time being. He prefers this to involvement with the mining side of the business. I agree. It also gives me the opportunity to make my own contribution, with no little experience from the Harrington estates. He agrees. Eustace is perfectly sensible about everything when it is properly explained to him. This is far from always the case with Mr Thirwell.' And so on, only just reaching the beginning of a fifth page, in Charlotte's large but cramped writing. Near the end, what passed for concern in the Charlotte way: 'the papers, which Alice reads with fanatical thoroughness, seem to believe a final push will take Sebastopol and hopefully end the war. Tell them to get on with it, Charlie. It's time you were back with us, being loud and untidy again. Eustace misses you too. Do take care'.

Charlie turned to the big lined office pages where were Francis's trademark; Francis would see it as wasteful and rather showy to write to his brother on elaborate stationery. Charlie still secretly lamented his lost Frank; over the years, the few people who'd called him Frank had faded until Charlie and no-one else did it, mostly, Charlie felt, because Frank the chuckling kid, the easy playmate, which he'd once been way, way back when they were both little children, had gradually been usurped by this so-serious, careworn creature who seemed to relish the burdens accumulating on his back.

As usual, most of the letter was concerned with the mining business; Francis had never fully understood Charlie's indifference and disinterest in what earned the family's bread. Lately Charlie had been forcing himself to pay more attention, because he wanted – needed – to believe he still had a future somewhere as far away from this present hellish place as possible. Nothing the family business could do to him, nothing anyone could ever do to him again, could begin to compare with the several lives he'd crammed into the last few weeks.

'The remorseless tug of war between safety and profit goes on', Francis wrote. 'I think, after a lot of time and effort, I can count on Burridge as generally an ally rather than a stubbornly determined neutral. He represents the views of the other partners to me as a devil's advocate, enabling me to outline my own arguments which I think he is increasingly prepared to relay back to them. Burridge is immensely respected by all, whereas I continue to be seen as George Howell's whelp, wet behind the ears and with milksop notions about feather-bedding the men. I try to tell them that more solid and well-established works, and more careful processes and procedures, will actually increase profits in various ways; less working time lost through injuries and accidents, less frequent replacement of equipment, easier recruitment of a better standard of hewers and hurriers, especially the former. But I remain clumsy with them, in all honesty. At the last Board meeting, Mr. Thirwell intervened to say I must at least be heard, amongst a generally unsettled atmosphere of chair-scraping and paper shuffling. His tone was so much that of humouring the importunate youth that my patience was stretched and I said, with some asperity, that as the Howell share of the Company at 40% was the largest single block, I could and would be heard now and at all times in the future. Thirwell is much the most sympathetic of the partners and he looked hurt, though Mr. Foster seemed perversely pleased; 'there, gentlemen, we hear the authentic Howell voice once again'. Burridge looked at the floor, and they were on to the next item on the agenda before I could continue'.

Francis, too, was courting, but in a much more indirect way than Charlotte. He had clearly set himself at the Rector's daughter, Emily Salter, but in such a tentative, circuitous fashion that Charlie doubted whether he would ever actually make any significant progress. He also spoke of her more as a paragon of virtue, a walking angel whose pretty shoes he was not fit to kiss; he didn't even seem able to refer to her first name. 'Miss Salter was gracious enough to show me the progress being made in the Rectory garden, and I was able to learn a number of interesting stipulations regarding the successful growth of several salad vegetables'. Charlie smiled and lamented simultaneously. He knew for a fact that Francis was not a virgin after a couple of extremely daring trips to Newcastle, ostensibly on Howell business, in 1849 and 1850, when his brother's shock at discovering Charlie knew the whereabouts of a brothel was immediately moderated when Charlie assured the younger man – Charlie was 20 and Francis 18 – that he knew someone who could carefully and instructively relieve him of his virginity. And the lady in question did, and Francis could not stop talking about it for weeks afterwards, even though, in true Francis fashion, his delight at the whole business had to be tempered with constant anxiety at the possible appearance of disease. Which never happened, as Charlie swore it wouldn't, because he knew the lady personally. Francis, he thought, had the same young man's delusion that a whole ocean of time was ahead for him to do whatever he chose; Charlie knew well enough that he had already only just cheated death at least four times since arriving in the Crimea and it might well be waiting for him tomorrow, even today. For pity's sake, Francis, he thought, if you want the Salter girl to the extent that you're prepared to put up with her hell fire and damnation thundering bore of a father, then hurry the courtship along before the poor woman despairs and turns her head elsewhere.

But Francis, as ever, at least knew the right words for his brother.

'I can only imagine what you must be going through and the risks you must already have had to take. I sometimes feel the blood draining from my face as I read the Times. You are in all our thoughts always, brother; we can only wonder and applaud your courage and sense of duty and hope you will be spared to come back to us. Your ever faithful brother, Francis (Frank)'.

Charlie looked again at the final bracketed word, and a sudden shame of tears had started to his eyes before he recalled the men nearby and controlled himself with a huge effort. Then he seemed to feel cold, in spite of the heat of the day, as if his being was struggling to escape the bleak futility of its present surroundings and return to normal, blessedly normal, life, bringing an end to this whole pointless posturing of his declaration of independence, a gesture he could now begin to see became obsolete as soon as his father died.

But, as he and his fellow officers had often observed and occasionally dared to discuss, the Crimea rarely left anyone time enough to think very much, and so it proved now. Another commotion outside, and this time it wasn't just the tedious bawling of irate men, it was the occasional dull boom of artillery guns against the staccato crackling of musket fire and the customary dreadful accompaniment of noises both human and inhuman. Ever since the failure of the assault on 18 June, the Allies had been inching their lines forward, keeping the advance troops in trenches and making sure each new fortification was protected with thoroughly built parapets. Unusually, the Allied armies were suffering the majority of casualties; the vast numbers of dead and wounded on all sides since the beginning of the war had been particularly heavy for the Russians, both within and outside of the city. But now, they were using the tactics of sending out relatively small raiding parties to snipe at the Allied soldiers, men who could kneel in their trenches at distances of no more than fifty or a hundred yards and shoot down whoever appeared. Now it was happening again. Big guns loosing off at targets they couldn't see was as pointless as ever, but they continued to do so, and if they couldn't hit the snipers, they could make life more difficult for the defenders in the city. As ever, two armies prepared to hit at each other, wherever, whenever, they could, even if just for a few men here or a few fallen walls there, walls which the Russians still remorselessly managed to rebuild during the night.

The men in the forward trenches particularly were unsettled and expectant, and understandably so. Everybody remembered Inkerman, on 5 November 1854, when over 20,000 Russian troops emerged from Sevastopol to join up with a field army of another 20,000+ , a total Russian strength of 42,000 men and 134 guns against 8,550 British and 7,500 French troops mustering fifty-eight artillery guns between them. The Russians had resolved to either drive the Allied army back to the coast in chaos or massacre them where they stood. Nobody could ever forget the carnage of that day, endless waves of Russians with their old Napoleonic flint lock muskets pouring forward to be slaughtered, their sheer

weight of numbers killing or wounding hundreds and hundreds
of the Allies. Only when almost half the Russian Army had been
killed or wounded themselves did Prince Menchikoff end the
slaughter and withdraw, leaving the Allied armies horribly mauled,
but in charge of the field. The 55th lost five officers and sixty-six
men that day, the numbers and memories etched on the minds of
Charlie and his men, more blood-letting, death and maiming on
a single day than any man, even the veterans, had ever seen before
or would wish to see again, worse than either Balaklava or Alma,
both battles with which the Russians had intended to end the war.
Even now, every skirmish, every minor Russian sortie out of the
city, aroused suspicions in all British and French minds that they
were ready to make yet one more attempt with the same readiness
to take massive casualties and keep coming.

As Charlie watched, a man moving something about behind
one of the parapets nearest the city raised himself too high for too
long and his head was quite literally shot off, the remaining corpse
hovering, as if in indignant surprise, before collapsing out of
sight. Not so long ago, such a sight would have been sure to make
Charlie's guts heave; sheer numb shock got him somehow through
Alma, but at both Balaklava and Inkerman he had vomited almost
casually, doing his best to find any kind of disguise available until
he saw numbers of other men in similar difficulties. Now he
was conscious of the ever-present trickle of sweat on a July day
accentuating in various places and the questions he'd been asking
himself ever since the beginning of this gruesome business echoed
in the back of his mind again. What had he expected warfare to be
like? What had he thought battles were all about? He felt foolish
and somehow cheated, because he suspected the disillusionment
of a young man, even if it was inevitable, should follow a slower
and less brutal course, that youth to middle-age should be more
elastic than a three-month epic blood bath for a collection of
reasons which Charlie regarded as flimsy at best. He had asked

Alice, who seemed to know more about world politics at the tender age of sixteen than he had ever known, to try and explain the thinking behind the war with Russia, and she'd done her best at enormous length, though Charlie remained unconvinced and found himself startled that people in high places could make such dubious decisions, for which thousands of men had to pay with their blood, lost limbs and mutilated bodies. His tentative attempt to have a dialogue with Colonel Travers on the issue had been firmly, if gently, rebuffed.

'The situation is, Lieutenant Howell, that their job is to make decisions about what we are to do and ours is to make decisions about how we are going to do it. We may have opinions about the efficacy with which they do their jobs, and they certainly have similar views about the effectiveness of the way we do ours, but mixing the two is a recipe for confusion and reversing them is a recipe for chaos. Our business is how; their business is why. So be it.'

The Russian breakout proved to be no more than a few minutes' skirmish and exchange of fire; more lives lost as if an afterthought to excite the day. Charlie was eventually able to return to his tent and his mail. Even after the returning Travers and Hartley had been sighted, he remained determined to keep Mary's letters for last, and for a time at night when the prospects of interruption, though never non-existent, were as low as they could be. He felt the same about Alice's writing, but for different reasons; Mary he could follow easily enough. Alice at times made him feel out of his depth and her letters usually needed silence and concentration.

He contented himself with a first reading of his mother's neat and very eligible copperplate, a style taught her by Lady Harrington, her mother. Unlike the others, Elizabeth Howell didn't spend the great majority of her time talking about her own life; there was more than enough now, Charlie knew, to fill a dozen letters in every mailing, though she usually contented herself with two, both written over several days and, in the winter when deliveries were more problematic, weeks. They were mixtures of reminiscences, encouragement, information on self-help in protecting health, smatters of local gossip and events, but the dominant and recurrent theme was about bringing him home.

'I know well enough you felt you needed to go away and prove yourself; young men do, and not just young men. Alice has been plaguing me with the monstrous idea of her going off to join the group of nurses at Scutari; she wants a medical career and she thinks to begin with care at its most challenging. I am holding the fort as well as I can, insisting that, whatever the medical career may be, it will start neither at sixteen years of age nor at Scutari, and especially not for a girl so vulnerable in infancy that she spent most of it ill in bed. But I will not be able to hold out for much longer; Alice is already an adult, perhaps because her young life has already contained so many trials and dangers. For her sake and yours, Charlie, I can only hope that this wretched war finishes soon. While I hope you won't think of it as interference, I have spoken to my father, who has various connections with the military, and his information is that those young officers who feel, and rightly so, that they have served their country well enough after having gone through this hellish campaign will find tolerant attitudes being taken on discontinuing their commissions, and those who have distinguished themselves – which, it seems, will include you, Charlie, from the very strong hints your grandfather has received – will be treated with particular sympathy, perhaps even with some of their commission costs returned to them to help their start in civilian life, which will clearly mean problems for some. My father is quite adamant that he will use his influence to help if and when it becomes necessary, and please don't think ill of him because of that, Charlie; he has always loved you dearly, even when you were at your most impossible, and no one else with any place in society seems reluctant to use it; it is the way of the world.

'I know your reasons for leaving had much to do with your father, and I have little doubt that, were he still with us, you would be finding new ways to antagonise and annoy each other. But, unhappily, he is not. The burden of man of the house has fallen on Francis and he does his best, which is not inconsiderable, but Francis has more than enough on his plate with the company and I think he finds the now almost exclusively female household rather trying at times, as I confess I do myself. While you arrive at decisions about how much the Army needs you when, God preserve you, this war is over, please reflect that our need is probably at least as great as theirs, and much easier to meet.'

He had only begun to digest the intentions and implications of this when the order for all officers resounded through the camp and the whole regimental officer complement was shortly gathered in and around Travers' tent, sitting and standing, while the man himself laid the situation before them as cogently as he was able.

'There is a feeling amongst the High Command that, while there must be no further question of another winter spent on this campaign after the dreadful privations the men have already endured throughout last winter, enough time is now available through the summer to work on ensuring the success of the final assault on Sevastopol. As you know, the Tsar who brought Russia into this war, Nicholas 1st, died in March; his successor is reputedly much less keen on the conflict and it is suspected that the fall of Sevastopol would probably cause him to sue for terms. Therefore, we must ensure this time that everything which can be done to pave the way for a successful lifting of the siege will be done before an attempt is made. We are to redouble our efforts to move our fortifications ever closer to the city and strengthen them so that the Russians continue to waste manpower and ammunition in trying to force them back. The enemy is already severely weakened, gentlemen, as is well known from the accounts of the many deserters now leaving the city. When we are ready to strike the final blow, we will do so, and at last bring this bloody business to a triumphant end.'

In the dead of night, a night for once almost silent, Travers countered his sleeplessness by working on correspondence and administration, of which there was always more than enough. He felt slightly ashamed of what he now thought of as his weak feelings of earlier; it is known well enough, he reflected, that war requires a discipline of thought, the ability to establish channels which the mind may wander along and channels which are out of bounds. Fatalism and trepidation were not positive emotions for military situations. Soldiers could not avoid the necessity of a blinkered approach. Their natures and characters were questions *for* men; the predominant question *of* men concerned whether or not they were, *en masse*, equal to the tasks they were set. It implied a collective spirit, a companionship in adversity, and whether they had the unity and determination, as a group, to succeed in their aims and do their duty. He believed the regiment did, and intended to work hard to prove the supposition a reality.

The bliss of solitude was a new phenomenon for Charlie, who had steadfastly tried to avoid it since childhood and had largely succeeded. Weariness with the press of people around him was not a problem he had envisaged, but the brief Crimean campaign had taught him that any snatch of privacy was usually restorative and essentially liberating, without the persistent clamour of expectation from superiors, equals and inferiors alike. With a carefully gathered and protected candle collection, he enjoyed the luxury of being able to give his final two correspondents, sister Alice and lover Mary, his exclusive attention, not least because they both demanded it in their turn.

In Alice's case, she seemed to be able to lead him to a point where he knew they were in disagreement, but he couldn't trace accurately back to identify the moment where their paths diverged.

This present communication, like a number of its predecessors as much political analysis and treatise as family correspondence, took him to the conclusion that the whole idea of going to war with the Russians was absurd.

'Even if it were true that the best way to arrest Russian imperial ambitions is to fight them on their own soil – and it is not, it is patently absurd – taking and holding their major cities is not sustainable without massive garrisons which neither ourselves or the French could afford for any long period of time, and would in any case always eventually be retaken by the Russians, given their vast reserves of manpower and weaponry. The trick with any potential invader is to be too strong for him to launch a successful invasion in the first place. Mercifully, we are, because of our island position and our superb Navy, and if we are to render really valuable assistance to our Allies abroad, it is that naval power and tactical assistance which makes most sense of all.'

Charlie found his eyes narrowing at Alice's straggly little lines, thirty or forty to a page. He found it difficult to understand in what way he was supposed to find Alice's insistence that he was fighting an entirely futile war helpful. But, of course, Alice had an interpretation of that as well. 'Of course, what you're really doing, dear Charlie, is what all young people must do sooner or later; we need to find ourselves as individuals and I don't think it's really possible to do that while one remains surrounded by the people of one's childhood. If it was entirely my choice, I would be at Scutari and learning my trade with Miss Nightingale's nurses, but Mother is adamant that I am too young and she will not countenance it. She has suffered much since Father died, as has Francis, and I will not sulk or withdraw whatever I can do to help them, but sooner or later I need to begin to do what as an adult I will need to do, though if I was at Scutari now, my attempts to help deal with the consequences of the war would not imply my approval of it any more than I suspect your attempts to win it do.'

Charlie found himself becoming conscious of a kind of dull ache behind his eyebrows and realised he could no longer hold back his need to read Mary's letters. He packed Alice's letter away carefully, resolving to return to it whenever enough time and silence was available, and turned to the bundle within a bundle, Mary's little collection.

They had a secret, quite a big secret, which gave the whole tone of their correspondence an extra piquancy. They had already made love several times and, extraordinarily, the first time was on Mary's initiative. A summer ride, and Mary reining in suddenly, trotting her horse gently through a fallow country field, one belonging to her father's farm. The breeze was bouncing her hair very slightly; her eyes were glistening, and her voice had a hypnotic tone to it, as if he was dreaming and making her say what he wanted to hear.

'You will soon be going back to the Army. I am tortured by the idea that we will never actually make physical love, Charlie. I know it is widely seen as wrong for a woman to admit to such desires, but even if I could convince myself that I am indifferent to you in that way, I cannot avoid knowing that you are not similarly indifferent to me. Your face and your body are at least as communicative as your words, Charlie. I know well enough that I will not be the first woman you have made love to' – Charlie had blushed, absurdly, as his suspicions about his terrible reputation preceding him had proved to be true – 'but that is perhaps not such an unhappy circumstance. I confess that I have loved in that way before and I pray that you will not be dismissive of me because of it. There have only been a couple of misadventures, the foibles of a passionate if unwise nature, and I cannot claim to really understand the full meaning of sexual love, though I yearn to. I cannot even put up a credible defence of ignorance; having grown up on a farm, very few of the biological aspects of life are beyond my knowledge. I eventually determined that it would not happen again until I met the man I wanted on a permanent basis, and now I am sure enough of that, I would rather not risk the chance of some Russian bullet depriving me of knowing the full truth of it.'

She leaned across from her horse and touched Charlie's leg, her slight hand with all the impact of a sudden scald.

'Please let us make love, Charlie, and not in any clandestine, fumbling way. There is a disused small barn on my father's land here which I have converted into a studio, where I can paint as and when I choose and stay entirely safely and comfortably overnight when I wish to. The simple fact of you visiting my studio would not excite remark, and in any case it is in an isolated spot where any who approach can be heard from a far distance. Yes, we will be deceiving some who love us, but the war has changed things and it is an issue for us to resolve and no one else. We both know what the outcome might be if we do not take care, but we have already spoken of marriage on your next leave and when we are married, only old ladies counting days or particularly well-informed curates will notice or be outraged, and I don't, in any case, give a fig for their outrage.'

So they used the neat little room at the back of the studio, a converted cattle shed, for making open and fully naked love, and Charlie wondered at her insistence on watching him strip as he had watched her. He also found himself taken aback by the classically inspired male and female nudes amongst her paintings, though most of them took the theme of the local landscape and wildlife, transposed to situations and settings of her imagination. They seemed to him to be startlingly good, he thought, with the caveat that he did not see himself as any kind of expert on art. When she had first talked about painting, he had interpreted it as an occasional hobby, a lady's amusement, and her initially casual, almost throwaway reference to selling them surprised him even more.

'Oh, yes, they do sell quite well,' she said, as they sat with a post-coital glass of wine in a couple of armchairs in the living area at one end of the studio. 'That's what finally persuaded my father to help me set up this place. I demonstrated to him that three paintings sold at my friend's gallery in Durham would pay for all the necessary work, which seemed to finally gain acceptance for me, because he put up half of the cost. Though he still looks at the classical nudes dubiously and stipulates that they must not be sold in this part of the countryside, the landscape and wildlife studies have excited his admiration. They continue to sell tolerably well, and it has enabled me to make this my province entirely. My parents know well enough that I could and would set up a studio elsewhere if it should become necessary; my role in life is already established, it seems, though that does not mean you will not have a part in it, Charlie.'

Now their intimate knowledge of each other made her correspondence at times very personal indeed, and Charlie, who saw daily physical obscenities quite relentlessly, found himself blushing ridiculously at one or two of her more outspoken references.

'Your nakedness was nothing short of a revelation to me; such beautiful, controlled power, such economy of form, such smooth, deep touches of the sun, and yes, Charlie, as this is for your eyes only and if there are any others who pry, let them be shocked enough to prevent further such intrusion, I miss those parts of you which women will sometimes refer to with dread and apprehension or a mountain of mealy-mouthed euphemisms, the sight and the sensitivity of them, the joy they can bring to both of us.'

In the hot darkness of the Crimean night, the organs of which she spoke reacted in their usual inconsiderate and demanding fashion, and Charlie closed his eyes. Try as he might to evoke Mary, the gentle soap and lemon aroma of her, the long pale thighs like sculptured ivory, she was worlds and aeons away and the surrounding morass of ugliness too dominant. For the physicality of pictures, it was easier to bring to mind occasional flashes of dirty, steamy romps in Newcastle back streets, but sometimes he could recall the passion so thoroughly and uninhibitedly touched off in Mary, how even tousled, sweat-streaked hair and ungainly positions could not compromise her ravishing, unconfined sexuality. And yet she knew patience, too, the sheer relaxed relishing of love-making; she had taught him to hold and anticipate final orgasm to the point where every ounce, every drop, of frustration, impatience and unhappiness inside him could, temporarily at least, be expelled in a single, glorious release. Everything else had been rendered inadequate and ultimately unfulfilling by comparison. A kind of relief was not difficult; the squads of travelling whores shadowing his and every other army were instantly available on any leave or even between them, but for Charlie the risk of disease was no longer just his and he would not countenance it.

He contented himself with her final words, written the way she spoke, and at last a very evocative picture in his mind of her saying them, openly, freely and to his face, her hand propping up her head next to him in her long thin studio bed while her hand ranged languidly through his hair, while they both lay naked after their last time of making love, only a day before the foreign posting.

'Charlie, I think of you every day, I want you every day, your voice, your body, your being. Please for the love of God be careful and do everything you can honourably do to make sure you get through this dreadful time and bring us back together. Come back to me, my love. God preserve you.'

And Charlie became conscious of an enormous tiredness again, a feeling introduced to him by the Crimea and, alien as it still was, sometimes immensely valuable. He had no sooner lowered his head than sleep arrived overwhelmingly, uncompromisingly, a sleep so deep and quiet that even the battle images were, for once, unable to penetrate it.

The morning brought Mr Fenton and two assistants, and an initial polite if slightly impatient conference between Mr Fenton and Colonel Travers. The photographer listened gravely to Travers' assurance of co-operation, his head and body held so studiously immobile that Travers rightly concluded that the experience of listening to officers' set speeches was beginning to reach levels of repetitiveness which Prince Albert's appointed nominee found tiresome. When Travers then outlined his own personal request, meaning that the photographer's services were actually being welcomed rather than tolerated as an infernal and irrelevant nuisance, Mr Fenton was the very model of graciousness, though, even so, the individual portraits were allocated to an assistant while Fenton himself went off to examine the terrain, the soldiers and the situation, before he decided what his official photographs of record were going to be.

As first the Colonel and then those officers who had agreed to be portrayed – Travers had retreated, on this occasion, from compulsion – sat for Fenton's assistant, usually in stiff, self-conscious poses which reflected not only their contempt for whatever supposedly encouraging and relaxing remarks were coming at them from the gentleman concerned, whose name everyone carefully contrived not to retain, but also the low discontented humming noises from other ranks. Officers in the Crimea, dealing with units with casualties numbering up to half of their manpower already killed or wounded and many men who felt they had nothing left to lose, were becoming increasingly unhappy at hearing that buzz with its mutinous potential. Charlie, whose knowledge of the men already excelled that of some of the more genteel officer types, even if he was junior to them in length of service, remained unconcerned; he knew the character of the men's noise, individually and collectively, and the character of this one was mainly about the sardonic, alienated incredulity which gave them a kind of emotional protection, all items not within their realms of experience being instantly dismissed as yet more bizarre manifestations of the generally hopelessly insane world inhabited by officers and gentlemen. Fenton and another assistant were arranging gun teams and groups of infantrymen, wonderingly and not always helpfully assisted by non-commissioned officers, the portraits seemingly calculated to persuade whoever saw these pictures that the men were well-equipped, adequately prepared and ready for action whenever or wherever it should come. While Charlie was waiting for his turn to pose, he could see men being excluded or included for various group pictures on no sensible criteria he could make out, but he suspected states of uniform, boots and visible battle damage might have something to do with them.

But it wasn't that, or the men's noise, or his embarrassment at facing a camera for only the second time in his life, which caused a slight air of uncertainty and doubt in the eyes and the carriage of the body to compromise Charlie's perfect facsimile of an active and capable infantry officer. It was, primarily, memories in her absence of Mary Prentice, and likewise subsidiary but far from insignificant similar thoughts concerned Elizabeth, Francis, Charlotte, Anne and Alice Howell and a whole crowd of more peripheral relatives and friends inhabiting Charlie's real world, the one he became more and more eager to return to as soon as the grotesque fantasy which had usurped his life could finally be shuffled off back to whatever storage cupboard in Hades had originally allowed it an escape.

But release would not come easily, and when the Russians under another aristocratic general, Prince Gortschakoff, did make a second, Inkerman-like attempt to break the siege on 16 August, Charlie spent several hours watching their army in desperate struggle against the French and the Sardinians and found himself wondering if the siege would ever end. Finally, however, the Russian effort proved to be another carefully planned and ultimately disastrous failure. The battle over the Tchernaya river cost them over 3,000 fatalities and over 8,000 casualties, compared with an

Allied total of 300 and 1,600 respectively. From that day onwards, there was no longer any real doubt of the eventual outcome, though the defences of Sevastopol remained strong and the Allied officers and men knew well enough that victory would still come at a price.

After endless rounds of conferences and discussions and a growing restlessness amongst the men, all regimental officers were summoned to Travers' tent on Monday 3 September. As usual now when any officers were called to the Colonel, many eyes followed them. Whether the men were working, eating, cleaning or sitting down, noise and movement generally ceased and even the loud and profane insistence of the more conscientious non-commissioned officers could not immediately restore the camp's normal bustle. Rumours had stoked everyone's anticipation for days, and even the iron discipline of the British Army seemed on the verge of being unable to stop the widespread belief that the time had come either to make a last assault or call off the entire business. In view of the immense sacrifices already made in the effort to take Sevastopol, the latter decision would be very poorly received, but the point was being reached when indecision had become the greatest evil.

Travers waited for complete silence and only had a few seconds to do so. He looked pale, tired and even more emaciated than usual, but there was a grim gratification in his eyes which spoke volumes to all of them before his mouth had opened.

'In two days' time, gentlemen, in the early morning of the 5th, a general bombardment will begin on the city from all the Allied guns. It will continue for three days. On Saturday the 8th, an assault will be launched on all the major and minor batteries surrounding the city, with the main French objective being the Malakoff and the main British the Redan. The column of 1,000 men making the initial attack on the Redan will consist largely of soldiers from the Light and 2nd divisions; as you know, gentlemen, this regiment is part of the latter and is therefore to contribute some of its strength to one of the storming parties. There will be one hundred men from this regiment in the assault party; I will, of course, lead them personally, and the officers accompanying me will be Captain Moss and Lieutenant Howell.'

Charlie felt the heat of many eyes upon him, and dared not try to return any glance, in case he should be seen to exhibit arrogance or any kind of triumphalism. But there was a sudden groundswell of noise, and Charlie could read officer noise just as well as men noise. The excited mumblings were about congratulation, goodwill and, so obviously undeniable as to coat his heart in growing, spreading warmth, approval. He told himself that it was aimed at Travers and Moss, but the warmth knew all of it wasn't, and such knowledge was more satisfying than he could express. Travers had already resumed speaking when Charlie heard Mary's words again, loudly and distinctly in his ear: 'Come back to me, my love.'

'Now, I wish to make one aspect of this decision clear to everyone. I have no intention of embarrassing Captain Moss and Lieutenant Howell with eulogies extolling their worth in order to justify my choice; there are a number of logical reasons for it which would take too long to explain and it is in any case invidious for a commanding officer to be doing so. What I wish to emphasise with all the power at my disposal is that the decision does not reflect in any way on any other officer in this regiment, and it has not been made on the basis of suspicions that any man here would lack conduct. We have been at this business for some time now, gentlemen, and this regiment has been at the forefront of action throughout. No officer here has failed to serve according to the best traditions of the British Army.'

Another bout of approving and gratified murmurings, in which Charlie could properly join, though the heart warmth had now been joined by a deep sickness in the very pit of his stomach and an inability to expunge the scarlet lips and marble nakedness of Mary Prentice from his mind. His eyes caught those of Nicholas

Moss and, astonishingly, the Captain, a dour, monosyllabic and duty-obsessed Cumbrian, actually smiled, a thin, quick expression rather like a grimace with which Charlie was so unfamiliar that he didn't immediately recognise it for what it was. Travers continued with detailed descriptions of the positions the chosen men would take and the objectives as they were anticipated during the day, and when he came to describe the two days' rations each man would carry with them in the expected contingency of them forming an advance party into the city itself, a smattering of applause broke out which Travers decided he would indulge, and everyone could hear the NCOs outside now quite frantic in trying to quell the burgeoning noise of reaction from the men. The applause was continuing when Charlie joined eyes with Moss again, and this time Charlie returned the smile, apparently with some sincerity and communication, because Moss took a few strides across to him and, rather than react to Charlie's hurried salute, took Charlie's hand in his and they shook hands warmly as the applause mounted all around them. Moss, slightly shamefaced at such an unprecedented show of emotion, then nodded apologetically to the Colonel and tried to move back into one of the groups of men, but the hand-shaking had started and was inevitably going to continue. Charlie and Moss found themselves hailed on all sides and the sickness grew in Charlie's stomach almost in proportion to the redness spreading all over the Captain's face and neck; these men were now relying on him to get *them* home and taking it for granted that he would give his life to do so if necessary. Charlie knew he still wasn't entirely sure that he would.

Travers allowed it to continue for a few more minutes and then stopped it with a word. As immediate silence fell and their mostly younger faces all turned towards him, their eyes gleaming and at least a slight flush on every face, a man much less subtle in reading men could see that relief and expectation were not all the eyes were gleaming about; respect, even veneration, for him,

Colonel Travers, personally, spoke to him on all sides and for a moment, he was almost unmanned by such esteem and, it seemed, affection. For the commanding officer, he thought suddenly, there was only one really relevant question relating to men: would they follow him, not just in the forced observances of saluting, respectful address, obedience to orders, but in their hearts and minds, would they see him as a man worthy to lead them? And, patiently obviously, in spite of – or perhaps, even, because of – the sweaty, unsure nights, the staring, terror-struck eyes in the darkness of the small hours, they did.

'We will speak together again, gentlemen,' he said, hoping his voice didn't sound quite so hoarse and choked to them as it sounded to him. 'In the meantime, Captain Moss, Lieutenant Howell and myself must list the names of the men we will take, and in this respect we may have to seek the opinions and recommendations of some of you; however, for the moment, please return to your duties and regain control of that hubbub outside.'

The officers left and Travers nodded to Moss and Howell to sit at the table with him. The Colonel allowed a few minutes to pass while the shouting, stamping and fierce low rumble of talk ebbed away outside. He looked at the two other men and saw that the emotion and sentiment of such a short while ago had marched out with their fellow officers; the expectancy now was about the practicalities concerning how viable they thought the attack plan was and who they would consider it most advisable to take with them. The plan, of course, came first. Travers spread a large chart with the whole Sevastopol area, its troop gatherings, gun emplacements and city defences, laid out before them.

'Now, gentlemen. To business.'

On the morning of Wednesday 5 September, a huge cacophony of noise erupted over the whole siege area as the Allied batteries opened fire, rapidly from the left attack batteries whose men were not to be in the initial assault and more gradually from the French and British units of the right attack who fired steadily, but reserved some of their energies for the coming assault. The Russians made little or no reply at first, and the natural pessimists amongst the men, by now numerous and with many sympathetic adherents, maintained that the enemy was reserving his fire until the assault, when every gun would suddenly be found serviceable and every battery would swarm with artillerymen.

On the night of the 5th, a large Russian frigate was seen to burst into flames and was burnt to the water's edge by midnight, and if that ominous event for the Russians was not sign enough, on the afternoon of the 7th, one of their line-of-battle ships caught fire and burnt fiercely all through the following night. The whole harbour and town of Sevastopol were lit up by this great conflagration, and the other ranks' Jeremiahs were temporarily silenced as the omens of Russian disaster were there for all to see. During the bombardment, the Russians were seen to be using the bridge across the harbour connecting the Crimean peninsula to the mainland to move people and equipment out of the city. Thousands of carts passed over from the south to the north and returned empty for more.

Shortly after 7a.m. on the morning of the 8th, the troops of the Light and 2nd division moved down to the forward trenches and took up the positions assigned to them. It took a long time, as some of the approaches didn't allow more than two men to go abreast in comparative safety. The artillery fire continued more intensely than ever before until almost midday; it then gradually ceased, as it usually did because of the intense heat at that period of the day, and even though the day itself was comparatively cold, the calculation was that stopping the bombardment would lead the enemy into the belief that no assault was about to take place. At 12.00, the French rushed out of their most advanced trench in front of the Malakoff and at about 12.10 p.m., the French General Pelissier signalled that French troops had taken possession of the

Malakoff battery, so classically placed to maintain withering fire on the besieging armies and equally destructive bombardments if turned to point down into the city. The French were to face an epic and bloody confrontation to hold on to the Malakoff, but their initial possession of it was the agreed starting point for the British assault on the salient arch of the Redan battery. The ladder and storming parties dashed out of the forward trenches and came immediately under heavy grape shot fire. Charlie, beside Moss and behind Travers in the third storming party, saw the horrendous situation of the troops' exposure, the rocky ground giving them no chance to prepare sheltered ditches for a gradual approach. Charlie watched as the advance troops were mowed down at the front of the column, and even those who managed to cross the 200 yards to the front of the Redan were being massacred as they reached it. What no one could see at that time was that the Russians had lined their troops up behind the parapet at the rear of the Redan, leaving the body of it empty, and simply continued to pour murderous fire on to the arriving British without the British soldiers yet being able to see most of them, let alone return fire. It was the kind of inexplicable, disastrous situation when only courage and blind faith kept the assault party pouring forward to their deaths.

In spite of the carnage in front of them, Travers' third storming party struggled forward, though it was clear enough that no ladders had been put up to the body of the Redan and no assault had begun. A brigadier had been shot in the face almost immediately after leaving the trenches, a colonel was lying mortally wounded. Colonel Windham, left as acting Brigadier, eventually appreciated the gravity of the situation and the position of the Russians, and dispatched officers to beg for reinforcements, as it was clear enough that there simply were not enough men to take the objective. None of the messengers ever arrived at their destinations.

Charlie looked wildly around him. In front, behind and beside him, men were being quite literally shot to pieces. In a kind of arrowhead triangle, Travers was standing in front of him and Moss was on his left; everyone, including Travers, had momentarily stopped uncertainly. The men in front of them who had actually made it to the Redan were simply being mowed down; some were trying to detour away to the left and get at the back of the battery where the Russians were lined up with the guns resting on walls and being fired through holes they had made. Windham was making loud, screaming efforts to get his men to move forward and more quickly, but they could see what they were moving forward into and they were hesitating and being shot down where they stood.

Travers looked down at the ground and ahead towards the Redan. Already the ground was an obscenity, a bloody mush of mud, blood and body parts. This was the nightmare as it really worked out, worse than anything his imagination could devise; no glorious standard to pick up – they had been left behind, as providing too easy markers for the defending artillery – and no visible enemy to fight against, just an incessant stream of unanswerable fire to strike them down and tear them apart like some dreadful nemesis, some particular day of judgement for him and his men.

Howell and Moss were looking to him with questions in their eyes. Moss had already been hit with something, as blood was seeping down his neck and across his jacket. *This hell must end*, thought Travers in one split second, and a curious quick reflection passed through his mind, that the nightmares never had allowed for the fact that there would be no time.

'This storming party moves forward to destroy those Russians,' he screamed behind him and jumped forward, blazing his gun blindly at where the fire seemed to be coming from.

The next period of Charlie's life, he would reflect time and time again, could not have lasted for more than thirty seconds at most, but the universe had somehow slowed to a grotesque, deliberated mime, a dream dance of unreal, impossible people and events. Deafened and seemingly unable to speak, Charlie approached the very edge of total panic, and something insistent, some inarticulate but clamouring voice, was saying to him that he should quit the field now, run as fast as he could to anywhere, forget everything and everyone here and associated with this debacle, this insane war, the brutal, life-squandering Army, the determined, suicidal Russians marching remorselessly to their deaths, the heat, the stink, the blood and gory shame of it all. Charlie hovered for a moment like a perplexed child, looking from the men still gathered behind him and reluctant to move anywhere but back and Travers still beckoning at them, still bellowing something at the top of his voice.

And then something hit Travers' right shoulder so hard he leapt backward at a forty-five-degree angle to his left and lay crazily arced over a body, his head thrown back, his eyes staring madly behind him. He turned to his left and Moss was screaming into his face.

'Retire! They've given the signal to retire! We can't—'

As Charlie stared, Moss's face and torso suddenly disintegrated, a scattering of grape shot hitting him in at least five separate places. His left eye and forehead blew away, a great red gash appeared in his stomach, and his right arm detached itself after making a lurching movement behind him. Charlie still watched, hypnotised by the horror of it, and the top half of the Captain's body fell directly towards him, detached at the waist and leaving his lower half bizarrely stranded alone until it toppled backwards.

'What, sir? What now?' said someone, Corporal Ben Fenwick, Charlie thought it was, and Charlie shook himself awake enough to realise he was now in command of the men. He could hear the signal from the forward trenches, and it was to retire clearly enough.

'Move back now!' he said. 'That is a retire signal; move back to the forward trenches and re-group there. Now, now!' The last two words were screams as more grape shot cut up the ground around them.

'Thank God,' said Fenwick. 'Fucking madness, this lot, it is,' he muttered as he turned.

'Be quiet, Fenwick, and move, damn you!'

Charlie looked forward again and saw that Travers was trying to move, one hand clutching his shattered shoulder and the other pushing down on the ground to try and heave himself off the body underneath him. Charlie cursed under his breath and heard himself muttering an apology to Mary, now and for always, as he rushed the twenty yards to where Travers was lying.

'Sir,' he said. 'Come, quickly, please, one arm around my shoulders, now sir, please!'

The men were falling back rapidly now and Charlie was afraid they would become isolated targets in no more than a few seconds. He hauled Travers to his feet and the Colonel screamed with pain at the touch of a hand on his shoulder, but they contrived to get Travers' good arm around Charlie's shoulders as bullets and grape shot still crashed and whistled around them. Together, they took a few awkward steps as if starting on a three-legged race.

An enormous crash only inches away resounded in Charlie's right ear, followed by a noise approximating to a very loud dull thud, and then oblivion, nothing but blackness, fading noise, and the hard rocky ground. There seemed to be an age of terrifying notions of Russians above him with bayonets at the ready, ready to pierce him like a stuck pig in every tender spot they could find, and then he blinked his eyes open to see Fenwick at an illogical angle above him, the man's head and torso seeming to bounce up and down.

He glanced to each side; there were three of them holding him, one on each side and Fenwick on the head and shoulders. Almost parallel with them, another three men were carrying Travers, and Charlie could see the forward trenches now only five yards away.

'Fenwick, I will never forget you for this,' Charlie muttered at the bobbing head above him.

'All in a day's duty, sir, I'm sure. Wouldn't do it for every officer, sir, pardon my frankness, me and the boys, but the ones with as much fucking balls as you and the Colonel, we're not about to leave you on the field for those fucking Ivans and their knives.'

Ben Fenwick, Charlie reflected half-consciously, as they settled into the forward trenches, out of range of the Russians, was a criminal, like a good number of other men in the ranks, with convictions for violence, drunkenness and affray, but he had a casual and apparently unassailable courage and was classically the kind of NCO the men looked up to and followed. As he lay at the bottom of a trench waiting for them to get stretchers organised, his mind was musing confusedly about how anyone can possibly make accurate judgements on the worth of soldiers when the realisation came to him that something was dreadfully, catastrophically, wrong with his lower right leg; the trouser cloth and boot were a mass of congealing blood. He tried to move, and pain swept over him so overwhelmingly, so irresistibly, that he passed out.

He woke slowly, groggily, to find himself in what he could easily identify as a field hospital; he knew the sights and sounds of them well enough. The difference this time was that the naked figure on the bare wooden board was himself and the words he heard froze the remains of his courage so badly that he could neither move nor speak.

'If we don't take it off now, he'll not last the night out. You know that just as bloody well as I do, McCann, so stop being a damn fool and let's get on with it.'

Charlie's open, unmoving eyes caught sight of one of the surgeons, Major James Glaister, a slight figure often with the bemused air of a rural schoolmaster visiting the big city, but now red, red and red – red in his tired, sore-rimmed eyes, red in the face with sweat and streaks of blood, and with his coat soaked with huge red congealing patches. He looked to be a man nearing the end of his physical and mental tether.

'Oh, God's teeth, he's awake,' said Glaister. 'Hewson, some of that whisky, here, now.'

'Not much of it left now, sir, half a dozen after this at most,' said a half-naked orderly, whose shirt had been wrung out of blood and fluids and tied around his waist.

Glaister's irritation snapped again. 'Just give the man a decent glug or two, Glaister, and bloody hurry up about it.'

Charlie found he was still unable to move, think or speak. The sweat of the orderly crowded into his nostrils as his head was held by the neck and he was made to swallow several huge mouthfuls of the foul, throat-stinging brown liquid. He passed out again, knocked out by the ingestion of strong alcohol, and then began a whole eternity of pain, pain more persistent, more severe, more mind-numbingly brutal, than anything he'd ever known, and accompanied by wild dreams of gathered groups of Russian soldiers, their bayonets fixed, thrusting down again and again into the bloody mass of his leg. In the back of his mind was an endless wild screaming and he realised he was the one doing it, screeching and barking his pain out as rivers of sweat coursed down his face, back and crotch. As the pain continued, on and on and on, he felt his crotch dampening and a full flow of urine emerge, and he cared nothing for any of it, or the rumbling voices around him, or the ever-pervasive stink assailing his mouth and nose. They had strapped him down across his chest and his ankles and they watched with amazement as his great heaves and screams threatened to snap the powerful leather apart. At last, at long, long last, the pain subsided to a nagging, incessant dull ache and he lost consciousness again, just after hearing Glaister's voice once again raised in petulant, exhausted anger.

'Get him off the fucking table, you bloody fool, now, and get that sergeant on here before the man breathes his last, and on your head be it!'

Now his dream became the interminable torment, as he wandered through darkened, burnt-out rooms and across endless wind-blown fields where men lay in their hundreds, with every conceivable kind of pain and injury visible and an ever-present low, unearthly moan echoing behind the distant crashing guns. He wept and wept, or at least he seemed to be doing; they were the noises he could hear, close at hand, unmanly and mortifying for an officer, a sorrowing so thorough and exhaustive as to expel every last drop of moisture from his body. But silence did come again, and this time he gradually accustomed himself to the idea that the darkened room around him had become the new reality.

A few hours passed before he had fully realised and adjusted to the fact that he was in a hospital, but this was no stinking, screaming field hospital; the place was pleasantly warm rather than oppressively hot, and the building was not precarious canvas, flapping in the wind and sagging in the rain, but solid stone, high-ceilinged and sparsely furnished, containing no more than five beds, all of them occupied with sleeping or resting men, a high arched window facing him and showing nothing but scudding clouds. The beds were decently spaced, his neighbour a good two yards away. He was dressed in a clean nightshirt and there were actually clean sheets on the bed. For Charlie, whose notions of religion were half-formed and rarely thought about, even in the heat of battle, a few unsettling suspicions of where and what he might actually be had begun to creep into his mind until he saw the nurses moving about the room, taking and putting objects in the large storage cupboards at either end of the room.

The light had started to fade through the arched window and Charlie had been brought water for washing and shaving purposes when the figure of Glaister entered the room at the far end. He looked very different from Charlie's last sight of him; he was clean, smooth-haired and presentable, once again with that vague, academic air about him and wearing a decent, if rather worn, dark blue coat over his waistcoat.

Glaister seemed entirely pre-occupied with walking towards Charlie's bed, with no more than a nod at the two other men who greeted him.

'Lieutenant Howell,' he said, and they shook hands. 'We meet in rather easier circumstances than our last encounter, I feel.'

Charlie took this to be an attempt at a pleasantry and smiled, receiving a wintry, rather vacant momentary grin in return.

Glaister seemed to settle himself to get his business done. He sat on the end of the bed and folded his hands slightly primly in front of him.

'We have taken Sevastopol,' Glaister began, making this monumental pronouncement in a slow, semi-murmur. 'Or, more accurately, the Russians have given it to us. They have moved out enormous amounts of material, mostly warlike apparatus of one kind or another, and fired some of the public buildings. However, our own supplies added to what they left behind have made us more sheltered and comfortable than I can recall anyone being since this whole wretched business started. Colonel Travers has specifically asked to see you—'

'Colonel Travers? So he survived? Thank God.'

'Yes, indeed,' said Glaister fussily, 'though the Almighty cannot be said to have been especially active in this part of the world recently. But the Colonel will bring you the narrative of the whole siege conclusion in due course, and I will also enlighten you concerning his current state of health. In the meantime, however, it is you, Lieutenant, we must discuss.'

Charlie sat up and made himself look attentive; whatever it was, he had wept enough now, if only in his dreams, and he would take it with a little more self-possession.

'It became urgently necessary to amputate the lower part of your right leg, with a first incision a good six inches below the knee. It was already badly infected, and had we not done as we did, it would have spread rapidly and killed you, without a shadow of a doubt. No amputation, in the current state of our medicine and with the lamentable lack of equipment we were suffering at the time, can be anything but a desperately and inhumanly brutal business and some men do not survive. It is a great tribute to your strength of mind and body, Lieutenant, that you did and have.'

This time Glaister did smile; Charlie nodded his thanks, but words would still not come.

'I will leave Colonel Travers to deal with the subject of your future with the Army. My concern is the future of your health. There is no point in me attempting to mitigate the seriousness of what has happened; the loss of even part of a limb is a great challenge for any man, perhaps especially a young man. But the consequences of war are not all evil, thankfully, and our now widespread experience of amputation has enabled us to progress rather beyond the wooden stumps on offer to veterans in the Napoleonic wars. I have every reason to believe that you will be walking unaided by the time you leave this hospital, Lieutenant Howell; not as easily, nor as fast, but walking unaided nevertheless. So please don't despair or arrive at any too desperate conclusions about the rest of your life. We will do our very best for you, Lieutenant'.

Glaister stood up and nodded amicably. He seemed on the point of leaving, but he hesitated and began to speak again in a hoarse, slightly embarrassed tone.

'I should also say that your enormous courage both on the operating table and, I have been very reliably informed, on the battlefield, is well known to all of us here. It is, of course, not our policy to have favourites in such a place, but please be confident that anything and everything which can be done to make you comfortable and assist your recovery will be attended to, on my personal assurance.'

Charlie found his voice at long last, and he had a moment of oddly detached curiosity at how normal, how ordinarily conversational, it managed to sound.

'I thank you for your care of me, Doctor. I owe you my life, and I will not forget it. You mentioned Colonel Travers earlier; is it permissible for you to give me any further information about him?'

With a curious twist of impatience with himself, his lips grimacing and his hands spreading apologetically, Glaister sat again.

'Of course. There is so much information to be retained at the moment. Forgive me. Your Colonel had one of the truly luckiest escapes I've ever seen. A sizeable musket ball passed right through his body no more than three inches below his right shoulder. A few inches here or there and it could have punctured his lung or shattered his shoulder blade; as it is, it caused a good deal of visible harm while remaining relatively superficial. He lost a great deal of blood and would certainly have died if you and the soldiers who came after you had not removed him from the field when you did. Some internal damage will remain, but he is unlikely to be seriously discommoded for long and he is already on his feet, attending to regimental matters. As I mentioned earlier, you will soon be able to talk with him yourself. Good day to you for the moment, Lieutenant Howell.'

They shook hands again. A nurse was hovering about at the door of the ward, and Glaister left rapidly, with a glance and a wave behind him.

Day had only just turned to night when Travers appeared. Charlie had been bed-bathed; he marvelled at the ingenuity with which they contrived to ensure that the lower half of his body was never exposed to the whole room at any time, but entirely concealing any part of his body from the nurse's attention was not possible and he found himself as awkward as a gauche boy in the presence of a nurse who couldn't have been older than her early twenties. But she handled him with such gentleness and succeeded in ignoring his missing half-leg with such care that he made himself simply enjoy the blessed sensation of even greater cleanliness than the clean clothes and sheets had provided. By the time Colonel Travers walked into the ward, his shoulder still heavily bandaged, some colour had returned to Charlie's cheeks and he was managing to sit right up in his bed.

Travers was unhealthily pallid, tending more to grey than white, and his heavily bandaged shoulder emphasised even more his gangling height, but the smile he directed at Charlie was not an expression the younger man could ever remember seeing before, and somehow outside all their previous military relationship. With an air of rueful apology, Travers extended his left hand to be shaken.

'Lieutenant Howell,' Travers said, and his words sounded as if they had been prepared and possibly even rehearsed. 'I am enormously glad to see you looking so much better. We have all been very anxious over the last few days, when you seemed to be sleeping for so long. I am very mindful of the fact that I would not be standing here but for your courage. Please accept my most heartfelt thanks, on behalf of myself and the family who I will now shortly be seeing again because of your actions.'

Travers offered his left hand again and Charlie felt himself reddening with the formality of it.

'If true, sir, it was both my duty and my pleasure, and the two cannot always be so happily conjoined. But please, sir, do sit down and make yourself more comfortable, and enlighten me on the recent campaign success. I do not even yet fully know what happened to relieve the siege.'

Travers collected a wooden chair from where a few were standing near the door at the end of the room; sitting on beds was clearly still too informal for him, even in this situation. But his stiff dignity and grey features seemed to have relaxed a little as he took his seat.

'What happened, essentially, was that the French took the Malakoff, and the Little Redan, and a few of the other minor batteries. They paid an enormous price for the Malakoff particularly, not only in taking it but in holding it, but they did so, and all praise to them for it. Even during the bombardment, the Russians were moving out vast amounts of material and people, as we saw, and when they realised they had lost those batteries, particularly the Malakoff, where the French would have been able to continue a bombardment right down into the city itself, they finally gave up and marched out over the bridge on the north side, destroying the bridge behind them. And though they took all the munitions available and fired several of the major buildings, there wasn't time for them to march everything out by any means and we are already more comfortable in this place than we have been for many a week, especially as we can now be copiously supplied with the protection of our warships using the harbour. We are told that the new Tsar is already negotiating terms.'

'And you, sir? Will you be going home?'

'Yes, I will. I undertook to serve with the regiment for the duration of the war and the war is clearly over. My beloved family and the Lake District are in prospect, where hopefully this shoulder will continue to heal.'

The Colonel's eyes sought some unknown spot on the floor and then forced themselves back up directly into the younger man's.

'You, Lieutenant, have lost more and have that which will not heal, and I am more sorry than I can say. As you can imagine, the plans for the assault on the Redan have come in for some fierce analysis after the event. It was understood that the three-day bombardment would so weaken the defences as to cause the Russians to be spread more thinly. However, they somehow received information that the Redan would be the British target and packed men behind it, with holes placed for shooting through the walls as well as over them. In a gruesome way, we did eventually achieve a kind of revenge, because when they tried to fortify the Redan again, the generals ordered every British gun to be trained on it and it was reduced to rubble with a fair few of them still in it. It is no longer of any use to either of us and they have, in any case, left the field to us.'

Travers stood again, and the words slowed as he chose carefully.

'But I see the question in your eyes relating to yourself, of course, and you have been extraordinarily patient in listening to other circumstances while I take far too long about addressing yours. You are to be invalided out, Charlie. At one time, when we were in our death struggle with Bonaparte, even men who had suffered the damage that you have would continue in some capacity, but now the Government is increasingly obsessed with the ruinous cost of the war and determined to cut back, even after making the Russians pay handsomely for it. I have already ensured a pension for you and there is even a possibility that some of the price you paid for your commission will be returned; there is still a streak of generosity in them for brave men. And I am going to ensure that you do receive the full glory of whatever campaign medal is devised. You will also take with you a framed and enlarged copy of Fenton's assistant's portrait of yourself in uniform, which may not be of enormous concern to you but I think may please your family.' Travers almost added 'and, I understand, your prospective wife', but stories of former amputees filled his head and he desisted. The young ex-lieutenant's face looked shocked and somewhat bewildered, as he tried to assimilate such emphatic changes in his life and circumstances and wondered dully whether he really had heard Travers address him as 'Charlie'.

'But we have no need to say goodbye as yet, Howell. I am based here while treatment continues and I will start dealing with the paperwork concerning our withdrawal. We will talk again very soon. In the meantime, try to get as much rest as you can, and be assured that you will be well treated here.'

And in a few seconds, Travers had stomped away, the ward was quiet again and Charlie could see a growing respect on the faces of his fellow patients. But everything whirled through his mind more chaotically and demandingly than he had the strength to handle. Only he knew how close he had been to fleeing the battlefield in a demented panic, and a question mark from that would reverberate in his mind for all the foreseeable future. And, of course, his changed circumstances meant he would not be able to marry Mary and not long ago, that would have been enough to end his will to live. But now the war was over, now the theatre of horror would cease and now, above all, he was going home.

4

THE JANUS
YEAR – 1860

Charlie was duly invalided out of the Crimea and left the Army with a pension to his name. To his surprise and gratification, but also, to some extent, his apprehension about the future, Mary was not prepared to renege on the plans they had made and they married in June 1856. Sir John and Lady Charlotte renovated an ex-gamekeeper's lodge on the main Harrington estate for the couple and they confessed themselves quite happy with the comfortable, if relatively modest, accommodation. A daughter, Elizabeth, was born and proved strong enough to survive infancy in May 1857. Mary's success continued and she eventually decided to move her main studio from her parents' land to a more accessible house with generous studio quarters upstairs on the outskirts of Durham. A nanny was employed for little Elizabeth, and the family set up house in the Neville's Cross part of Durham in March 1858, Charlie finally confirming his non-involvement in the Howell family business. Mary found an agent, Will Gelson, and they drew closer as her success increased. Charlie's job, jointly funded by local organisations, was officer in charge of the local militia, the kind of organisation which partly gave rise to the modern Territorial

Army, but little threat of invasion or mainland warfare remained and Charlie began to see it as a pointless sinecure, which to some extent it was. As his tormenting nightmares increased with the intensity of his drinking to relieve them, he also conceived of a growing jealousy of Gelson, who he believed, without justification, had cuckolded him. Among the artistic circles Mary moved in, Charlie found himself increasingly out of place and unable to establish a compensatory network of his own friends and colleagues.

Francis continued to fight an uphill battle with the other partners in the mining company for more attention to be paid to safety issues and the number of very young boys employed in the company's pits to be cut. The numbers of accidents, injuries and deaths in the area overall began to drop slightly, largely because of the company's figures, but so did the company's profits, and Francis didn't always battle successfully, with only the reliable support of Burridge and Thirwell on the board. In 1858, Emily Salter's patience with his long and overly respectful courtship gave out and she forced the situation, telling him he must either propose or end their relationship. Startled and gratified that marriage was what she actually wanted, Francis did propose and was accepted; they married in July 1858, living at Howell Grange, and Francis found more comfort and support in their happy if undemonstrative marriage than he'd thought possible, though a first child continued to elude them in spite of their best efforts.

Elizabeth, now aged fifty-six, continued her matriarchal and sometimes challenging presence in the lives of all her family, even if rest and recreation had become increasingly necessary. She took enormous pleasure in the birth of her first grandchild, though her diaries reveal a continuing anxiety for Charlie and her sadness at the difference in him. In November 1857, a second grandchild appeared, this time a boy, called Eustace after his father, as a result of the business-like marriage between Charlotte and Eustace Thirwell in the autumn of 1856. Elizabeth felt a little ashamed at her relief that Charlotte's formidable energy and sharp temper had moved to the Thirwell house, where Eustace and his widower father had adjustments to make to the arrival of an exacting new head of household.

Anne surprised her mother in 1857 by suddenly distancing herself from Thomas and taking upon herself some of the household duties vacated by Charlotte. Attempts to find a new suitor for her continued to fail cruelly and Elizabeth was beginning to feel that Anne would inevitably remain a spinster when she discovered towards the end of 1859 that the relationship with the still unmarried Thomas had secretly started again.

Alice formed a friendship with a local doctor, Samuel Spencer, married, in his forties and with a wife and three children, after she volunteered in 1858 to help him and be trained by him as a nurse. Mrs Spencer's initial hostility was superseded by a more sympathetic response when she realised that Alice did genuinely consider herself to have a sense of medical vocation. In any case, Alice, nineteen in 1858, was thin, pale, bespectacled and obviously not qualified to be a young siren with ideas of ensnaring her husband, even if the redoubtable and stout Samuel was inclined to such affairs, which he decidedly was not.

Alice continued to insist that her ambition was to become a doctor. Her friendship and successful working relationship with Dr Spencer could be partly explained by the fact that he was one of the very few people who did not either ridicule her ambition, if they dared, or simply maintain a diplomatic but incredulous silence, as most did.

Alice's relationship with her mother deteriorated gradually, Elizabeth being the only person in Alice's life who insisted to her face that her ambition was unrealistic and who would protest at the very short shrift Alice gave to the few suitors brave enough to attempt to secure her affections. Elizabeth's temper was also not improved by the declining health of her father, whose eightieth birthday celebrations in 1859 were rather compromised and subdued by the obvious reality that his life would not continue for very much longer.

MONDAY 24 DECEMBER 1860, 2.52 P.M.

Two diaries and one local history refer to a picture taken on Christmas Eve 1860, though the photograph has not survived; the following is an approximation based on their descriptions.

The family are ranged on the right of the elaborately and gloriously decorated Christmas tree, whose height towers above even the tallest of the men, who are standing in a row behind the sitting ladies. The number of ladies cannot but emphasise the depleted numbers of the men and, for anyone acquainted with the family, there are two particularly poignant absences; for Elizabeth, in the middle of the sitting row, the mixture of emotions is particularly noticeable.

The two children sitting cross-legged on the floor in front of the ladies are dressed as miniature adults, as Victorian children tended to be, and both carefully avoiding any acknowledgment of each other's presence. The girl, Elizabeth Howell, dressed in an absurdly frilly little formal dress and wearing an oddly familiar lop-sided smile, is a more festive figure than the glowering Eustace Thirwell, in a sailor-like suit which he clearly despises. At the feet of his mother, he clearly yearns for escape at the same time as realising the impossibility of it. They are both three years old, and even though Eustace celebrated the occasion rather more recently, he is already a heftier figure than his very feminine cousin.

Lying in Elizabeth Howell's lap is a third child, almost invisible in a mass of spreading shawls, whose recent arrival is evident not only in his tiny form but in the dignified pride of his parents, beside and behind Elizabeth.

The whole group seem to share a tacit understanding that, after such a year as 1860 with its endless wild fluctuations of fortune and circumstance, those who survive must seek to celebrate what they can when they can, especially in view of whatever new trials and misadventures might be even now hiding only just around the corner of the arriving 1861.

MONDAY 24 DECEMBER 1860, 9.56 A.M.

Elizabeth Howell stared out of her bedroom window at the unpromising greyness of the morning. Seasonal as it might be, she felt grateful that the snow had not so far appeared this year and her guests at the Grange would all be spared the hazards, sometimes even the impossibilities, of travel. Charlotte and Eustace had already arrived, and however she felt about the relative calm which had settled over house and servants ever since Charlotte's departure, her no-nonsense eldest daughter's organising abilities could be very useful at times. Elizabeth had felt, in the weeks leading up to the Christmas celebrations, almost numbed to insensitivity by this extraordinary year. She could remember how difficult it had been to remain in this room after the incident with Dan Robson and the strangling inability to discuss or even mention it to anyone around her.

Robson had subsequently made the best of the offered opportunity for himself and his family and honoured his own side of the bargain, and Elizabeth had forced herself, in due course, to walk outside on to the terrace in good weather and even to manage something like the calm contemplation it had once so easily provided. But distance of time and comparisons with the still raw pains of 1860 made her feel that a hundred Dan Robsons would be more tolerable than two events overshadowing the recent past. She knew, in any case, that not even the most remote possibility of the Robson incident now remained, with the ivy creepers long gone and a permanent window created in the butler's quarters downstairs with a view which took in every direction of access to the wing of the house.

Armstrong, as intelligent as he was well informed, had managed to conclude enough of what might have happened without a series of intrusive questions; he accepted on face value her reasons for removing the ivy, and then added the window on his own initiative, making up as inventively fictitious a collection of reasons as she had done for the plants. Once again, his discretion and quickness on the uptake made him invaluable. Neither the terrace nor the bedroom could quite return to the innocent bliss of her former perceptions, but she now used them without fear and sometimes even without recall.

It occurred to her, as a dispassionate reflection on the realities of the household, that it would now be at least an hour before she need stir from her room and there was every chance that she would be left in peace. Curiously enough, Charlotte and Armstrong generally got on rather well, seeing themselves as natural allies in dealing with the deficiencies of everyone else in the house. Charlotte's husband Eustace would, as ever, melt into a relatively anonymous background. Eustace, Elizabeth had been happy to note, could and did assert himself when he considered it absolutely essential, and was at present holding out on the subject of little Eustace's name being put down for a northern public school with a fearsome reputation and astronomical fees. The other members of the family had yet to arrive, and definite lunch arrangements had not been made to allow for any winter hazards causing delays. For the moment, Elizabeth's time was her own.

Mrs Granger had moved on in 1851, thankfully forestalling any need for dismissal or demotion, for the less demanding business of a pie shop in a nearby village, where food preparation was to a relatively predictable and less versatile pattern, and the present younger incumbent, Rose Fenwick, had a competence and unflappability about her which had proved a great gratification to Armstrong, so long used to dealing with the Granger high dramas; they were now mutually professionally supportive, and Rose had shown she could even hold her own with Charlotte. While Elizabeth had some mixed feelings about being reduced to irrelevance, even temporarily, in her own household, she was by now aware that only lengthy periods of rest would enable her to manage the hectic, crowded day this would become by the afternoon. The extent of her fatigue quite startled her at times, and Dr Spencer, to whom Alice had attached herself with such leech-like tenacity, had made some very pertinent observations concerning her heart and the increased vulnerability of ladies in the post-childbearing years. 'The desirable and the beneficial do not always contradict each other, Elizabeth,' he'd said, the years of miscarriages, infant mortalities and family illnesses having long since done away with much of the formality between them, especially following George's death. 'Sitting restfully in your room, with or without a good book and well away from the hubbub of the household, reduced as it may be these days, is not only a pleasure but much to your advantage in preserving your continued good health.'

Elizabeth moved her chair to the French windows opening on to the terrace and emboldened herself enough to open the windows slightly. The breeze was quite emphatic but not unbearably so, and the fresh, crisp air, that northern country bouquet which she'd always found so intoxicating, flooded into the room. A few hours' reading was tempting; Alice had finally prevailed upon her to read Mr Trollope's *Doctor Thorne*, published in 1858 but only recently available further north, and, wary as she sometimes was of Alice's opinions and recommendations, the book had proved to be intriguing and readable. But she knew another essential task, for her, had to be undertaken before the arrival of the family – the entire, hateful as it was to have to use the phrase, surviving family.

The afternoon and evening promised to be emotional and very demanding for everyone. Rightly or wrongly, everyone did still seem to look to her for their precedents regarding mood and behaviour. Were she to be mournful and overburdened with grief, the chances of the family, including the children, having anything like a festive time of it would be severely compromised, if not destroyed. She dearly wished to avoid such an outcome. Apart from the innocence of the children and what she felt was their entitlement to something like a happy Christmas, everyone else had felt the turbulence of this remarkable year and needed a period of calm, a way to regain roots and ground themselves for whatever lay ahead. 1860 had appeared to them like the Mask of Janus, now ecstatically happy, now desperately miserable, with no one quite sure at any particular time which of the faces they would find themselves encountering. They had all been bruised and cosseted, and much of the family were in a state of some confusion, disorientated and intimidated, and she needed to take the time to calm herself, partly by enduring enough pain of recollection to postpone further invasions of her peace of mind until the Christmas festivities were over, and partly by boosting her own morale with the achievements and great satisfactions which had also characterised the year.

As she knew very well, the starting point was all too clear, even though it was a day in March. Wednesday 14 March, a quiet if rather bleak day, found the household sheltering from a deeply chilling north-easterly wind. Samuel Spencer was visiting her, and had given her a routine check-up – even before the year had really got underway, she had been showing some signs of fragility. They remained in her room for a short while after the examination and then went down to the drawing room; it was mid-afternoon and she'd called for tea. Some of the minutiae which always came back to her was absurd; their talk over the tea was entirely inconsequential, but she remembered with precision that, at the point where they were interrupted, he was discussing bits and pieces of damage which had been done by the recent strong winds to his vegetable garden, at the same time as she tried to frame questions about the health of her father which he would not see as breaching confidentiality and would be prepared to discuss with her.

The door opened slowly; she could even recall the creak and her noting that she would need to speak to Armstrong about it.

She felt sure it would be Alice, who would never be far away when the doctor was present, though Elizabeth had accepted that Alice's interest was entirely professional. The person who entered sedately was Armstrong himself, though with a pallor to his expression and a tongue-tied, appalled demeanour that she could rarely remember him exhibiting before. He seemed to be on the verge of announcing someone, while too overcome to successfully do so. In any event, he wasn't given the time; the someone himself, Mr Burridge, came into the room seconds later, wearing such a grimace of pain and horror that both Elizabeth and the doctor got immediately to their feet.

'Mrs Howell, your servant, ma'am. Dr Spencer, I am glad to find you here. There has been a massive explosion at the Heddon Hill colliery – firedamp, probably inadequate ventilation. Scores of men may be injured or worse. I have sent urgent messages to Mr Howell; as fate would have it, he is in Durham today meeting some merchants. Please, Doctor, will you come?'

'Of course, Mr Burridge. Elizabeth, excuse me, will you?'

She nodded at both of them and they were heading for the door when it opened again, and this time Alice did make her entrance, dressed, as usual, in her plain blue, which Elizabeth had mentioned made her thin, pasty features look even more so, though Alice's indifference to her own appearance could not generally be moved one iota.

'I heard and saw what your men are so unsettled about, Mr Burridge. May I accompany you on this occasion, Dr Spencer?'

Elizabeth rather expected the girl to be summarily dismissed with as much politeness as each man could muster, but her progress was resoundingly demonstrated by the doctor's immediate and enthusiastic agreement.

'I would be most grateful for your assistance, Miss Howell; I am all too afraid a great deal of work may be involved, and possibly more than I can deal with alone.'

Elizabeth had gleaned the subsequent events of that dreadful day from the three participants who left the house in the morning and a number of other sources, both first and second hand. Dr Spencer and Alice prepared in a long, low wooden room, normally used as a storeroom, at the pithead, Spencer having made it abundantly clear that casualties would have to be treated on the premises and messages sent out to the nearest available hospital in Durham. Alice spent the first hour gazing out at the gradual accumulating crowd of silent, shuffling people, some content to simply stand and wait, some talking, occasionally shouting, in small, clustered groups. She knew from the glances shot in her direction that she had already been identified as a Howell, and she knew from what Francis had said that this would once have been an automatic prelude to angry stares at the very least, and quite possibly obscene gesticulations and threatening movements in her direction. However, in eight years Francis had changed the mood at least to the point where open hostility towards all Howells had become relatively rare. In any case, the dark, poorly clad local people gathering around the towering pithead looked so numb with grief and shock that exhibiting aggression and hatred would mean an expenditure of energy they could not muster.

Then the first casualties started to arrive and the full horror of the explosion became apparent. What the men called 'firedamp', gases contained in the coal and adjacent strata especially in bituminous coal, could and did precipitate huge explosions when the coal was pierced and remained a major hazard even after the Davy and Stephenson lamps were developed, because of the constantly bad ventilation of the mines. The owners refused, in any case, to supply safety lamps, and the miners had to supply their own; many preferred naked flames which made the situation worse.

At the beginning, all that appeared in the improvised candlelit treatment chamber with benches pulled together for operating purposes were bodies and bits of bodies, men sometimes horribly mutilated, in several cases with their heads or limbs literally blown off. Many had little or no clothing, and Alice noted, as much as she was able to note anything with coherence, that this did not give rise to the constant stream of anxious and doubtful glances in her direction from the doctor whenever anything connected to male nudity had to be dealt with. Nakedness paled into insignificance beside the outrages perpetrated on their bodies. Eventually, men and boys who were still alive began to emerge, most of them suffering from the after-damp, or choke-damp, of the released carbonic acid gases. She helped Spencer do everything he feasibly could, including amputations where inevitable and one feasible restoration of an almost severed limb, a boy's forearm, with Spencer believing it was possible that his youth would prevent the traumatic rejection of the carefully stitched-back limb. In spite of the most recent regulations and the fact that none of the boys was supposed to be less than twelve years old, several of the corpses and patients were no more than children. Alice knew from the occasional rueful outburst by Francis that many of the mine owners would quote the difficulty of proper birth registration and the malnutrition of some local people to suggest the impossibility of knowing how old many of the boys were. In spite of herself and her best efforts at control when engaged in serious work with Spencer, the tears flowed freely, though mercifully quietly and almost unnoticed in the endless stream of blood and body fluid. She had already conceived of an enormous respect for Samuel Spencer, whose slightly comical, tending to the rotund normal being changed so drastically in such circumstances as these, his sleeves rolled up and his shirt deteriorating slowly to a soaked, soiled, bloody mess. He could do no more for the dead than pronounce them so, to be taken and covered until the burial groups dealt with them, but if there seemed to be a chance, even the remotest chance, that anyone might be revived, whatever the shocking condition of the body, he would do everything he could for as long as he could. It dawned on her quite suddenly, with a little mental nip at herself for not realising sooner, that sheer sweat was one of the worst hazards he had to face in this unaired, subterranean-like spot, and she made it her business to open what windows were available and to use whatever she could find, usually rags of discarded clothing, to mop at his head and neck. At first, he flinched from her, with a questioning look, but she muttered to him, 'Samuel, you can hardly see what you're doing', and he smiled grimly and nodded.

Both of them lost all track of time; their ordeal amongst the limbs, blood and filth seemed to continue as if a condemnation, an everlasting torment in some futile hell of inevitable defeat, but there were just enough victories – the boy's arm, men slowly recovering when their inhalations had been relatively light and they were firmly placed in open air, a few cases where amputations did at least save the life – to keep their sagging bodies and tortured minds afloat. At last, when dawn was beginning to break over the silent, ghost-like crowd outside, help arrived from the hospital and the two of them were able to sit outside, propped up against the wall, and let some life return to their own agonised limbs.

Alice could remember Francis and Burridge appearing in the room at some point in the dead of night, though the memory had some disconcerting dream-like characteristics and she needed to check with Samuel before she could be sure.

'What? Oh, yes,' the doctor said, closing his eyes and continuing his speech even as his chin sank on to his chest. 'Francis did appear in the early hours, though I would not find myself able to identify exactly when. I think we were checking on the faint life signs of some hopelessly mutilated boy at the time, but we must have seen upwards of thirty corpses or near corpses by then and I could no longer maintain any notion of numbers or even retain separate features of the poor souls.' He struggled up to hoist his back more squarely against the wall, and his opened eyes turned towards Alice; she could see in the red raw rims and the stiff white skin, like stretched parchment, what the night had cost him.

'I know your brother quite well, I think,' Samuel said. 'I did actually contribute to bringing him into the world. I looked up from what I was doing, as I think you did, because I had a sense that the door had opened – a sudden expansion of the odd, unsettling agitated hum of noise from outside the building, a clump of wood on wood. He was silhouetted against the window, next to the rather more substantial figure of Mr Burridge. I remember the straightness of his figure; there was no sign of his elbows at his sides and it registered briefly in my mind that he must have his hands folded before him, entirely quiet and still, like a waiting monk. He stayed there for some little time, I think, though my sense of it by then was flimsy; he seemed to still be there, quite constrained, unmoving, unspeaking, when I had time to glance up again. Some passing lamp lit his face very briefly; he looked to be watching you rather more than me. Then he said something to Burridge which I didn't catch, and when I looked up again, he'd gone.'

Alice heard the words emerging from her mouth and acknowledged that the voice was hers, but the dream ambience was still everywhere around her and, in spite of her awareness that the time and occasion were scarcely appropriate to say what she intended to say, she knew in a quite cold and detached way that she was going to say it anyway.

'Samuel, a friend and correspondent informs me that in May, the first advertisements will be placed for probationers, or trainee nurses, at Miss Nightingale's School of Nursing and Midwifery. Sufficient funds have been gathered and the school will open later this year. With your help and support, there may be a chance for me, even at such a distance from the proceedings. Would you at least consider of it?'

She looked across to see his head dropping again and his arms seeming to fall away from his sides. She turned back to see various singles and small groups of the local people gathered around appearing to be heading in her direction; a few of them seemed to be carrying objects beside or in front of them. She knew she had no strength and even less will to resist them if, God forbid, their intent was hostile.

A large hand enveloped her slim forearm and she glanced across to see Spencer's exhausted eyes now looking straight into her own.

'I will do more than consider of it, Alice Howell. I will support it with every scrap of influence I possess, inadequate as it is. But you must not let the scepticism which surrounds you prescribe the limits of your ambition. Becoming a doctor is within your ability and I believe it will probably be within your power; it should be a realistic summit of your ambition, whatever obstacles may be placed in your way.'

She was still absorbing the significance of his words and the communication in his eyes when they both became aware of various dim figures, mostly women, looming over them and no more than a few feet in front of them. For a few moments they stood awkwardly, and then several nudges were landed on one of the older women, a small, bare-headed, square-faced figure, her jaw a determined jut even if her words were halting and touched by self-consciousness. The County Durham accent they knew well enough.

'Miss Howell. Dr Spencer. We all know, like, what's been going on in there, all them poor smashed lads, and the sort of thing you've had to be doing all night. We've got together some soup here, like, nothing fancy, just the sort of stew we do around here, and a bit or two of bread, bit black in bits but fair eating all the same. I think for the likes of yous, we'd manage whatever we had, like, Howell or no bloody Howell, pardon my tongue.'

Alice took what was offered and did her best to eat and drink, though her tongue was lizard-dry in her mouth. Within minutes, the women had formed a seating semi-circle around herself and the doctor, almost like an umbrella of protection against the agonies around them, the still ubiquitous shuffling confusion of milling, purposeless people forming unwanted escorts and spectating columns around the carts trundling bodies away. Alice had never known this kind of warmth and acceptance from the colliery people and she held herself very hard against a floodgate of tears which, once started, the long horror and fatigue of the night would not allow to stop for too long and too awkward a time. She had wondered more than once in recent years how she could feel so solitary and isolated in such a large family and why it was that she only seemed to be able to communicate with most of them, even her mother, in the most superficial and carefully negotiated terms, knowing how to avoid the danger areas and stepping into them only when all the other choices were exhausted. Francis, the only brother left to her now that Charlie seemed to have abstracted himself to a convoluted world of his own which even his wife found barred to her on occasions, had always been closer to her than either of her sisters, but Francis spent almost every waking hour these days with a greater burden than any man still to attain the age of thirty should reasonably expect to have to carry. Their companionable if often rather aimless conversations in his room or hers, an occasional delicious conspiracy of two siblings to exclude the others, were now long departed indulgences, replaced by brief, brittle morning or evening encounters with nothing of any great note being said or implied. All the affection and confidences of which Francis was capable were now, correctly and predictably, reserved for his self-contained, philosophical wife, whose gratitude at her release from a loudly evangelical and permanently outraged father could be seen in the genuine peace and content which now surrounded her. Alice sometimes found herself feeling like a visitor to her own household.

Samuel had moved back into the room to help with the final stages of what medical care could do to mitigate the disaster for the area and its people on the accident site itself. Alice relished the easy talk and companionship she now seemed to have with the local people. A carriage could be heard behind them clattering into the pit yard, and one of the younger women left to investigate, returning with a half-smile in Alice's direction.

'It's Mr Armstrong from the Grange, Miss Alice. Saying he's to take you home.'

And in a few seconds the competent and utterly reassuring figure of Daniel Armstrong appeared, the man whose first name she had even used once or twice, mostly for the pleasure of seeing his mock-outraged face and that rare grin, surprisingly full of mischief and wayward boy. Now he was at his most butlerish, standing by the very best two-horse Howell carriage gravely, as if about to accompany a funeral procession. She signalled five minutes to him. Samuel, seeing Armstrong's arrival, had emerged from the building. She smiled her thanks and the women shuffled away, but not without touching her, gently and sometimes with a rub or a pat like a consolation. She pointed him back into the room; even with the still prevalent sights and smells, she couldn't say her farewells to him in public.

'You have forever encouraged me in this, Samuel,' she said. 'I hope I have finally reached some position of usefulness; I would rather be an asset than a burden as soon as possible.'

He took both her hands in his and she felt the disturbed, callous breakages in his smooth skin, like torn leather.

'Alice, if you hadn't been with me, my assistant would have been the normal well-meaning clodhopper, standing where he shouldn't, getting under my feet and useful for nothing but heaving corpses about. You are an invaluable asset to any doctor; you have been for some time, as a matter of fact; tonight has just arrived at a consummate maturity. Make your overtures to Miss

Nightingale's school; you will have all the help I can devise and provide.'

As the carriage pulled away, she turned back to see him wave, briefly, a wave like a salute, before he turned back into the room for such finalities and formalities as there had to be.

She passed people now standing in their hundreds, mostly in small groups, some simply holding on to each other, and above the low, melancholy, mutinous growl, occasional shrill voices of women and children would shout or sob their grief at the great looming mass of the pit, gigantic, dark and immovable in the morning mist.

So much Elizabeth had gleaned from various accounts of the events of the night, including Alice's own and the eventual long, intense testimony of Francis, though it was several days before he could be brought to talk about the night at all. The total death toll after three full days was seventy-four; by no means the worst mining accident in the North during Victoria's reign, but for Heddon Hill, the nearest pit to the Grange, and its surrounding community, devastating and traumatic to the point where people would still gather for services and commemorations on the anniversary for decades and even centuries afterwards. In the mellow evening light of the Howell Grange drawing room, Francis, almost in tears, faced his mother over a week after the disaster, the first time they were able to have each other's company exclusively to themselves since it happened.

'It was the old story, Mother, except worse, much worse,' he said. 'Inadequate, shoddy roofing, neither properly constructed in the first place, nor subject to any sufficiently rigorous kind of inspection process. Insufficient attention to checking for gas leaks or accumulations; sparse if not non-existent use of safety lamps. Not enough urgency applied to getting men and boys away from the scene of the accident rapidly enough to stop the choke-damp affecting them. As ever, scanty or simply non-existent ventilation.

At least they have no case to deny me, this time, the opportunity to reconstruct the pit on safer lines, as a good proportion of it has been blown to pieces and must be rebuilt in any case. But, as usual, they will fight the costs every inch of the way, interpret such regulations as exist in the loosest possible fashion, protest at the chunks taken from the profits, refuse to provide the safety lamps themselves, and the whole sorry business will all repeat itself in due course as another community is torn apart in a similarly brutal manner. I don't know how long my heart and soul will allow me to persist in such an endeavour.'

Elizabeth remembered looking across at him, all those months ago just after the disaster, and seeing his long thin features more lugubrious than ever, his eyes still shot with lack of sleep and his body moving from sparseness towards emaciation, and thinking how long it was, probably twenty years, since she had been permitted by his childish years to simply embrace him and reassure him of support and understanding. That, of course, was now his wife's place and Elizabeth owned that Emily did not seem deficient in offering the support he needed, but she knew now, as she always had, the steel in him, the worth which amounted ultimately to more than either his father or his brother could command. Defeat left him morose and meditative, but without the drink, violence and self-hatred of George or, sadly now, Charlie; George and Charlie's great unhappiness with each other, she could now look back and realise, was that of two men looking into mirrors and hating what they saw there. In the time since Heddon Hill, Francis had had no more drink than his usual modest wine quota and a couple of stiff brandies on returning from the pit in a state of shock not long after dawn. He railed against the men who obstructed him, but he used the anger to advantage, letting it confirm his own moral certainties and adapt them to an oral battering ram against those who opposed him. Elizabeth sometimes regretted the necessity for her to develop the highly sophisticated information network she had constructed around the business. She knew that assuming an official position within the company, which she would be entitled to do as George's direct heir, would compromise Francis's position, undermining him in the monolithically inflexible notions of masculinity so many of his partners and colleagues possessed, but she was not without a certain political acumen of her own – no one married to George for any length of time could fail to have such a gift if she wanted any kind of successful survival – and she had known well before her father's plans for Francis were brought to fruition, that, frustrated and angry as he often was, Francis *was* making progress, slowly but certainly. Most of the company's partners and managers were older than him by a good margin and their days of control were numbered, while those of Francis's generation tended to more sympathy with his opinions; time was definitely on the young man's side.

Sir John, her ailing father, had done no more then than hint in vague terms of taking steps to give Francis much more power to his elbow; how dismissive she had been at the time, ascribing it to condition and senility, underestimating his ability to relieve her anxieties.

Anxiety, Elizabeth now reflected, seemed to be so much of what her life was about, even as she gazed out over the Howell Grange beautifully landscaped gardens on a Christmas Eve morning which promised a gathering of family and, on Christmas Day itself, a portrait to commemorate them all forever afterwards. She knew she was clever, tough and with enormous economic and bargaining power at her fingertips – she did not in any sense allow herself the kind of womanly self-deprecation which would refuse to acknowledge the strings she had pulled to help Francis achieve the now extraordinarily powerful position in which he was finishing the year – but in his case, the question mark would always hover above the physical constitution. Mentally, Francis was also tough enough and clever enough; physically, the enormous reserves of stamina he drew on from his thin body would not last forever. But he continued to allow her to mingle great pride with the anxiety, in a succession of bizarre contradictions which shouldn't mix but somehow did. When she had heard from a number of sources that he had made himself dress as an ordinary miner and do a full shift in exactly the way they did, something which she knew none of the other partners had done or would ever do, she had been simultaneously furious and enormously proud, the two emotions seeming to thrive on and feed from each other, making the silence she forced on herself about his escapade all the more difficult to maintain.

And now Alice, she thought, had started to produce a similar combustible mixture in her at a younger age than even Francis had managed, and elicited her brother's respect and admiration in the process. In the same evening conversation when Francis revealed his frustrations with the partners, he'd also described, for the first time, some of his detailed memories of Alice's contribution during the night, having first ensured that his mother wanted to hear enough to deal with however difficult the hearing may be.

'When I eventually walked into that room, after all the distractions and discussions based around the main scenes of the accident, and our struggle to arrange the removal of the living and the dead from the tunnels and faces, it could not have been far off three o'clock in the morning; all the help from the hospital didn't actually arrive until nearly half past four and that is yet another issue which will need to be investigated, thoroughly and probably expensively. Dr Spencer and Alice had by then been at their gruesome business for the best part of seven hours. I walked in and saw that the light was barely adequate for them to see five yards from them, let alone carry on detailed treatments and operations. To my right, there were at least fifteen covered bundles laid out on pallets, for the carts which had already started trundling bodies to the graveyard; believe me, many of them required a rapid burial. Several men were spasmodically walking in and out to collect bodies or give Spencer and Alice some basic physical assistance. At the moment when I first saw them, Alice was holding the head of a thin young man, white and as naked as the day he was born, a strange sight to see one's youngest sister engaged in. The youth was turned completely towards us with his head raised by Alice, who was trying to introduce some water into his mouth; Dr Spencer appearing to be working on the boy's back with some kind of preparation. As we watched, the boy suddenly arched backwards, clattering Alice's cup to the floor, and he fell on to his front, revealing the most horrendous of burns covering almost his entire back from the shoulders to the knees. He must have been fleeing from the scene – he must have realised, Mother, ten seconds beforehand, what was about to happen and started to move away. They had done what they could; five minutes later, the boy was himself on one of the pallets, covered with a sheet, and they had another man already up on the table, his arm looking as if removal was the only possible option. I'd already had enough; the smell and the fetid atmosphere were almost beyond belief, as was the collection of filth and degradation already accumulated on the floor around what they were using as an operating table. I wanted to shout to Alice to stop now and come away from there, I wanted, for a moment, more than anything, for my sister to leave the place, immediately and forever, but Spencer at that time seemed to be heading for the last stages of exhaustion and there was no one, absolutely no one, who had anything like enough medical knowledge to help him other than Alice. I loved her for her profession and her dedication to it, even as I despised the experiences which it made her undergo. I spoke some fatuous words of encouragement and admiration to them, but I don't think they heard me. I went out and ordered in some more physical help for them; I also ordered that all the stock rooms available should be turned upside down if necessary to provide them with

extra medicines, bandages, whatever could be found. I sent yet
another horseman towards the hospital to meet them wherever
they were and convey anyone qualified out of the carriage and on
to horseback. And now I will have some kind of medical training
introduced to the collieries, I will have proper treatment rooms
organised, I will have better organised alarm systems. They will
prevaricate and obstruct, as they always do, but I will have it and I
will overbear their arguments about costs by quoting just what the
bald figures will be for lost Heddon Hill production, the extensive
repairs and rebuilding now required and the local consequences,
including many who would rather now finish in the workhouse
than take further risks in one of the company's pits.'

Elizabeth saw a first carriage approaching in the morning mist
and realised she would somehow have to lift her mood before
people started arriving. The matriarchal role thrust upon her since
George's death was not always so easy to sustain; they all looked
at her to act as a kind of informal master of ceremonies, filling
any awkward conversational gaps and setting the mood of the
gathering, and at times it was more influence and power than could
sit comfortably on her shoulders. The misery side of the Janus
mask was not done with after the Heddon Hill disaster, not by any
means, and she knew well enough what its legacy would be in the
case of Alice. They had finally come to terms with each other in
mid-April, some weeks after that dreadful night, and Alice, restless
as she always was with static conversations, suggested a walk in the
pleasant freshness of the spring morning air.

'Dr Spencer has specifically pledged me his support and has
undertaken to describe in some detail the areas where I have
experience as a consequence of his training. I will earn a minimal
amount of financial and board support, I gather, if successful,
though I would hope that you might be prepared to sanction some
further assistance if I require it. Francis may control the books of
the business, Mama, but you have the family purse strings, as we

all know. I am still not entirely sure of how you feel about the whole venture, in spite of your tacit approval. It seems you have little enthusiasm for it, and I know you were absolutely opposed to allowing me to join Miss Nightingale earlier—'

Elizabeth had resolved that confrontation should be avoided if humanly possible, but this way of expressing her feelings was too much to accept. She stopped in her tracks, just as they were about to turn along the path leading down to the lodge at the gates, and Alice did likewise; they turned to face each other, eyes seeking for clues.

'Alice, at that time you were sixteen, Heaven help us, a slip of a girl proposing to go to a theatre of war populated by thousands of men of all nationalities, and you still had much of the physique and frailty of a young girl. It would have been outrageously irresponsible of any parent to allow you to go to such an intensely unhealthy place, riddled with death and disease. In a matter of weeks, you will be twenty-one and I will no longer be in a position to stop you even if I should wish to do so, and I would certainly not be so mean-minded as to deny you some additional financial support should it become necessary. If I am not ecstatic at the prospect of my youngest daughter, who I watched cheat death on at least three separate occasions before the age of five, heading into a profession where daily contact with diseases, including contagious diseases, is an essential duty—'

Elizabeth turned her face away and Alice placed one bony hand on her mother's shoulder.

'Still I am so importunate; still I do not return enough of your affection and care for me. Forgive me, Mama. It's just that if one is lucky enough to discover early on, with some certainty, what it is one needs to do, there seems no good reason to delay or deny. But you know, however I felt, I would not proceed against your expressed wishes.'

Elizabeth turned to gather her daughter's hands in her own.

'I am so proud of you,' she said.

'Are you?' Alice looked momentarily genuinely taken aback.

'Of course I am, Alice,' she said, surprised that the girl should think otherwise. She turned to begin walking again, allowing herself to organise her thoughts.

'Apart from what you yourself have told me, Francis has spoken of that night and how he saw you and Dr Spencer working together, with pride ringing in every syllable.'

'Francis is a dear brother and a good friend. I shall miss him; I shall miss you all. I do what I know to be necessary, Mama, not what I would prefer for my comfort.'

So, Elizabeth reflected, even if the settlement between them hadn't been entirely satisfactory, yet another fledgling flying the nest and probably not quite as ready to do so as she herself imagined, it had at least been amicable and the opportunity to see to it that Alice was provided with decent and comfortable accommodation had been conceded. She knew well enough that forbidding Alice from making the attempt was no longer possible and what had been negotiated between them was the best which could be made of the situation, but the whole business implanted a perpetual uneasiness in her and she tried, with the increasing volume of sound from downstairs pointing ever more clearly to the imminence of the coming gathering, to reflect on how positively and soon Janus turned his face around to show a smile again.

His first effort was predictable, though none the less gratifying in its confirmation and with the added congratulation of her own very prominent part in it. In early May, Elizabeth had made a rare morning visit to the library, rare because the room was on the extreme opposite side of the house to her own suite and because it aroused mixed and not very satisfying feelings in her. It was, essentially, George's idea of what a library should be, meaning more about show and prestige than attractiveness of decor and full of strange and indecipherable old volumes – indecipherable to the Howell family, in any case – which George had obtained from various sources, concerning himself more with their age and appearance than any literary or utilitarian content. The light was poor, even though there were two very substantial windows, because George thought libraries were about dark expensive wood and London club-like armchairs. The whole had cost an inordinately large amount of money and its effect depressed rather than impressed. She had made efforts to introduce brighter and more contemporary reading material and brighten up the decor with flowers and a few less imposing items of furniture, but respect for her husband's memory prevented any more drastic upheaval, even if she had arrived at definite conclusions on what she wanted to do with it. A large room almost equivalent in size and height to the front hall, it constituted a great deal of space to remain redundant, but with her children leaving or left, alternatives to it seemed far from obvious. And it did have a few very attractive corners and niches, usually facing out to the gardens and grounds rather than inwards to the mahogany dominance. One of these was a bay window which overlooked the approach to the house and was high and well-positioned enough to take in a distant view of the county beyond, particularly on a clear day. She was enjoying the view and a letter from a friend when she saw a horseman approaching and recognised Thomas Henderson, though not immediately; he appeared taller than she remembered, and he handled his horse superbly, an ability of his which she didn't seem to have noticed before. Her sources told her that Henderson was doing well and might soon be considered able to sustain a substantial promotion. At twenty-seven, he was two years older than Anne and, though he could hardly be described even by his most ardent admirer as good-looking, with dark, severe sideboards and odd darting little black eyes, he was clearly a fine and lean figure. His constancy for Anne, even during the period when she had broken with him, had surprised Elizabeth, and bearing in mind that Anne also could not be considered any great beauty, it would seem that he did love her for herself and was not looking to detach himself even when the opportunity arose. As Elizabeth watched, Anne came running out of the house to meet him and their meeting could not be construed by anyone with any sensitivity at all as other than indicative of deep affection and familiarity. He kissed her lightly on the cheek; she giggled and drew away, then, in almost the same movement, flung her arms round his neck with such warmth that Elizabeth was genuinely touched. He drew her attention to the horse he'd been riding, standing steaming gently in the warm air, and Anne considered the virtues of the animal as he pointed to various qualities it visibly possessed. Anne spent a lot of time in the stables and was no bad judge of horseflesh. Then he suddenly said something which made her move back from him and stand quite still, her index finger to her mouth in the way she had, a leftover from childhood, of showing distress. He was explaining something, gently, patiently, his palms spread in appeal, his head leaning in towards her. She turned and flounced off towards the stables and Thomas, with a long sigh and a gesture of eternal male resignation, led the horse as he followed her.

Soon they were out of sight.

Elizabeth stood up. Her mind was made up. All of the children except the two youngest were now married, and in every case their partners were estimable and worthy, well situated if not major heirs, and in any case, her family were not royalty and she was not in the political business of looking to gain territory or prestige by marriage. She had misread Thomas as something of a dullard who pursued Anne because of her comfortable family connections and because he had a lack of alternatives, but she knew now there was more to him and the career he had would be sufficient to keep Anne content, though Anne, with her competence in domestic and equestrian knowledge, could also earn if she needed to.

Something had happened between them, something upsetting for Anne. Asking Anne directly about it would mean having to admit that her mother had been watching her and her lover for some time and may well cause resentment. Elizabeth at Christmas casting her mind back to Elizabeth in May found it strange to recall how calculating she had been, how the experience of handling such a diversity of siblings gave rise to a subtle variation of approaches if the likelihood of success could be increased in every case. Anne's collection of strengths and weaknesses presented their own dilemmas. She was often more difficult to read because of a greater inclination, perhaps common to younger siblings, to allow her own concerns to be overshadowed by her elders, and she had always been more reluctant to confront other members of the family, especially her parents, lacking the self-assertion of her brothers and sisters, even her younger sister. Elizabeth could see no other way than to allow a few days to pass and then announce to Anne that the marriage could now go ahead, as far as her mother was concerned, if Anne still wished it so. Part of Elizabeth's reasoning was that, even though Anne was generally more biddable than any of her siblings, she had a 'boiling point', as did all the Howells and, for that matter, most of the Harringtons, and if Anne had reached the point where she was prepared to meet her suitor on the front steps of the house, a breakaway marriage would not now be out of the question. At twenty-five and with all her brothers and sisters married bar one, Anne might decide on a bid for independence with the man she had chosen, and Elizabeth would be sorry to see such a break. Part of her success in coping with the potentially unruly Howell brood, minus her husband for the last eight years, originated in an ability to see approaching confrontations and forestall them, preferably with beneficial results for all parties.

Anne said nothing of the incident and Elizabeth had to discipline herself not to ask tactless questions. Six days later, Elizabeth invited Anne into her bedroom and they sat facing each other on two chairs inside the open French windows, looking out at the remodelled terrace, colourful with new flowers. Anne managed to look both flattered and apprehensive at the same time; this special, individual attention was rare and could presage trouble, though Anne couldn't begin to imagine what she could have done.

'Anne, my dear,' Elizabeth said, 'I have been giving further thought to Mr Thomas Henderson and his aspirations towards your hand in marriage. As you know, I have harboured certain doubts concerning his suitability and prospects, though I'm happy to say that the reports I have received of him recently have been able to finally overcome my former reluctance. I know that you did end your association with him for a while and you may not yourself now see him as a prospective husband, but if you do and, most relevantly of course, he does, then I will embrace and sponsor the marriage rather than continue to place impediments in its way.'

Elizabeth had not specified in her mind exactly what effect her words would have on her daughter, but the trickle of tears forming little parallels beside Anne's carefully constructed ringlets while the girl's little hands twisted a handkerchief in her lap was not what she believed would happen and she found herself momentarily speechless.

'Oh, Mama,' Anne said faintly. 'For you to come to such a decision at such a time!'

'Why, dear, whatever's happened?'

'He has almost finally decided to leave. An opportunity appears to have arisen for him with a company in the City of Durham, the offer to be confirmed when the company's board next meets in a few weeks' time. There is a family connection; Mr Henderson's elder brother, Tom's uncle, who has a manufacturing company on the outskirts of the city, has need of a chief bookkeeper, a position of some seniority and enhanced wages compared to the clerical position Tom currently occupies.'

'Has he told any of his present employers that he wishes to leave Howell service?'

Anne became even more distraught at the question, and Elizabeth felt a pang of conscience that her daughter had so obviously been struggling with this burden for some time.

'I have said too much already,' Anne said unhappily. 'He has discussed matters with Mr Burridge, who has said that a more senior position with our company is not available at the moment and that he will not stand in Tom's way – indeed, he has promised some support. The last thing Tom wants, Mama, is to appear ungrateful to his existing employer, find the position in Durham is not to be offered and even the situation he already enjoys compromised. Oh dear, Mama, these are waters too deep for me!'

Elizabeth suppressed an inner twist of irritation; she had forgotten how ready Anne could be to embrace a melodrama, but in truth the girl was being placed in a very difficult position.

'If you were to marry, would you go to Durham with him, my dear?'

Anne was suddenly quieter and more controlled, with an expression in her eyes that could not be misinterpreted.

'Mama, I would go anywhere with him. I love him. I have, over time, come to love him.'

'Very well. If his hopes in Durham are realised, you will obviously be able to set up in reasonable comfort. If they are not, I will arrange for him to enter Harrington service at a suitably senior level as befits my son-in-law, after having discussed with Mr Burridge and Francis whether the prospects in the Howell company are as limited as Mr Burridge appears to believe. We will raise him to the levels his industry and service have deserved, and you shall have a working husband, my dear, and be none the worse for it.'

'Mama, he proposed once and was rejected by both of us. He has not yet proposed again. Are you suggesting that I must shame myself by proposing to him?' Anne returned to something like her former anguish.

Elizabeth simply smiled.

'My darling Anne,' she said. 'There are ways of giving a man to understand that his proposal will be accepted, should he brave himself to it. It is their fear of rejection which makes the deed so difficult for them to undertake; if that fear is removed by a signal clear enough for anyone but the most stupid man to understand, and Thomas Henderson is assuredly not that, then I feel you will gain the result you seek.'

And so, within two weeks of the conversation, she did, both the marriage proposal and the Durham offer having been made and accepted by her and her fiancé respectively. As it was intended that Thomas Henderson's new duties would begin in July, a June wedding was now in prospect. All of her children bar the very youngest would now be married, all of them happily so far, at least on the face of it, and a properly managed and fully subscribed marriage festivity would take away some of the gloom pervading everywhere since the events at Heddon Hill. Janus had turned his face again and smiled broadly.

And, in the very middle of the wedding planning, he smiled again, and again it was no less satisfying for being predictable. Elizabeth had first noticed the change in Emily in February, not usually a month for women to be glowing with pride and health, and not usually a state particular to Emily, whose sober demeanour tended to be reflected in her quiet manners and unobtrusive dress. Elizabeth, however, already knew that Emily had some characteristics of the wolf in sheep's clothing, having been present when the Reverend Salter, astride his own drawing room fire and seeming to gain warmth from it in proportion to his mounting indignation, denounced the lax morality and haphazard observation of proper religious ceremonies and strictures which he saw like a plague around him. The minor restraints placed on him by his now deceased wife, Emily's exhausted and outgunned mother, had now disappeared, but Emily proved increasingly less easy to browbeat and overbear as she got older. Emily would be crocheting or knitting with an odd half-smile on her face as the vituperation continued until, when the Reverend Salter had reached the crescendo of his righteous fury, she would say, quietly but quite firmly and audibly, 'Yes, Father, thank you. I think we all understand perfectly', and while the clergyman, usually with mouth still open and features ruddy with the effort of his exertion, looked on in astonishment, Emily would turn to whoever the current guest was, including Mrs Elizabeth Howell, and begin a much more mundane conversation which was, if nothing else, at least a conversation in which more than one person could contribute. Mr Salter, whose ideas of correct behaviour fortunately included not interrupting ladies in mid-discussion, would either have to retreat from the room or take a seat while the ladies ensured no gap in their speech would be long or hesitant enough to allow the Reverend to return to his theme. Elizabeth also admired the way Emily had determinedly adopted the position of mistress of the house since the death of her mother when Emily was only fifteen, to such an extent that any conflicts of loyalties which may arise amongst the few servants at the Vicarage would always resolve themselves in her favour. On her marriage, she had left the Vicarage entirely and stoutly resisted any attempts by her father to induce her to return, even partly, though she did find a suitable housekeeper for him who could be relied upon not to be bullied by him or allow him to bully others.

With only ten days to go before Anne's marriage, Elizabeth and Emily were sitting companionably enough in the drawing room, discussing a few details concerning arrangements for guests' travel from the Grange to the church and back.

'I think unpleasant surprises are what one most seeks to avoid,' Emily said. 'When I married Francis, one of my bridesmaids, my cousin Henrietta, chose to disappear into the surrounding countryside until the very last minute, leaving about three minutes for us to get her dressed. I was also quite sure that Charlie had left the ring somewhere – he had already partaken of a good deal of ale before arriving at the church, but he managed to produce it with quite a theatrical flourish just in time.'

'Yes, Charlie partakes of ale and a number of other drinks rather more enthusiastically than is good for him. I think in some respects it is a case of the devil making work for idle hands; country militias are not occupation enough for him, wounded as he is. In mind as well as body, I fear. The Crimean War was a truly dreadful business.'

They were silent for a few minutes, Elizabeth reflecting once more on the appalling accounts she had eventually managed to prise out of her Uncle William concerning the field of Waterloo and its spectacular, remorseless carnage. Charlie, however, would not be drawn beyond the most banal generalities, and Elizabeth, used to his openness and honesty, had drawn her own conclusions. For her own sake as well as Anne's, this occasion being one of the few times she had been allowed a little family limelight, she postponed the whole challenging contemplation of Charlie's present condition until some more appropriate post-wedding opportunity. She looked at Emily, whose modestly cast-down eyes, edging occasionally towards her current reading while she wondered whether she dare read while facing her mother-in-law like this, did not fool her; she seemed to have a bigger, healthier presence, a quality of comfortable maternity which most certainly had not been there before. She decided it was time to test the water.

'I think perhaps you may have a surprise in store for Francis, Emily, have you not, though I would venture to suggest it is not an unpleasant one? If you have already informed him, he is concealing his delight remarkably well, and such concealment is rather unlike him.'

'Oh, Elizabeth.' Emily glanced across – the first name use was the most comfortable for both of them, Elizabeth having firmly repelled 'Mama' again and refused to countenance either 'Mother' or 'Mrs Howell' – and seemed to go, if anything, a little ruddier. 'I was trying to be so clever, thinking that such an announcement would distract everyone from what should be Anne's special day. I see you are, of course, cleverer still, as I should have realised. What would you have me do?'

Elizabeth saw that what she had intended as sympathy and support had been misread. She leaned across and took Emily's hand.

'Nothing whatever, my dear, except what you wish and what you judge to be right. I sympathise with your consideration for Anne, and her day is imminent enough now, though I am not unique in my perceptive abilities and your secret will not be safe for much longer. How many weeks is it?'

'Dr Spencer confirmed the fact in March and it had then been several weeks. Now it is almost exactly four months. Oh, dear. Do you think Francis will suspect now?'

Elizabeth smiled.

'Francis has many virtues and perspicacities, but it would surprise me if they included the detection of pregnancy. No, my fear would be that one of the women in the house, perhaps even a servant, might inadvertently refer to it before Francis is told. I think your wisest course would be to tell him, my dear, and we will try to ensure that such celebrations as are fitting do not disturb Anne's special time. But the decision, I say again, is yours and I will happily concur with whatever circumstances you feel most judicious.'

So, two days later, with Francis's thin face positively glowing, Elizabeth acted a convincing surprise and delight that her third grandchild was on its way, and a muted celebration, consisting mostly of a dinner a little grander than the usual rather haphazard family affair, took place, Anne seeming to take as much genuine pleasure in the announcement as everyone else, though Elizabeth noticed one or two fleeting, anxious glances shot towards Francis and particularly Emily, as if Anne was trying to establish whether or not Emily's condition might produce some unpleasant surprise in the middle of her wedding day.

But it did not, and six days later, on Saturday 16 June, Thomas and Anne married in St Cuthbert's church in the village of Harrington, where Anne's sister Charlotte had married three years before, the bride once again being escorted down the aisle by her determinedly sober (before the ceremony, at least) elder brother Charlie, still an imposing figure, even if the complexion had less of the outdoors than it used to have and more of the pallor of the alehouse. Everyone studiously ignored the thump-thump of Charlie's leg, and the swelling wedding march in any case drowned it almost to obscurity. Elizabeth vowed not to allow herself to become too upset, disliking the cliché of the weeping mother, but Anne's transparent happiness, lighting her to such an extent that certain qualities of prettiness showed which no one had much noticed before, touched her to the very heart, contrasting so drastically as it did with Charlotte's smirk of business-like satisfaction. And the substantial promotion Thomas had achieved had its own effect on his looks, Elizabeth noting his dignified bearing and easy confidence with satisfaction.

Elizabeth gazed again at the approaching carriage and now she could tell quite clearly whose carriage it was. Her mother cared no more for those who carped about her extravagance than she did for any other criticisms of the Harrington dynasty into which she had married. Very few other people in the area even owned a coach and four, and those who were lucky enough to possess such a conveyance might not see a family gathering on Christmas Eve as sufficient justification for such an indulgence as transporting a solitary person twenty miles across country. But Elizabeth had the ability to understand what her flamboyant mother intended even when she disagreed with the consequence and, in any case, a lady of seventy-nine travelling in December was probably entitled to be as comfortable as she could afford to be. Nevertheless, Elizabeth watched the coach's stately approach with a weary eye. She had wanted to dwell longer on that June day and Anne's delight in it all, and now the imminent appearance of her mother had irreversibly cast her mind back to when Janus turned his face again, this time to take from her one of her nearest and dearest, possibly the nearest and dearest of them all. And yet Sir John had still managed to wrench a last tight smile out of the friendly Janus side before the mask turned to present its sad face in his direction for the last time.

Clearly so ill at the wedding that he needed to be supported or wheeled about, Sir John had nevertheless maintained the presence of mind to ask for a private hour in the study which Francis had inherited from his father and enlivened with occasional lighter panelling in the dark wood and a few more local landscapes on the walls. Neither man had any reticence about describing their meeting after it had happened, but Sir John's tight-lipped refusal to discuss the matter in detail beforehand only added to Francis's bemusement and his mother's frustration. Sir John, amiable as he usually was in most ways, retained a belief in men's business being just that, even in what were now fairly obviously his last days.

However Francis had expected the conversation to begin, the events at Heddon Hill were not what he could have predicted and he resented being reminded of them when a happy occasion had just been enjoyed and his sister was still on her way to her honeymoon.

'Perhaps we do not need to discuss that just at the moment, Grandfather,' he said, gazing at the wheezing, shrunken figure propped in the armchair facing him.

'Unhappily, my boy, we do, and if you will be patient, you will understand why.'

Francis did as he was told, in the way he always had with this man, whose easy authority and benevolent decree so definitively outdid the volume of noise and the violence so typical of Francis's own father.

'I have heard you, on many occasions, speak with some disenchantment of the difficulties you have encountered since your poor father died, in dealing with his erstwhile partners, particularly in view of your relative youth. I suspect that, following on from Heddon Hill, your desire to make them see sense regarding proper safety regimes has become all the more urgent and their refusal to commit the necessary time and resources to these issues all the more frustrating, even though they must know that Heddon Hill has at least weakened, and possibly entirely defeated, their reasoning.'

The old man had to have time to regain his breath and Francis curbed his impatience; whatever rambling or incoherence this might ultimately represent, this man was very dear to him and had to be heard, even in his dotage.

'What you say is very true, Grandfather. Being simply wrong is not, I regret to say, an impediment to their obstinacy, though I continue to fight as best I can with my few allies.'

Sir John heaved his torso a little higher and raised his head with an effort.

'Perhaps your assault on them might be more effective if somebody could enable you to come at them from a different direction. If they cannot be brought to heel by persuasion, they will have to be by legislation.'

A glimmer of understanding spread through Francis's mind, but what was being implied seemed more than he could reasonably hope to achieve.

'As you know, dear Francis, I have been Member of Parliament for this part of the county for over forty years. I had intended to bow out gracefully when a general election became due; I fear now that I may have to surrender my responsibilities a little sooner.'

This was said in a resigned, gentle tone, so much that of a man at peace with himself saying his farewell that Francis momentarily needed to turn his face away.

A few more deep breaths and Sir John ploughed on.

'I intend to recommend you as my successor and ensure that the influence which has kept me in the situation for all these years be transferred to yourself. I have generally seen fit to support the Whig interest, but, not having any intention of seeking a government post, I attempt to act independently in the best interests of all my constituents and I hope you will do so as well.'

'But, Grandfather,' Francis felt bound to protest, 'Uncle Randolph – I always assumed—'

'Randolph manages my extensive estates, with the invaluable help of your dear mother, and he is not only content to do that, but prefers to do so. He is, in any case, now fifty-six, and while that is not an age which would forbid him politics, he feels it is probably too advanced an age to begin such an involvement. I have discussed the matter with him at length, and he is as prepared as I am to support your candidature. He feels, as I do, that you not only have the necessary energy and ability to make your presence felt, you also have a highly worthwhile cause. And, however entrenched your opponents may be on the mining company board, none of them will dare defy the law of the land if you should get your more stringent measures on to the statute book.'

Francis was silent, lost in contemplation of what he might now be able to achieve. Sir John, reading the silence as doubt, took further breaths and plunged on.

'And you would not be alone, Francis. By no means. At the beginning of this century, there were no human beings of any age or sex who were excluded from working in the mines, and the butchery and immorality which flourished in those depths beggars description. Now we are restricted to boys who must be over the age of twelve, and men. It is only a question of time before boys under the age of sixteen will also be excluded, and it will be only a matter of time before certain safety measures will become statutory and offending companies will be forced out of business. It will need your generation of politicians to ensure that progress can only proceed with sufficient regard for humanity.'

Francis found his voice.

'I am deeply grateful to you for this opportunity, Grandfather, and I must think of how to reconcile such a calling with the Howell mining company interest.'

'That is up to you, my boy,' the old man continued, his voice fading now. 'But if you will be advised by me, you will sell the Howell share in the business. In the present state of the market, you should have no difficulty and you will obtain a good price, enough to put you beyond intimidation and coercion for the rest of your life. You may feel that you are abandoning the workforce you seek to help, but if you remain in partnership with the men who fundamentally oppose what you are trying to do in Parliament, the day-to-day working arrangements will become impossible and your commitments in London will, in any case, leave you no time to reverse their machinations in the mining company.'

Sir John only just got to the end of his sentence before being subjected to an apparently unstoppable bout of coughing; Francis went to him and patted his back gently. Francis had almost reached the point of deciding that a doctor would have to be summoned when the coughing faded at last. Sir John spoke again, so faintly now as to be almost a whisper.

'I have always believed you to be destined for great things, Francis. With all due respect to your brave, good-hearted brother, I have always believed you were Elizabeth's most promising son; Charlie is of too quixotic a temperament, and he seems to have managed to make his relationship with his father an even greater handicap to his progress after your father's death than it was when George was alive. You and Alice are the most gifted members of the family; I do not have time enough left to me to help Alice towards the great deeds she is destined to achieve, nor am I at all sure as yet what help I might provide in her case. But, for you, I believe Parliament is the answer, and you will not need to break your back wading half-naked through filth and muddy water for ten long hours to discover what the shift of an Honourable Member entails.'

Francis looked at him open-mouthed, this being his first inkling that any member of the family knew about his shift experiment.

'You knew about that, Grandfather?' An appalling thought struck him. 'Does my mother know about that?'

'Of course she does.' The old man grinned in spite of his pain, and wheezed again, creating some anxiety in Francis that his coughing would begin again. But he resumed laboriously; Francis kneeled beside his chair, as he'd been accustomed to do as a child.

'Your mother is no fool, Francis; never, ever underestimate her. But you have no need to be so anxious on the score of your discovering the lot of a miner at first hand; her admiration overcame her anxiety and anger, as did mine. Both that and the dignified way you behaved when your father died convinced me that you had arrived at a most promising maturity. Did you ever discover exactly what happened that day?'

Francis's eyes narrowed and he glanced away, deflecting a measure of pain.

'No, sir, we did not. Wherever we went and whoever we spoke to, the answer was the same: no one saw anything. The whole community seems to have been simultaneously seized with an extraordinary mass bout of blindness. But the shaft is filled in and the spot marked and protected with a solid stone building, and I have made the consequences of tampering with that building clear enough to forestall any attempts to do so, with regular checks and maintenance visits being carried out by company staff from other areas. If I have to after leaving the company, I will maintain such a regime out of my own pocket. Whatever their opinions of my father, he was not directly responsible for that boy's death at all and they are all indebted to him for employment they would not otherwise have.'

Sir John nodded deliberately and thoughtfully.

'Your father was not an easy man, but he created industry where there was none and was true to his own lights. You do well to honour him, though that does not require you to follow in his footsteps. Times have changed and, in truth, Francis, you are the better man and your filial loyalty and duty should not blind you to the fact.'

Francis recounted the experience to his mother with his normal detailed recall, but without the last two sentences of Sir John's words, not wishing to put his mother in any position of having to agree or disagree. Elizabeth listened intently, trying to force down her irritation at not having been more closely consulted before the conversation and concentrate on the potential of what Sir John had suggested. At this distance of time, and with her mother, now Sir John's widow, approaching the house in her spectacular conveyance, Elizabeth could see that Sir John would consider it inappropriate to put such a matter so closely concerned with Francis's personal future to anyone before discussing it with Francis himself, though she still believed a theoretical discussion about the possibilities of such a strategy would have been perfectly legitimate. But now, of course, it was too late, and no resentments about one or two possibly slight mistaken moves in the last days could so much as deflect by one iota the mass of loss she felt as the Janus face suddenly turned its lips down again. On the final day of June, just two weeks exactly after Anne's marriage, Sir John had died peacefully in his bed – as it happened, in the company of Elizabeth alone. With her mother and Randolph, the intention had been to organise a rota of attendance at the bedside in the huge imposing main bedroom of Harrington Hall, a riot of Lady

Charlotte's much favoured pastoral colours in silk and velvet, encompassing the four-poster bed and the immense sofa in front of it where, six days before, Sir John had, with a considerable effort and the gentle assistance of two hefty male servants, sat outside his bed for the last time. Three days later, he appeared to have lost the power of speech, and attending his bedside had become a difficult and morale-sapping business, with nothing left to do but watch the shrunken, pale head and shoulders, a small, inert protuberance from the magnificence of the bed and its coverlet. Elizabeth had known that she was bearing more than her fair share of the rota, with Randolph protesting his reluctance to leave at the same time as he stressed the urgency of the huge estate's needs, which Elizabeth knew was not an exaggeration. Lady Charlotte's lack of attendance was more directly explained, in that even a fairly short stint would reduce her to floods of tears, and Elizabeth could not but understand that reaction as well. Her mother had known John Harrington all the way back to the full vigour of his youth; even in his later years, he had been a handsome man, if greyer and more misty-eyed, and Elizabeth knew from a portrait of him, painted when he was a very young man of twenty-two, what a fine, well set-up figure he had been in those distant days of the turn of the century, before she was born, when Napoleon continued to threaten the country and John Harrington expressed his desire to join Nelson's navy, only for his politician father to quash such ambitions and insist on him learning his political business as his father's secretary and bag man. And Elizabeth had a few detailed memories of her own about this room in which her father lay dying, a room which had once been the holy of holies for her, William and Randolph. The memory which seemed to cause her most pain took her back to an approximate age of five, the visual vividness of the picture in her mind not being matched by a precision of the exact day and time. She had been kneeling on that very sofa, looking to left and right of her at its beautifully upholstered vastness, and slowly her head edged up and over the end of it, to peer at the two (to her) huge bundles of her mother and father at an entirely horizontal angle. The site was so strange and unprecedented to her childish mind that she stayed there for some time, simply staring, presumably the main reason why the memory had lived in her mind for so long. After what she experienced as a whole aeon of time, when some fiend had crept into her mind the notion that they had both died, her mother's head rose up from the bed, appearing comically first in a strange velvet night cap, followed by pale, unmade-up features, a vision of her mother she had never seen before, and Charlotte, as she was then, gave a little squeal of anguish before realising that the little face at the end of the bed was her daughter Elizabeth. Charlotte had not been pleased, chaffing and tutting at such an intrusion – Elizabeth realised, years later, that it must have been in the very early morning, as she eventually recalled the faint silver light around the room. But Sir John's big, whiskered face appeared soon afterwards, and the eyes were twinkling with glee, soon expressed in a great, hearty deep-throated chuckle. She even remembered his blue and white striped nightshirt and the soapy smell of his neck and cheek as he bent down and kissed her, still enjoying their private joke while Charlotte fumed in the background. So wrong, so unreasonable, the conspiratorial little alliance between them, more or less from the start, against her poor mother, whose grandiose ideas and pompous manners originated so directly from the slur constantly slung against her, a 'grocer's daughter', no fit match for old country aristocracy like the Harringtons, as if the Harringtons didn't owe most of their advancement to a tax collector elevated to a sort of peerage by the miserly old Henry VII, who valued his collected taxes more than he did titles. And Charlotte's father had not been a grocer, he'd been a merchant of various foodstuffs and every bit as middle class as the original Harrington tax collector. But Charlotte would talk so about 'form', 'bearing', 'the acceptable and the contemptible', 'above stairs and below stairs', that she and her father would be set off grinning at each other in spite of their best efforts.

Her mind on the past Sir John had made her stray from the present Sir John, and when she'd looked again, she was astonished to see his eyes were open and he was gazing at her fixedly, balefully, as if something was left to say and, knowing that he couldn't, he was trying to look it instead. One of his arms had half-stretched in her direction, and she took his hand in hers. For a few seconds, his mouth moved slowly and she could see the frustration in his eyes. Then, somehow, his cold hand managed to squeeze lightly on hers. Then his head simply turned on its side, his eyes closed and he died.

At the very moment when the specific memory lived most freshly in Elizabeth's mind, Lady Charlotte's coach and four clattered up to the front of the house. Now the conspiratorial smiles and winks were over; Lady Charlotte was putting on a show, keeping the flag flying, as she always had, and Elizabeth was pledged not to make even the ghost of an attempt to burst any of her mother's pomposity bubbles, at least until she had helped her make her way through her first Christmas without her husband.

And, of course, Sir John's legacy, in terms of assets and influence, had raised a plethora of issues which needed to be talked about. Elizabeth was not entirely convinced that a political and London-based career was most suitable for Francis, though she did recognise that there was a selfish element in her objections; now that Anne had married, if Alice succeeded in her objectives and Francis in his, she would be left alone in Howell Grange with only Emily and her new grandchild remaining in permanent residence. She reflected on how many times she had wished for a more peaceful, sedentary household, and now that it was in prospect, her enthusiasm for the hustle and bustle of family life seemed to renew itself. Elizabeth hurried down to meet her mother, envisaging that the next few days, much as she would like them to be about simple festivity, would certainly involve some more complicated events and conversations. And, of course, the last and greatest downturn of the Janus face, the most pitiless, unforgiving scowl of all, could not but hover over the proceedings like a great grey ghost at the feast.

She invited Lady Charlotte back up to her own room, her own private quarters, and Elizabeth knew that her mother particularly liked this spot, gazing out through the French windows or, in more clement weather, sitting out on the terrace itself, in either case having the opportunity to take in the wide-spreading vistas of Howell and Harrington land – for Lady Charlotte, the two were indivisible. Lady Charlotte knew nothing of the incidents of 1844 in this room and, as far as Elizabeth was concerned, she never would. In this respect, it helped that the old lady's well-known tendency was to talk only to family or people who she considered equal to her station in life, an exclusive enough bunch, or, failing either of those, people who would tell her what she wanted to hear, which included all the local clergy and all the Harrington tenants. Evil rumours concerning intruders at Howell Grange were most unlikely to ever reach her ears and would probably be ignored if they did.

Lady Charlotte sat resplendently in her armchair, straight-backed and filling the chair with splendid shades of purple, her walking stick clasped to one side. She looked admiringly on the terrace and the land beyond it and, typically, made no complaint about the breeze wafting in on the December day.

'Dear Elizabeth,' she said, and her daughter did not detect any announcing voice, any prelude to the ringing declamations characteristic of the lady. 'I suppose we should fall in each other's necks and weep yet again, two women so seriously bereaved. But the family must have a Christmas at least a little worthy of the name, if only to give them the strength to brave the New Year. I do not mean to suggest a complacency – your losses are more grievous than mine, my dear – but it behoves us to make some kind of a show of it. And it is true, is it not, that the year has had its saving graces, not least the fact that your son is now one of the richest and most powerful men in the North. John was adamant that the sale of the Howell interest in the mining company would not be a difficult matter, and how right he was. He had a habit of being right, doubtless a most desirable characteristic in a husband, if a little galling at times. I gather the concern in question, a consortium of families, was so keen on the purchase that even the stated approximate price was exceeded.'

'Yes.' Elizabeth took her cue in a spirit of slightly shamed relief that the emotionalism of the day might yet be controlled. 'It remains something of a mythology that King Coal is the road to easy fortune, in spite of so much evidence to the contrary. The partners were politeness itself when it came to the last attendance at the board for Francis – many fine speeches and presentations, concerning the pride they all felt at one of their own, as they put it, going to London to "speak the voice of the North", I think one of them said. It was left to Mr Thirwell, mischievous as ever, to point out that what the voice of the North might finish up saying may not be what some of the gentlemen most wanted to hear. Francis simply beamed on them, I understand, confident to sit in the warm light of their approval for the moment. "Because," he said to me, with that glint he gets in his eyes, "their approval will be short-lived. They will soon be denouncing me from the rooftops, and I shall not give a fig for it. They can vote me down with their share majority between them; they cannot vote down Parliament." I watched him at County Hall when the result was announced, still as slim as he's always been, poor boy, but taller now, and quite imposing in his long dark coat.'

'And now, of course, a son as well. And the grace – if that's the right word, Elizabeth, which I leave to you to decide – to christen the infant George, though going through life with the name George Howell in this area may not be the easiest path for the little mite.'

'Mother, please,' Elizabeth said evenly. 'Your thoughts about George are well known and there is no need for you to repeat them to me, especially on this occasion. I am not strong enough at the moment for such persiflage, especially in the light of the sadder events of the year. We are all somewhat weakened this Christmas, and if it is to be a remembrance for those no longer with us, please remember that one of them was my husband and the father of my children, who have already, I might add, presented you with two great-grandsons and a great-granddaughter.'

Lady Charlotte looked for a moment as if her mind was not entirely made up on whether to be hurt or indignant or both. The silence stretched to a potentially awkward length, then the old lady saw, on the basis of the minute signs which had always enabled her to interpret her daughter from early days, just how raw and open to damage Elizabeth was. There were times with Elizabeth, she knew, when discretion was very much the better part of valour, and Lady Charlotte did not relish any possibility of her being left in the magnificence of Harrington Hall to wander aimlessly from room to room, alone but for disgruntled servants. Less than half a year of relative solitude had brought home to her that tact, a little more political acumen in close family matters and a little less of the Grande Dame, had now become rather more necessary. Her eyes met Elizabeth's and she smiled.

'The remark was not meant to be contentious, my dear. I am merely remarking that the Howell legacy is a formidable one, one which the boy may struggle to honour. Were there any complications, at all? Is – erm – Emily to be amongst our circle?'

'Yes; Emily lives here, Mother, as I think you know. Dr Spencer attended her, as he did with Charlotte and Mary. Perhaps it is pure good fortune or the strong constitutions of the young women concerned that have so far given us three healthy births, but I think

Dr Spencer's skills may have served at least as much. As you know, the boy was a respectable seven pounds and only a few days early, on 7 November; Dr Spencer's insistence on preparedness even several days in advance of the due date, was, I think, invaluable.'

'This is the medical gentleman who is encouraging Alice in her – erm – ambitions?'

Elizabeth sighed, and her eyes dropped. She turned her face away.

'Another debate on Alice's intentions is a venture for which I don't currently have the strength, Mother, I confess—'

A sudden, urgent grasp descended on her forearm and she turned, startled; the old lady was leaning towards her, her head turned to one side in an odd mixture of appeal and apology and her face awash with tears. Elizabeth immediately saw through everything, the coach and four, the sniping at George's memory, the mounting disapproval of Alice's nonconformity, all skins over a badly bruised inside, and the two of them embraced closely and quietly, allowing, for a short time at least, dues to be paid to the year's sorry damages, so that its victories might ultimately create some spirit of optimism to be taken into a new year. Assimilating pain without reaction, a process apparently so favoured by men, could leave the person entirely controlled by pain, damaged beyond repair to the ultimate point of self-destruction and, though Sir John had died peacefully in his bed after a long and mostly contented life, the example in the near past of a damaged self-combustion was so close and so acutely hurtful that it was the one matter they so far had not been able to discuss or even refer to.

The click-clack of a more modest chaise sounded from outside the house, and Lady Charlotte got to her feet.

'That, I think, must be the arrival of Anne and her dark young beau. We must clean our faces and go to meet them, Elizabeth, after which I believe my most advisable course would be to take an hour or two's rest after my journey and before the evening's events. Do you feel ready for more family meetings, my dear?'

'Yes, Mother, I think I do, and being witness again to Anne's happiness may lift both of our spirits. There will be something of the glad occasion about this festive season, come what may. And a little rest before this evening's exertions is eminently sensible.'

The family assembled in the hall for mutual greetings, including Francis, Emily and their baby son, Charlotte and Eustace with their own boy, and the arriving Anne with her husband, Thomas. The latter couple were a little overawed with the proceedings, Thomas because the Howells *en masse* made him feel out of his depth and rather intrusive, as if he'd impertinently insinuated himself into the private lives of his employers, and Anne because her towering happiness at being in her own house, modest but comfortable, with her own husband was still so fresh and strong that even the year's more tragic events could not seriously or permanently dampen the completeness of her satisfaction.

They had a lunch of sorts, consisting mainly of bread and the local hams and cheeses, laid out informally in the morning room and sufficient to assuage the appetites accumulated by the travellers while leaving them capacity enough to deal with the substantial Christmas Eve dinner later. Everyone took pains, for the moment, to avoid distressing topics and the attempt to keep the atmosphere unemotional caused several bouts of banal conversation about house interiors, weather prospects, travel difficulties and the like, but at the end of it, those who remained largely strangers to each other, such as Eustace and Thomas, Emily and Charlotte, felt a little more familiar and less intimidating for being better known. Lady Charlotte presided over the proceedings with a benign and indulgent air which earned Elizabeth's admiration and even included, at one stage, making a determined effort to talk casually to Thomas Henderson and put him more at his ease.

Two members of the evening's gathering had yet to arrive; it was known to all that they would be late arrivals and their names were not mentioned in criticism or displeasure, though the mood of the company towards them could perhaps also be indicated by the fact that their names were not mentioned at all.

After they'd eaten and talked enough to acknowledge each other's arrival, they all gradually dispersed and drifted off to various parts of the big house, waiting for the main events of the evening. Elizabeth had always felt that one of the main reasons for the family's successful survival through the children's childhoods and maturing years was simply the size of the house; it provided a kind of sanctuary for everyone, places where confrontations could be avoided or withdrawn from once they had started. George and Charlie always seemed to manage to run into each other, to their immediate and mutual antagonism, but this train of thought Elizabeth determined to stop instantly, or she would be in danger of losing the day before it had properly started.

She realised that she was no longer in the frame of mind to simply withdraw to her room. Competent as Armstrong was, it seemed arrogant and a little negligent to simply leave him to it, especially on such an occasion where, with so many people gathered in the house, he could be placed in positions where decisions were forced upon him which were not really his to take. His shoulders were broad, absolutely, and he would take them rather than disturb her if that's what he thought she wanted, but she saw it as an abdication of her ultimate responsibility to simply withdraw at this stage of the day.

She made her way to the foyer area inside the main entrance, and a comfortable group of chairs under and next to the central staircase. In a high-backed armchair, convenient for her occasionally troublesome back, she sat down and examined some of the local newspapers and magazines left on an adjoining occasional table. The unwritten codes of the house would enable it to be understood that this indicated her intention to remain unobtrusively in charge, forming a focal point, a higher authority, like a little monarch, as she sometimes mocked herself, giggling into the bathroom mirror as she examined the latest ravages of advancing age. The position gave her awareness of most of the comings and goings of the house, as it did now, with the Thirwells audible in the day room, Charlotte's deep command reverberating through the whole foyer area: 'Eustace, you will come here this instant, or you will, I assure you, be close to incurring my deepest displeasure'; Elizabeth wondered wryly whether she was actually talking to her husband or her son, but the man's even deeper but somehow kinder rumble followed soon afterwards – 'Eustace, my boy, obey your mother' – and the ensuing settled silence suggested that the father's authority was not non-existent, simply gentler. Lady Charlotte had withdrawn, as she had stated she would, and Elizabeth took that at face value; the journey from Harrington Hall was tiring, especially at her age. Emily and Alice she could see walking together across the grass in front of the portico, talking quite animatedly; Emily seemed to have recovered well from the experience of her first birth, in spite of previous frustrations, and Elizabeth knew she had allowed, with some initial misgivings, Alice to help Dr Spencer in attending intimately to her; the experience seemed to have succeeded in drawing them closer. Alice herself had realised her ambition and would be leaving for the Nightingale School of Nursing and Midwifery early in the New Year, as part of their second wave of admissions. Samuel Spencer's whole-hearted championing of her cause, boosted by more highly placed friends and colleagues than his habitual modesty would allow him to refer to in everyday conversation, and his detailed categorisation of the now lengthy list of treatments with which Alice had become familiar, had secured her admission. Elizabeth steeled herself against feeling hurt by Alice's evident sense of triumph and eagerness to leave the house and disciplined herself to think of it as another of the Janus smiles alleviating the savagery of his grimaces, but in her heart the anxiety remained. Whatever Alice was or would become, she remained the precious youngest child.

She had become quite absorbed in a *Times* news story when she became aware of Armstrong nearby. She always was aware of him, his tall, patient figure, hovering at arm's length, immaculately if soberly dressed, and had more than once quite shocked herself by imagining what he might look like when not soberly dressed, or perhaps not even dressed at all. She was not, and never had been, unaware of him as a man, even if rather junior to her, like a dutiful younger brother, perhaps, though now, of course, he was in his mid-forties and the still ample and carefully groomed mop of hair had more than one or two streaks of grey running through it. His feelings towards her, she knew, and had always known, were rather more complicated than just employer and employee and were not entirely unreciprocated, though they both knew there was nothing to be done about it and respected the knowledge even while acknowledging the emotions.

'Armstrong,' she said without looking up. 'Is everything in hand, the day progressing?'

The question was superfluous; the quiet if occupied feel of the house, the traditional Christmas cooking smells beginning to drift up from the kitchen, were clear enough, but the formalities continued to have to be observed.

'Yes, madam,' he said. She looked up; he looked pale, a little more tired than usual, she thought, and cursed herself for a fool, to imagine the servants to be so indifferent and withdrawn that they would not feel themselves some of the blows that had shuddered on to the family during the year, including the recent and most grievous. She smiled, thinly but reassuringly – another item in their long, private lexicon of non-verbal communication.

'I have not the slightest doubt that everything will proceed most satisfactorily. But I would like to be seen to be available for the family and in the event of Mrs Howell arriving rather sooner than we presently expect. So I will remain here for the time being.'

'Very good, madam. Will you take tea?'

Elizabeth looked at her tiny gold wrist watch, a fortieth birthday present from George.

'In about half an hour, I think, Armstrong, please. Thank you.'

He nodded and withdrew. Elizabeth sat on quietly in the foyer, already seeing, in her mind's eye, Mary and her child stepping down from their carriage and fighting a sudden mounting panic inside her by sedately turning another page of her newspaper.

Francis sat alone in his study, the severe room inherited from his father. Ostensibly, he was checking on details of past legislation before the House resumed its sitting in 1861, as well as acquainting himself with more information on his political friends and opponents by looking up some of their writing and other people's writings about them. In fact, a contradictory and enervating combination of grief and fury had him entirely in its grasp and he could do nothing, for the moment, but stare out of the small window on the other side of the room, the only light allowed into it and offering a less than inspiring view of the stables and pastureland beyond.

Once, though now it seemed like a very, very long time ago, this room meant nothing to him but fear and intimidation. Here, he had been summoned by his father to be beaten on several occasions, and while they lacked the frequency of his brother's visits, they were nevertheless a source of resentment on his part, partly because he rarely – in fact, never – committed most of the outrages which Charlie would recklessly perform, his own sins being lower key and sometimes non-existent, such as the occasion when he had been beaten for not completing a piece of school work which his father had confused with another piece. He had a theory that he and Charlie derived some kind of pleasure from it – not sexually, but as a kind of mutual physical contest, a form of substitute fighting, the man insisting on proving his superior status and authority, the boy determined on defiance, exhibiting he could take it and was indifferent to it. Whatever it amounted to for them, for Francis it constituted a horrendous and deeply mortifying experience. After many years of a Victorian school and home regime, the pain elements of it did not discomfort him to any great extent, but the ritual had included strong elements of embarrassment and humiliation which could leave him sobbing, mercifully on his own in the night, when the experience recurred in his mind. After his initial reservations about using this severe room with its unhappy associations, Francis took a vicarious pleasure in neutering the beast, assuming, through his present ownership of it, control of what the room amounted to. The adjoining plain-tiled, functional bathroom and spartan little bedroom did take him aback; he'd never known that they were there, concealed as they were behind a wooden panelled door entirely the same as the wooden panelling on either side of it. He hadn't appreciated that his parents had come to spend so much of their time apart. On first inspection, he had resolved that nothing would induce him to use them and not be with Emily, but on occasions during her pregnancy when they both felt an uninterrupted night's sleep might be best for her, he had broken his vow and slept next to the study, as he had during the period of the child's birth. He told himself the facilities were now his alone, and their previous use or user was no longer of any account. And there was another kind of satisfaction in annexing his father's spaces to his own world. At that time, he had begun to feel that this year had chosen him to anoint him in happiness and success; he had become a Member of Parliament without a great deal of effort, because even without the formidable posthumous endorsement of Sir John, the retiring MP, and the convoluted but highly effective string-pulling of Lady Charlotte and his mother, his views on mining safety and investment were well known and especially pertinent after the Heddon Hill disaster. His single shift down the mine had also entered local folklore and enhanced his popularity enormously, though he seemed to be the only one who found it rather strange that the employees were expected to perform such feats on six days a week every week, while his one twelve-hour shift, which had almost crippled him for days afterwards, young as he was, could earn him such political capital. The opposition had been token at best, and making speeches proved to be little effort after years of ploughing his verbal furrow on the company board. And, to put a tin lid on it, he now had a son and heir, little George, and it seemed highly probable that the child would survive. Even though the year had taken Sir John, over eighty and in some pain, Francis felt his life had achieved greater purpose and promise than ever before. And then Charlie, whose aggressive masculinity and easy-going ways had always overshadowed his younger brother, had found a way to throw a pall of dark over Francis's new shining lights.

Francis put his papers down on the desk and ran his hand through his hair. Today was about the whole family taking their lives back into their own hands and setting off on their journey again, buffeted, bruised but ultimately undefeated. Probably in less than two hours now, Mary and her daughter would arrive. He could, with an effort, thrust everything to do with Charlie to the back of his mind until the festive season was over and he once again had time to mourn and reflect. But he knew such a suppression would make the latter part of the day all the more difficult to control, and he felt that he needed to try to understand and rationalise his own feelings before he could expect to be of any use in helping other people, including Mary herself, to deal with theirs.

He had visited Charlie in August, on a warm but breezy summer day in Durham. He hadn't seen Charlie face to face since Sir John's funeral some five weeks previously, which was a longer gap than he would have wished, especially remembering the particular vulnerability, the apparent weary fatalism, the rapid drinking, which he remembered featuring in Charlie's attendance at and after the funeral. Had she not already been so devastated, Lady Charlotte would probably have found much to be offended about in Charlie's behaviour that day, and one of the last sentences Francis had to say to his brother was to hiss at him, during the reception at the Hall which followed the church ceremony, 'Charlie, Brother, let me not mince words, we are not wont to between us; you are talking too loudly and drinking too heavily. This must be an occasion for a certain sobriety, for Gran's sake.' A haggard face turned towards him and momentarily flushed, Charlie seeming to debate rapidly with himself whether or not to be angry and deciding against it, more from tiredness than diplomacy. He spoke in an even, tense but mercifully quiet tone.

'Francis, how many men do you think I've seen die? Tell me – would you guess it to be in the scores? The hundreds? The thousands?'

'This isn't any man, this is your grandfather, for pity's sake.'

'For pity's sake? He was an old man in his eighties, Francis, who had had a rich and comfortable life and was seriously ill and in pain. I'll tell you about pity's sake. Pity is for boys, dead before they're twenty-five, bleeding to death on a battlefield, wasting away to cholera death in their own excrement. That's for pity's sake, Francis.'

Francis knew Lady Charlotte was now watching them from her chair, surrounded by consoling locals, but with her eyes fixed firmly on her grandsons. The subject of Charlie's speech surprised him, reluctant as his brother generally was to make any mention of the Crimea. He needed to abort the conversation rapidly, but with a suitable conclusion.

'I will happily debate these issues with you, Brother, but Gran is watching and I would sooner it was not here and now. Please understand that if your behaviour does not become less inappropriate, she may well reach such a point of distress as to ask you to leave and bring shame on us all. Have a care, Charlie.'

Charlie's eyes turned towards Lady Charlotte and Francis moved rapidly away. Twenty minutes later, during which he was mercifully unable to hear Charlie's voice declaiming anywhere in the room, he saw Charlie slinking unhappily out of the room and Mary leaving the people she was with to follow him. By the time Francis had disentangled himself from a group of Harrington tenants, including some electors, and made his way to the Hall entrance, Charlie's carriage was already in the distance.

Francis remembered the number of times he had considered riding across to Durham and making whatever peace with Charlie needed to be made, but the aftermath of Sir John's death became so hectic that all other family matters tended to be squeezed out. Eventually, towards the end of July, Francis made time to write to Charlie and Mary and arrange a visit; he knew well enough how damaged his brother had been by the Crimean campaign and suspected Charlie's superficial indifference to Sir John's death originated mainly in a refusal to pile hurt on hurt. To his pleasure, Charlie himself wrote back; correspondence in the past had more often than not fallen on Mary's shoulders. Charlie's big rambling writing made no mention of the funeral, but the tone was uncomplicatedly friendly and the letter proposed a specific date and time for Francis to come which Francis discovered, to his further relief, he could do, and he wrote back confirming the arrangement.

On Friday 17 August, a pleasant day for travelling, without the deluges of rain which could make the roads difficult in summer and which again suggested to Francis's reluctantly superstitious mind that his post-funeral meeting with his brother might be well-omened, he set off for the Neville's Cross area of Durham where Charlie and Mary had set up home. As almost everything connected with Charlie seemed to have, there was a battle connection, with the eponymous cross erected by Lord Neville to commemorate a victory over the Scots in 1346. Placed on the better-heeled west side of Durham, Charlie and Mary had arranged a comfortable life for themselves, though Francis knew enough to be aware that the marriage, after four years, could not be described as idyllic. Mary had soon realised the impossibility of living and working at home – Charlie was too ever-present and too needy to allow for concentration on her work – and she had rented a top-floor studio, which she could now well afford, nearer the centre of the city. While she worked and moved between her studio and the local galleries, often accompanied by Will Gelson, Charlie was trying to flog life and meaning into his militia post or stomping around the house, frightening the nanny or little Elizabeth or both, in between fitfully reading military literature, including retrospective reports and opinions on the Crimean War which almost invariably antagonised him. And, of course, drinking, a habit he'd picked up in much younger days which had intensified considerably after the Crimea. Most of the income available for their comfortable standard of living was provided by Mary, whose still lives, landscapes and classical studies were commanding higher and higher prices as her reputation spread far beyond the North.

Francis's open carriage drew up outside the neat, six-windowed Georgian house built by a wealthy merchant some seventy years before, though the house had outlived the merchant's prosperity and Charlie's family were its third owners. He expected to see Charlie watching for him or emerging to meet him on the path dissecting the neat front garden. He had important, perhaps life-changing news, for Charlie, and though Charlie didn't know that, Francis still hoped his brother would be eager for their reunion. No one appeared for several minutes, and then Francis caught a glimpse of a young woman, either housemaid or nanny, peering out of the window on the left of the imposing blue front door. Francis felt a little foolish and puzzled; Charlie himself had named the day and the time. He sat in his carriage for ten minutes, frowning at the young groom appointed to bring him to Durham, who kept glancing back at him and making questions with his eyebrows.

Patience and attending to his own business, Francis was thinking testily, were perhaps qualities his groom might need to acquire, when a neat little cab drew up next to his own carriage and Charlie climbed awkwardly out of it. Francis watched him as he paid his fare; the lurch was very slight, almost imperceptible, but it was there, and it told him a good deal. Charlie, who had a head for alcohol and an enormous capacity to absorb it, rarely showed signs of it affecting him in any way, and when he did, the consumption rate had already reached considerable proportions.

However, Francis was determined to avoid any kind of confrontation if he humanly could. He snapped instructions at the young groom and adjusted his features carefully into a wide smile as Charlie turned to greet him.

'Francis, old fellow,' Charlie said, and there was a real warmth in his voice and the firm grip of his hand, though Francis could detect the ale from several feet away.

'Charlie, well met. Have I mistaken my time?'

His tone was neutral enough and he did not intend it as a reproof, but Charlie elaborately took a watch from his waistcoat and inspected it.

'Oh, yes, I see. A little tardiness has crept in. I am nowhere near as well with that as I was, I'm afraid. I met some of the Northumbrian men, spare-time militia officers, in an alehouse near Mary's studio, and they had something to say to me of military service not so long ago, and we got a little involved with fighting old battles. But, anyway, old man, here I am, and here you are, so let's get ourselves inside and have a fraternal wet to match the military one. Such a surfeit of good company today is rare and should be enjoyed. Mary will join us this evening, so I understand, that is, so as to spend some time with you before you have to return in the morning.'

Francis, who rarely, if ever, drank anything in mid-afternoon, again decided to bide his time and let events follow Charlie's course; it was, after all, a peace-making expedition, though he had an uneasy feeling that perhaps the clearest reason why Charlie remained undisturbed and apparently unoffended by their last meeting was that his recollection of it was haphazard at best. He reflected on the lurch in the road and then on how much more must have been imbibed to lead Charlie to behave in the way he had at the funeral.

Nevertheless, that incident was in the past, and seemed very much so when the two brothers sat on the lawn behind the house with two tankards and a jug of ale on a table between them. Francis excused his indulgence to himself by acknowledging his need for refreshment after a fairly lengthy journey on a summer day, and Charlie's ale was cool and invigorating. They spent some minutes on pleasantries concerning the weather and the garden, Charlie mixing praise and blame in his comments about the gardener, a man called Hodgkinson. While the flower beds were pleasant enough in places and the lawn looked reasonably well kept, Charlie thought Hodgkinson over-emphasised the rear garden at the expense of the front and considered his gardener a little long in the tooth for the work he had to do, with too much 'prettification' and not enough 'spadework'.

'He means well, and his wages are reasonable, but he lacks the strength and endurance. There is some kind of connection with Mary's family, ex-labourer or something on the farm, and she sees him as a kind of family retainer, I think, close enough to be sinecured, in any case, it would seem.'

Francis grinned. 'Perhaps you should take to it yourself, Charlie; good exercise and fresh air, after all, and a chance to work off the ale.'

The remark, for Francis, was a bit of fraternal badinage, amounting to nothing very much, but Charlie suddenly seemed to grimace and turn his face to one side, as though acknowledging he was at fault and had been found out in dereliction of his duty. Francis felt suddenly afraid, for no immediately comprehensible reason.

'How are the militias?' he said, in a tone of voice which could not allow the question to be taken as anything other than serious. Charlie gulped lengthily at his beer and wiped his mouth with his hand, the whole gesture somehow dismissive of the entire militia business.

'A little outdated, or at least many appear to think them so. Their particular heyday was the Napoleonic threat, I suppose; Sir John used to say that there were many in the North who felt that Boney was trying to fool us all and he'd come in on the north-east coast where the defences were lighter. But our spies on the French side of the Channel thought 100,000 troops and 2,500 boats in 1798 was an extremely elaborate hoax. Now, of course, persuading most people here that there is any serious risk of invasion is very difficult. As we have this year concluded a free trade treaty with the French and joined them in a war against China to force the Chinese to continue taking our opium, a fairly catastrophic sequence of events would have to take place for there to be any chance of a threat from France, and no one else seems immediately dangerous. And, of course, there hasn't been a battle on British soil for over a hundred years, since Culloden in 1746. But governments have to appease their voters if they wish to remain as governments, reassuring the populace that they will not suddenly be murdered in their beds, even though they're not prepared to spend very much to do so. It provides me with an occupation, though I'm seriously considering rejoining the Regular Army.'

Again, Francis saw an uncharacteristic look, a glance away as if in disgust, doubting the veracity of his own words. The question which had formed itself in Francis's mind was 'Would you be accepted?', but he could already see that the habitual frankness between them had the potential to bruise Charlie when he seemed so easily bruised, and he chose a more circuitous route.

'Would there be medical difficulties in offering you a commission?'

'Probably.' The tone was weary and lacking conviction. 'But – how shall we put it? – everything has a price. And, of course, Brother, I will soon have an even greater friend in high places, will I not? I take it your election will be a formality?'

Francis was happy enough to talk about his progress for a while, though it seemed to him that the abrupt departure from Charlie's plans signified a lack of faith in them from Charlie himself. The reference to influence made him uneasy, as he suspected that his status as a parliamentarian could well be compromised if it became known that he had insisted on a commission for his one-legged brother. He saw himself once again on this lawn trying to explain the impossibility of it while watching Charlie's face grow ever bleaker with disillusion and self-disgust. But, he reflected, there could still be another way.

And, as the afternoon wore on, Francis appreciated more and more that Charlie's frustrations were not confined to his professional life. The fact that he suspected his wife of drifting towards an affair with Will Gelson was never articulated in so many words, but the implication remained after almost every reference to Mary's activities:

'Mr Gelson is ever-present, it seems; where my wife is, Mr Gelson needs to be.'

'Mary is with Mr Gelson again today, for most of the day, I gather, though it is not unusual.'

More drink and the company of a long-standing intimate like his brother also made Charlie bolder in his reminiscence, referring to his early courtship of Mary, even before Sevastopol, with occasional uninhibited frankness which made Francis, a man delicate and discriminating when speaking of women, especially his wife, feel decidedly uncomfortable.

At about half past five, Charlie retreated to the house 'for a little rest and recuperation, which has become necessary with this infernal hobbling around on this accursed thing all day', the first allusion he'd made to the artificial lower half of his right leg. He also, curiously, apologised to Francis for 'talking incessantly about nothing in particular, while you must be tired after your journey', which was both highly uncharacteristic of Charlie and oddly inappropriate given some of the subject matter discussed.

Francis unpacked to the limited necessary extent, rinsed his face and hands in the basin in his room and went down to wait for Mary. The door of the nursery was open and he smiled at the startlingly youthful nanny and her little charge, Elizabeth Howell, who was engrossed at the time in colouring a picture but stopped for long enough, on her nanny's urging, to smile and 'say hello to Uncle Francis'. The little girl's smile, though clearly easily produced 'to order', was nevertheless quite stunning, illuminating her whole face with its intelligent brown eyes and something of her father's perpetual air of amused mischief, or rather, Francis thought unhappily, that which had belonged to the pre-Crimea Charlie.

'Will you come and talk to me later, Uncle Francis, before I have to go to bed?', she announced to him, in a clear, determined tone with no hint of childish reticence.

'Of course I will, my dear; I see little enough of you,' Francis said, and turned to the nanny. 'Jenny, when does my lovely little niece normally go to bed?'

'About seven, sir, as a general rule, after a little story read.'

'Good – well, tonight, I will do the reading. May I do that, Elizabeth?'

His heart warmed as the smile appeared again, and he was still wearing a smile on his own face when he returned to the front living room. It faded at the sight of Mary being handed down from her chaise by Will Gelson. Francis had never seen the man at close quarters before, but even Charlie's scanty, grudging descriptions were enough to identify the perfectly dressed, slim, good-looking and surprisingly youthful figure. Francis watched both of them carefully as the little ritual proceeded in all its absurdity; Mary was a superb horsewoman and could leap in and out of every kind of carriage entirely unaided if need be. Not for the first time, Francis wondered about how galling it must be for women to have to take part in these little charades of manners. However, Gelson was grinning and holding his hand out in a kind of elaborate half-bow, making a pantomime of the whole business in any case, and she couldn't prevent herself giggling at him. Francis was intrigued and somehow reassured by them. He was, yes, a well-presented and very good-looking fellow, clean shaven, the eyes, even at a distance, a striking light blue, and a long, graceful sculpture of a neck only partly covered even by his high collar. But Francis, who had spent most of his twenties as a single man with such an urge to be a lover himself that he could detect easily enough the signs of it from people he met, did not see Mary and Will as lovers; their manner towards each other seemed more sibling-like, in Gelson's semi-mocking of courtesy towards the woman and Mary's answering high-spirited glee. Francis watched them for some minutes, discreetly where a curtain would cover most of him. Even allowing for their awareness that they were in a public place, none of the covert signals which passed between lovers, the glances, the supposedly incidental touches, the bodies leaning in closer than necessary, were apparent. What they were about was making some kind of business arrangement concerning a further meeting convenient to them both. The voices and faces were friendly enough, and there was a grace between them born of mutual respect, but Francis knew he could not have persuaded himself that they were lovers on the basis of their behaviour, and did not really believe anyone else could, unless they especially wanted to, and his anxiety about Charlie's state of mind intensified. When Mary, walking down the path, caught sight of her brother-in-law and her face broke into a smile almost as wide and fulsome as her daughter's had been, there was no sudden break in it at the recollection that Francis had just seen her talking to Will Gelson, no swift, anxious glance behind her at what her parting with Gelson might have revealed.

Mary offered him a cold drink, which turned out to be cool lemonade stored in an outhouse, and she took what had been Charlie's seat on the lawn. Most of the initial conversation was taken up with Mary's inquiries about Emily. Having not long since gone through the whole business of her first child, Mary was an expert on the process and some of the questions she asked were beyond Francis's competence to answer, but he emphasised that Dr Spencer and Alice were maintaining a close observation to ensure any irregularity was attended to as soon as it appeared. A curtain briefly seemed to fall over Mary's face at the mention of Alice, and her comment, 'Well, if the good doctor remains in control, all should be well, Francis, I suspect', specifically seemed to exclude Alice. Their relationship had been streaked through with tension from the start; Alice hadn't believed that Mary, however gifted she conceded her to be as an artist, was the right partner for her brother, and Alice being Alice, the fact that it was not her business did not require her to keep her opinion to herself. Even when Mary had made clear that Charlie's amputation would not alter the marriage plans as far as she was concerned, Alice had remained sceptical – the more so, in fact, because she couldn't see how a woman as dedicated to a career as Mary was would be able to take care of a crippled man. However, by that time a condition of armed neutrality had been established between them, and Alice had at last begun to develop more discretion with greater age.

Francis tried to be as discreet and disinterested as possible in his inquiries about Will Gelson; Mary was no fool. However, he had obviously not been discreet enough.

'I suppose Charlie has been plaguing you with his fears and suspicions, as if I was some silly girl whose head is turned by any young beau who happens into her life. Will is a very good agent and not without talent of his own, though his particular gift is nurturing that of others. He is careful, patient, very well organised and capable of talking to almost everyone in language they will understand; he is a good friend and an extremely useful partner, but that's all he is, Francis. I could tell Charlie something which would finally make his suspicions look as ridiculous to him as they are to everyone else, but I see no reason why I should. If I did not see Charlie as the only husband I wanted, even after the Crimea, I would not have married him, Francis – I certainly didn't marry him out of pity. He is the most beautiful man I've ever known – even now – and possessed of a boundless generosity and good nature that I hope and pray may return to him when the distance of time allows him to get more of that ghastly war out of his head. I would wish that he could leave military matters altogether; he protests he knows nothing else, but I am sure he could find himself in something else with an effort – he has a good eye for horseflesh and a deep understanding of agriculture. We could leave this place for a country house, for a farm – I have volunteered, Francis, even though it would make my life less convenient because of the need to travel in and out of Durham. He doesn't say yes and he doesn't say no, apparently content to stew in his unhappiness until he makes it mine as well.'

This, for Mary, was a highly emotional statement and she stopped for a moment, taking a couple of deep breaths.

'When he first returned from the Crimea, he had a good deal of trouble sleeping. Would that still be a concern, Mary?'

For a long moment, her head didn't turn directly back to him. When at last it did, her eyes were gleaming and the mouth had tightened; Francis saw he had prodded a hornets' nest.

'Nightmares. Again and again. Anyone's mind can distort the routine events of the day into the most hideous sights and sounds, Francis; the difference with Charlie is that he needs no exercise of imagination, nor even any distortion. He has seen everyone's worst horrors, seen everything most to be dreaded, every distortion of flesh and blood. Sometimes there can be several in a single night. He wakes awash with sweat, exhausted, sometimes shaking; there are days when only drinking himself into insensibility will allow him any kind of rest. He will not attempt to define for me the images he sees and the sounds he hears; I have tried to encourage him, in the hope that sharing them, articulating them, may take some of the sting from their pain, but he will not attempt it for my sake. I can only begin to imagine the nature of tortures which cause a six-foot-tall, tough country boy and soldier to sweat, shake and whimper in the night like a sick child—'

Charlie appeared at the French windows and she turned to see him; Francis wondered how long Charlie might have been standing there and how much he had heard. As it was, he betrayed no sign of pain or reaction and seemed taken aback when Mary suddenly ran at him. He returned her embrace while smiling ruefully at his brother over Mary's shoulder.

'My dear, I am always grateful for your affections, but our guest—'

She turned, still with her arm around him, and they both regarded Francis benevolently.

Francis, remembering in his study their faces turned to him on that day, still consoled himself with the thought that the moment he chose could not have been bettered, though from that summer day to this present winter one, he could not decide firmly in his mind whether the news he then gave them constituted a blessing or a curse, or whether simply leaving them alone with their assumptions and their independent lives might not have made more sense from the first.

He saw himself again, trying to be a detached judge, standing up and addressing them, almost as if he'd decided to make a speech.

'For the moment, I seem to have your undivided attention, and it is as good a moment as any. I have something to say on behalf of Mother and myself, something in which I believe you may have a very substantial interest, and I really need to say it to both of you. It might be better if you sat down.'

He nodded to the two chairs on either side of him. Charlie grinned, and Francis saw the country boy could still surface in him occasionally, even now.

'Perhaps it would be best if we *all* sat down,' he said, and when he'd brought a chair from inside the house, Francis sat to the right of them, with Charlie next to him and Mary forming the other side of their little semi-circle. Francis could recall every facet of their expressions, every nuance of eyes and mouths, as they reacted in their different ways, silently but expressively, to what he had to say.

'As you know, the Howell share in the mining company has been sold. You will not yet know the precise amount, whatever the speculation in the press, because all concerned have been sworn to secrecy – not, of course, to their own immediate family.'

He told them the amount, swollen by competition, good Howell lawyers and the eagerness of some partners to remove the Howells from their immediate vicinity, and their stretched eyes and open mouths told of utter astonishment and a kind of fear.

'Mother, of course, is Father's direct heir in this matter, and her wishes are that the bulk of the money be invested so that the family can exist comfortably and lend assistance from the central fund to any family members who may need it. You know, Charlie, that Mother's hope is that you will soon leave military service, but she has no more wish than I do to enforce her will on you. What she does desire, as I do, is to put you – both of you – in a position where whatever you do in the future will be your own choice and not forced on you by financial need. She will make a substantial sum available to you without conditions, but she would be particularly pleased if part of it was used to settle on and farm a parcel of Harrington land, bought for enough to appease the business instincts of Uncle Randolph.'

'Back in the family fold, eh, Francis?' Charlie's voice was quiet and dangerous. 'Back under the umbrella of my father's money.'

Francis stood his ground; the brothers' eyes met and seemed to lock with each other.

'Mother's money, Charlie. Mother's money. Father is dead.'

'Is he, Francis? His body is dead, right enough, but his influence and spirit live on, I think.'

Even in the safe haven of his study, Francis remembered the exposure and confrontation of that moment, when he and Charlie had once again worked themselves into an impasse, their eyes registering the level of irreconcilable difference there once more seemed to be and Mary looking from one to the other in mute sympathy that even mutual goodwill didn't seem to be able to bridge the gulf between them. How long they would have stood there on the neat back lawn glowering across a chasm, Francis could not have guessed, but Mary came to their rescue, not for the first time.

'Gentlemen, there begins to be a chill in the air and I believe we would do better to retreat to the house. These are weighty matters which will need a great deal more thought and discussion and are not to be resolved in a few minutes on a summer evening. Let us make ourselves comfortable indoors while I establish what provisions are being made for our evening meal. We do not see you as often as we would wish, Francis, and when we do, it behoves us to make the hospitality suitably appreciative.'

The spell was broken; Charlie stood back and beckoned Francis in ahead of him, and they were both settled, within minutes, with pre-prandial drinks, the conversation remaining correctly neutral and uncontroversial.

An amicable enough evening had followed, which Francis now treasured to himself in the light of what subsequently ensued. Some undefined understanding between them seemed to have the result of each of them in turn talking about what was happening in each life and the importance or otherwise of the recent developments. In deference to the carefully bred chivalrous instincts of both of the brothers, Mary talked first, describing some of her most recent clients and taking care to clarify exactly what Will Gelson's role had been in securing and pursuing her interests. Charlie looked unhappy and occasionally indignant, but he listened, and Francis felt that even as he became more in his cups, the way she talked about Gelson could not be interpreted as that of a lover in any way. She also made clear enough that Gelson was only part of the story and she had a sense of being something of a pioneer in her field.

'Ever since the Great Exhibition, a decade ago now, people have been looking to broaden their cultural interests and be seen as having taste enough and wealth enough to collect worthwhile *objets d'art*. The legacy of the romantic poets has sustained nature as a constant theme, and this part of the world is so beautiful, outside the cities and the industries. There also seems to be a constant sense of the rise of an empire, Great Britain as the new Rome, reawakening interest in the great classical heroes and legends of the past. It is a grandiose and far-reaching canvas on which I can work, and I mean to do whatever justice to it that my poor talents will allow. Men cannot expect to entirely monopolise the creation of worthwhile portraiture and interpretation; neither should they consider themselves exclusively entitled to suffrage, Francis. If it should fall to you to have to vote on a new and sensible Reform Act, please bear in mind that many women do not see themselves as having to wait patiently in a kind of queue while men have the vote doled out to them in stages; universal suffrage must be the aim.'

Francis took this moment to remind them both of Alice's formidable recent achievements and the fact that her ambition to become a doctor was now being taken a great deal more seriously than it had been. Both of the men watched with carefully restrained amusement as Mary fought between her delight at a woman winning pioneering breakthroughs in such an important a field as medicine and her personal misgivings and suspicions of Alice.

Charlie spoke of the anomalous position of the militias, usually county-based, and the contrasting understandings of what they were for and should do.

'For the old-money northern families, it seems their main purpose should be to ensure that all the Chartists and radicals are kept firmly in their place, and they should be on hand to be mobilised swiftly against even the hint of armed insurrection. Those for whom us Howells are simply *parvenus* no longer seem to take seriously the idea of having to contain invasions; the enemy is amongst us, so they think, though some people in the militias are precisely opposite to them. Some of them, I'm quite sure, *are* Chartists and radicals, whose notion is that the militias should be able to protect people when regular troops are sent in to deal with demonstrations; I have heard Peterloo mentioned on more than one occasion.'

Charlie spoke of his frustrations with the amateurism, the obsession with drill, the problems with supplies and finance, and the world he described was so far removed from Mary's that Francis wondered how often and how closely they could ever establish any form of contact. And Charlie's frustrations were different in intensity and distance; while Mary was closely involved with her world and such problems as she had were mostly about being able to work hard enough and organise exhibitions quickly enough to satisfy the growing demand for what she was doing, Charlie's weary detachment had a fatalism about it, an oddly contradictory note of nodding to the inevitable from a man who must know now, after what Francis had said, that he could step completely away from what he was doing at any point. Even the tone of the conversation had changed as a result of their move from Mary's working life to Charlie's; Mary paused briefly and only long enough for the men to ask intrigued questions about the places she was visiting and the people who bought her work; Charlie paused often, and let the ensuing silence ease the discontented rumble of his words while his companions nodded their sympathies.

Finally, the host couple realised that all the normal obligations towards a guest were being outrageously disregarded and insisted that Francis regaled them, in equal detail and length, with his own activities, accepting for the moment the stresses, pleasures and anticipations of his coming fatherhood. For Francis, his impending parenthood loomed over everything else, but he realised, after a few questions had been politely dealt with, that these parents had assimilated bringing up their child so far into their daily routine and farmed so much of it out to servants that it was no longer an issue which exercised them to any great extent either physically or mentally. He suspected, however, that their reluctance to examine the present and future of young Elizabeth stemmed from an awareness that the whole subject had become such a bone of contention that this assumed acceptance of routine served as a camouflage to avoid disputes erupting in front of him. There were undeniable echoes in Charlie's, 'I spend as much time with her as could be considered necessary between fathers and daughters at this stage', and 'She is already mastering such skills as will be relevant to her future', of an unspoken but undoubted disappointment at his first born not having been a son, allied to an acceptance of his limited part in the girl's life. Mary, on the other hand, hinted at very different ideas: 'There is already a versatility and spectrum of interests which will call for a broad and substantial education'; 'She will not remain for too long in the nursery, and certainly not for long entirely confined to the home.' Once again, Charlie did not contradict, but simply looked slightly incredulous at such statements, while Mary's own opinions of Charlie's ideas for the girl's future could be seen in the dismissive glances elsewhere and general lack of attention when he referred to them.

At last, at their insistence, with the night now ebbing away and the dinner long consumed, Francis was induced to speak in detail of his own plans and concerns. Within fifteen minutes, Charlie and Mary had both been struck into silence, Charlie notably taken aback at this eloquent firebrand of a brother who had somehow been lurking inside the uncertain exterior for so long, and Mary with her eyes now glowing and flickering with some incredulity from one brother to the other. Francis was speaking of matters of life and death, matters which were killing and maiming people now, at this time and in places they all knew well. His fury at the carelessness and immorality associated with present-day mining practices, still with scant regard for even the most elementary safety procedures, still asking men and boys to work either largely or entirely naked in sweltering conditions with inadequate and sometimes dangerous equipment, subjected to threats from various diseases and ailments which could be at least eased with no huge amounts of time and money, gave him an evangelical, fervent air which contrasted sharply with the normal self-deprecating and undemanding Francis.

'Grandfather, in the great graciousness of his heart, saw that I was fighting with at least one hand tied behind my back and he determined that he would hand me such a sword as can take the battle to them with such a new excess of strength and cutting power as to make it impossible for them to continue in their criminal indifference. This tide will be taken at the flood, I'll warrant, and lead on to fortune enough for those poor souls condemned to such a subterranean existence without the most elementary regards for their well-being.'

For Mary, who had never known Francis particularly well, this side to him was a revelation and an explanation for the third-hand accounts she sometimes heard of him in the county, varying from enthusiasm for his abilities and the promise of his elevation to Parliament to the reservations, from those of a more conservative nature, that reform could damage the profitability of the mining industry in an area with few other alternatives to sustain its economy. This, she saw, was the wolf in the sheep's clothes, his spare face lit up and animated with reforming zeal; Mary was fascinated and resolved that Francis would have to sit for a portrait before much longer. Charlie was silently astonished at what had been happening to his brother in the time when he himself had chosen to make his break for independence. Charlie's conviction that Francis was still in the shadow of the Howell monstrosity that was his father joined the other formerly solid pillars of Charlie's world which were collapsing around him.

Eventually, Mary retreated to bed, confessing to a busy day in the morning and bidding Francis an affectionate and, Francis felt, a more intimate, farewell, as if they understood each other better, in case they did not meet up again in the morning. The whole process took place to a background of non-committal grunts from Charlie, and Francis internally despaired at the way his brother bid his wife only the most cursory of goodnights.

For the final part of the evening, on either side of the dying fire, the only other light being mantelpiece candles, the brothers seemed to have arrived at a comfortable accommodation with each other, though Francis still found he had to consciously suppress occasional spasms of irritation at Charlie's tendency to wallow in his difficulties, weaving them around him like an entrapment web of his own devising, rather than determining to confront them directly or even work out more circuitous strategies which might lead to them being confronted and overcome in time.

'She can hardly be blamed if she seeks solace elsewhere,' he said at one point. 'I am limited, without doubt, in what I can offer her as husband, breadwinner or both.'

Francis had felt bound to point out, even while he questioned whether or why he should need to, that Charlie was a senior member of a very wealthy family and entitled to a share of its wealth, though even the obvious seemed unable to penetrate his brother's pessimism.

In recollection, Francis realised that his grip was so tight on the arms of his study chair that his knuckles were white. Long immobility also seemed to have deadened one of his feet. The books and papers in front of him on the desk remained in almost exactly the same places as they had been when he'd first sat down. But the years had already taught him something about how time should be prioritised; thinking time was not an indulgence, but an absolute necessity, especially in matters concerning relationships with people. He needed to remember the rest of this, to allow the day its recollection of Charlie before the day was taken over by remnants of Charlie. The recollection did not take from the remnants their power to hurt and disturb, but it did give the potential victim a greater balance, a capacity to look at the whole range of what Charlie did and was, and not just a last desperate glimpse of the unhappy conclusion. Footsteps were approaching the study, footsteps which Francis knew very well to be Armstrong's; there could be several reasons why Armstrong wanted to see him, but one was much more likely than any of the others, and Francis wanted to fix in his mind the last words Charlie had spoken to him, because in the morning, when he had had to leave, Charlie was still snoring steadily in the next room, usually, Francis noted, a spare bedroom. In the light of the fireside, Charlie's now red and blotched face, set in a grimace with the need to express his thoughts carefully, turned to Francis and said, slowly, 'I do make you this promise, Brother. I will think of the matters we have discussed in relation to the Howell fortune, and I will give serious consideration to what has been suggested concerning the future for my family, though I have to say, Francis, that I fear a deluge of Howell money would drown my marriage and fatefully compromise the principles of independence for which I have paid such a price. But I do thank you for your care of me, Brother.' As the study door clicked open, Francis wondered how long and how badly he would now be haunted by the final sentence.

*

'A message relayed from the very edge of the estate, sir. Mrs Howell's conveyance is approaching the edge of our land, and it is anticipated that she and Miss Elizabeth will arrive in between forty and fifty minutes, sir. I believe you intimated that you would like to be warned in good time, sir.'

'Yes, Armstrong, I did, and thank you. Where is my mother?'

'In her favoured position in the main foyer, sir.'

'How is she?'

Armstrong never made any attempt to duck or deflect the more awkward questions.

'Fairly relaxed, I believe, sir. Reading papers and having occasional snatches of conversation with our various guests.'

'Please tell her I will join her in twenty minutes.'

'Very good, sir.'

As the door closed, Francis stood and stamped life back into his foot. Abandoning all pretence of work, he made himself stride, as he often had across the main Howell office, like a captain on his bridge, organising and controlling the thoughts in his head.

He had, now, what he believed were the essential details of that day, Tuesday 16 October, constructed from not only Mary herself but incidental characters who came into contact with Charlie at various points until the last, long blank. Compared with the pernicious and still extant obstructions he had encountered in trying to piece together his father's last few hours, Charlie's story was comparatively simple; the main difference was that, while he had never had any doubt at any point as to what his father's motives had been or how his father would have reacted to what was done or said around him, Charlie's actions and reactions were frequently ambiguous and, at certain stages, almost indecipherable.

In the morning, Charlie and Mary had argued; nothing very unusual, so it seemed, about that, though this one ranged more widely and touched them both more closely than most. It began with Mary's complaints about Charlie's physical state in the morning and moved swiftly on to the extent of his drinking.

'Charlie, for heaven's sake. You are dishevelled, half-dressed, your breath is foul. What kind of a sight is this for your daughter to see? Even if you are indifferent to my feelings, you could have a care for Lizzie's; she's only a little girl.' Mary could remember having said that, and more, and her anger mounting at his refusal to respond, either in contrition or anger. 'Your drinking is moving out of control, Charlie. You must be able to see it for yourself. How you can reasonably expect to keep the respect of bodies of troops, I cannot imagine.'

And so on and so on, without counter from Charlie beyond an occasional grunt or angry glare. Only when Mary told him she would be back on Thursday did he fully turn his attention to her.

'You are leaving for three days? Why?'

'Oh, Charlie.' Mary was oddly touched by his genuine bemusement and an edge of fear in the bleary morning eyes. 'I told you all about this yesterday, and a couple of days before that. I have an exhibition in Newcastle, a large and prominent affair, with a number of local dignitaries taking the time to visit it. Will is organising the whole event...'

'You're staying in Newcastle for two nights with Gelson? Where?'

'In a hotel, Charlie. Mr Gelson in one room, myself in another. We are neither of us so poor as yet as to need to share rooms.'

Charlie was on his feet, unsteadily and odorously angry.

'This is too much, Mary! This is not to be borne! Shall I wear horns to walk out around the town? Why do you treat me so?'

Mary stood up too, keeping her contact with his eyes. She made a decision.

'Charlie, please. Lizzie is only just two rooms away, with the nanny. There is something I need to tell you about Will, but I need to say it to you quietly; it is between us and for no other ears. Sit down, Charlie, please.'

She leaned into him, ignoring the night sweat still hanging around him; she knew what the night sweat was about, and what really caused him to wake in such a state.

'When you were in the Army, you must have known well enough that there were men, in it and the Navy, for that matter, whose affections are mostly directed towards others of the same sex as themselves.'

Charlie frowned. 'Yes, I knew such men, officers mostly, but not always. They were not men to my taste, but they could be cruelly persecuted at times, and I saw little sense in it. Often, they were brave men, and especially when it came to protecting and fighting for their own kind. What of it?'

'Will has never said anything of the kind to me in so many words, which is why I have remained loath to say this to you and it is also why I must entreat you not to repeat it outside these walls. But I believe he is like the men I have mentioned. He does not look at me as other men do – you must surely have noticed that, Charlie – he does not seize on any excuse to touch my shoulder or arm, or kiss my hand, as other men try on occasions. He also has a close friend, slightly younger than himself, a clever, articulate young sculptor called Henry Mills, and they spend a good deal of time together, walking, riding, swimming. It's my firm belief, Charlie, that I could spend several nights, several weeks for that matter, with Will in the same hotel, and probably even in the same room, and nothing would happen other than both of us discovering a surfeit of each other's company.'

Charlie, she remembered, looked thunderstruck, and still that fear, that edge of bewildered, damaged fear, stayed in his eyes.

'I see,' he said. Those, she said, were his last words to her. 'I see.'

She said several sentences more, realising she was late and the carriage still standing outside. He said nothing more. As she bustled out of the room, naming a time on Thursday for her return, he was sitting at the table, quiet and unmoving, his eyes dully following her every movement.

From this point onwards, Francis recalled, Charlie's actions were known; his motives were not. About an hour and a half after Mary left, Charlie told his groom to saddle him a horse. The groom, a boy who had not worked in the stable for long but was already wary of Charlie Howell and the old soldier reputation, described how Mr Howell looked clean and well dressed, 'set up as if he was off visiting gentry'. As Charlie swung up into the saddle, the boy noticed the weird shape of the man's right foot – 'He always amazed me, how he could ride with only one real, proper foot and the other that strange big foot-shaped bit of wood'.

The next sight of Charlie was in the late morning, when he thundered through the village of Welston on horseback; several people saw him, inevitably, it not being too frequent for that quality of horseflesh to be seen travelling through Welston. One person, a shopkeeper standing outside his butchery at the time, definitely recognised the rider as Charlie Howell – another mention of the wooden foot, yes, but it would be surprising for him not to be identified in Welston, near the edge of the main Harrington estate and a frequent destination in Charlie's younger days, well away from Howell land and much closer to the grandfather he loved and respected than to the father he didn't. Charlie passed through Welston with hardly more than a vague wave in the shopkeeper's direction.

By twelve o'clock, Charlie was sitting in the Harrington Arms, a coaching inn which actually was on Harrington land, though the landlord, Ben Flaherty, an Irish ex-soldier known to Sir John, rented the place and ran it independently of the Harrington family. Flaherty was not the kind of man to tell tales out of school, and though Charlie had been getting drunk in his establishment since boyhood, he had never relayed any of the worst excesses to either Harringtons or Howells.

'Charlie Howell is the boyo of the world with a devil living in him,' he'd said. 'He'll either grow up and sweat and fight the thing out of him or it'll eat him up.' In their disconsolate conversation in Flaherty's back snug, reserved for family and very close friends only, Flaherty confessed to Francis that he thought he'd played a part in pointing Charlie towards military service. 'I always thought, he'd either get his fool head shot off or it'd be the making of him. With respect to your family and yourself, Mr Howell, he was fretting his poor heart out around here, and nothing, not the liquor or the wenches or the fighting, could satisfy that demon of his. When I first saw that wooden leg of his, my heart turned over inside me; that, Flaherty, you great gobshite, should be laid at your door with putting ideas in boys' heads.'

The landlord described himself as taken aback at the sight of Charlie. 'He's hardly been near here ever since taking his bride, the artist lady. The lads who come in here had accepted that Charlie was moving in more exalted circles these days, up there on the gentry side of Durham, and he was better dressed than any man needs to be to come into this place. When he came bursting in, usual Charlie style, except now he's got that leg stamping on the floorboard every second of the time, I said, "We've not seen you in here in a while, Lieutenant Howell" – he always liked being called that. "Flaherty, you old villain," he says, "cut your cackle and put me up a jug." Just that; no explanations, no where he's been or where's he going to, his business only, as ever was. But I'll tell you this,' Flaherty had said, leaning towards Francis's stricken face, 'if that was a man, Mr Howell, who had it in mind to do away with himself, he was putting on a brave disguise of it, so he was.'

Francis gave the quick, ashen grimace which passed for a smile during those horrendous few days. 'So you said, Mr Flaherty, and I appreciate such consolation. But you mentioned before an argument, a fight?'

'Well, I'm not sure you could say it was a fight that it amounted to, Mr Howell. I didn't see any blows being thrown, though there were some colourful words exchanged, for sure. Charlie took his jug and sat minding his business, then Abe Slater came in; he doesn't get in so often now, Abe, he's something akin to respectable these days, runs his farm and makes himself a fair living. Now and then he comes in here for a wet and a crack. It took him and Charlie a minute or two to make each other out, it's been so long, and I'm already feeling trouble waiting round the corner. Charlie and Abe go right back to boys, to way before they started coming in here, and they're what you might call dangerous mates, Mr Howell, one minute old pals, the next at each other's throats; even as little lads, they'd be after larruping each other. But I mind my business, that being my job. After a while, a few other lads come in and it starts getting noisier in their corner of the tap room, and when coach passengers stop off for a wet, they're giving nervous little looks at this bunch of overgrown boyos shouting the odds round their table and lining up jugs like no tomorrow. I take no mind of it, they're just reminiscing, all the daft things they were at as lads, and enough of them, God knows. But then, as it will with Charlie and Abe, the mood changes, and I know why because as usual, I get lugged into it, Mr Howell. "Flaherty, you old Fenian wretch," Abe's shouting – the drunker Abe Slater gets, the less he cares what he's saying – "come by and listen to this. Old Charlie here's talking about setting himself up for a farmer – can you believe that? He's all doled up to go see his grannie, bless her heart,

Lady Charlotte herself, to talk it over. Let me tell you, Charlie, listen to your old mate, Abe" – and I'm watching your brother, Mr Howell, and I know that glint he gets in the eye, and he's got his back jammed right up again the wall while he looks down his nose at Abe Slater – "One, you'll need to sober up, you old bastard, before that stuffed shirt butler of hers'll let you anywhere near her, my son, and second, Charlie, you ain't got the patience to be a farmer and you never will as long as you breathe, mate, and that's the truth. What's more, you old bugger, you've only got one fucking leg; you'll do alright chasing cows round the field with your peg leg, now won't you, Charlie?"

'Abe laughs fit to bust and shoves his head in his tankard, trying not to notice no one else is laughing. Charlie's eyes are narrowing, and now he's up on his feet, and peg leg or not, Abe's not laughing no more. "I got this in the service of my country, Abe Slater," he says, very quiet. "While you were tupping maids or sheep or whatever you could get your filthy hands on, I was fighting for England." "Charlie, mate, listen—" Abe's starting to say. "Step out into the yard, Abe Slater, for so help me, I'm going to knock your scrawny head right off your fucking shoulders, and you can tie a hand behind my back as well, because even with one arm and one leg I could still do you, Slater." The whole place has stopped now, Mr Howell, and I'm trying to make my mind up what's the best thing to do; the lads don't like noses in when they're setting about each other, and I don't keep anything in that tap room that's of any value, for sure I don't. But Abe's as mixed and strange a combination as Charlie himself, and Abe makes a little speech right there on his feet, looking into Charlie's eyes. "Charlie, I'll go into the yard, but when you take your fist to me, I'll do nothing, because I'm not the man to raise my hand to an old soldier and especially one I count as an old friend. It's only because I think of you as an old friend that I speak so. I meant no offence, but it's obviously been taken, so you can knock my fucking head off and whatever you said, Charlie, and I'll not deny you the satisfaction." They stand there, the two of them, eyeing each other up like bantam cocks working up to their set-to, then Charlie's face suddenly breaks into his old slanted head grin and he says, "Well, I'll have the satisfaction of seeing you putting a tankard down in one, you contrary old bastard", and then everybody's clapping each other's backs and shouting, all misty-eyed like you English are, and I'm starting to reckon the pack of them will drink me out of ale before the day's over.'

Francis reflected, on the chair in his study, the number of times and places he'd felt the relative hopelessness of his own role in his relationship with Charlie, unable to influence events or help in any way, a classic case of a kind of responsibility without power. And on the one occasion when he had actually tried to intervene decisively in Charlie's life, he seemed to have succeeded only in lobbing a bomb into a confused and directionless existence. Flaherty finally got to the most telling part of his narrative, the minutes before Charlie left the inn.

'I'm thinking, these boys'll still be here when I'm lighting the candles, but suddenly they're all up on their feet and Abe's saying he's got a market to go to, though how he'd ever manage to buy any animals in the state he's in, I don't know. I got a sort of feeling, which you do with groups of men sometimes, that they'd all just had about enough of Charlie; they'd crack on with him for old times, but he's not one of them any more, in his fine clothes, and he shouldn't be making as if he is. Just as Abe's going out the door, Charlie says, "You're right enough about one thing, Abe Slater, and that's Lady Charlotte's reaction when I roll up like this. I'll have to douse myself or drink a load of black coffee."

'Abe leaves the door and moves back to him, with that mischief look on his face, like he's going to say something which will have Charlie laughing, right enough.

'"Wharton's Hollow, wasn't it, Charlie? Where we swam as the skinny little tiddlers we once were, did we not? Then when we got old enough to start taking Flaherty's poison, we'd go down there and swim as naked as the day we were born, and laugh at who's got a new hair or two to show, so that when we got home, all the fathers would smell on us would be the river and not the ale, so they'd not thrash the living hell out of us, and sometimes it even worked. Not to mention being a bloody good laugh, eh, Charlie? You know," – and he's suddenly all serious, like Abe does – "I don't think I've ever been as free, as carefree, all your life to go like a big picture to paint on, as I was swimming through the fresh water of Wharton's Hollow with nothing on but my skin. Grand days, Charlie."

'They shake hands and Abe's gone. For a long time, Charlie just stands there, looking at the door. Then he downs the rest of his ale, wipes his mouth with his sleeve, and he's gone, and, God help us all, Mr Howell, we know what to.'

Charlie's naked body was found miles down the river, there being a small gap at the side of the Hollow where the full tide of river goes sweeping past the edge. The boys all knew that and avoided it; Charlie, befuddled with ale and probably stunned by the freeze of the October water, rather different to the summer water of his boyhood, didn't. His fine clothes were piled neatly on the bank of the Hollow, and Francis could now remember that having that neat little bundle delivered on the back of Armstrong's cart was probably the moment when he came closest to losing his self-control.

No one could prove that Charlie had any intention of taking his own life; on the contrary, the fact that he obviously had it in mind to discuss the possibilities of starting as a farmer directly at Harrington Hall itself clearly indicated he saw a different future ahead, so no clergyman dared talk to the Howells about any lessening of ceremony because of a suicide. Charlie was given a full and proper funeral, and the whole family were amazed at the number of local people who turned out to mourn him – many more, he might have been gratified to know, than had for his father, and including a shattered Abe Slater. Francis was also deeply touched that Charlie's regimental commander in chief, the now retired Colonel Travers, travelled across from the Lake District and paid his respects in his full dress uniform, presenting the family after the funeral with his own personal print of the Crimean picture of Lieutenant Howell, with a new gold-plated frame.

But Francis, with the new relentless self-honesty and merciless logic which he was determined to impose on himself before the political world had the chance of corrupting him with wealth and position, still found himself lining up a few facts. Charlie, drunk or sober, was a superb swimmer and always had been; even the loss of the lower part of a leg would not detract from that to any great extent. Drunk he may have been, though Flaherty's testimony suggested that Charlie was drinking ale throughout; even on neat whisky, it took a great deal of it to cause Charlie to lose control of speech or movement. Even so, the impact of the water temperature would very likely cause a rapid sobering process. And swimming in Wharton's Hollow was such a commonplace in Charlie's life that the notion of forgetting the point at the edge of the Hollow where it touched on the river flow was not as credible to Francis as he would have liked it to be. Yes, perhaps Charlie was stunned; yes, perhaps he lost consciousness. But Francis could not rid himself of at least the suspicion that Charlie, when he found himself drifting dangerously away, could not summon up enough resistance, enough simple will to live, to arrest the process.

Francis made himself breathe deeply, pressing his palms down on the desk top. He had hardly had time to properly mourn his grandfather when another grievous loss, so much less expected or considered even as a remote possibility – Charlie was thirty-one years old – had distracted him from the attempt. It seemed to be symptomatic of the whole year, no time available even for sorrow, the family simply swept along in a remorseless tide of events and powerless to influence or alter the weird inevitability of it all, good or bad. But now was not the time to start seriously mourning Charlie; now there had to be some sense of the family pulling together and, perhaps most importantly of all, extending support and sympathy to Charlie's widow and child. Francis knew how Alice in particular felt about Mary and he had already had to take issue with his sister when Alice had implied, albeit obliquely, that Mary's absence from the house that day and her trip to Newcastle with Will Gelson had contributed to, perhaps even instigated, the day's other events. Francis also knew that Mary had not and would not tell anyone else but him of her summary of Will Gelson's inclinations: 'I tell you of this, Francis, because it is your entitlement, as the relative closest to him in the world, to know the character of what passed between us on that day. But I must ask you, for my sake and Mr Gelson's, not to divulge this knowledge to another living soul. It is and must remain a confidence for your ears alone.' It was indicative of Mary's strength of character that she was prepared to take the odium which would result from Charlie's death and the widespread rumours about her and Gelson, the flames liberally fanned by the many retainers and hangers-on of the Howell and Harrington families, without uttering her ultimately conclusive defensive argument to anyone but Francis. Such a confidence could not honourably be broken, but Francis felt that he had other means at his disposal to defend Mary if necessary. Her most obvious move would be to Newcastle, where much of her work was now to be featured and her previous association with Charlie would not disadvantage her in any way, but the choice was hers and no one else's and Francis knew that his mother would certainly regret her little namesake grandchild being permanently so far away and potentially with a stepfather who would be a stranger to the family.

Francis made his way downstairs and saw as he approached that the entire family had gathered in the foyer area to welcome Mary, though the expressions on the faces of his sisters Charlotte and Alice in particular did not speak of welcome. Francis exchanged glances with his mother; there were times when there did genuinely seem to be some telepathy between them, and when Francis raised his eyebrows, Elizabeth nodded slowly.

Armstrong walked in to face the family from the open main doors.

'They are in sight now, sir.'

'Thank you, Armstrong.'

Francis took a deep breath and began to speak. A growing experience of public speaking on the company board and on the hustings had provided him with a greater volume and authority than many, especially his sisters, would ever have expected from him, and even now, he could see that one or two pairs of eyes were reluctant to turn in his direction. But the year had toughened Francis and already given him a different perspective on what was and wasn't important; the former now concerned the treatment about to be accorded to Mary and her child, and the latter, his sisters' current good opinion of him, for the moment was not.

'I must and I will make clear that Mary's name remains Mary Howell and that there is no indication of any kind that Mary was culpable for recent events in any way. Everything that I know, and let me say I now know a good deal, points to Charlie's death as a tragic accident and this family needs to model its behaviour on that basis.' Francis raised and quickened his voice at the sound of Mary's carriage clattering up to the main entrance. 'I know I speak on behalf of Mother and myself in emphasising that any discourtesy or ill manners in speech or gesture towards Mary during the celebrations will incur our deepest displeasure. I think you would endorse that view, Mother?'

'I certainly would and do, Francis.'

Elizabeth looked at the faces around her, and thought that nothing could more accurately sum up the differences of character of her children and their partners than their reactions to the approach of Mary Howell, nee Fenwick. Anne looked intimidated and a little anxious, her smile on the edge of sadness and her eyes too bright; her husband Thomas looked as he always looked at Howell Grange, wary and defensive, lowering under his dark eyebrows. Alice's head was held high, as usual, and though her expression remained neutral and she had managed to arrange her face into something which resembled a smile, her little body was too stiff, with her arms tightly into her sides, for a convincing attitude of welcome. Charlotte looked cheerfully fierce, a combination which many would find difficult but came almost as second nature to Charlotte; she looked as ready to fight the newcomer as to fall on her neck with affection. Eustace, hand placed as ever just on his wife's shoulder, watched and waited like the perpetual bystander he was, though Elizabeth had begun to appreciate that he did not watch and wait without thought and judgment. And Francis, who somehow seemed to have become taller in the last two years, was very clearly and perceptibly the master of the house, with the kind of attitude of pleasurable anticipation that he now seemed able to produce at will, even in such fundamentally unpromising circumstances as these. Emily, who had been sitting on Elizabeth's right while they discussed certain details of the catering regime for the next two days, had stood up and moved to the right of Francis with an adroitness and ease which showed how used she was becoming to the position.

Elizabeth stood up herself. The Janus year had yet to play itself out, and she felt unable to deny to herself the possibility that another turn of the masks might yet startle or terrify them. 1860 had played with her family like gods to mortals, and what she resented most of all in the loss of her father and her son was the unfairness of not having had even the slightest chance, in either case, of preventing the disaster occurring. The Howells and the Harringtons were not mortals who cared very much for being pawns in the gods' games, and whatever else they would have flung at them, it would be taken on the chin and fought against with every means at their mortal disposal.

Mary moved nervously through the entrance doors, shepherding little Elizabeth in front of her. Francis stepped forward and embraced her, kissing her carefully on both cheeks; Elizabeth saw Alice shuffle from one foot to the other and tighten her mouth into a line.

'Mary, sister, you are welcome to this house and our festivities and we thank you for coming to spend these days with us.' He looked down at the little girl and knelt in front of her, embracing her gently. 'Such a pretty niece I have, and prettier by the minute, I declare. Eustace, my boy, it is marvellous that I have a dashing young nephew to take care of his cousin; perhaps you could take little Lizzie and show her our wonderful Christmas tree and all the presents assembled beneath it. Will you do that, Eustace?'

The little boy's face went a deep shade of beetroot and he glanced up at his mother, whose pointed answering look allowed not the slightest ambiguity. Eustace edged nervously up to his cousin, who laughed happily – Alice shifted feet yet again – and ran off in front of him before she knew where they were supposed to go.

And suddenly, appearing from no one quite knew where, the generous figure of Lady Charlotte Harrington appeared in full and resplendent imperial purple, grasping Mary in both arms and speaking softly into the younger woman's ear as she did so.

'Such a year, my dear, such a terrible year. But my life is not done with yet, and assuredly, dear Mary, neither is yours.'

The rest of Christmas Eve passed without untoward incident, which was as much as Francis had hoped for. Even if his own authority with his sisters, one of whom was older than him, would not have been sufficient, the commanding presence of Lady Charlotte and Elizabeth was enough to negate any potential explosions of temperament or emotion in an age where age had a status of its own. Only two late-night liaisons took place, neither of them involving anything more than conversation and both concerning the decisions of widows.

Shortly after the gentlemen rejoined the ladies in the drawing room, Mary announced her intention to withdraw to her room on the not unreasonable grounds of tiredness and bid her goodnights, which were returned by all, even if Alice's had the timbre of gun metal. As she moved away, she leaned into Francis.

'If you could spare me a few minutes, Francis, before you retire, I would be most grateful.'

Francis had a discreet word with his wife and went up to Mary's quarters about ten minutes later. Mary had been given the compliment of the generously sized Blue Room, to Elizabeth's design, with a sitting room next to the bedroom, used more than once by the Howell company's distinguished guests, otherwise and more accurately described as people George needed for some purpose or other. The easy, regular breathing of his little niece could be heard from the bedroom. Mary looked tense and apprehensive, her face reflected in the light of the fire stoked up against the night chill.

'Francis, I wanted to tell you alone about my decision concerning the future, in the hope that you will be prepared to relay it to the rest of the family rather than me having to make an announcement in the middle of a festive occasion.'

'Of course,' said Francis. 'But do you absolutely need to make a decision so soon?'

'I'm afraid so. I know the time span is short, little over two months since Charlie's death, but even Durham is not far enough, it seems, for Mr Gelson and I to be immune from suspicion and abuse, and however I may feel about tolerating it myself, I have

Elizabeth to think of and it grieves me intensely to think that she may come to some harm as a consequence of totally unwarranted slurs. I caught something of your words on my way in earlier, and it is clear that only you and your mother's authority has prevented your sisters, Alice in particular, from speaking their minds. I cannot defend myself to them as I have to you without further compromising Will; he would have me do so – as your dear brother so considerately said, men of his kind are not without courage and honour – but I refuse to allow Charlie's fate to ruin any other life. It is assuredly not what he would have wished, and I will always believe that what happened on that day was a case of terrible, alcohol-induced misjudgement, even though he had obviously determined on a new course in life. I tried, Francis, I really did try; I cannot tell you how many nights he would wake screaming, sweating, sometimes even weeping, and alcohol could at least distract him. Will's presence and encouragement enabled me to hold something of my spirit and ability together, and gave me some time to escape from Charlie, which I found, I confess, an increasingly urgent need. I will not have Will and his friend's lives ruined for their good intentions.'

Francis stayed silent and waited. He had known the months between Charlie's return and his marriage and there was nothing in her words which he could doubt.

'Will, Henry and I are to rent a house with a studio in London, which we can now afford easily enough, when I will divide my time between my art and bringing up Elizabeth; a nanny will be employed, but only for a limited number of hours each week; I will not neglect my daughter, and she will retain the name of Howell. Will and Henry, who are physically quite similar, will take the identity of brothers and live in separate quarters from me. The house in Durham will be sold and part of the proceeds put in a fund for Elizabeth's maturity. I deeply regret taking your mother's grandchild away from her in this way, but I think she would no more want the child to be harmed than I do, and some of the threats already made anonymously against us have been disturbingly specific. Certain aspects of the coverage of Charlie's death in the press are an utter disgrace and I would take legal action if I felt strong enough to endure courtrooms, but I do not, nor do I want to squander the resources I have for Elizabeth and myself. I should tell you, Francis, that our London accommodation has already been found through Will's contacts, and I intend to leave, with Elizabeth, almost immediately. I determined that, because of the kindness of yourself and your mother, that I would not leave without facing the Howell family again, otherwise I would look as though I have something of which I should be ashamed and I have not.'

Francis rose and crossed to her, taking one of her hands in his.

'No, Mary, I don't believe you do. You will have my full support in this. I shall use the full influence of the Howell connections to mount a gradual defence of you without incriminating Will; I shall emphasise that, war hero as he was, Charlie had paid a severe price for it. In due course, I feel you will be able to pay visits to us and, of course, your own family, without risk to yourself and Elizabeth. As you know, my new position as a Member of Parliament will necessitate my spending a good deal of time in London and I hope you will permit me an occasional visit. My mother cannot now undertake such distances of travel and she will want to know how things are with both you and Elizabeth.'

Francis kissed her lightly on the cheek and she felt a sudden thrill at his touch, a hint of the raw sexuality of his brother as he used to be, before the anger, paranoia and accumulation of memories had unbalanced Charlie's mind. As he resumed his seat, she felt herself looking at him as a man, a long, lithe young man, attractive in his health, power and ability, and immediately counted it as one more strand of the mental scourge she had recently constructed for herself, paying a price for Charlie even as she heard herself deny that there should be a price to pay.

'Of course you shall visit us, Francis, and very welcome to do so,' she said, even as a vague, faint figure in her mind seemed to be shouting a warning from a far hillside.

Beside her windows overlooking the terrace, Elizabeth sat with her mother again, the old lady having asked for a little company before making 'an attempt at sleep, though lately such attempts have not always been successful'. Lady Charlotte had also arrived at a decision for the forthcoming year.

'I shall move out to a house on the estate, Elizabeth, I think,' she said. 'Your brother and his wife, with their grown-up children and associates and friends, make it difficult for me to entertain my own people, the friends past and present cultivated by John and I. Privacy is also not always as I would wish it. And, of course, the place is perpetually full of such bustle and noise. I shall take a few of our own particular people – Robbins, the butler, probably – managing such a huge house is really getting rather beyond him. Mrs Winterton is also the member of the cooking staff most suited to my precarious digestion, and I shall have a couple of gardeners to manage my own grounds as I would wish it. And, of course, after all those years of John's cigars and now Randolph's, I will impose and maintain a regime of good fresh air to breathe in on the spring and summer mornings.'

Elizabeth's mind was wandering as she watched a few country lights glimmering faintly in the distance behind the house. Not for the first time with her mother, she had the vague impression that she was listening to a speech and not wholly registering the details. She was also, once again, excessively tired and hoping she could persuade her mother to bed without resorting to overt rudeness.

'Of course, Mama,' she said. Agreement was invariably the most politic response and she had managed to retain the general gist. 'It must be entirely as you wish it to be.'

The next day, a photographer arrived at the appointed hour, and a family portrait was arranged in the drawing room with some fitful December sunshine appearing through the large window to the photographer's right. Francis knew that a number of tensions in the family were now beginning to simmer ominously, and both the facial expressions and body language of the participants suggested a not entirely comfortable co-existence. No arranging of subjects or inclusion of as many people as possible can disguise the two missing family figures, belonging to three generations of Howell men: the determined, ruthless industrialist, the uncomfortable patriarch and the detached, defiant boy. In the years to come, Elizabeth would need no more than a glance at the photograph to bring back the Janus year, and in the spirit of the turning mask, she would mourn at the departures and rejoice at the arrivals, reflecting on the fine balances between damage and survival.

5

FOOT SOLDIERS
OF SATAN - 1866

The intervening six years for the Howells were characterised by frustrations rather than tragedies, though 1866 itself was to see some major achievements. Lady Charlotte carried out her stated intention of leaving Harrington House for a comfortable smaller house on the estate and taking most of her staff with her. Randolph continued his able and energetic management of the estate, and the well-received assistance from Elizabeth enabled Lady Charlotte and her daughter to spend more time together, which proved to be surprisingly pleasurable for both of them. However, Lady Charlotte's increasing frailty and absent-mindedness, culminating in a bad fall at her house in 1864 at the age of eighty-three, made it clear that the 'matriarch' could not continue for very much longer.

Anne's long wait for a successful marriage was compounded by further cruelties as a result of a miscarriage in 1862 and the death of a little girl in childbirth in early 1865. Materially, she and Thomas were comfortable enough. Thomas continued to be the major breadwinner, making further progress in his administrative work, but Anne found her services in demand at a local stables for handling, breeding and training. They both wanted children and Anne increasingly felt as if she was letting her husband down. Her problems were exacerbated by the apparently effortless success of the Thirwells in adding to their family, with a further son, John, in 1859, and two daughters, Amy in 1861 and Caroline in 1863. With the death of Eustace's father at the end of 1864, Charlotte made clear to Eustace privately that she considered her childbearing days at an end and she and Eustace jointly undertook the considerable demands of overseeing the now extensive Thirwell estate, which had proved enough to break Mr Thirwell's health in his increasingly desperate attempts to remain responsible for everything and improve land yields and profitability for the growing family.

Francis found his first few years as an MP based mainly in London difficult. His fellow Members seemed to believe that his inexperience and youth qualified him for no more than a gradual introduction to the customs and practices of Parliament before mounting any major initiatives or attempting to bring forward legislation in his own name. He also faced a widespread perception that mining safety was an area which was being tackled and improved at an appropriately responsible rate, without what many termed 'faddishness' or reckless innovation. The Act of 1855 had provided seven general rules, relating to ventilation, very relevant to Heddon Hill, and the fencing of disused shafts, to particular and personal Howell relief and approval, if too late. It also introduced proper means for signalling, proper gauges and valves for steam boilers, and indicators and brakes for machine lowering and raising, the last of real significance to Francis after his coal face shift experience. A further provision stipulated that detailed special rules submitted by mine owners to the Secretary of State might, on his approval, have the force of law and be enforceable by penalty.

This last measure Francis could not bring himself to see with anything other than cynicism, however, as the reluctance of many mine owners to even acknowledge the need for tighter regulation made the number of likely submissions to the Secretary of State too low to effect any major improvements. He also knew well enough that the measures passed into law could only bring about permanent and verifiable change if they were supported by rigorous inspection regimes, which they were not, in his opinion. His efforts at persuasion seemed to be perpetually dogged by members' reluctance to directly confront the economic and political muscle of the mine owners and their allies, some of them peers of the realm. Even after a series of disastrous accidents and explosions in 1859-60, when several inquests produced strong evidence of incompetent management and neglect of rules and the government was pressurised into strengthening some of the safety provisions in the Mines Act of 1860, the crucial reformers' demand for enforcing employment only of qualified and certificated managers for coal mines continued to be ignored. Francis felt that hidden hands were working assiduously against the changes so urgently needed, and began to look into the ownership details of various mining organisations. In June 1866, Lord Russell's Whig government fell because of Liberal Party splits over electoral reform, and the ensuing minority Conservative administration under the Earl of Derby seemed to put paid to any further chance of greater safety regulations being enforced for the foreseeable future. Francis resolved to overcome his naivety and get to know his enemy.

The second surviving child of the marriage, Caroline, was born in 1863, after a son called Edward had died in infancy in 1862 not more than three days after being christened, and Dr Spencer advised Emily that complications arising before and during Caroline's birth meant further conception might carry considerable risks for her health. With Caroline's survival to a noisy and vivacious three-year-old, and son George now a hefty boy of six, Francis and Emily determined that future childbirth would be avoided and took confidential medical advice on how this could best be achieved.

The Florence Nightingale training school for nurses had opened on 24 June 1860 with Sarah Wardroper as Superintendent of the school and Matron of the adjoining St Thomas's Hospital. Alice, devastated by the loss of her grandfather and brother in the space of a few months and unwilling to leave her mother in such circumstances, continued to work with Samuel and there were further pit accidents for them to attend, though Francis, before selling the Howell share in the business, had taken firm and decisive measures to ensure that the two of them would never again find themselves coping alone by meticulous arrangements for each pit to have people with medical experience either near or on the premises. In the crucial board meeting, Burridge, closely involved at Heddon Hill, threatened to resign and take significant members of staff with him, clinching the decision for Francis in spite of the budgetary implications and ensuring that such arrangements would continue even after he left.

Alice joined the nursing school with its 1862 intake. It had become clear that ladies with affluent backgrounds could purchase their instruction, although the school did look for some kind of medical knowledge and experience even for them. Alice's considerable experience secured her a place without difficulty, and she was given all the support the considerable Howell resources could offer, though the students lived modestly enough, in their own private rooms surrounding a central 'social room'. Much of their training took place in St Thomas's Hospital. Training courses lasted a year, and in early 1863, one of the doctors who habitually visited the hospital for various purposes, including recruiting possible help for their own practices, was a Dr Nathaniel Heckford, who worked in Wapping and was almost overwhelmed by the number of the poor and ill in his area. Alice admired Dr Heckford's zeal, energy and idealism – in 1866, Nathaniel Heckford was twenty-seven years old – and she believed that the challenge of caring for the poor in the East End would be no greater than dealing with the aftermath of accidents and negligence in the coal mines. She joined Dr Heckford and his wife Sarah in Wapping and was allocated a comfortable room in their house.

In July 1866, when Alice had been working with the Heckfords for three years and was contemplating on how she could match the achievement of Elizabeth Garrett Anderson in becoming the only woman as yet accredited as a doctor, cholera broke out in London, beginning in the areas close to the docks…

SATURDAY 15 SEPTEMBER 1866, 3.28PM

A faded family photo, dingy with bedraggled edges, shows Francis and Alice sitting on either side of a neat, white wrought iron picnic table which has been spread with a laced tablecloth. The chair between them is vacant, but its occupant has obviously just shared a meal with them, because the remains of three lunches, including empty wine and water jars and plates still spread with bread and cake crumbs, are waiting on the table to be taken away. Whoever took the photograph, probably Mr Reece Wharton, a local press man who had become a friend and associate of Francis after their meeting in 1852, seems to have just said or done something funny, because both of his subjects are grinning widely and their friendship with the photographer is very obvious. Francis is leaning forward in his chair with a smile which has a hint of anticipation that Mr Wharton might yet do or say something else equally diverting; Alice, with one long thin hand on each of the arms of her chair, is leaning back and her expression speaks of mock outrage, her eyes wide and smiling. Francis is now thirty-five; his figure is a little fuller than it was, with flesh broadening his thin face and his hairline beginning to recede, the greater expanse of forehead giving him a rather more academic and professorial air. Nothing which could conceivably be described as approaching middle-aged fat is evident, but he is markedly less emaciated and oppressed than in previous portraits, most notably the press pictures of 1852. A few faint age lines have appeared under his eyes, very slight and ghostly in this picture even at close quarters, but the eyes' life and animation is still very clear, partly as a consequence of Reece Wharton's relaxed, less posed methods, arising from professional expertise.

Alice is still only twenty-seven, but most observers would place her as the older of the two subjects. Her heavy dark dress seems to emphasise the slightness of the body within and the gaunt hollowness of the face; her hair, much longer than it was and seemingly darker, is tied behind her neck and makes the fact that she is recovering from recent illness all the more apparent. However, there is a world-weariness, a sophistication, in her expression and bearing which certainly wasn't evident in 1860.

This photograph, or rather the best reproduction of it achievable, has been a favourite of the family's since Reece Wharton first presented it to them in the late autumn of 1866. It hung for a time in what was then called the drawing room, until the room was enlarged, redecorated and renamed the Blue Lounge, when an even better pride of place was accorded to it on a wall facing the large bay window, where what light there was would always fall on it. The two people are as happy in each other's company as a man and woman who are not lovers can possibly be – perhaps even more so, with the tensions and additional emotions of physical love absent. The joy of an unexpectedly pleasant autumn day and a guest who is congenial to them both emerge very clearly from the picture, and the overall effect is one of great optimism, *joie de vivre* and apparent triumph over what have obviously been recent difficulties, especially depicted in the physical condition of Alice, but also present in a complacency and confidence about Francis which suggests an important victory recently achieved.

SATURDAY 15 SEPTEMBER 1866, 8.10AM

Francis reclined in the generous, warm bath water, his head resting against the back of the bath and his eyes occasionally closing against the stream of sunlight coming in from a large window, high enough for modesty even when the bather stood upright, but well made and positioned enough to flood the whole room with light when there was light to be had. September mornings like this were rare in the North, and even rarer were days when he was in a position to be at his leisure, should he so choose, for the entire day. Morning baths were also relatively infrequent indulgences, usually because of pressures of time, and when they were possible, he preferred his London valet Railton to attend to their preparation. Francis found himself growing more particular with maturity, and Railton knew precisely what temperature, amount of water and addition of bath salts was required. He had been bringing Railton with him to the Grange for a couple of years now, ostensibly and quite justifiably to relieve the burdens on Armstrong, who had started to show a greater age and frailty. Armstrong's initial suspicion and slight resentment had faded quickly enough; Armstrong was a practical man and knew an extra hand would be useful. Railton worked only as a valet to Francis, and had enough discretion to defer to the butler of the house without needing any fatuous strictures from Francis. Railton was moving about in the adjoining bedroom, no doubt putting out exactly the weekend clothes required, and Francis felt pampered and indulgent enough to keep to the water for a little while yet. The grime, sweat and dust of the long journey from London had not been entirely dissipated by a night's sleep, and recent events had left him feeling entitled to live life at a rather more relaxed pace, at least for a while.

His anxieties about how Alice would be when he returned were allayed quite quickly. He had only beaten the evening dinner gong by half an hour, and saw not only a recovering colour to her cheeks but a growing appetite in her, as she made what he could at last accept as a decent meal of it. But her physical state was not his greatest anxiety. He had long since accepted her as a brave, capable and accomplished woman, but for a while, the light and life seemed to go out of her. Emily, as obviously sympathetic as she was, would occasionally give him slightly pained sidelong glances when it seemed that his concern for his sister outdid his interest in his wife and children. Francis could make no apology.

He had always known and accepted Alice as his closest sister, but it was only when she became seriously threatened that the prospect of losing her grew a cold anxiety in him and an awareness, for the first time, that personal loss might have a finite point, an extremity which would take him beyond the ability to assimilate and continue yet again. The consequences of arriving at such a crisis were unthinkable, if not, unfortunately, unimaginable. The sinister quality of Alice's predicament was also intensified by the fact that, while the menace did eventually prove to have emerged from natural sources, his first and wholly justified suspicions were that its origin was entirely man-made. The very idea that Alice's death might be merely an adjunct to his own feud with a mortal enemy made even the prospect of such a reality inconceivable and put his four family bereavements – father, brother, grandfather and, equally as devastating in its way, young child – into a place where there were still at least movements and shadows, rather than an utter blackness of total defeat, a lost and lonely hell on some barren rock in a distant universe.

A sudden, intense shaft of new morning sunlight recalled him to the day and his place in it like a friend's tap on the shoulder. He sunk a little lower in the water and let it caress his chin and neck. Alice was not only still very much alive; her spirit and resilience were returning quickly now.

Then, right in front of his closed eyes, like a vision invading a dream, he saw again at close quarters the dark, hypnotic eyes and supercilious, half-twisted mouth of William Michaelson, 6th Earl of Melbury, philanthropist, friend of government, industrialist, traitor, thief, lecher and adulterer, a man of such monumental arrogance and confidence that he would see young people maimed and killed for his basest personal appetites.

It was, Francis reflected with some amazement as he opened his eyes against such an immediacy of memory, still only just over a year since his first encounter with Melbury. It had all the feel of being summoned by his father yet again, except that Melbury's surroundings were infinitely grander than his father's dark wood, restrained sobriety, with commissioned portraits of Melbury's antecedents on the walls, expensive, velvet-upholstered furniture crowding the room and gold candlesticks lining the ornate mantelpiece, there for decoration only. Melbury had placed his mountainous Regency desk, an antique of now incalculable value, in the generous space of a large bay window at the far end of the room, so that light would flood into the eyes of whoever he happened to be interviewing and Melbury could examine his interviewee at leisure while he himself remained largely in shadow, a broad-shouldered, immobile silhouette against the magnificence of his spreading acres.

'My people tell me, Mr Howell,' Melbury began, and his voice was a languid growl, the inquisitor addressing the racked man, 'that you have been making inquiries about my business. Attempting to establish, it seems, what I own of your wretched northern mines, and the extent of my professional interest in the whole tortuous processes of extracting British coal from the ground.'

Francis had already determined that he would not be intimidated, and he took pains to keep his voice steady and his eyes fixed firmly on the dark shape against the window.

'Yes, my lord. My parliamentary colleagues and I feel that it is entirely reasonable that all who have a stake in possible reforms should be invited to contribute to the debate, and the patterns of colliery ownership can tend to be rather opaque. I would hate anyone to feel that changes had been introduced without their voices having been heard, and anyone who acts as an agent for a higher power has no choice but to refer decisions to the ultimate authority. It seemed to me more sensible to go directly to the ultimate authority, thereby saving time and simplifying procedures.'

The shape seemed to consider for a moment. Melbury moved back in his chair, and Francis had an impression of being peered down on, a celestial being surveying the ants below from Olympian heights.

'I don't know what the hell you mean by your parliamentary colleagues, Howell,' Melbury said, and the tone now was more schoolmasterly, a tedious but necessary prelude to punishment. 'For the kind of profit-wrecking extremes of reform you're talking about, I very much doubt whether you could raise enough votes to be counted on the fingers of your hands.'

'You are quite familiar with what is being proposed, then, I gather, my lord?'

The shape clanked petulantly to its feet; Melbury turned to gaze over his domain, and Francis kept his eyes firmly on the back, held militarily stiff as if surveying a parade.

'I know as much as I need to know, I think. Obstructionists, complainants, prevaricators, like yourself, Howell, do cross my path from time to time, people who think the making of money is somehow criminal in itself, people whose own modest talents and accomplishments create in them a certain envy which causes them to delight in sabotage and interference with those of loftier aims and abilities. Let me deal with some of what you are happy to describe as your reforms.'

Melbury then began to detail his objections to a number of the measures which Francis and his little band of allies wanted to introduce to improve safety and efficiency, though he dismissed the former as largely irrelevant ('Perhaps we should transfer this approach to our armed services, and order the men not to initiate any attack unless the enemy is entirely disarmed or immobilised.') and the latter as bogus ('The logic of arguing that, in order to save a great deal of money, we should spend a great deal of money, is so obviously flawed that I wonder how any intelligent man can countenance it'). Melbury had a thorough grasp of many of the technicalities and procedures, and in another man, Francis would probably have begun to warm to him as a fellow specialist, an aficionado in various highly complex areas. But Melbury, though far from an old man, had a detached hauteur, a place in his imagination far removed from what he obviously saw as the pygmies and inadequates around him or opposing him, and Francis felt his resentment rise as he continued to be addressed in the manner of a headmaster towards a truculent, precocious youth who needed a thorough grounding in reality. Melbury moved around his desk as if a public lecture was underway, and his eyes, sometimes widening in surprise and outrage, sometimes actually flashing with anger, dark, translucent circles against the light from the great window, would do no more than dart at Francis occasionally for a few seconds before turning away, their distance emphasising the disciplinary oration.

Francis took little notice of the arguments being raised. He had heard all of them many times before; some had a grain of truth in them, such as the possibility of greater ventilation creating some problems as well as solving them, but in the main they were self-serving, blinkered and dismissive of the idea that the safety of the workers should be a serious issue in the first place. Francis thought of his unlikely mentor, the cynical, saturnine Silas Fletcher, also a northern MP for a sizeable chunk of Cumberland, who had approached the very new and lost Francis Howell MP in the first division when his vote needed to be cast.

'Your late brother's commanding officer, Stephen Travers, or Sir Stephen as I should now call him, is a good and long-standing friend of mine; we were at university together. He greatly esteemed your poor departed brother and does not disguise his admiration for the rest of the Howell family. He particularly asked me to be as helpful to you as is within my power, and I know from my own experience what an infernally difficult and perplexing place the House can be to a new man'.

Francis had not been too sure about it; Fletcher, pale skinned and rather dandified with his elaborate frock coats and carefully groomed moustache, seemed an unlikely man to be concerned with the troubles of pitmen and their families, which he must have known from Travers was the main point of entering parliament for Francis. But, in the more intimate atmosphere of a private room in one of the better London taverns surrounding Westminster, Fletcher had described some of the Cumberland, Lancashire and Westmorland disasters with a combination of meticulous detail and suppressed emotion and indignation.

'The problem remains Melbury,' Fletcher had said. 'Melbury is an oddly specific and concentrated tyrant. He keeps well away from anything in the south, where he mainly resides and where various dark rumours circulate about his private life, in spite of his best efforts at suppression, which are considerable, let me tell you. Melbury's tactics are to control at a distance, carefully placing a whole network of agents and underlings between himself and any possible scandals relating to mining disasters. If you look closely enough into it, Francis, you will find Melbury behind a staggering number of the mine owners and coal traders; he practically owns half of the north and midlands. He also controls a number of northern members and contributes generously and tactically to his party's coffers – hence his peerage, of course. No significant reforms of mining, especially in the north and midlands, are likely to ever come about without the opposition of Melbury being overcome or neutralised, and he is very rich, utterly ruthless and much cleverer than he might seem.'

And Francis, reflecting in his bath and shuddering slightly as the water cooled around him, could not deny to himself the fear and foreboding he had felt even while answering Melbury bravely and thoroughly. Fuelled by anger and frustration, Francis had listened to Melbury's monologue for over ten minutes before his patience snapped. He found himself suddenly on his feet without remembering at what point he had stood up; his left hand was pressing down so closely on the desk that it was whitening, the fingers pushed hard into the wood.

'Lord Melbury!' he snapped, rather louder than he'd intended. Melbury was by the window, and turned as if struck, his figure rigid, his head held high as if looking down at a madman.

'I am an elected member of the House', Francis began, with an entirely intentional emphasis on the 'elected', 'and my family have been associated with the mining industry for generations. I do not need to be instructed by you or anyone else about the processes and technicalities of mining'.

And Francis took his turn at oration, taking each of Melbury's arguments and demolishing them with a mixture of reasoning and comparison – 'making war is inevitably associated with weaponry and therefore death and mutilation; all soldiers know that. Mining is not and should not be, and all pitmen know that' – which surprised him with its controlled, analytical passion. After what must have been about six or seven minutes, during which Melbury had hardly moved at all, his eyes still flicking on and away from Francis as if uncomfortable in the presence of a raving lunatic, his lordship gave loud and savage vent to his feelings, barking as if at an errant servant.

'Recall yourself, sir! Do you presume to stand and rant at me in my own house, damn you!'

Francis saw the outraged face and the defensive, unmoving bearing and momentarily cursed himself for a fool. He had come here to try and turn Melbury to his cause by personal contact and persuasion, not to make an implacable enemy of him. He sat down and framed his words slowly, taking care that they could not be interpreted as a kind of capitulation.

'I do not mean to cause offence, my lord. I have seen, on more occasions than I care to remember, the brutal consequences of the often wilful and careless disregard for even the most simple and uncontroversial precautions and procedures, maimed and bloodied men and boys, sometimes little more than children. Suddenly-created widows with no feasible means to support them and their children; men deprived in a moment of any reasonable chance of continuing to earn their livelihood. I have seen my own valiant sister working alongside medical colleagues in indescribably bad conditions to save what lives and limbs she could. I fear my passion can sometimes cause me to pay insufficient attention to my manners. I speak only in defence of my cause, sir, not to create personal antagonism.'

Melbury moved slowly back to the chair and Francis found himself facing the dark shape again. Melbury's tone was much softer and more modulated; at first Francis had taken it to be conciliatory.

'Yes, Mr Howell, I have heard something of this sister of yours, who satisfactorily completes her Nightingale training course and immediately disappears into the human cesspit of the East End. Wapping and the docks, I gather. You are obviously a family full of reforming zeal.'

Now Francis caught the tone of mockery and he raised his head and sat to his height.

'The trouble is, Mr Howell, that we are all so vulnerable, are we not? Especially when our cause brings us up against determined opposition. Your dear sister, for example. Who knows what dangers might befall her, working in such a place? Accidents and mishaps, infections and disasters, are not, unhappily, confined to coal mines. You would do well, I feel, to look to your sister's safety in such a situation, Mr Howell, as much as your ex-employees, I feel.'

The dark shape moved forward, the head now emerging from the shadow. Melbury's eyes were glittering with an odd, disturbing kind of satisfaction, a relish in such talk of blood and injury.

'You would do very well, Mr Howell. Even your own Grange, there in your northern heartlands with an ageing butler and a few grooms and underlings. Even here, my London home, stoutly appointed and defended. Who knows what can befall us,

Mr Howell, at any time? Who knows what intruding presences might be on hand to persecute us, even if the places we consider ourselves and our loved ones to be most safe and secure? Your beloved mineworkers are not the only people to face daily dangers, Howell, are they?'

Melbury leaned back into the shadow and turned his chair slightly, to gaze again over the spreading land behind him.

'It is always wise, Mr Howell, for those with reforming zeal for the vulnerable to take care that they do not, as a consequence, increase their own vulnerabilities. And those of the people they love.'

The electric charge which seemed to pass through Francis, bringing him immediately to his feet then, returned in much the same way as if the memory was an instant jolt in itself, and he stood up in the bath and stepped out, grabbing a towel in the hope that a vigorous drying down would allow him to subdue the great choke of anger which also returned to him. He had once believed, as did most of his boyhood friends, in the essential gentility of peers, people of innate taste and sophistication whose birthright was to rule by example, using their instinctive, inherited knowledge of the way things should be done. He still could scarcely believe that he himself was moving amongst these people, caught up in the day-to-day business of actually running the country. It seemed that the consequence of such naivety was to listen to a peer of the realm debase the most basic rules of hospitality by threatening a guest in his home in the most gross and shameful way.

At the time, Francis still managed some control, some way of detaching himself from the encounter with his dignity and temper intact. He had risen slowly to his feet once again.

'I see our conversation, such as it is, is at an end, sir. We are *all*, as you so rightly say, vulnerable, whatever we may see as the privileges of our birth. Good day to you, sir.'

Francis stepped out of the bathroom and into the bright, spacious adjoining bedroom, where Railton had, as always, left the required clean clothing neatly laid out. George Howell's grim study and adjoining little apartment had been adapted to an extra guest room, Francis having tired of its darkness and unhappy memories quite quickly, and one of the nicer guest rooms which his father had usually reserved for impressing his wealthy visitors, with a mostly light green decor, less heavy and forbidding furniture and a comfortable bathroom, had been commandeered for his own use.

Emily was similarly provided with her own room, though hers was lighter and more graciously appointed, full of flowers and pastel colours. The masculine nature of Francis's quarters could be seen in the sparse ornaments and the plain colours. He allowed himself a full-length mirror, though on the inside door of the wardrobe so as not to invite unintended revelations. Francis was not a vain man, but he had come to the realisation that his physical fitness and sometimes personal appearance could be important in providing properly for his family and achieving his professional aims. His love life with Emily was also far from concluded, even though the childbearing decision had been firmly taken. Even after they had taken to separate rooms, Francis would still ask if he could visit her on certain nights and it was rare for her to decline. Very privately, and with a degree of frankness which neither of them would once have believed themselves capable, they had arrived at ways of giving each other pleasure which would be safe from any prospect of childbirth. Emily's father's assertions about any sexual contact being entirely about procreation Francis couldn't and wouldn't ever accept, and the very fact that it was her father's creed was enough to ensure that Emily would not ascribe to such a belief. To the restrained but very heartfelt delight of Francis, Emily would even, every now and then, invite herself to his quarters, and he knew from the code they had developed between them what that would mean, allowing him to pass such days in warm if slightly shamefaced anticipation. To turn into another of the malodorous, overweight, prematurely middle-aged specimens now too numerously represented amongst his contemporaries was a particular horror for Francis, and an occasional, brief detached examination of his naked body was permissible for that and the other reasons. He allowed himself one now, for no more than ten seconds. The chest still had the same slightly concave, pigeonish quality as ever, but there remained no extraneous flesh on the stomach and buttocks, which is where it seemed to begin to appear and already had with a few of his contemporaries. Francis grinned briefly at himself. He never had been and never would be anyone's dashing young beau, but his body was still a young man's and he intended to keep it that way for as long as possible.

Emily, for the moment, was away taking care of her much reduced and ailing father, whose health had been deteriorating steadily for some time and who no longer had either energy or inclination for loud lectures and bombast. She had relented to the extent of visiting him for several days at a time, since the Reverend Slater's own remaining days seemed to lessen with each passing one. Now she had, quite fairly, rated taking care of her father at least on a parallel with Francis's care of his sister; an interlude of largely separate existence had been accepted between them, though it sometimes made Francis morose, as it did now.

He dressed in his usual systematic way, gazing out over the approaching fields, where the memory of seeing Charlie's horse in the distance could still remorselessly return to him. He wrenched his mind away to the immediate aftermath of his confrontation with Melbury.

Back with Silas Fletcher in their favourite London snug two days later, Francis described what had happened, his still smouldering anger almost reducing him to inarticulacy at times. He also became gradually aware that Fletcher was listening to him with an air of sad resignation which was beginning to be annoying in itself.

'My poor, dear Francis,' Fletcher said, with a sidelong, slightly disbelieving look. 'When I said to you that Melbury was the main threat, I didn't mean that you should immediately proceed to ask people direct questions and make your interest in his lordship's affairs so manifest. This is London, Francis. It's like a big, decayed village, where everyone is looking to protect themselves at all costs and pre-emptively attack whoever looks likely to attack them. Those who appear to be a little too inquisitive will find their actions being rapidly reported to whoever it is they are being inquisitive about. Melbury has people firmly in his pay in the House itself.'

'Well, the truth is, Silas, I don't really know how to go about it in any but a direct manner.'

'God bless your pure soul for that.' Fletcher took a long drink from his tankard and spoke slowly, meditatively, as if looking back on a being he could still hardly reconcile as himself.

'I used to think well of the aristocracy when I first arrived in this place. I blush to think of it, simple little puppy dog as I was, rushing round to do the bidding of Lord This and the Earl of That, even though what I was being asked to do often went against my own instincts. I've never managed to absolve myself for the responsibility of lugging Stephen Travers into that dreadful Crimean business, though none of us could have foreseen the monstrous miscalculation and ineptitude which characterised that campaign. Government was looking for at least a fair contingent of honest officers who could be relied upon to regard military service as a public duty, rather than an invitation to line their own pockets on various black markets. Poor Stephen was almost killed and still suffers from various ailments, including nightmares of remembered horrors, and, of course, your own family have paid an even heavier price.'

They exchanged glances and Francis had to look away momentarily.

'However,' Fletcher hurried on, 'that is all the more reason to protect the remaining Howells and their interests, including your laudable aims of trying to inculcate common sense and humanity into the present carnage of the coal mining industry. I would like you to meet a friend of mine, a man who most definitely does not have any aristocratic lineage.'

'Rather the opposite, I take your implication to be,' said Francis.

'Quite so. His name – very strictly *entre nous*, Howell – is Renfrew; I have never heard anyone use any Christian name before it. Those who know him in London usually refer to him as R. I suppose he's of what most of us in the House would describe as low birth; his father was a kind of itinerant carpenter, self-taught, working wherever he could find work and moving on, chiefly to avoid gambling debts built up in his foolish youth. R was originally what used to be known in London as a thief taker, working for bounty, collecting money for arresting wanted criminals or causing those who needed to know to find out where they were. Not a very honourable and certainly a very dangerous profession, but he started it as a contribution to his father's attempts to stay out of Newgate and he became wily enough to begin turning the tables on the debt collectors and bailiffs. Eventually, other gentlemen in trouble started eliciting his help.

'During this time, he moved extensively through the underworld, as you might imagine, though, unlike many wastrels and ruffians in those circles, R had a remarkable kind of native intelligence and a genius for obtaining and retaining information. He discovered in time that information was a profession in itself, and he has a vast spreading network of agents and allies across London and beyond. He is something of a legend on both sides of the law; he has helped the authorities apprehend particularly vicious criminals, but it is also well known, though he himself would never admit it and neither would any of his many associates, that he has protected the weak from the strong in criminal and even occasionally political circles, usually by helping people away to places of safety and effectively putting up an obscuring smoke screen behind them. R is very clever, ruthless when he has to be and totally discreet.'

He stopped and looked around him, as if to demonstrate his last two words. The snug was one of the private rooms which gentlemen could hire for meals involving confidential discussions; in the areas surrounding Parliament, such meetings were frequent.

'One of the reasons I choose this place so often, Francis, is that its geography is such as to ensure the physical impossibility of anyone hearing us; immediately behind my head is the thickest wall in the place, some two solid feet between the tavern and the stables, the original owner having insufficient land to build his stables at a distance and wishing to ensure beyond all possible doubt that no bolting horse would come charging into his place of business and ruining his trade. I am now so acclimatised to the feverish conspiratorial atmosphere of this city that I find myself always taking the most stringent precautions.'

Francis nodded sympathetically. An uncomfortable feeling of being out of his depth had preoccupied him ever since arriving in London, and he was realising slowly how unsubtle his moves against the rest of the company board had been in his younger days and how easy they must have found it to plot against him. Even now, he didn't immediately grasp how he would be able to use 'R' in his cause; because he trusted Fletcher, however, he decided to be honest enough to say so, and was surprised to have his question taken so seriously.

'That we don't really know at this stage, which is the leap of faith you have to make with this kind of thing and dealing with the ubiquitous R. What we will get, however, without a shadow of a doubt is some information regarding Melbury. It may be that he is whiter than white, a politician and industrialist purer than the driven snow, but I know, Francis, and I believe you are beginning to realise, that such innocence is unlikely. As my lord is happy to point out, everyone is vulnerable, and using the services of R may enable us to discover something about Melbury that R himself would probably term 'leverage'.'

Francis looked dubious, and felt a growing uncertainty about where this might be heading.

'So are you suggesting that we meet this man here?'

'Good Lord, no!' Silas Fletcher took another long draught of ale to deal with his shock.

'No one can hear us, yes, but people can see who is coming in and going out of this place and I don't doubt Melbury has people who have people who keep an eye on all the politico London taverns. No, I will arrange with intermediaries to meet up with R at his brother's farm; he provided it for his brother partly out of fraternal affection and partly because of the advantage of having somewhere well out of London and owned by someone he could trust totally for meetings with his "special clients", which I flatter myself would probably include us.'

So, Francis thought, as he finished his dressing and gazed over his own share of the countryside, another of his preconceived ideas was demolished, the notion that plotting was for smoke-filled dingy rooms down city side alleys. Railton came in as he was finishing and the morning pleasantries were exchanged; Francis, who had known servants since birth, still didn't live with the idea particularly comfortably and always made sure that he remembered his manners scrupulously.

'How is Miss Howell, Railton? Have you heard from Susan? It is Susan who's attending her, isn't it?'

'Yes, sir. Susan tells me Miss Howell is still sleeping – deeply and comfortably, sir, it seems.'

'Good. Excellent news. Ask Susan to let you, and subsequently me, know when she wakes up, please, Railton.'

'Yes, sir.'

Railton was hovering near the door, his reliable signal of a further matter.

'Something else, Railton?'

'Yes, sir. An early morning rider from Mr Reece Wharton's house, requesting that he may be allowed to pay a social visit in the capacity of a personal friend this afternoon?'

'Oh, Reece.' Francis smiled to himself, a habitual reaction to thoughts of a man who had been his well-spirited ally all the way from his first fumbling dealings with the local press.

'Yes, of course he may. And I wonder, Railton, that if the day stays as well as it has started, whether we may not have a picnic tea in the garden behind the main Grange? Could we make arrangements for the food and what have you? If the weather turns or Miss Howell is not yet well enough, we can always move the whole thing into the conservatory. Could you ask Mr Armstrong, please?'

'Yes, of course, sir. I will report back to you if there is any difficulty, sir.'

Francis breakfasted lightly and then went to the library, which he now used as his most frequent workplace when he was at home, with views to inspire and sometimes console. Such generous spaces and bucolic peace was the unlikely backdrop to his meeting with the legendary R, though a man looking less like a legend on first meeting would have been difficult to imagine. R was a smallish middle-aged man with a squat muscular build which gave a first impression of fat until closer quarters revealed little spread round the middle and an awareness that most of the bulging arms and wrestler's legs was sheer muscle. His calm, contemplative eyes seemed remote, and in truth, he would not always look directly at whoever he was talking to or whoever was talking to him; he seemed permanently to be weighing up what he was hearing and carefully phrasing what he was saying. His features were entirely unremarkable, with a man on the street anonymity which Francis suspected he used as a professional asset, enabling him to see and hear everything as a detached, unthreatening face in the crowd. He moved with surprising and initially bewildering grace and athleticism, which suggested a sporting background to Francis, easy, unhurried physical abilities well preserved even though he had to be at least in his early forties.

On a terrace at the back of the Renfrew farm, with country smells wafting over them and as quickly disappearing in the June breeze, the three men shared a jug of ale. Fletcher looked out of place and slightly ridiculous in his town clothes; Francis had seen R's quick little eyes dart over both of them when they arrived, with a twitch of a grin for Fletcher and an almost imperceptible nod at the looser, lighter garb of Francis. Fletcher, of course, had to initiate their discussion.

'Our curiosity about his lordship is not an idle one, R. We believe he will use his extensive business interests in the North to block all legislation which he sees as ill-advised and contrary to his various companies' interests. We think that Melbury is actually the controller and guiding hand in most of the mining industry based in the North and Midlands, however many different nominal companies there are – ownership of individual collieries or groups of collieries can be traced to companies which have been taken over by some larger group, which in its turn will frequently be found to be related to Melbury's parent company. As Mr Howell has discovered to his cost, having been effectively summoned to Melbury's presence to have both himself and his family threatened, official inquiries into what Melbury owns and how he controls it are likely to be traced back to him. We are hoping you may have associates who can do the necessary investigations in as clandestine a way as it takes to prevent Melbury from hearing of it.'

R nodded and seemed to begin speaking only when he was quite sure Fletcher had finished. Francis expected him to have a strong accent, perhaps one of the more impenetrable Cockney brogues, but R spoke so neutrally that most would find it impossible to identify any part of the country over any other in his speech. The voice was gentle, unassertive and certainly lacking stridency or any particular emphases, but its care and deliberation seemed to ensure that the listener heard and registered every single word.

'I shan't need to do much investigating to be able to tell you a good deal about Lord Melbury already, gentlemen, for reasons which I'll come to later. I've worked for you in the past, of course, Mr Fletcher, and I know I can rely on your discretion and probity. I hope sincerely that the gentleman with you, Mr Howell here, won't take it at all amiss if I ask him to enlighten me as to what kind of legislation's interests are so urgent and demanding that he is prepared to take on such an obstacle as his lordship to achieve them.'

Both pairs of eyes turned towards him, and Francis, even as he reflected in the totally secure heartland of his own library, could remember the pang of doubt which assailed him under their cool scrutiny, these metropolitan men who moved easily through the most savage, convoluted and dangerous city worlds. Were they already humouring him as a country bumpkin? Were they leading him by the nose into labyrinthine places from which he would never be able to extricate himself? How much, when it came to it, did he know of either of them, and how could he be so certain of their bona fides, practised as they must be at playing all sides against each other and remaining themselves invisible?

Unsurprisingly, he began the business of explaining himself hesitantly. R did not appear to change the close and attentive politeness with which he was listening to him one iota, or if he did he gave neither facial or physical sign of it, but Silas Fletcher's expression seemed to stray off into the expanses of the surrounding fields as if in the garrulous company of a tedious relative. But Francis had a passion about his subject which could not fail to impress in time, and when he related the personal tragedy which had befallen his father, he knew they were attending fully. As he told of the Heddon Hill disaster and related the sights, sounds and smells of the subterranean rooms where his sister and Dr Spencer struggled for hours with burns, broken bodies and the most ignominious of deaths, all because of a profound ignorance and wilful disregard of the nature and content of poisonous gases and the most elementary of ventilation procedures needed to deal with them, R seemed almost to have stopped breathing, his face immobile, his eyebrows lowered in concentration and his eyes fixed unswervingly on Francis Howell's lightly flushed, intent features.

Francis made a passing reference, as an aside or a footnote, to his own shift when he was little more than a boy, and this R picked up on immediately, looking genuinely surprised for the first time.

'Forgive me, Mr Howell, but are you saying that you yourself have done one of these infernal shifts you speak of, those that are expected of the men?'

Francis felt his habitual annoyance that a single shift could be so esteemed against those who did it every day, every week, every month of their working lives, but he saw that he now had their full interest and sympathy and was able to describe the experience of working a shift with such graphic detail concerning sweat, blood, grime, nakedness and fatigue that, by the time he stopped, both of the metropolitan men were almost pallid in amazement, Fletcher never having heard this particular part of Francis's experience before.

R was the first to speak. The easy tone of his voice had not changed, but his demeanour towards Francis had; he was now leaning into him as if to an old colleague or partner.

'Well, I used to wonder why it was that London was so full of rum Northerners ready to take their chances with the cut-throats and the purse snatchers rather than rely on a steady wage. Now I know. And there's precious few employers in my experience who'll go anywhere near what their poor workforce are expected to do, especially in the factories and mills and what have you. I honour you, for it, Mr Howell, I really do. I believe I would be happy to provide you gentlemen with what assistance is within my powers, and the fees will not be at all unreasonable, I do assure you.'

For a moment, the three men enjoyed the harmony which had been established between them, shaking hands and exchanging smiles, and then into the brief uncertain silence about what happened next stepped R, with a quiet authority and assurance which the other two found themselves accepting readily enough.

'There are several very essential matters here which it behoves me to make clear to you, gentlemen. Lord Melbury is very rich, very dangerous and very powerful, and if we are to stand any feasible chance of opposing him, we must approach our business with the most scrupulous and stringently observed caution. I will not spend too long a time explaining what has happened to previous enquirers into his lordship's affairs, beyond saying that the most recent one was probably dredged up by those men who have the desperate task of removing such objects from the Thames, though by the time Melbury's men had finished with him, he would have been entirely unidentifiable. A journalist who had got wind, so the rumour goes, of some of Lord Melbury's curious recreations, of which more later. Your status as a Member, Mr Howell, and if you'll forgive me saying so, sir, your somewhat ham-fisted way of going about your inquiries, has saved you and yours so far, but I would most earnestly advise you, sir, to prevail upon your sister to remove herself, not only from the dangerous area in which she now lives and works, but from London altogether.'

Francis looked taken aback, and spent several seconds scratching through his memory to recall the time when he'd told R about his sister, with no immediate success. R saw his expression and immediately provided the explanation.

'Your sister, sir, if I may say, is almost as well thought of down there by the docks as Nathaniel and Sarah Heckford themselves. I have many connections in that area, because many clients in high places find themselves in need of information about what and who is going into and coming out of those docks, and part of my endeavour, in line with several local gentlemen, has also been to protect the Heckfords from anything the less salubrious outfits in the East End might have in mind for them. Your sister is now very much within that protectorate, Mr Howell, which comes as no surprise to me now, because the efforts you have so articulately described in the coal mines would inevitably mean that even the poorer East End hovels would have few terrors for her. But I must ask, sir, for a reason which will become immediately apparent, when was the last time you met and spoke to your sister?'

'A little over two weeks ago now,' Francis said, and an edge of anxiety had already crept into his voice. 'Alice has forbidden me, with all the emphasis at her disposal, which is considerable, from going to see her in the East End, and when we do meet, it is usually somewhere in the city. But you have information, sir? Is something amiss with Alice?'

R sighed and his voice softened.

'There are rumours, sir, and no more than that as yet until the full facts can be verified, that your sister is ill. It's said that she hasn't been seen on the rounds she usually does so assiduously for about nine or ten days. When I knew I was going to be meeting up with you gentlemen, I made inquiries, though Dr Heckford is repeatedly saying to callers that Miss Howell is exhausted for the moment and is resting before taking a much needed rural relaxation period. Short of pushing past Dr and Mrs Heckford and examining the entire house, sir, which none of my connections or agents would be prepared to do, rough types as some of them are, we cannot exactly establish the truth of the case.'

Francis had found himself slowly freezing with horror and he was now on his feet; even Silas was shaken out of his usual *sangfroid*.

'But there's cholera in the East End! Reports are emerging that cholera has again found its way in through the docks!'

R was also on his feet now, but the easy tone of his voice had not changed; it seemed to remain as a reassurance in itself.

'Please, Mr Howell, calm yourself. There is very little possibility of your sister having cholera. An experienced London doctor such as Heckford would most certainly not have allowed a patient with cholera to remain in his house; she would have been taken to a hospital without any doubt at all, sir, and Miss Alice Howell being admitted to a hospital in that part of London would be known to many. In any case, cholera is not the rampant killer that it was, especially after Dr Snow's discoveries in Soho. I believe you know something of that, Mr Fletcher?'

Silas Fletcher had made little contribution so far, and even as he seized the opportunity to do so, he was reflecting ruefully that he had probably been putting out signs of some kind of juvenile sulkiness at being so peripheral to their considerations which R's sensitive powers of observation had noted.

'Yes, Snow effectively demolished the obsession of so many of the authorities, that cholera was a result of "miasmas", or bad air, in 1854 in Soho. He simply removed the handle of a drinking pump infected by leakage from a sewer – and stopped an outbreak of cholera that, in two weeks, had killed almost 700 people in just this small area. He has recommended boiling water before use, and the disease is retreating in every place which has taken Dr Snow's measures into its controlling efforts. The man should have a knighthood, though the medical establishment's sour grapes will probably prevent it.

'So you see, Mr Howell,' R continued, 'it may well be as Dr Heckford says; Miss Alice may be resting after her exertions, and it would be no surprise to anyone who knows the standards she demands of herself. She has the added protection of being for the moment entirely confined to Dr Heckford's house, and you have the added advantage that taking her away for a rural convalescence would be entirely in keeping with what the Heckfords are saying.'

R paused, but with such a distinct air of not having finished what he wanted to say, whilst reluctant to deal with what had to come next, that Francis felt bound to encourage him.

'Please do tell us what you feel you should, Mr Renfrew. I admit that much of this is new and bizarre territory to me, but I want above all not to fail as a result of simple naivety, and you are clearly a man well able to enlighten me.'

R had winced slightly at the use of his name; he sighed and his eyes flickered momentarily to Silas Fletcher, who nodded encouragement. Francis registered that Fletcher might well have had to work quite hard to set up this meeting at all. However, there was no point in a northern ex-mine owner pretending to a London worldliness that he didn't have.

'Thank you, sir. I would sooner you use the single letter as a name, sir, if you wouldn't mind. As you say, it is bizarre, as is much of the world in which I move and have my being, but there are a number of evil men who would love to know such details and still do not; for the safety of both of us, such subterfuges are unfortunate necessities. My hesitant pause was because I know what I am about to say may shock, sir, but I cannot, in all duty, not say it. Would you say your family seat, Howell Grange, I believe it's called, is well protected, sir?'

Francis, in spite of his best intentions, was momentarily nonplussed at this.

'It is quite generously staffed. My family and the Harringtons, with whom we are closely associated, do believe in providing the local people with as much employment as we possibly can, and neither of our families can be said to be less than wealthy.'

'My advice would be for your establishments to be increased, sir, as much as they can be without undue alarm being spread, perhaps in the name of a new agricultural or building project and with the aim of employing strong, young men. It has been known in the past for Melbury and his kind to operate with bands of brigands committing supposedly random crimes when opportunities arise. Men with some military experience would be especially useful, sir.'

So, Charlie, Francis thought, with a deep pang of regret and dismay, *your time would have come for us after all. The pity of it.*

'And each new employee in whatever area should be vigorously investigated, sir, particularly any who appear suddenly from outside your area. Melbury may well already be considering ways of putting pressure on you, sir.'

'It's quite extraordinary, really,' Francis said. 'The man struck me as reasonably intelligent and capable of mastering his arguments. Is it not enough for him to rely on his experience and status as a peer of the realm to make his case without such tactics of violence and intimidation? Why would he take such alarm at a relatively new member in the House without much of a network of supporters and sympathisers attempting to further the interests of mining safety?'

A long pause, during which Fletcher's eyes slithered to the ground and R was examining Francis with an intensity which became unnerving. Francis had opened his mouth to protest, but R began speaking first, and with a tone of harshness and a speed of speech which he had not used before.

'Mr Howell, it would be less than honest of me not to confess that when Mr Fletcher here first approached me about this matter, I had a number of reservations. Lord Melbury has tangled successfully with some of the most experienced and well-supported members of the London criminal underworld and some of the finest thief-taking and detective minds the country can offer. To take him on with a – forgive me, sir, but it must be described so – simple Northerner ill-versed in the ways of the Smoke as a leading member of the team struck me as more dangerous than an old hand like me could seriously contemplate. But your passion, sincerity and eloquence have won me over, sir, and I believe your natural intelligence will bring you to an understanding of the need for careful and complete discretion at all times. I am therefore going to tell you certain facts about Lord Melbury and put a trust in you, sir, to realise very seriously that the simple knowledge of these facts would be enough to kill you if it gets back to Melbury that you know them, as they are enough to kill me should he come to understand that I know even a fraction of them. Both of us could well die in a particularly brutal and unpleasant way, sir, while his agents attempt to extract such knowledge from us. I intend to impart this information to you because without it you will never entirely understand Melbury, why he is so dangerous, and why his opposition, once invoked, is implacable. But I hope I have made it clear to you, sir, that there are grave and inevitable implications of the course on which Mr Fletcher and yourself are considering embarking, and I should also say that there are only two possible conclusions to a successful campaign against Melbury: his imprisonment, for a very substantial length of time or, and very much preferable, his death. If he remains alive and at liberty, he will act quite ruthlessly against anyone who consistently opposes him, even if it is only within the chamber of the House of Commons, and he will act in such a way – assaults, accidents, robberies – as to shield himself entirely from any consequences, because his involvement at any level will be absolutely impossible to prove.'

R paused and looked at his companions. Neither of them doubted for a moment his sincerity and neither of them had any serious doubts about the truth of what he was saying, meaning question marks about their own involvement were already embedded in the backs of their minds. The most obvious one was articulated by Silas Fletcher, whose pale features demonstrated that even he, from within the shelter of his metropolitan sophistication and cynicism, was shocked at the gravity of what he had originally seen as a matter of influencing or pressurising some of Melbury's industrial and personal allies in such a way as to put pressure on Melbury himself.

'While Francis is considering his own position, R, I have two questions which I must put to you myself. You are not obliged to answer them, of course – you are not, nor will you be, under any obligation to us at any time – but I think they pertain so relevantly to the success or failure of our enterprise that I feel I must have some answer to them before I can confirm my own intention to go ahead with what must be done.'

'Ask your questions, sir – please do. If I can answer them, I will; if I can't, then we will end your own part in this here and now without, I hope, bad feeling, and certainly not on my part,' said R quietly, his eyes fixed on Fletcher's face with what Francis thought was the first hint of a kind of suspicion.

'And not on mine, sir, I do assure you. I count it as a privilege to know of your existence at all, a confidence advanced to me by someone I much respect only under the very strictest injunction not to spread it further, and I may have other cause to ask for your services in the future. Only my faith in the absolute integrity of Mr Howell caused me to speak to him. But please don't be offended if I ask what your own cause is in this matter. For Mr Howell, it is the need to advance legislation on mining safety without the unrelenting opposition of a hugely powerful aristocrat to add to the already formidable list of obstacles; for me, it is a belief in Mr Howell's cause and its pertinence to my own constituents. But you, sir – I do not mean to be intrusive or impertinent, but my understanding is that you are not a man who needs our money or anyone else's to live comfortably for the rest of your days, after your record of successful ventures. What is your concern with Melbury? That, essentially, is my first question. My second is why does our action need such draconian outcomes? In previous parliamentary campaigns, when opponents have proved to be intransigent, success has often been achieved by influencing their allies, mounting effective sanctions against their business interests, using the gentlemen of the press to further one cause and diminish the other. Why are these inadequate for dealing with Melbury?'

A long pause followed, and Francis began to think that the whole enterprise might yet end acrimoniously, with trust insufficient between them to allow further confidences. R rose from the table and carried his tankard over to the edge of the terrace, looking out in a distracted, absent-minded way over his brother's well-tended acres of crops and animals. He took several sips at his beer, apparently in a brief but tortured silent debate with himself. Silas and Francis looked at each other and Francis spread his arms in puzzlement, wondering whether they should simply leave, though it seemed a feeble way to end their deliberations. Silas held up one hand as if to ask him for a little more patience.

R arrived at his decision. He turned back and the tankard was slammed down on the table as he spoke with greater fire and animation than he had at any time up to this point.

'I confess that I needed to talk to you gentlemen to satisfy your bona fides, and please don't be insulted by that; in my world, care is an absolute essential. I knew Mr Fletcher, of course, but this enterprise is a pricklier business altogether and every precaution has to be taken. I will tell you enough for you to decide for yourselves, gentlemen, without irretrievable commitment. I referred earlier to Melbury's recreational tastes. These are such as to disgust even some of the notorious figures of the London underworld, and an attempt is already being planned to put a stop to his lordship's activities once and for all. He operates two aliases in two much more modest areas of London than the one which includes his grand London residence, and imagines himself incognito when he goes to these places, and in truth it has taken a lot of time and investigation to establish beyond all possible doubt that Melbury and these two men are one and the same. That, at this stage, is as much information as I can reasonably give you without firmly implicating you in the conspiracy. Suffice it to say that the outcome can only be Melbury's death or his permanent and irretrievable exile if the attempt is successful. If it is not, then the probable result for me and my fellow conspirators, perhaps including you gentlemen, will be either to exile ourselves to the most remote corners of the globe or face the certainty of a hideous and lingering death at the hands of Melbury's many agents. There is no compromise, no middle way, for this, gentlemen. As you will know, I suspect, from my record and the circles I move in, I am not a man given to melodrama or overstatement, and I do assure you of the deep seriousness of what I say.'

Both of the other two men, but particularly Francis, were now feeling out of their depth and their doubts had become visible in pale countenances and lowered eyes. R saw the effect his words was having and continued in a slightly gentler tone.

'The way I see it, sirs, is this. Melbury and his kind are the foot soldiers of Satan; both their destinations and the means they use to reach them are intrinsically and dangerously evil. They will maim, kill, lie, cheat and dissemble in any and every way possible, without conscience or a second thought. Those who seek to oppose them successfully must, of necessity, temporarily join the foot soldiers of Satan themselves, hopefully remembering that the evil they use is to a noble purpose and hopefully managing to keep themselves aloft of the deep pit until their aims are achieved. I am not what I suspect either of you gentlemen would define as a good man; I have done myself or caused others to do innumerable acts of violence, deception and occasionally, yes, treachery. But the unarmed, chanting monk, the angel with his harp, the pious man with his Bible and peace offerings, while they may seek and earn God's approval for their martyrdom, do not stop or even hinder the likes of Melbury in their rampage on this temporal earth, and this temporal earth is where we live, gentlemen, and now is when we live. There are those who seek a heavenly future and those who want a less tortured present, and I am very much in the latter camp. If I must sometimes walk in the uniform of Satan, then so be it. If you gentlemen are to make common cause with me, this is the reality you must face and accept when you shave in the morning mirror.'

He saw that their eyes were back with his and decided the meeting had taken the matter as far as it reasonably could for the moment.

'I would now urge you gentlemen to take at least a few days to consider your position. If you do choose to join me and my fellow plotters, I will tell you in much greater detail exactly who Lord Melbury is and of what our plot against him consists, but I'm afraid none of us would consider your membership of our group unless we have clear evidence that you have armoured all of your obvious weaker spots – exposed relatives such as your sister, Mr Howell, who is exposed even in Dr Heckford's house, scantily defended homesteads, predictable and regular patterns of movement, and so on. You must also arrange your affairs so as to ensure that you never, under any circumstances, travel alone, accept any invitations however cordially or innocently they seem to be advanced unless you know the person offering the invitation personally or travel after dark unless in a conveyance with a substantial number of other people. Public events of any kind, except debates in the House itself, would also need to be avoided. And also you must accept that you will probably be an accessory to a murder and your conscience must allow you to live with that. I need hardly say to gentlemen of your understanding and intelligence that discussing this project, even though as yet you know little enough of it, with any other human soul, however intimate you may be with them, will immediately disqualify you from joining our group and you will be subjected to serious questioning in the early stages to establish that this has not happened. If you can accept all that, dear sirs, then we will become brothers in conspiracy, pledged to destroy either ourselves or Melbury. One final caveat must be added in your case, Mr Howell: being rid of Melbury will undoubtedly make your path easier, as many who work against any measures regarding mine safety do so primarily because Melbury is their ultimate overlord or because they fear him. But not all, Mr Howell, not by any means all; you may remove the largest single hurdle, sir, but others will remain. Melbury's contempt for the working classes and total indifference to their welfare is not Melbury's alone. There, gentlemen, I have done, and I believe my good brother and his lady are to provide us with some sustenance for the long journeys we all face.'

Francis stared out of his library window, looking hard but seeing nothing, and heard again R's hypnotic voice challenging his listeners to have the courage of their convictions in such stark terms. He had probably sacrificed his peace of mind to R's conspiracy, and he could not bring himself to feel any shame in the thin tears which habitually gathered in his eyes, to be blinked back and remain unshed, when he recalled the unblooded, whiter than white young parliamentarian he had been before Lord Melbury and R came into his life.

He recalled himself to the moment, thinking of Alice and Samuel Spencer in quick succession, and was about to call for Armstrong when he realised the man was already in the room. The man had the professional butler's genius for unobtrusive entrances and exits, but it could sometimes be disturbing; he wondered if Armstrong had been there long enough to see the staring eyes and the involuntary tears.

'Armstrong, I'm sorry, have you been standing there for long?'

'No, sir. I had only just entered the room, I do assure you.'

He protests just a little too much, Francis thought, and as he looked up at Armstrong's benign and respectful features, he once again sensed that the man had somehow contrived to know all about recent events, even though he knew such a suspicion was ludicrous and entirely impossible. Armstrong always seemed to carry with him an indefinable but unmistakable air of knowing everything but acknowledging nothing.

'Is Miss Alice awake, do you know?'

'Yes, sir. She has received Dr Spencer in her room.'

Francis got to his feet.

'Samuel? Why? Has she relapsed?'

'No, sir. Dr Spencer found himself with time available after a cancelled appointment, and his concern about Miss Alice being so great, he came to check on the situation. I concluded, while you were preparing, sir, that you would not disapprove.'

'No, of course not. His ministrations have been invaluable ever since we returned. Where are they now?'

'In the conservatory, sir.'

'Very good. I'll come down.'

The butler withdrew as noiselessly as he'd arrived. Francis looked again at the view which had meant so little to him before his recollection of that first meeting with R had returned so powerfully. Howell land, Howell people, and probably safer now than they had ever been. His time as a foot soldier of Satan may have been a heavy price to pay, but he could not fail to be surrounded by its glorious consequences. One of them was the proposition for Alice which he had been nursing to himself for some days, determined that he would not put it to her until she was strong and receptive enough. Whether or not that time had come was his, and only his, decision to make.

Alice woke again, and this time the near past returned to her at once; the drifting in and out of consciousness, the confusion as to who and what was surrounding her, was fading away at long last. She knew Samuel had been in the room, and he had talked to her on various intimate matters before leaving, but when he'd arrived and when he'd left were still vague and undefined recent episodes.

The presence in the room she now became aware of was Mary, bustling about with towels and clothes. Mary could be a little scatter-brained on occasions – she was still young and in training

– but she was grounded enough to know what was happening in the house at any one time.

'Mary, I must have fallen asleep again. Is Dr Spencer still here? How long ago is it that he left me?'

She stopped dead and the smile was natural and seemingly grateful.

'Oh, only ten minutes, Miss Alice. Anyway, Mr Francis wanted to talk to him.'

'Yes, about me, I suppose. Well, if I am to go down and talk to the gentlemen, I'd better make myself decently clean, hadn't I? Run me a bath, please, Mary.'

'Yes, miss. Shall I stay and assist?' Mary said it because it was her duty to say it, but Alice could hear the trepidation in the voice at having to face the sight of the pale, emaciated thing which was her young woman's body at the moment. Alice knew she had always been a much better nurse than she ever could be a patient, and she was determined to make an effort of will enough to re-assert her independence in the intimacies of life.

'No, Mary. The fever has passed, and I will not regain my strength unless I start to do things for myself. But Dr Spencer is a busy man and he will no doubt need to return to his work after he has spoken to my brother. Please ask Mr Francis to arrange a further visit from the doctor in another few days, because I will need time to bath and dress. Thank you, Mary.'

Alone, Alice stayed in bed for a few more minutes. She had been aghast at how her constitution seemed to completely disintegrate at the onset of pneumonia, and how it had taken every ounce of will and strength that she possessed to fight it off – only then with the resolute help of Nathaniel, Sarah and eventually, Francis. This bedroom in Howell Grange, another of the brightening and modernising conversions brought about by her mother and Francis, with its spectacular views to the rear of the Grange over lawns, hedges and eventually fields and its ultramodern, immaculately tiled bathroom, was such a drastic contrast with the narrow, dark green and brown room just under the garret in the Heckfords' Wapping home that Alice, in her confusion and overlapping wakefulness and sleep, sometimes saw the room as a kind of dream or vision. In Wapping, the washing facilities amounted to a small basin with a face mirror above it, and the room was almost entirely bare of ornament and decoration except for the ageing, green (inevitably!) curtains. With the best will in the world, and her fervent desire for medical experience which would not be mostly about pandering to wealthy hypochondriacs, her first look at that little bedroom had daunted her spirits, even as Nathaniel stood beside her making a long series of explanations and apologies.

As she forced herself into the bathroom and through the still amazingly exhausting simple motions needed to remove her clothes and clamber into the bath, she reflected on Nathaniel and whether or not, as her brother obviously suspected but would not openly state, she had actually fallen in love with Nathaniel rather than the idea of working in the East End, even though he was happily married and was looking only for a nurse, not a mistress or an affair. Certainly, he had cut an impressive figure on his visit to the school, his appearance belying the rank curse of poverty he described.

Nathaniel Heckford was to die in 1868, to Alice's great distress, only months after he had established the Children's Hospital he had worked with Sarah to create. Not long before his death, his appearance was captured for all time by Charles Dickens, in a chapter called 'A Small Star in the East' contained in Dickens' *Uncommercial Traveller* magazine.

'An affecting play was acted in Paris years ago, called *The Children's Doctor*. As I parted from my children's doctor, now in question, I saw in his easy black necktie, in his loose buttoned black frock-coat, in his pensive face, in the flow of his dark hair, in his eyelashes, in the very turn of his moustache, the exact realisation of the Paris artist's ideal as it was presented on the stage. But no romancer that I know of has had the boldness to prefigure the life and home of this young husband and young wife in the Children's Hospital in the east of London.'

So Heckford had appeared to Alice, and so Alice had answered his appeal in his ministrations to the people, and most especially the children, of the East End. The Heckfords lived in a modest but comfortable town house on the chapel side of Union Road, separated by no more than a few hundred years from the grimly ironic Paradise Street and the rows of houses sweeping down to the wharfs, many of them half-derelict and all of them with ridiculous numbers of people crammed into narrow, poky spaces breathing foul air and still drinking, despite the relentless efforts of Nathaniel and others, water polluted with London's sewage. When cholera had broken out again and the Heckfords were frantically advising everyone on the treatment of water, Alice felt she could do nothing else but spend every moment possible helping them to stop and reverse the outbreak. She saw and took very seriously the precautions the Heckfords took to prevent themselves from contracting the cholera, and her disappointment and frustration at falling ill and being immobilised threatened to worsen the pneumonia already contracted from the damp, freezing little houses and the myriad of germs circulating around them. Alice experienced the rare agony of being rendered useless in a situation where she was desperately needed. Looking down in the bath on her spare, waif-like body, she remembered the innumerable times she tried to trick, persuade or force her tired limbs to get up and get on and how assiduously and eventually imperiously the Heckfords insisted on her staying where she was.

The argument, or more accurately gentle tug-of-war, was suddenly taken out of her hands by a prolonged nightmare, quite literally, when she found herself beset by intense, garishly coloured and disturbingly vivid dream worlds, some of which would stay with her so strongly after she woke that she could not properly adjust until drifting into the subconscious caverns again. Some she remembered, like her standing on a Wapping street looking into a dark house where all the local people seemed to have gathered, standing almost shoulder to shoulder in their tiny two-up two-down decrepit little building, but refusing her entry and grinning their blank-eyed stares at her even as the low growl of drunken young men could be heard approaching from the end of the street. But there were other situations whose details did not stay, full of grotesque unrecognisable creatures and bestial noises of pain and anger.

All through this seemingly interminable feverish spell, she was sometimes aware of people in the room, almost invariably the Heckfords, singly or together, whose shapes and gentle smells she often held on to for reassurance that there was still somewhere a base of reality, a retreat, an ever-present truth. And ultimately and incomprehensibly, when the fever seemed to be fading at last and her sheets were no longer perpetually soaked with sweat, the lean figure admitted by the green door was Francis. Her notion that he was part of another dream, that the tormenting dreams had moved on to a new and cruelly realistic level, and her subsequent attempt at indignation that he had so defied her stipulations as to bring himself into the East End, were both brushed aside; this was the assertive, irresistible force which her once hesitant, pasty-faced brother had somehow metamorphosed into from boy to man and no sooner had the Heckfords conceded that she could be moved, at least a few miles across London, now that the main fever had passed, than she was in an altogether different place, the London residence of Hon. Francis Howell MP, with a maid in attendance on her for twenty-four hours a day, fresh, sweet-smelling sheets and a detail she seemed to treasure more than anything in those first few days, the sound of bird song in the trees outside the window.

Piece by piece she prised information out of Francis, the normal strains of sibling rivalry compounded by the additional complexities of patient and well person. In spite of having been driven almost to breakdown, the Heckfords and their allies had controlled the cholera outbreak and it was already clear that it would not take the terrible toll of earlier outbreaks. Francis eventually conceded that Nathaniel's health had been compromised to some extent and he did not seem to be as active and energetic as he had been; he also let her know that the Heckfords were both upset at not having been able to do more for her than they had and would visit as soon as the opportunity arose. After three days they did; they were full of apologies, entirely unnecessary as far as Alice was concerned, and solicitude. By now Alice had begun the period of almost constant sleep which enveloped her for days to come. Then came the inevitable set to, determined sister meeting implacable brother. Alice insisted that no more than a week or so of recuperation was now necessary and she could return to the East End; Francis, at first blustering and almost shouting, declared that she would go to the East End and work until she killed herself literally over his dead body, that he'd heard all the details of her spending all day and every day in one Wapping hovel after another, regardless of temperature, sanitation, precaution, and pointing out that a dead nurse is no good to anyone and a dead nurse has sacrificed forever the prospect of being a doctor. Far from going back to the East End, Francis ranted, she was returning to Howell Grange for however long it would take to effect a full and lasting recovery.

Alice had raised herself up on her pillow and made herself sit up, her eyes flashing against the gaunt white cheeks.

'I would have taken this from Father; I wouldn't have had a choice. I would have taken it from Mother; I might even, depending on the circumstances, have taken it from Charlie. But I will not and cannot take it from you, Francis. You can advise; you cannot control. That's a right I would not concede to a husband, if I should ever have one, let alone you.'

And all at once, the new authoritarian Francis had regressed to the vacillating adolescent Francis in the space of a few seconds, and he was sitting on the bed beside her, holding her hand, with tears clouding his eyes.

'Alice, dear Alice, if you've ever given a snap of your fingers for a devoted brother, please understand that I am as certain as I can be that you will be in desperate danger if you return to the East End, and I don't mean from illness or squalor, I mean from certain agents of a certain powerful force with whom my allies and I are in dispute. The Heckfords remain entirely unaffected. I swear, and I will swear on anything you hold dear, my dead father's soul, that if I could tell you more than that without the further certainty of you then being irretrievably incriminated, I would. I'm sorry to have used such crass and ill-judged strictures, knowing how it would annoy you; please do what I ask out of love, not obedience. Please, Alice.'

And so she had conceded, albeit with something like a promise that he would tell her if and when he could, and she had even managed to eventually concede to herself her relief and gratitude at being treated so gently and considerately from then onwards. A huge coach appeared, hired at heaven only knew what expense, which moved more sedately and with less disturbance in its stately interior than any she had ever known, while she lay comfortably bedded like some queen riding to meet her victorious king. On her occasional hours of wakefulness, she felt like waving regally to her passing subjects, though there were precious few of them to be seen; precious little of anything to be seen, but the opulent satin-covered roof of the coach and a sky varying from morning blue to turgid grey.

Her return home had also been touching and enormously gratifying, with the splendid conversions undertaken by her mother and Francis making the whole place brighter and more convenient and all of them so genuinely solicitous as to make her feel ashamed of having been so determined to get away from them – to places and circumstances, she now began to admit, which could easily have been disastrous and very nearly were. Her mother in particular had been so distraught and concerned that Alice felt yet more stabs of shame at her relief that Elizabeth, like Emily, had eventually succumbed to the demands of an older, now more vulnerable relative. Lady Charlotte's grip on life was drifting away in much the same way as the Reverend Slater's, and Elizabeth was now spending much of her time at her mother's house in the grounds of Harrington Hall.

Before she left, however, her determination to attend to the care of her youngest daughter was meticulous and relentless. Even now, Alice felt herself cowering absurdly in the bath at memories of her mother's remorseless stewardship. Her suspicions that her mother might even come right through from the bedroom to the bathroom with no more pause at the door which Alice always forgot to lock, or sometimes even close, had been confirmed in every particular only two days before, when even Mary was struggling with the whole bathing and dressing routine and Alice had to undergo the mortifying experience of both Mary and her mother assisting at her most intimate moments. Alice's embarrassment was mercifully tempered by her apparently almost insatiable desire for sleep as soon as she had been returned to her bed and the extraordinary tenderness and consideration with which they handled her, carefully leaving her as much dignity as the situation would permit.

The children were another firm contribution to the success of her homecoming, blonde-haired nephew George, now six, showing what his father said was an untypical tongue-tied shyness in her presence, and fat little Caroline, not long firmly up on her feet, having to break the ice with her chuckling and gurgling routines. Charlotte and Eustace's children had only briefly appeared, briskly supervised as ever by their mother on a transient visit – 'We don't want to exhaust Aunt Alice even more than she is already suffering, now, do we?' But even Charlotte had surprised her with the emotion of hand-holding and a long cool kiss on the forehead at the moment of departure. Eustace, her eldest, who she remembered as only just beyond babyhood, was a little boy of nine, looking tall and strong for his age and unable to conceal his boredom, but a long meeting of eyes and a mutual exchange of grins suggested that this was a relationship with interesting future possibilities between the oldest of one generation and the youngest of its predecessor. Charlie's daughter Elizabeth, growing up in London but unseen since babyhood – Mary and Alice still had too many obstacles to overcome – would also now be nine, Alice realised, before making herself not dwell on it.

A sudden loud trill of bird song, startlingly close, came through the slightly ajar window above Alice's head. An urge for a final moment of total privacy overcame her; climbing laboriously out of the bath, under her own grateful steam, she made her way to the door and did lock it quietly, unobtrusively. Then she climbed back into the bath to enjoy just a few stolen minutes of being completely to herself, now aware of the summer air drifting gently in and the noises of the countryside's more melodic performers.

Downstairs, in the light, delicate ambience of a mid-Victorian morning room, before the rich, dark tones in wallpapers and textiles and large quantities of highly decorated furniture and ornaments became widespread in the 1870s, Francis and Samuel Spencer sat in two windows arranged before a square bay window. This was normally Elizabeth's preserve and her daily centre of operations, the place where she briefed the senior servants and received the more informal household visitors. Elizabeth felt able to make more concessions to current fashion than she had been when her husband was alive, and many objects in the room reflected the popularity of French style in England during the 1850s and 1860s, including the exuberant, brightly coloured curtains and the carving on the side chairs. Francis didn't feel his austere library, softened as it had been in recent years, was the appropriate reception venue for an old friend and family associate like Samuel Spencer.

Now the message had been received from Mary, and Alice had clearly decided, rightly in Spencer's opinion, to take her time about finally rising from her bed, Spencer needed to go. Francis seemed to be in a contemplative, abstracted mood, as he often had been recently, and Spencer had already made a note in the back of his mind to insist on examining Francis at some time in the near future; if the young man was beginning to wilt a little with the burdens placed on his shoulders, it would hardly be surprising. Spencer reflected ruefully on the differences between this and the previous Howell regime. In George's day, he would be lucky to get five minutes of the man's time and had suspected on more than one occasion that, if he hadn't taken his leave promptly, he would have been almost physically thrown out. Now, Howell Grange would receive him for as long as he pleased and, pleasant as that was, the clamour for his time and his need to tick items off during the day to prevent anything vital being omitted made him perpetually impatient, and with the likes of the Howells, peering at watches and straining in doorways simply wasn't permissible, especially when Francis was dealing with matters of such importance to all of them.

'Well, Francis, I do genuinely feel that the situation which you have in mind to offer Alice is one which she will find interesting and stimulating. I entirely accept that you cannot tell me in intricate detail about the precise backgrounds of the young people you have brought, or I think perhaps rescued might be a better word, from London, but I would emphasise once again that the quite shocking injuries many of them have will take time and care to address and

I think the task is one for which Alice is eminently well suited. It also cannot do harm to her still very extant ambitions towards qualifying as a full doctor. The medical authorities seem to think that conceding qualification for Elizabeth Garrett Anderson as an exceptional and singular case will put the genie back in the bottle, though the evidence is already clear that it will not. However –' Samuel could hear his wife's gentle admonitions – 'Wandering away through the paths and alleyways again, my dear?' – 'I must attend to my duties, Francis, if you will forgive me. I will return the day after tomorrow, if I may, when I will hope to see further improvement in Alice and all the more so when she receives the news you have to give her. I should also be able to give you the latest news on the situation at Lady Charlotte's house in the grounds of Harrington Hall, where your poor mother and I, I fear, can achieve little but delay the inevitable for a few more days.'

'Thank you, Samuel, on more than one count, as ever.'

As Spencer left, Francis felt the weariness which was still an unaccustomed and intimidating intrusion so relatively early in the day, and probably another price being paid for the long crisis from which he at last believed he was emerging. But he had no patience with it; his recovery and redemption were in his own hands. He headed for the stables, for the vigorous answer which usually served at such a time.

Thomas watched him approach with that surly wariness of his, eyes peering suspiciously from under the dark eyebrows. Thomas had seemed intent lately on making him feel like a presumptuous intruder into his own stables; men who had known you since you were a boy had an unreasonable advantage which even their silence could exploit.

'Peg, please, Thomas. It's a decent morning for a ride, and Peg is always game.'

'Sir.' He heaved himself away from what he was doing; yet another disturbance on a busy day. Francis suspected he would sigh if he dared.

Peg was a sturdy and spirited young mare, with an incredible turn of speed when she had a mind to it. Peg was a shortening of Pegasus, the winged horse, a name which Francis had tired of explaining to the stable staff. Peg had been settled on, an acceptable compromise to all parties.

She nudged up against him gently and momentarily. She was mature now, but she still liked to gallop, feeling the exhilaration of speed and rushing air, and he had a number of merits as a rider which particularly recommended him: his weight made him easier to carry than the hefty Thomas, and he had an easy way of control, using the reins more as suggestion than command, asking rather than insisting. He'd found earlier on in their association that she was a highly intelligent creature and didn't need heavy hands; she was also surprisingly resistant to sudden, noisy distractions, such as approaching farm carts, yapping dogs or even the crack of a hunting gun. During the dangerous period which had now passed, beyond further dispute or anxiety, he had made himself take R's warnings as seriously as the man clearly meant them, and only with a band of companions or employees had he dared take Peg riding. Now this particular escapist delight was restored, to the mutual satisfaction of man and horse.

Thomas watched him ride away intently, with his usual muted appreciation of horsemanship combined with his own brooding, ponderous anxiety. He had known Francis since boyhood and shared the general astonishment of the staff both at the succession of twists of fate which had propelled Francis into the position of senior Howell man and at how well Francis seemed to have handled his fate. But Thomas worked in an area where the real self was more difficult to disguise. When men depended so much on horses for the proper conduct of their daily lives, their relationships with them were infallible barometers of their state of mind and reliable clues to the kinds of men they were. Thomas was much quicker on the uptake than almost everyone except his nearest family and associates realised. He knew with near certainty where Francis was going this morning; he knew that a very serious crisis had only recently subsided in Francis's life and he strongly suspected that something had irrevocably changed his employer, and not necessarily for the better. Thomas watched developments with unobtrusive vigilance and picked up on whatever clues appeared.

Francis worked up a speed; he knew this country intimately and he suspected Peg had already worked out where they were heading, which was the same place they had been together the last time and the time before that. It seemed he was fated to hear words returning to him against the rush and noise of the wind. On the day that his father had died, the news of the accident had been relayed to him against the wild insistence of a cold north-easterly, and he would forever hear his own half-cracking voice standing at the top of that mine shaft trying to find words which would make sense even to his sullen, resisting audience. The more devastating the words were, the more chance they had of surviving in all their deliberate diction and irresistible volume against the numbing wildness behind them, and now, almost as if he knew where Francis was yet again heading in search of peace and some kind of forgiveness, the words of R to the new and persuaded converts to his cause, Francis and Silas Fletcher, returned in their brutal if deadpan description of a world which Francis had hitherto known nothing about.

'It isn't hard to understand, gentlemen, why Lord Melbury is indifferent to maiming, injury and even death. Melbury's pleasure lies in inflicting it. In each of his two modest London houses, a number of young people are kept in virtual imprisonment, their ages ranging from as young as sixteen to nineteen or twenty-one at most. The majority, but by no means all, are girls; about a quarter to a third are boys. Melbury will visit each house on a regular basis, his incognito carefully preserved – I referred in our first conversation, gentlemen, to the time and sacrifice which has been needed to make the necessary connections. Not content with brutally thrashing his victims, very occasionally, actually to death, the remains attended to by means of the river or other contrived disappearances, Melbury also derives pleasure from all other forms of degradation and humiliation imaginable, which he will inflict, or cause to be inflicted, or even force his victims to do to each other, girl on boy, boy on girl, boy on boy, girl on girl. His subjects, or perhaps objects would be a better word, are hopeful young runaways arriving in London, sometimes from the kind of areas you gentlemen represent in Parliament, to seek work. Quite often, they are lured to London by Melbury's agents with the promise of work in domestic service, or training for it to be followed by the employment itself. Some have actually finished up as employees of Melbury or his associates, continuing to provide the curious services which these gentlemen enjoy well into their twenties, too scared to attempt escape or contact the authorities, knowing as they do the dreadful fate of those who attempt such a thing.

'I don't doubt that you gentlemen will find such tastes abhorrent and probably inexplicable, and who knows what extraordinary warps of fortune or experience have caused men to relish such practices? Some of them, of course, have attended public schools whose regimes of premeditated and officially sanctioned brutality are legendary, apart from the cruelty of senior pupils to younger, and to have witnessed and experienced such things in youth can create wounds which remain for a lifetime. It is also known that Melbury, in spite of now being married to his third wife and having dispensed with her two predecessors on the basis of their failure to provide him with heirs, remains childless. The clear conclusion is that it is Melbury himself who is unable, for some reason, to successfully procreate, however much odium he heaps on the supposedly barren women. Perhaps, given time and patience, some saintly medical man might be capable of making Melbury and his associates understand the iniquity of their behaviour. However, neither time nor patience remain available while young people are being scarred for life, robbed of all pride and dignity and even sometimes killed. I do not condemn the entire aristocracy, many of whom have and do undertake invaluable public service. But Melbury belongs to a group of very rich and very powerful men who have long ago decided that no normal rules, no laws of the country, can or will apply to them; their will, however perverse and evil, must be done. No doubt their like exist in almost every country, an army of the most savage and dangerous foot soldiers of Satan, sometimes moving from one generation to the next without anyone having the determination, resources or power to stop them.

'Many London people are not easily shocked, gentlemen, especially those whose daily business is in the depravity of the underworld, but there is a widely held view, even amongst those immured to vice in the normal way of life, that Melbury is more than can be tolerated. When I first spoke to you gentlemen, the notion was that he could be incapacitated or exiled. Since then, however, other arguments have been considered, and in short, gentlemen, we are agreed that nothing can ultimately resolve this situation than Melbury's irrefutably proved death.'

Francis could remember glancing across at Fletcher at this point and wondering whether his friend's drained face and wide eyes reflected his own. They were being asked to be accomplices to murder. R, who had obviously already been through this experience a number of times, seemed to have already realised their trains of thought.

'None of us, that is the gentlemen who are contriving to put a final end to Melbury, will be the immediate physical agents causing his extinction, but that should not cloud the necessary questions in your minds. No jury is likely to see any of us as less guilty because of that. But, if the attempt fails, those of us who are unable to flee the country in time will not live long enough to face a jury in any case. It is a desperate situation, gentlemen, and it calls for desperate measures. As I believe I said on our first meeting, piety and scrupulous honour are balm to the soul, but they will not stop the foot soldiers of Satan from what they have elected to do.'

A patter of rain and Peg tossed her head in momentary protest, but she was enjoying the pace and the fresh air; September rain was ultimately as much refreshment as imposition. Francis heard again R outlining the plan, his words as definite and absolute a condemnation as if he was putting on the black cap of the judge while speaking them.

'Our band of hired men, well over 200 strong, will target one of Melbury's houses at a time when our observers have revealed him to definitely be in attendance. His guards and any other staff in the house will be bribed away or otherwise restrained so that Melbury and whoever is with him in the upper room where his depravity is taking place are isolated. Our men will break the door and enter the room in force, removing any of Melbury's companions, who will be taken to the ports and forced to leave the country on pain of being immediately handed over to the authorities if they return. Our men will then release and arm with knives and swords all the boys and girls contained in the building and will inform people in the locality about what has been going on in the house. Our men will then remove themselves from the house and watch all the available exits. If his former victims and the neighbouring people do not cut him to pieces, our men will shoot him as he emerges from the house. At the same time as this is taking place at the house Melbury is visiting, our agents will also be breaking into and releasing the young people in his other house. Then everyone will melt away; the young people will be taken to a place of safety to recover and be out of the range of any inquiring authorities, the local people will say nothing for fear of incriminating themselves or their friends, Melbury's companions will be out of the country and any of Melbury's agents who prove recalcitrant will be threatened with a similar fate to his lordship should they approach the authorities. Melbury will be dead, his infernal business terminated, his victims rescued and rehabilitated. Your chances, gentlemen, of bringing greater humanity into the dirty, dangerous business of mining will be greatly enhanced and any other high-ranking aristocratic tyrants who believe themselves to be beyond justice or retribution will have a great deal to think about.'

Peg pounded on enthusiastically, knowing their destination was now within minutes. The rain had passed and the September morning seemed to be quickly returning to an imitation of a summer day.

Francis saw the little church in the distance, St Cuthbert's, a simple stone construction dating back to before the Civil War, on the edge of the Thirwell estate and therefore ultimately Harrington land, as so much of the area was. St Cuthbert's was the adjoining church to the village of Lower Thirwell, until the disruption of the Civil War, when the Commonwealth and the Restoration sent the men away to war or in search of work away from the devastated land. Lower Thirwell simply died, most of its largely wooden buildings now long since taken for firewood and the remainder no more than overgrown little stacks of rubble or rough and ready animal shelters.

St Cuthbert's, however, had survived intact, probably because it suited the Thirwells and eventually the Howells to have somewhere they could use for a private chapel without the expense of building a new one on their own land and without having to go to services through rows of staring country people. It was understood that only the Thirwells, the Howells and their respective retainers were entitled to use the place – the Harringtons had much grander worshipping quarters near the Hall.

Francis dismounted and left Peg near the patch of grass to the east of the church, where she could lie down to rest if she chose. He never bothered to tie Peg to anything, knowing full well she could be waiting for him in almost exactly the same spot. St Cuthbert, one of the very oldest of the north-eastern saints, was rumoured to have visited the very spot on which the church had been built, and sceptical as Francis had always felt himself to be about the whole paraphernalia of relics, past holy deeds and associations between saints and places, the atmosphere around the peaceful little church had a kind of profundity which demanded a certain respect and obeisance. The graveyard stretched to the west and many eminent, mediocre and occasionally villainous members of the families were buried there, as well as some of their more senior and respected servants.

It had been in the much grander surroundings of St Paul's Cathedral that Francis, after an unaccustomed and self-startlingly lengthy session on his knees, had contemplated the irrevocable decision. Ever since first arriving in London, St Paul's had made a profound impression on him with the sheer size and magnificence of the witness it bore to a faith which had only marginally touched him before, in spite of the lip service paid to the many rituals, services, weddings and funerals he had had to attend. His childhood had been subsumed by his awe of his father, the Master of the World, and his father's scorn and dismissal of so much of what the Church was supposedly about was such that Francis's immature logic could only imagine that one or the other were wrong and that it could be his father's was not a feasibly tenable conclusion at the time. Losing both his father and Charlie, and then his own child, spoke of a need for some sanctuary or escape, at the very least somewhere or something to enable a regaining of strength, a quiet rebuilding. It also made him think that his very mortal father was actually in the wrong after all.

He thought going on to his knees in such a place – St Paul's was never anything like empty, even when its vast spaces did not seem to echo to human voices – would be an over-ostentatious piety for him, a monkish charade which would make him self-conscious and feeling a little foolish. As an integral part of a well-established service or occasion, when all around him were similarly engaged, the action did not require any thought, any independent analysis. But in St Paul's, he was praying alone and outside any regular service.

He did not expect to find answers and he didn't; in fact, what drove him to stand again was a kind of impatience, a feeling that he was simply trying to push the need for decision in another direction, like a soldier requesting orders or a schoolboy looking for precise instructions. God, whoever or whatever He might be, could not make this decision for him or spare him from the very human and temporal consequences of getting the decision wrong. And since that was the nature of the consequences, so it must be the nature of the decision. There were no moral absolutes; if killing is understood to be entirely evil, intrinsically and regardless of circumstance, then the foot soldiers of Satan would have to include every military force which had ever sallied out to defend its own country and people. And if the sanctity of life included Melbury, how many more pitmen would have to be crushed, burnt or mangled to death, how many more young victims thrashed and destroyed, to preserve a sanctity which Melbury himself so callously disregarded? If he needed to stand before St Peter and answer for why he had deliberately chosen to aid and abet a murder plot, he could point to the piles of corpses and broken hearts which Melbury had already created before the plot had been hatched. And, if hell was his destination, and hell was a concept which Francis, having worked and observed the workings of many subterranean pits which put hell into a visible, tangible human form, could not associate with any notion of a merciful God, then at least he would have the satisfaction of seeing Melbury and his kind alongside him.

Francis used a key to enter the little church of St Cuthbert's. The place was well looked after, an outpost in the formidable administrative empire of his sister Charlotte, who allowed her husband Eustace to control certain aspects of the Thirwell estate's agricultural production while extending her own well-organised and thoroughly efficient hegemony over everything else. St Cuthbert's even had its own curate, though it was one of his several livings and he visited rarely, usually for some Thirwell or Howell connected event. A group of Charlotte's ladies regularly inspected and cleaned the church, while men from the Thirwell maintenance staff would take care of any repairs the premises, graveyard and surrounding grounds might need. Francis had been coming to the church for various reasons ever since boyhood, but to attend on his own and then have the place entirely to himself was a satisfaction which he appreciated more with increasing age.

He closed the low, arch-shaped wooden door behind him and then, after a moment's thought, locked it. If the place was truly inhabited by a holy spirit, he was seeking to communicate with it or for it to communicate with him, hopefully to ease his troubled mind in one sense or another. He felt that involvement in a murder plot was a Rubicon which, once crossed, could never be retraced, and perhaps the first of an accumulation of compromised principles, political dirt, which would ultimately drive whatever holy spirit may once have lived inside him remorselessly away. He gazed around the neat, unpretentious innards of St Cuthbert's, enlivened by an occasional vase or flower arrangement from Charlotte's ladies. What little the place had of coloured glass, gilt, silver and paintings had been destroyed or taken in the Reformation, but the arched window which allowed light to fill the whole space from the end of the church Francis faced was still impressive, and the simple table altar with its wooden cross complemented that flood of light very effectively. The pews, no more than a dozen rows of them, were hewn wood and not very comfortable after those with little protective flesh had been sitting on them for a while, as Francis had discovered as a boy, but the whole building had a quiet, unassuming dignity and peace, an uncomplicated pleasure in its own survival and, like all buildings which were carefully tended, a kind of pride and contentment.

The fact that his involvement in the plot had been so relatively withdrawn did not ultimately make things any easier, somehow. He had envisaged waits in darkened houses and physical violence at least in one brief, intense burst of activity and possibly something much bloodier and more prolonged. Growing up with his father and Charlie had left him not entirely unacquainted with the use of his fists and the handling of swords and guns, but he was not an outstanding or natural performer in these areas and he knew it. However, such a substantial moral commitment seemed to demand action, whether it suited him or not. Once again, in the rural peace of R's brother's farm, the man himself explained to Francis and Silas Fletcher what their part in the plot would entail, in R's familiar tone of decisions already taken for the very best of reasons.

'I mean no disrespect to you or any other of the gentlemen who have contributed, like yourselves, to providing the essential funds to enable this conspiracy to make progress. On the day itself and for the necessities of the action, the type of men needed are those whose training and experience has been of the London streets, who have proved their ability in this kind of enterprise and have a thorough enough knowledge of our great city to be able to conceal themselves totally and for as long as possible. The attempt itself will be made in August of this year. Melbury is particularly active in his nefarious recreation during August, knowing as he does that so many of his fellow aristocrats and parliamentarians have gone to the country or are travelling abroad. Wherever you gentlemen are, and you would be best advised to be in your country homes, not in London, you will receive a message, which I will either deliver myself or will arrive under my personal seal – you will recognise that because I will show it to you before you depart today. The message will tell you the day when the attempt will be made, not more than three days in advance of the attempt. If you have heard nothing further from me or my seal by four days after the attempt, gentlemen, then you must, and I repeat this with all the emphasis I can muster, you must flee abroad and either take with you as many of your nearest and dearest as possible or arrange for them to be heavily and permanently protected. If I do not survive, certain other gentlemen in the group have been authorised to use what methods they can to get messages to conspirators abroad, but unless and until you receive such a message in such a way as to make it plainly credible, you must stay where you are. Failure means either death or exile, gentlemen, and please understand that they are absolutely the only two alternatives available.'

Francis realised the simplest and more pertinent explanation for his recent troubling habit of locking himself into a local church was simply privacy, the state of being away from all eyes and all need to maintain appearances. He did not want to behave extravagantly, weeping or shouting or doing anything much except sitting in contemplation, but the pleasure of knowing he could do so here in absolute isolation was what was sustaining him through this difficult aftermath. Recall and reflection had a healing quality about it, providing the mind with the time and leisure to assimilate and consider what had happened and stripping it of the immediacy of its horrors.

R did deliver the word personally, partly, it seemed, because he wanted to test the defences and readiness of the most far-flung northerly of his allies. He could remember both Howell and Fletcher looking at him askance at the idea of bands of brigands appearing before their respective main homesteads, Howell Grange and Fletcher's rather less grand but equally rural Milverton House. He mentioned their scepticism and his greater ability to understand it when visiting the North itself, as the three men sat in the modest but comfortable drawing room of one of Fletcher's wealthier tenants, currently enjoying the sun and beaches of Italy. The house was almost central to the Milverton estate, inherited by Fletcher from his wife's father, and vast spaces of Cumberland stretched away on either side of it.

'A happy choice of venue, Mr Fletcher,' R said, 'and admirably remote, though I am fortunate to have arranged teams of horses and riders to enable me to move around the larger spaces of England more easily. As for your main residence, it is difficult to see any feasible attempt being made on it without the men concerned having been seen in the area long before arriving. I take it Howell Grange is much the same, Mr Howell?'

'Oh, yes, very much so. When I tell you that a cart with more than three occupants would excite remark in the area, the idea of a substantial group of men, especially men who seem intent on evil purposes, not being noticed long, long before they arrived at any local destination is really quite preposterous, and if they were seen to be heading for Howell Grange, I would not only be able to fortify the house with a large number of local men, I would even be able to arrange various obstacles and raids on their group before they ever arrived,' Francis said, and Fletcher nodded.

'Good,' R said. 'And London is so very different. Today is Tuesday 14 August; our conspiracy will come to fruition on Friday 17 August, and there are already over one hundred of our men gathered within half a mile of the target, without anyone in the area apparently noticing anything remotely untoward. In a certain area of South London with fading claims to gentility, a comfortable-looking Georgian house is owned by Mr Marcus Field, supposedly an antiquarian, with four hefty man servants and a very large and commodious attic. Two extraordinarily brave and spirited young men, one aged seventeen, the other eighteen – their names will remain known only to me and my immediate assistants – escaped from this house not long ago, half-clothed and still suffering from various wounds, with an admirable mixture of initiative and speed. Due to the remarkable and heartening good luck of them seeking shelter in a shop belonging to one of my men, we have managed to spirit them out of London altogether, rather than leave them to be captured by Melbury's agents and subjected to treatment which, men of the world as you are, I will not particularise, gentlemen. They are well protected and recovering in a place even more remote than this spot, and they have given us our first eye witness accounts of the contents and activities of Mr Marcus Field's attic. Suffice it to say that it is thoroughly equipped for all Mr Field's purposes, and so thick are the ceilings and roofing around that the hellish noises which the boys have curdled our blood by describing do not emerge from that attic into the outside world to the extent of a single faint peep, though my agents do say that suspicions have arisen in the locality about the house, because of the unusual absence of any female servants and a number of clandestine comings and goings, sometimes clearly sounding like forcible entries or removals. My agents have been working very discreetly on informing some of the more robust and active local people about the allegations being made by the two boys. Melbury, we understand, is not particularly alarmed at their escape, apparently concluding that they were lucky enough to find someone to spirit them out of London – as, indeed, they were – out of pity; he doesn't believe that anyone is likely to take any of their lurid accounts very seriously. They are, after all, boys, and boys who have tried to enter the London crime scene, interfered with the territory of much more seasoned practitioners and been well served out for it are a common enough feature of that and other areas. Mr Field, alias, of course, his lordship, with two companions, one of whom, we understand, is the brother of a cabinet minister, are planning a weekend in South London discussing and valuing new items which Mr Field has acquired for his collection, while adjourning in the evenings for their curious amusements. I now even have one exceptionally brave man actually in Melbury's domestic service. All is set, gentlemen; we have planned and considered with the now inestimable advantages of an intimate knowledge of the precise geography of the house. It is no easy matter to plot an assassination, as this must be understood to be, but before we become too steeped in any premature regrets, we should bear in mind that one piece of foolishness or miscalculation could see any of us secured in that attic for his lordship's amusement assuredly unto death, after who knows what lengths of time and agony have been suffered.'

Francis remembered R's words almost exactly, and his flesh crept again on its own in his favourite church, as it had done on first hearing. The challenges of physical endurance and the ever present question marks about how strong each man's will to resist will be if and when it needs to be had remained largely unanswered in his mind, and he had eventually, glumly and realistically, acknowledged to himself that he was afraid. However lauded he might have been in some circles for undergoing a shift as an ordinary pitman would experience it, he could not avoid the certainty within him that it had driven him to the very limit of his endurance, young as he was at the time. All the mitigations – inexperience, naivety, an unprepared body for such endeavours – could not disguise the truth of it, and he had long ago told himself that if he ever reached the stage where self-deception became as natural to him as it clearly was to some of the people he had to work with, he would no longer be able to see himself as working to greater and more valid purposes than they did.

By the time he had met up with Peter, now long gone to a large practice in Newcastle, Francis was aware of the extremes of exhaustion and an invasive humiliation at the ruthless exposure, not so much of his nakedness but his sheer blundering incompetence and inadequacy. Fraternal comparisons, all too often to his disadvantage, had not stopped with Charlie's death; in fact, he had been unable to prevent himself reading avidly whenever yet another account of the Crimean War came to light, and he doubted his own physical ability to have survived the experience at all, let alone distinguish himself as his brother had done.

But the streak of obstinacy and determination revealed to his family as Francis emerged blinking into the remorseless spotlight which the loss of his father and subsequently his brother had thrown on him caused a repetition which had grown into a character trait. Repercussions and difficulties there may be, and some of them might be drastic enough, but when some long churning inner debate resolved itself and a decision had been taken, there was almost no imaginable human consequence which would prevent him going through with whatever it was. Even as he'd contemplated the dreadful business of being subjected to the torments of Melbury's agents or Melbury himself, quite possibly in a situation where Melbury had contrived to make the world believe Francis was already dead and there was therefore no chance of rescue or relief, and shaming beads and streams of sweat would appear in various places while his insides chilled and shrank, he had jumped and now there was no possible movement but forward. He realised that St Paul's was one of the processes along the way; the final, irrevocable commitment had been made here, in St Cuthbert's, when the remaining vestiges of opposition had been swept away. Here was where the strength finally arrived, and if this place and St Paul's really did mean anything, if what they represented meant anything at all, there could be no other ultimate outcome for the likes of Melbury but defeat.

So, having cast the die, Francis took another decision, and it meant a long and potentially tortuous conversation with Armstrong. The butler, he had always known, was discreet and utterly trustworthy, but that would not have counted for much in this affair if discretion was countered by single-mindedness, stupidity and an insistence on knowing every aspect of the situation. But Francis knew the ageing senior servant very well, and he already knew that an inability to trust even those who were demonstrably worthy of trust was a sign of stupidity in itself.

'Please believe that I am speaking from reality and the imperatives of the situation I'm facing, Armstrong, not from any desire to create melodrama or self-aggrandisement. I cannot, and I use that word because it is literally true, tell you exactly why I want you to undertake the duty I will shortly describe.'

'You have never, since childhood, been very much given to self-aggrandisement, sir, if you'll forgive me for so personal a remark. And it is in the nature of my duties at times, sir, rather like the aide-de-camp to the general, that I must take responsibility for certain actions being taken without necessarily knowing the reasons behind them. If it is conceivably within my limited powers and abilities to carry out your instructions, sir, I will do so.'

Francis smiled his relief quickly but perceptibly, and Armstrong gave thanks once more to whatever guardian angel had arranged the eventual Howell heir to take so much after his mother and so little after his father.

'Thank you. I should have known better than to ask the question. Is it possible, at very short notice, meaning no more than a day or two, to engage on our staff in the region of thirty to forty young men, strong and fit? The reason given would be that I have a building project in mind, to begin within two or three months – which I well might, Armstrong, but that's another idiosyncrasy of my instructions which I cannot be as precise about as I would wish – and I want to be satisfied that the men I employ will be reliable and hard-working before the building begins.'

Armstrong showed no hint of doubt or hesitation.

'Mr Francis, there are in this vicinity literally scores, hundreds, more accurately, of young men who would undertake almost any conceivable employment if it meant an escape from the inevitability of mine work. You know, sir, that mining remains a difficult and dangerous occupation, even allowing for recent improvements achieved by gentlemen such as yourself, and there continue to be injuries and fatalities on a disturbing scale. Work in the stables and on the estate always calls for numerous sturdy men, and an influx of the kind you describe would certainly enable a number of current undertakings to move forward much more rapidly and efficiently, as well as providing the possibility of adding to their number. I feel confident that such a workforce could be assembled within hours, sir.'

'This endeavour is connected with my mining safety concerns, Armstrong, though I am not in a position to be specific about that, either, yet. And weaponry, Armstrong – I take we are tolerably well stocked in hunting guns?'

This time Armstrong did look momentarily disturbed.

'Yes, sir, just so. And, again, our supply could be enhanced within hours.'

'Good.' Francis paused and searched for the right words, knowing that the right words were now very important. Armstrong was superficially as unperturbed as ever, but the inclination of his eyebrows and his slightly paler features suggested a whole cauldron of questions ready to boil over at any moment.

'I am involved in a conflict, an unfortunately very necessary conflict, with a very powerful and well-connected gentleman. If my involvement is successful, all the measures described will probably be unnecessary; if they are not, there is at least a possibility that an attempt will be made on the house by a group of armed men, or men singly or in pairs might attempt an assassination.'

Armstrong made himself do no more than nod.

'I have not, as yet, confided this to my wife, my mother or my sister. My sister is, in any case, still far too ill to be receptive to this or any other similar news. In the cases of the other two ladies, I am hoping I will not have to so confide, Armstrong, which may be moral cowardice but is at least moral cowardice in a good cause. Both my wife and my mother are dealing with difficult parental situations and I do not wish to land a substantial extra burden of anxiety on them. I need someone I can trust implicitly, Armstrong, and I believe you are that person.'

'Thank you, sir. Your trust is much appreciated, and I will do my utmost to be worthy of it.'

'Then be prepared to act effectively and at short notice, Armstrong, and thank you from the bottom of my heart.'

Francis spoke such words with grim honesty, because he knew that he had already added to his criminal association in an assassination plot a premeditated and deliberated intention to defy the very man who had involved him in it. If R or one of his agents did not appear in the stated time, it almost certainly meant they were dead or had flown abroad, meaning his choices at such a point were no longer subject to their will. Even with Emily and the children accompanying him, as he could insist they should, he could not exile himself and leave the rest of his family to fend for themselves, however formidable Armstrong and his little army proved to be, and if anything happened to them in his absence, his sometimes strained ability to live with himself would break down altogether. He would stay where he was, stand and fight if need be, rather than eat his insides away in a foreign town worrying about what had become of them.

A padding of hefty animal feet paced past the little church and Francis listened intently; a second creature followed, of a similar size. This was not the first time his reveries in this church had been disturbed by such a noise, but the creatures had yet to present themselves. Francis knew the local rumours about wolves whose usual habitats were the dense woodland of southern Scotland moving south when their homeland pickings were meagre, and he knew well enough that the area was populated by a number of feral dogs, often employed by local people as watchdogs or ratters in their remote homesteads or vulnerable houses and subsequently proving to be unaffordable or uncontrollable. Left to fend for themselves, the largest and fiercest dogs supposedly survived longest by monopolising the food sources available. But everywhere in the North outside the few sizeable towns was always awash with rumours about wild animals, most of which Francis could not take seriously, and few of the species concerned included human beings in their natural diets, generally preferring to keep away from them. In a few seconds, all was quiet again, but for the usual easy, familiar sounds of the rural summer.

Francis looked directly at the wooden cross on the altar, its top illuminated by a shaft of brilliant white light hitting it directly from the window. He kept his eyes steadily on it as he made himself hear again the horror of R's words describing the last hours of Melbury.

'For my own vigil, I had chosen a comfortable house on the other side of the road, one belonging to a supporter of our conspiracy. It was noticeable from the start how Melbury's power was breaking as he lost some of his former discretion and rigorous leadership; Melbury, as you may know, Francis, from his reputation in the House, consumes alcohol in vast and regular quantities and I believe this has finally begun to take its toll. Certainly his men would once have swept the surrounding area with much more application and conscientiousness than they did on the Thursday before his lordship arrived, and their cursory efforts at inspecting the local taverns and coffee houses were risibly easy for our men to avoid. But we were unable to avoid them gathering up two young girls who had been given an address to apply to for domestic service and found themselves very much not required. Bemused and at a loss, their money having been spent getting them there, they were easy prey and did not even have to be talked into entering Mr Field's house. Whatever was needed to confirm my men in their intention, nothing could have been more appropriate than the sight of those girls smiling their relief and thanks at the two hefty criminals even as the front door opened and they disappeared into the darkness within, as if swallowed for a demon's consumption.

'The attempt was to be made at dusk; nine o'clock, at this time in August, when the great majority of those on the street returning from work had done so, the children had been put to bed and no more activity was visible than the occasional cab trundling up or down. We also knew that Mr Field and his companions would need to be about their depraved business for successful entry to be forced, because it would clearly be the case that, as no one could hear the attic activities from outside, so no one in the attic would be able to clearly distinguish what was happening below. Even in the dimness of the room where we were gathered, not wishing for any strong lights to draw attention to ourselves, I could see the tension set in the faces of my mainly young companions. None of them can be said to have had genteel paths from birth, but they all disliked deeply the necessity of leaving the young people we had seen taken in to their fate any longer than was absolutely necessary, and none of us knew exactly what his lordship and his companions might have done to them by nine o'clock. I have been in many tense preludes to action of this kind, gentlemen, but I have rarely experienced quite the silent, heavy burden of expectation being carried in that room, a dozen men armed and primed for the most violent of encounters – none of us knew for certain at that stage that Melbury had not detected the plot and a sudden influx of overwhelming force would not arrive as soon as we approached the house. We knew, from careful observation, that no substantial numbers had entered the place within the previous day; there were only the two regular and permanent janitors of the house and four burly individuals who arrived with their masters. The young people within the house would presumably be locked in rooms or otherwise constrained. But the list of our supporting conspirators contained a few names, not including your own, Mr Howell, I do hasten to add, which some of us were not as secure and sanguine about as most on the list.'

R was speaking in a private room in a hotel in Durham, and both of them were only too well aware at that time of the total disappearance of Silas Fletcher immediately after the attempt had been made. Much as Francis detested the implication, he could not deny that his friend should have been there and wasn't.

'The group I was leading, the men who were to make the frontal assault, were almost entirely noiseless as nine o'clock approached; the need for absolute silence at this point had been impressed upon them in the most uncompromising terms, and its observation was surprisingly absolute for a dozen young and heavily armed men. Two cabs were waiting outside Mr Field's house, their horses a little restless and bored, shuffling and occasionally pawing futilely at the street. One in particular, a colt seemingly not entirely trained, one of its owners' attempts at false economy, I suspect, was straying slightly to its left as it tried to get at a flower bed beneath some railings, plants which it obviously thought were edible. The driver was becoming increasingly irritable with it.

'At ten minutes to ten, assemblies of men at either end of the street were clearly happening to those with leisure to watch, albeit with a minimum of disturbance. At one end of the street, to the right of the Field house as we looked at it, the road stopped and a grass verge separated it from the nearby park with a set of railings, and the park was already very murky with no lights available, a perfect way for men to escape later into more or less complete darkness. The cabs were pointing up the street to the left, where a right turn would lead into a wider thoroughfare eventually finishing in the city itself and a left take the rider further into South London and, within no more than twenty to thirty minutes, the counties south of London.

'Figures were emerging from the park trees and moving up to the railings, two or three at a time, and difficult to detect as soon as they had hunkered down behind the railings, though already one or two curtains were twitching in the upper rooms of the houses nearest to the park. Only a few faint sounds and an occasionally indiscreet face peering round the corner indicated that further men were arriving at the other end of the street, gathering themselves on the main thoroughfare.

'I nodded at the men around me; no one spoke. We moved out of the house and covered the fifty or sixty yards to the front door of the Field house without a single word being spoken. I nodded again to my chief lieutenant, an utterly trustworthy man now married to my youngest sister, and he walked slowly up to the first cab driver, detaching a pistol from his inside garments as he went. I didn't hear exactly what he said, but it must have been to the point, because the cab and the one behind were scuttling away within seconds, the colt taking to the notion of movement with particular delight, so much so that the driver had to struggle to force the conveyance round to the left, away into the hinterland and the countryside, the man clearly determined that whatever was happening was not his business and was not going to involve him in any way. As we had anticipated, the cabs' noise drew an inquisitive person from inside the house to part the curtains and look out, and he saw me smile at him, though he could not detect my companions, lined up against the railings behind me. I moved to the door and he opened it. I felt I knew him quite well by then, as we had had him under observation for some days, but I had some knowledge of him even before that, having done my best to acquaint myself with Melbury's habitual lackeys. He was an ex-prize fighter, and the absence of marks on his rather bland, non-descript face showed how good he had been at it; on the strength of this, presumably, he had been taken into Melbury's employ. He could best be described as physically and violently efficient, a fairly typical East End bruiser and survivor who serves whoever pays him best and does not trouble himself too much about his employer's morals and predilections – scrupulous moral observances are luxuries few in the East End can afford. We knew enough of him to know that, limited as his intellectual abilities may be, he was neither stupid nor brain-addled as some ex-pugilists tend to be, and his rugged common sense was one of the lynchpins for the success of our enterprise.

'I greeted him by name, at which he looked surprised and a little suspicious. He turned momentarily at a few noises emanating from the rear of the house, our men from the main thoroughfare moving down and breaking entry through the enclosed rear courtyard, and in those few seconds, a couple of my most agile men had moved up so close to him that banging the door on them was already an impossibility; they were pressing pistols towards him at distances of no more than one foot.

'"Now, my friend," I said quietly, as a succession of dull clumps at the back of the house signified other members of the household being captured or expelled, "you find yourself facing a large group of heavily armed men intent upon their purposes, none of which need concern you. You can submit to being bound or you can withdraw with four of my companions who will take you far away from this place and keep you there until our purposes have been accomplished. I know you have a living to earn like all of us and this will doubtless be a blow to your professional pride, but you must by now know what kind of man your employer is and it is for you to decide whether it is worth your while giving your life for him."

'One of the four men who had been appointed for this purpose nodded encouragingly in his direction, his three companions arranged behind him, and our friend made an instant and quite admirable decision.

'"He is a demon and not what he appears to be" – there spoke the native intelligence of the East End – "and what he pays is not worth this. Do as you will, sir; I will withdraw with these gentlemen."

'At this moment, another of the house staff was emerging from the rear, also accompanied by four men; two of the six had now left. Our reserves were now emerging from the alleys, gardens and houses along the street and piling into the open door of the house. Lights were appearing up and down the street and some of the braver locals were beginning to tentatively emerge from their houses. Things would now happen very rapidly and we needed to retain control of the situation. I moved through to the back of the house. In a lobby next to the kitchen, I saw the inmate who had most worried me, a manservant of Melbury's who was intent on becoming his butler when the present incumbent retired, which was quite imminent, and seemed to be almost entirely immoral, concerned only with his single, obsessive career path. He had clearly refused to withdraw, and was being bound and gagged none too gently by some of my men who resented this complication to their plans. Another of Melbury's men was lying unconscious as he, too, was secured, having been foolish enough to attack several of the invaders. The remaining two of the staff occupants seemed to have fled, and my eyebrows asked a question to my chief lieutenant to the rear; we did not want men going off to raise a hue and cry, especially at Melbury's main London house where dozens were employed or one of the military men on his lordship's payroll.

"'I have a number of very fast men on their tail, sir," said my lieutenant in his gentle Suffolk burr, a man whose speaking voice was always totally at odds with his quickness of thought and action. "They won't get far, and when captured, they will be removed to a safe distance as arranged."

'My confidence was growing; it was already clear that the attack had not been anticipated and we were not walking into a trap, my main fear. Some of Melbury's agents in London were highly intelligent and able men, and as I said before, one or two conspirators had established tendencies towards playing sides off against each other. But Melbury was not now an employer to inspire any great degree of loyalty or affection in his staff, even if he had ever been when younger, and the consensus that something needed to be done about him had perhaps extended to such a point that even if one of his senior staff had been tipped off by a conspirator, they might still be tempted to let everything happen and rid themselves of an increasingly intolerable burden.

'In any event, if our success was to be sustained, speed of action was the essence. The noise, of course, was mounting enormously, as it will in such ventures; some of the poor young creatures imprisoned in the place were beginning to be confident enough to clamour to be released; a number of local people had gathered in front of the house, and the bound prisoners, or at least two of them, were trying to make some kind of noise to alert the gentlemen in the attic. It began to be less and less easy to believe that they had not by now been alerted, and I wondered anxiously as I charged up the stairs and groups of men broke open the various locked doors to our left and right on the way, whether the intelligence supplied by our brave young souls about the sealed nature of the attic was entirely accurate. After all, the circumstances in which they'd found themselves in that room were hardly conducive to dispassionate observation.

'But the room which gave access to the attic was reassuringly exactly in accordance with the boys' description. By this stage, I had only four chosen men with me, the rest dealing with the fracas downstairs. Although there still did not seem to be any clear indication from the attic that they had detected anything untoward, the prevalence of clumps and muffled voices at this proximity was difficult to interpret.

'I hesitated, for no more than about thirty seconds, I suppose, but long enough for the men around me, two of them long-standing friends and colleagues, to direct a few quizzical glances at me. They said nothing; whenever it is the case that one man has to go into a space alone, of necessity because of some operational reason, in this case the narrowness of the staircase leading up to the attic, his companions will wait for a moment of grace, as we call it. Every man who is to put his life in danger is entitled to such a moment. Even as we stood in that room, Melbury could be arranging furniture and friends in such a way and with such weaponry that at least the first five men who entered the room would be shot down where they stood.

'I saw the imaginary figure of a cross before my eyes' – Francis had still not allowed his eyes away from the wooden cross on the altar, as if it had a hypnotic quality, and these very specific words of R's had never left him – 'which suggested to me that my next action might well be my last. I'm ashamed to say that the part I had allocated to myself was not all about bravery and leadership, credible as that may have been to many of my men. We have discussed before, Francis, the repercussions of the failure of our plot, and I have to say that my decision to lead the assault was connected intimately with my desire not to survive the failure of the plot. I had made very careful and very thorough arrangements for the care of my family, who were already well away from any remote chance of being discovered by even the most ingenious of Melbury's men – I have long experience of covering my tracks. I did not want them to be blackmailed into revealing themselves by Melbury holding me as hostage and then bending me to his will forever afterwards, as he has done to a number of men in public service, nor did I want them to be distressed by graphic accounts of my mistreatment at Melbury's hands or return to them a disfigured cripple.

'I also further covered my exposure on entering the attic by shooting the lock off, so that the noise and smoke would cause confusion within, though I knew that would count for nothing if Melbury had already concealed himself and had a gun to hand. So if I have created any supposedly further legends around my name by being the first man to break into the attic, as some of my associated will insist on expressing it, I did so from a number of perfectly prosaic and not very heroic reasons. I say this, Francis, my friend, as I think I may now term you, because I know how little tolerance you have of your own conduct and how difficult you have found it to remain at such extended arm's length during this affair.'

Francis forced his eyes away from the cross at last as he heard the big dogs, if that's what they were, pad past the house again, and this time the passing was followed by a scrabbling at the wooden door. The remorseless enclosure process, dating back to the beginning of the century, had had many consequences, one of them being the relative scarcity of the stray and lost animals on which the feral dogs and foxes had once fed so generously. Some of the largest dogs were becoming so crazed with hunger, with their prey reduced and much more sophisticated ways of chasing them away from human habitation now in use, that the smell of flesh, even human flesh if it was clearly isolated, could impel them to desperate attempts at a fresh kill.

The scrabbling stopped, but the paws did not pad away. Francis felt that they would now be waiting. He thought of the rifle he kept at Peg's side and he knew that Peg would have had the sense to move herself downwind and at a distance far enough for safety. But he had come here for a purpose and he would not leave until he had allowed himself to remember the whole conspiracy in its entirety, remember it in this calm place and his now calmer mind, so as to reduce its proportions and its capacity to control his future life. New crises would have to wait for the moment. If Peg was seriously threatened, he would know, because she would head for where he was. And she was carrying the gun. He allowed R's remembered voice to get to the *coup de grace*.

'I could give you a lengthy description of the scene which met my eyes when I entered that attic, Francis, and it would live with you for the rest of your life, as it will mine. The atmosphere was heavy with terror and some of the basest human smells.

In the semi-darkness, lit by no more than nine or ten candles in a space large enough to run the entire width of the house, and the tormented figures held in the most abject and pitiable circumstances, it was as close to a vision of demonology, the very picture of hell, as I am ever likely to see and will ever want to. Let me try and confine myself to the essential figures in the scene and put away the dark recesses, the looming beamed roof and the blood and God knows what else spattered across the wooden floor. Three young people, two girls and a boy, all completely naked, lean and deathly pale where their skins were not lacerated or blotted with blood, were restrained to the point at which they could not move a single limb or utter any more than a suppressed scream through the thick gags in their mouths, their nakedness totally exposed in the most humiliating and dehumanising way.

'Melbury himself still had a whip in his hand, and now, when the attic door had been closed and virtually all noise below cut off, I could understand from the intent, absorbed expression on his face and the almost insane light emerging from his eyes in the gloom that nothing short of an artillery bombardment on the house would have diverted his attention from his activity. From his position and the angle of the whip, he seemed to be concentrating on one of the girls, and my anger mounted rapidly when I saw that it was one of the two girls his men had tricked into entering the house only a few hours earlier, probably no more than seventeen years old and now a sight so piteous that my men were sharing glances that confirmed their earlier fears.

'One of Melbury's companions was the brother of the cabinet minister I referred to earlier. He had no weaponry to hand, but when he stepped back from the restrained boy and the nature of his state of undress became clear, so did the type of activity in which he had just been indulging. The boy, his head no more than three inches from the floor, was sobbing from his heart and soul in a way which defies my abilities to describe it, but served to inflame my anger still further.

'The moment then arrived when I fear my self-control, the discipline which I imagined I had instilled in myself years before when moving in the sort of circles I do, snapped completely. Melbury was now smiling, or more accurately leering, and he moved across to the other girl, who had apparently been receiving inhumanly brutal treatment with a cane from a man who could not have been less than fifty years old and whose name I did not know, though I had seen him in Melbury's entourage occasionally, a banker or an industrialist, possibly. Melbury pushed him unceremoniously out of the way and grabbed at the girl in such a way as to make her cry out loud. Then his leer widened and his head dropped to peer at me; he lifted his whip towards me and seemed to be offering it, and presumably the girl, to me.

'I walked up to him and I remember the moment now as if it lasted minutes, every single slow movement of my body and his, the gun raising in my hand, the arm he raised as he finally understood my intention, and then the coldness of the barrel of the gun as I briefly ran my fingers over it, the weapon which now I simply could no longer afford not to use. When I placed it against his temple, he turned his eyes to me and I shall never forget the glaze of them and the suddenly desperate pleading they seemed to contain, a soul now so sunk in torment that it pleaded for release, and even though my wild anger had been created from a sense of retributive justice and not any desire to effect an end to his misery, I pulled the trigger all the same and his head blew apart, pieces of blood and brain spattering the wall behind him and his decapitated body hovering absurdly on its feet, as if startled and unknowing how to react, to lurch forward and land at the feet of the boy now released from his ordeal. The boy took a coat from one of my men and wrapped it against his nakedness, then he filled his mouth and spat copiously over Melbury's recumbent body.

'For several minutes, I grappled with my panic and self-disgust, and I eventually realised the scene around me was in danger of descending into chaos. Shooting Melbury in such a way had not been included in our original planning at all, and my men were unsure now, while the released victims were attempting to attack their two remaining tormentors, even before they had had the chance to adequately dress themselves. My men, on their own initiative, which pleased me, had secured both the cabinet minister's brother and the older man, and firmly but gently resisted the efforts of the poor victims to attack them. They were helped to find their discarded clothes from a careless heap in the corner of the room and, as they dressed, a little order and decency returned to the scene, everyone continuing to ignore the obscene mess which was the remains of Melbury.

'Finally, I forced my way back to the door of the attic; through the clatter and chaos below, I could hear the sounds of coaches approaching and I uttered a quick prayer to myself, incongruously enough in such a moment, that they were the conveyances which our plans included, to remove ourselves and our prisoners whether in success or rescue. I made myself heard and something like silence fell.

'"We are going to withdraw, and this attic will be fired behind us, gentlemen, using what we can collect from the stove in the kitchen. All the inmates of the house will also be carried away in the coaches assembling downstairs. Those men who are not included in the escort party will immediately disperse and lose themselves in the anonymity of the city as rapidly as possible."

'I turned towards the two captured men.

'"I will not use the word gentlemen when addressing you. You will be sent to permanent exile; you, sir," I said, looking at the minister's brother, "will communicate with that good man, your unfortunate brother, with whatever story you wish to tell, gambling debts, flight from an unwanted engagement, say what

you will, but if you ever set foot in England again, you will die."
This man had been a problem from the outset; his brother is a
man with such a misguided opinion of him, fraternal and well-
intentioned blinkers, that he would not credit his part in this.
His brother is a very able and well-respected man and the loss
of such a close family member would precipitate an investigation
which could be of such thoroughness and quality as to represent a
threat to the whole conspiracy. The exile I described was the best
choice available to us. Our captive himself had already realised
that myself and the escort I commanded were the only people
who could prevent him being torn to pieces by the assembling
mob outside.

'The next ten minutes were frantic and confused; putting
them into sequence is very difficult. We took our prisoners
downstairs and as soon as we had left the attic, more of my men
were setting up the firing. As we progressed to the pavement
outside, better order had been established than I had feared; the
house's wretched prisoners, ten girls and four boys, some of them
apparently crammed three to a bed, had collected in wonder and
bewilderment in a little protected group, the local people piteous
towards them and vociferous in rage towards their captors. Some
men had set up a shout about troopers, and when a forced near-
silence was formed, the clatter of a troop of horsemen could
clearly be heard, albeit still faintly; one of Melbury's men must
have somehow succeeded in setting up an alert before my men
caught him. We herded all the ex-prisoners into the coaches with
an escorting party of my men, and at this point, flames began to
billow thickly over the house as the attic took fire.

'As the coaches moved away and my close colleagues began
to lift the two captives into the coach, the older of them lost his
head completely and was foolish enough to try to run away, even
though his hands were tied behind him. Before I or any of my men
could do anything, the mob descended on him and quite literally

tore him to pieces; when the soldiers turned into the street no more than fifteen minutes later, his remains were unrecognisable and as far as my inquiries have been able to ascertain, his identity has not yet been established to this day.

'We fled the scene at the maximum pace the horses would allow, and still no sound of pursuing troopers had begun by the time London gave way to open countryside and we could disperse to our several planned destinations. By the time of the troopers' arrival, the house was ablaze beyond redemption, his lordship in it, and, as you may know from your examination of journals and periodicals, the baffling disappearance of Lord Melbury continues to exercise the cleverest of minds, there being no one in the area of Mr Field's house who knew his alias and none of Melbury's ex-employees prepared to involve themselves in investigations which could incriminate them in running that disorderly house.

'Melbury's surviving accomplice, the minister's brother, met his end in the English Channel when the crew of the ship transporting him found out from some careless fellow temporarily in my employment and who will not be so again who their distinguished passenger was and, more importantly, why he was fleeing the country, though at least the foolish fellow had enough sense not to refer to Melbury. The sailors arranged an accident, as sailors can and do, as our captive exercised on the deck in the evening, and my understanding is that his poor brother has accepted an unhappy accident while the fellow had drunk too much (his habits in this direction were well known). The fact that his brother was apparently travelling abroad did not disturb the minister; he and the members of his family did so quite frequently.

'So we have succeeded totally, Francis, in removing the iniquitous and dissolute peer from the face of the earth without any real prospect of repercussions, and have only now to discuss the future of the poor wretches released from Melbury's two whore houses, at present enjoying a pleasant rural confinement. They have been reassured that any of them who wish to return to their former lives will be allowed to do so after a suitable interval, but also given to understand that, should they not wish to do so, other more amenable paths will be made available to them. You have explained to me, Francis, your most generous and humane idea of establishing the kind of training in domestic service which many of them thought they were going to originally with the possible help of your dear sister, should her recovery continue and be consolidated, for which we hope and pray.

'But my trade is such that even triumphs can leave me heavy-hearted, and I can no longer think of myself in total honesty as anything other than a murderer, with a willingness to indulge in extreme violence which I cannot entirely convince myself was wholly justified even by the circumstances of my provocation. Those of us who convince ourselves that we walk with the foot soldiers of Satan for the best of purposes cannot entirely achieve absolution when we have to reflect on the base deeds done in such service. My peace of mind is an adaptable creature, Francis; it has had to be, but I fear this affair has dealt it a blow from which it may never fully recover.'

Francis was acutely aware that, in spite of his complete absence from the scene and his innocence of any direct assault on Melbury, he shared R's lament for his peace of mind and couldn't expunge the phrase 'accessory to murder' from his mind. He had helped to fund the project and willingly assented to its outcome being a deliberate and premeditated fatality, and the clearer it became that no repercussions would follow, the more his conscience, elastic and adaptable as he now deemed it to be in the worst sessions of sneering and self-denigration, seemed to adopt the prosecutor role which circumstances had spared him. There also remained the mysterious absence of Silas Fletcher, which R was less concerned about now that it couldn't materially affect the outcome of the conspiracy, but it remained disturbing and puzzling, and a certain look in R's eyes had appeared, albeit briefly, when Silas had failed to appear at the Durham meeting. Even though Francis's protestations about complete ignorance had appeared to have been accepted readily enough, R would not let the issue be, he knew, until the questions had been answered.

The need which had driven Francis to St Cuthbert's, to reflect once again on the whole Melbury affair in the hope that he could discipline his emotions into a more tolerable order, remained achingly unsatisfied, and alone in the church, a lean, crushed figure surrounded but not absolved by the modest virtue of its surroundings, Francis felt an insignificance and desolation he could not remember having experienced before. He felt his youth dying away and feared for what would remain of him after its ignominious death throes were finally done with, what perjured and spent shell of a man would be left to face the possibly even more formidable challenges ahead.

But he had no sooner begun to sink into the morass of pitiless self-analysis which the surrounding silence allowed when he was roughly and urgently hauled back into the immediate world. One of the dogs, obviously no longer able to contain itself at the undeniable scent of potential meat inside the church, clattered its body so violently against the door that the hinges creaked alarmingly and Francis got to his feet. The other dog, clearly not as large and powerful, repeated the exercise within seconds, and though it did not achieve the same impact, Francis judged that not many further attacks would be needed before the door would be opened to the extent of allowing the beasts to force an entry.

Francis thought quickly. If this represented some kind of retribution, if this was the fate which his agonised musings had summoned up for him, he was not prepared to accept it meekly. He was not prepared to accept it at all, in fact, and in no more than a few split seconds, he knew that his resolve to expunge the demonic Melbury from the world would have remained throughout an even greater set of obstacles and self-examinations.

Whatever the rights or wrongs, the truth was beyond dispute or denial.

The thought galvanised and exhilarated him, and even the great starving beasts crashing into his peace with no other desire than to feast on his flesh, dead or alive as he may be, were opponents he could face without fear or submission.

He moved to the side of the door, the dogs becoming even louder at the increasing scent of him, and, judging his movement to coincide with hearing the creatures' big feet approaching, he waited until they touched the door and then flung the door inwards. Both animals fell headlong into the church and momentarily became no more than a chaotic moving pile of limbs, while Francis whistled for Peg at the fullest volume he could manage. By the time the fallen dogs had risen, Peg was approaching at speed, and she drew up beside him, the four of them stood in a tense confrontational group, the dogs breathing heavily with their efforts to break the door.

Peg was whinnying quietly, reluctantly, her flanks moving slowly as she strove to control herself from taking flight. The dogs were slightly crouched, the hunters watching and observing, judging the moment to spring. They looked gaunt, non-existent bellies almost disappearing into their bodies, but still with immense power in the back legs particularly. They were mongrels, but Francis guessed both Alsatians and wolves were involved, the creatures probably being the offspring of some discarded guard dogs sent to fend for themselves, or the consequence of some wolf raid on an isolated Scottish homestead. Clearly, they were desperate; Francis knew enough about such animals to know that their desperation increased proportionately with their hunger, and to launch attacks upon humans, let alone buildings containing humans, they would need to be very desperate indeed. Even now, at the peak of their blood lust and slavering hunger, they had paused at the sight of the man and the horse with its size and potentially lethal hooves.

Francis knew he could jump on Peg and be gone; Peg's speed and assurance would leave the dogs behind in seconds. The horse was aching to be away and only her deeply ingrained loyalty – Francis had been close to her ever since she was a foal – kept her something like still. But the wild dogs were now very dangerous indeed. With so many creatures now fenced and barned in well-protected enclosures, they had nothing but small vermin and birds to feed on, and they were animals who needed a generous supply of meat to prosper. If they were prepared to attack a stone building because flesh was in it, they would find less formidable buildings and tear someone to pieces, probably before the day was out, and that could well include one of Charlotte's ladies coming to attend to church matters or the curate himself, resulting in a local scandal which would take an innocent life and rebound badly on the Thirwells. Francis had been a landowner and northern gentleman long enough to be able to consider the implications of a local situation in a matter of seconds. How the dogs had arrived at their state was not his immediate concern; no doubt there had been a time when the creatures were simply dogs and perhaps even of some use to someone.

But there were times, as in the exploits of Lord Melbury, when the present and future had to take precedence over the past, and when explanations mattered less than action. It might be an unpalatable truth at times, but truth it undeniably was.

Francis watched the dogs carefully as he removed his rifle from its bag attached to his saddle. He thought momentarily of R's advice to him to carry a gun at all times, and R's reassured, knowing manner when Francis assured him that he always did anyway. The kind of encounter with feral animals which Francis had just experienced was not common, but neither was it particularly rare, especially with the consequences of enclosure, and while an attempt on Howell Grange remained a very remote possibility because of the number of men required, the northern land outside the few towns and villages could be an inhospitable and dangerous place for human as well as animal reasons. Men who preferred robbery and living wild to pit work or domestic service, drifters looking for isolated opportunities, unemployed and desperate young men with no training in anything, there were reasons enough for a gun by the saddle and ready bullets in it.

As the animals moved towards him, edging apart as they approached, Francis realised he could not deal with a two-pronged attack or keep Peg from panic for much longer. He raised the gun to his shoulder and looked carefully through the sights as the bigger animal slunk to his left, shooting it cleanly and accurately in the side of the head. He watched for a second as it thudded to the ground, briefly convulsing, and then he turned quickly to his right and shot again as the other dog was in mid-flight, catching it between the eyes at point blank range. Even death could not stop the momentum of its leap, and Francis fell backwards with its inert body still on him, a body reeking with all the basest scents of the countryside. Peg had been on many a hunt and gunshots did not seriously upset her, but as he fell beneath the dog, she let out a high-pitched neigh of anxiety and moved towards him. He pushed the dog away, amazed at the weight even of its shrunken and half-starved carcass. As he swung on to the horse and began to move away, he looked back briefly at the two wretched corpses. Whatever causes a mad dog to become such, whatever the cruel twists and impositions practised by nature to create such a creature, every choice had consequences, and the more vacillating and compromised the choice, the more drastic the consequences threatened to be.

Francis had only ridden for five minutes before he realised his mood had changed completely. The weather was significantly better, tending more to August than September, and waves of sun were sweeping across the fields with the shadows and dull corners in headlong retreat. For the moment, foreboding and brooding anxiety had given way to triumph, an awareness of victory consolidated, and although he knew well enough the truth of R's caveat about those who opposed mining safety, he also could not forget the extraordinary verbal list of people in industrial and political life who were controlled or heavily influenced by Melbury, some of them men he knew and respected, and prospects were much improved now, beyond all question. The exhilaration of sun and summer breeze, clean country air and ground firm enough for Peg to fly over without her niggling discomforts on the hard winter surfaces, brought him back into the stables in an invigorated, redeemed frame of mind, which Thomas noticed before he had dismounted.

'Thomas, I had to shoot a couple of feral dogs outside St Cuthbert's; they are still there, now thoroughly dead, happily. Could you either get a couple of men over there to bury them in the wood, or, if you're short-handed, get a message across to the Thirwells?'

'Yes, sir; we've the men to do it ourselves at the moment. Mr Armstrong is being generous with the staff numbers these days, sir.' He nuzzled up to Peg and patted her steaming shank as Francis began to walk away.

'You shot your wild demons now, then, sir?'

Francis turned and looked back, wondering whether he could really credit Thomas with the implications the words had. The man was still easing down Peg, feeling the aftermath of her alarm and fear and soothing it as best he could. Francis had known Thomas since they were both boys, but he felt at that moment like he'd never really properly looked at the fellow before. Now he did, and saw behind the country accent and the surly manner an intelligence and sympathy which surprised him with its simple clarity. Thomas saw as much as he watched, he thought, and sometimes more.

'Yes, I think so, for the moment, at least. Thank you, Thomas.'

'Thank you, sir.'

As soon as Francis had passed through the portico into the grandiose lobby of the Grange, Armstrong suddenly appeared beside him in the disconcerting way he had.

'A personal letter has arrived for you, sir. It looked as if it might conceivably be of some importance, so I had it taken to your desk in the library, sir.'

'Good, Armstrong. I will attend to it now. Is Miss Alice actually up and about?'

'Yes, sir, she is.' Francis heard the ring of satisfaction in the man's voice, and warmed to it. 'On such a beautiful day now, sir, Miss Alice is in the conservatory, well wrapped up and comfortable, catching up with a few London papers.'

'Could you let her know that I will come to her in fifteen minutes or so, Armstrong?'

'Very good, sir.'

Francis looked at the letter, placed carefully and very centrally on his desk blotter. He did not recognise the handwriting, but that came as no surprise; he had become quite used to communications which took pains to disguise their sender in some way. But Armstrong was right; it did have a look of significance, and when he opened it, the handwriting inside was familiar enough.

4 September 1866

My dear Francis,

I have deliberately not addressed the letter; I am in the Netherlands, but for the moment I do not intend to specify my whereabouts more precisely. I know from various sources that our efforts have met with success, but I am remaining true to our friend's habitual counsel of caution.

I fear my disappearance will inevitably have caused a good deal of anxiety to you and all of my friends, and I cannot in all honesty blame anyone if some questions have arisen concerning my probity and my fidelity to our aims. However, I consider that when you have understood the situation in which I found myself, you will probably concede that I had no real choice and find some forgiveness for me.

I must necessarily explain myself a little circuitously in the interests of my stated caution, but my alarm was raised some time ago in the House when I saw a member who is a known associate of the man I shall simply refer to as M clearly eavesdropping on a coffee house conversation of a group of colleagues including two of our friends. One of our friends, I regret to say, was misguided enough to refer to 'our organisation', with significant glances at two others who I believe he wanted to join our friends, and was even reckless enough to utter the sentence, 'including Howell and Fletcher, amongst others'. Our other friend in the group coped admirably, laughing off 'such cloak and dagger nonsense, Routledge, it is simply a group to exchange knowledge and new information on mining technicalities', but something must have made its garbled way back to M, probably associating the mining issue, the existence of a group and our names together – not enough for M to arrive at any specific conclusions, but clearly enough to make him suspicious. You were already moving North with your sister in a heavily escorted and protected coach, so I had little anxiety on your behalf, and most of our other friends had left London or were about to do so. I had financial business which necessitated my presence in London for rather longer, and, I confess, a bravado at that time about not letting perceived threats interfere with my legitimate activities. Would that I had paid more attention to our friend's strictures and less to my own commercial concerns. Some days later, I heard from one of my usual sources, at very short notice, that a group of M's men were intending to take an early opportunity to waylay me as I moved from the House to my place of business and take me to 'a place of interrogation', under the guise of me simply being set upon by a gang of thieves and robbed, where severe pressure would be applied to obtain information.

A charitable reading of my subsequent actions over the next few days is that I acted expeditiously and in all of our best interests, though less forgiving souls might be more inclined to term it panic. However, whatever the interpretation might be, the facts are that I immediately changed my route, making it unpredictable and long-winded, and discussed the situation with my wife, with a certain editing of names and circumstances. Georgina and I have never had children, as you know, for reasons which need not concern us at the moment, and both her wider family and my own reside in places far from London. Everyone, certainly including M, who is not a fool, whatever else he might be, knows well enough that I do not confide my business to anyone but my wife, and then only when it contains information which she needs to know. I think it is not fanciful of me to claim that my reputation as a secure keeper of confidences is entrenched enough, perhaps one of the reasons for our friend's approach to me in the first place, and I flatter myself that M's intention to lay hands on me arose from nothing more than the situation of my being the sole member of our 'group' still accessible in London. But I cannot deny that it was probably not the only reason.

I know some think of me as tending towards the dandy or the fop, though dressing properly is not a characteristic which I would personally understand as sinful. However, I am not a soldier or a hunter or, as I rather suspect you are, Francis, a stoic. I could not guarantee to myself that being at the mercy of M's thugs for any length of time would not cause me to blurt out anything and everything I knew; I could establish red herrings and false trails if my wit remained with me, but M's hirelings are reputed men who will stop at very little. I concluded, Francis, rightly or wrongly, that our interests would be best served if Georgina and I decided, not unusually at such a time of the year, to visit the continent, without incriminating any of our friends by communicating with them before we went.

So, within two days of receiving the warning, my wife and I had crossed the Channel, and here we have stayed, moving about at regular intervals and continuing our incommunicado policy. Only last week, when I heard one of our friends was staying at a hotel not thirty miles away, did I finally approach one of our 'group' and discover the substance of what has taken place.

I regret, more than I can say, any anxiety I have caused to our friends and particularly yourself. I have also written to our main friend, if I may term him so, by circuitous means. It is also a source of some mortification to me that my entire contribution to our enterprise has amounted to a judicious and less than intrepid absence, but it is sometimes best, I feel, to understand and recognise one's limitations, knowing as I did that a few hours of the extremities of pain and humiliation which M's men would inflict could cause the ruination of all our hopes and many of the friends I most esteem and admire finding themselves subjected to the same fate.

So, try not to think too harshly of me, Francis, my dear friend, and I hope it will not be too much longer now before we can once again take the pleasure in each other's company which is such a delight for old companions. Which is how I pray you will continue to think of me,

Your sincere friend,

Silas F.

Francis stood for some minutes gazing down at the writing before him. Tears had risen unbidden to his eyes, another example of the phenomenon he was beginning to understand, the human spirit's equivalent of the calm after the storm, when the immediacy of action and the need for ceaseless vigilance has faded and the cauldron of doubts, fears and deep-seated insecurities could be finally stilled by reflection and contemplation. He could see now what an appalling wound Fletcher's treachery would have inflicted on him, had it been proved, underlining his naivety and lack of judgement in his metropolitan life and putting everyone close to him in mortal danger. Now Melbury was dead and Silas was true, but present realities could not entirely dismiss past suppositions. He placed the letter in a locked drawer and headed for his own quarters, there to wash his face and make himself reassuringly presentable to his ailing sister.

He looked round the door of the anteroom which led into the conservatory, with its abundance of windows within an ornate green wrought iron frame and a range of enthusiastically maintained plants, some of them very alien indeed, which allowed Robson the gardener to indulge his love of botanical diversity and experimentation. She was sitting in one of the beautiful armchairs, upholstered in yellow, which his mother had chosen to match the light surroundings. She was dwarfed by the chair and even to some extent by the newspaper spread widely before her. He could see her tiny, stick-like wrists emerging from her dress; the pallor of illness was still on her, and her hair, thinner and longer, had been subjected to no more than the few token strokes with a hairbrush which was all she had ever allowed since childhood. She was, as ever, entirely self-possessed and self-contained, the same fiercely defended if occasionally benevolent little island she had always been. For a moment, he could not move, as a long-standing reluctance to disturb her, a lasting sense that she had more important matters to deal with than him, returned again.

Now he remained dry-eyed. Mr Wordsworth had featured in his schooling, and 'thoughts too deep for tears' was a phrase which had occurred to him more than once since the outbreak of the Melbury business. What had turned him momentarily to stone was the sudden certainty that the loss of her would have been the unkindest cut of all; she pre-dated Emily and everyone else, she had been so often his only sanctuary in a mad household, she who could listen without impatience or even criticism until he had finished what he had to say and then address it with a directness and honesty which was, yes, sometimes uncompromising and outspoken, but never failed to be of some use, a pointer forwards or an indication of a new path. She had the real ability to help and a bizarre core of strength somehow contained within her bony little frame. He could remember overhearing Armstrong, having just come down from her bedroom, answering another servant's inquiry as he went into the kitchen area: 'She is improving, as she will; it will take much more than pneumonia to make an end of *her.*' Unlike almost everyone else in the family, she helped him rather than inflicted herself on him. He had missed her deeply and now planned an attempt to honourably ensure that they could at least be in some proximity, even after whoever it was who would arrive in her life had done so.

She greeted him with the same unaffected warmth as she always had, and he could actually feel a little warmth in her hands at long last as he took them. A few minutes of inconsequential conversation and a close examination of her eyes and face convinced him that she was well enough for them to talk with their old frankness and thoroughness.

'Alice,' he said, 'I have something to tell you, to fulfil my promise to you in London that when I could tell you, I would, about why it was not just your illness that necessitated the flight from London and about the kind of deep waters your foolish brother has been splashing about in. Even now, there are names I cannot mention and events which I cannot describe as thoroughly and explicitly as I would like, but the skeleton can be told, even with the addition of a little flesh here and there.'

Adult matters replaced those of childhood and adolescence, but the pattern of their communication began in the way it so often had, Francis talking, sometimes with great animation and gesticulation, and Alice listening, interjecting only to help his flow of speech, her eyes following him one minute and turning away abstractedly when he said something which made her thoughtful.

He told her everything he decently could, without naming Melbury or even using the initial R – R he referred to as 'our leader'. It took him a while to tell it all, and neither of them heard Armstrong open the anteroom door and gaze towards them. Armstrong was always the man whose duty it was to investigate when the routine of the house was disturbed, and there was a certain amount of below stairs disturbance at the lack of lunch arrangements and the possibility of them having their own meals immediately interrupted when the two Howells now in the house eventually decided what they wanted to do.

At that moment, Francis was standing before Alice in a stiff, dignified manner, his left arm apparently held with the palm outwards as if he was making a speech, and Alice was wide-eyed and leaning forward with, Armstrong was gratified to note, two distinct little flushes of red on her cheeks. Francis was actually describing his intimidating meeting with his lordship and momentarily taking on the part of his lordship, whose name he'd adopted from Silas – simply 'M'. Armstrong made his decision, moving away and closing the door quietly behind him. He felt sure that what they were doing would prove to be of more use to both of them than even the grandest lunch.

It took Francis a good while to describe even his skeleton in the detail he could, and by the time he'd finished, he was sitting in the chair nearest to her, staring straight into her eyes, which were more alive and aware than he had seen them for some time.

'So I am an accessory to murder, Alice; however it is dressed up or clouded, that is what it amounts to. I have connived at the death of a fellow human being. I tell you this because I promised I would, and I tell you more than I will ever tell Mother, Charlotte, Anne or even Emily. I have examined myself again and again, I have been to St Cuthbert's and flagellated myself in my mind, I have tried to persuade myself that my regrets are so deep and abiding that nothing would ever induce me to become involved in such a thing again. But my regrets are neither deep nor abiding; M is no more to me than the feral dogs I had to slaughter outside the church, and if I had to contrive to remove such a creature again, I would. This is the brother you see before you. Despise me if you must, but I beg you not to convey the knowledge you have, even in the most diluted form, to anyone else in the family. I share the burden with you because of my promise, and because I knew in St Cuthbert's today that I had to share it with someone, that making a totally internally held secret of it would make it some kind of poison inside me. Am I still to be your loving brother, when I come to you with blood on my hands?'

She took one of his hands in both of hers and was surprised to feel how cold and still it was.

'Blood on the hands,' she repeated. 'Tell me, Francis, those years ago at Gran's funeral, when Charlie asked you how many men do you think he'd seen die, would you ever have dared to ask him how many men he has caused to die? Charlie must have killed men with rifles, perhaps cannons, almost certainly, somewhere along the way, with his bare hands. Was he a demon to be cast into some wilderness, or was he a soldier doing what everyone told him was his duty? Our father, and let us not be mealy-mouthed about it, Francis, had caused hundreds of people to die, some of them no more than children, by the time he died himself, for no more reason than to maintain levels of coal production which pleased his board. For this, he would often neglect even the most rudimentary safety procedures.'

Alice's eyes fell and Francis felt her grip tighten on his hand.

'And I cannot deny that your sister also has blood on her hands, Francis. During the time when I worked with Nathaniel and Sarah, there were occasions when we had to deal with poverty-stricken wretches in the East End who were so ill and in such a squalor of pain and misery, with not the remotest possibility of ever emerging from it, that all three of us sometimes contrived to put them out of their misery, sometimes letting an ordeal which our treatments and medicines could have prolonged into days to end in hours, sometimes, God help us, actually administering a *coup de grace* in the guise of a new method of treatment. Even in the mines, there have been times when Samuel and I have looked at each other and tacitly agreed not to delay the inevitable or actively contrived to bring it about. Agony is almost as unendurable to the watcher as it is to the sufferer. You speak to me of foot soldiers of Satan, Brother; he, also his attendants and handmaidens, believe me, all of them seeing themselves, as we do, in a kind of righteous disguise and doomed to spend the rest of their lives wondering whether that is how they will be seen when judgement comes. If it comes, though it seems to me that judgment is more appropriate for the creators of such human disasters than it is for those who merely seek to ameliorate their effects.'

Francis stood up and she withdrew her hands from him as he bent to kiss her cheek, touching her shoulder as he did so and wondering at almost the sheer bone under his hand. He knew this was the time to put his idea to her, that following such a bewailing of the past with hope and inspiration for the future would assist her process of recovery, and when he talked of schemes and innovations, he invariably needed to be on his feet, as if testing whether or not the idea would be good enough to stand up to a public scrutiny.

'What's done cannot be undone, sister, but if we seek redemption or amelioration, we do at least have the means to do it. I cannot stop you from doing what you have decided to do, and would not even if I could. If you are intent on returning to the East End, I would only beg of you that you ensure something like a return to full health and strength, and ask you to at least consider the scheme I want to suggest.'

Alice looked up at him quizzically. Some of her worst invalid days had been spent in the debate he thought he had a way of resolving, and she clutched at the hope that he would. Whatever the defiantly independent spirit inside her might continue to assert, her reason told her that her health was not strong enough to sustain East End work for very long, especially if the dire living conditions of so many of the inhabitants stayed much as they were, and no one was doing very much to prevent that from happening. It was the height of vanity and foolishness to be so blind to one's own weaknesses that the crusade or whatever it is ends in nothing more than an early death. She knew that, sooner or later, others would walk through the gate which Elizabeth Anderson had so bravely opened, but it was taking time, and she did not want hers to run out before the chance came.

'As I intimated earlier, we have a number of young people in our care, still being provided for by the funds set up in aid of the conspiracy, which our leader insisted should be sufficient to allow for certain contingencies which didn't, thank God, arise. We took a total of fifteen girls and nine boys from M's two houses, some of them kept three or four to a room, all of them having been virtually imprisoned, many in chains or shackles. In almost every case, they had come from other parts of London or, more frequently, well out of London, in order to be trained in domestic service, or so they had been told. Our agents in London have already picked up another two poor souls who were clearly heading for one or other of M's houses and were highly sceptical of our allegations until they talked to some of M's ex-captives. It has been made clear to all of the young people that they are no longer captives and may leave whenever they choose, but we have also said that there are prospects of permanent arrangements being made, and so far none of them have left. They are all still deeply disturbed by their experiences and many have serious injuries, none of them now life-threatening but some likely to remain inhibitions and handicaps for the rest of their lives.'

Alice's face flushed anger, this time with raw anger, and it somehow heartened her that she could still feel injustice so deeply.

'I would like to think that this M is now receiving judgement, and that his expectations of mercy may be of the same stamp as those of his victims in his hands,' she said.

'Yes,' Francis said, 'and when you look at the living consequences of his iniquity, you can only wish it so. However, I have taken soundings and made investigations. One of our long-standing tenants, Ralph Robertson of Bucklands Farm, died last year at the age of seventy-nine, his wife having predeceased him by three years. Two of his children had already married and left the area for different trades in the South; the eldest, Jeb, remained only to assist his father until the end, but he is essentially a horseman and breeder and he doesn't want to continue the tenancy. He has accepted an offer from Eustace Thirwell to work in their stables, where he can live comfortably and does not face the unequal battle of maintaining Bucklands on his own.

'Bucklands is rundown, inevitably after the old man's declining years; he was offered estate support and sometimes took it, but he would try to manage with no more than himself and poor Jeb. If we were to establish an entirely reputable school for training in domestic service, there are enough buildings in terms of the farmhouse and the barns to accommodate living quarters and teaching areas for up to forty girls. The boys can be trained in the various stables, agricultural workshops, farms or domestic establishments we own, on the basis of apprenticeships, according to their particular abilities, and housed where the men live, with additional quarters added here and there where necessary. I believe that the girls' training school will pay for itself in a fairly short space of time. Many people in the area and beyond will appreciate a regular supply of properly trained and respectable servants and be prepared to support the school to ensure the supply continues. Likewise, demand for boys thoroughly trained on the premises where they are to work will sustain their side of it. I believe that the conspiratorial fund will contribute handsomely to the setting up of the school after my encouraging conversations with our leader on the subject.

'I think it very likely that the Thirwells and the Harringtons, Mother and her brother Randoph will do likewise, though I have yet to speak of this with them. I think Silas Fletcher would also help. And, as you know, the Howell coffers are still generously maintained.'

He paused and looked down at her. He had been organising his thoughts and talking half to himself, but he could see the eagerness and unfeigned interest in her face and he felt instantly encouraged.

'For the girls' training school, several staff will be needed who are experts in their fields. What I am suggesting to you, Alice, is that you become Superintendent of the school, responsible for the girls' health and welfare. Arrangements for the boys can be assimilated into the provisions already available in their workplaces, but you would be at liberty to take an interest in that area as well should you choose to do so. The world would understand you to be a senior nurse, but you would in fact be a *de facto* doctor in charge of all the girls who attended the school; admitting them, supervising their training and helping them to obtain employment. I could also arrange for our channels to London to be kept open for intercepting at least a few further unfortunates who stray into the clutches of the metropolitan demons, and establish local rescue networks if similar nefarious schemes are shown to exist in the northern towns nearest to us. Such investigations could continue to be an undercover concern of our conspiratorial group.'

Francis suddenly abandoned his public speech manner and sat beside her again, his eyes ablaze with hope and enthusiasm.

'Please say yes, Alice. You would be here amongst us, doing valuable and worthwhile work for which you are now admirably prepared. We have all missed you and feared for you; we all know and respect your wish for independence and making your own way, but is it not now true that you have made your way, that you have worked in the mines with Samuel and in the East End with Nathaniel and Sarah, experiencing the most grim and extreme conditions you are ever likely to see, facing the challenges and emerging from them? Of course, I must be in London for the House for some of the time, but to see you when I come back here is something else I would personally treasure, if you can bear to carry on listening to my confessions, doubts and miseries. But you will need time to consider, and you are still unwell. Perhaps we can return to the subject—'

'No, Francis.' He flinched back, trying to reconcile her words with her shining eyes.

'I don't need to consider, and I am well enough now. It is a calling which pleases me greatly, something which I know I can do and would take pleasure in doing, and your thought and consideration is to bring it about. Thank you, Francis. Thank you for giving me peace of mind and hope for the future; my recovery will be so much the sweeter and faster for it.'

They were still talking, fast and half-breathless like excited teenagers, when Reece Wharton arrived for the scheduled visit, and they realised they had not only completely forgotten about his visit, but that neither of them had eaten anything since breakfast. Francis realised how ravenously hungry he'd become after his morning ride and confrontation, and Alice felt something returning to her which felt remarkably like appetite – almost an alien sensation, like long lost aroma from childhood. Wharton himself was his usual extrovert and engaging self, having completely lost his awe of the Howells with the passage of years and the death of their grim patriarch. Francis had taken an informed interest in photography since the grim days of 1852. Reece had become a friend, with Francis able to put occasional commissions his way. Reece's extravagant dress and expansive manner amused and somehow heartened him, as if the world did not necessarily need to be entirely populated by serious men with austere manners and dark coats. Wharton, he knew, had some curious habits and preferences; on one unannounced visit to his city studio, Francis had found him engaged in taking pictures against a set representing Ancient Greece, and he was at first startled to see that the group of men being photographed were either scantily clad or, in the case of four of them, completely naked. Reece's explanation amounted to no more than a broad grin and the words 'Olympics, you see. None of the competitors wore anything at all. Historical accuracy, for some of my classical collectors.' Francis found himself returning the broad grin and, in response to Wharton's outrageous eye-rolling, bursting into laughter.

Reece was accompanied, as he always was these days, by a younger blond assistant called David, and the interplay between them did suggest that the whole basis of their relationship was not necessarily photography. However, Francis was the kind of man who generally believed in living and letting live, and knew very well that Reece was much too clever a man to allow himself or any of his friends to be compromised in any way.

The conservatory was suddenly transformed from a place of enterprise and serious discussion to a riot of noise and laughter. Reece was so genuinely and fulsomely glad to see Alice 'up and about, look at you, fresh as a new grown daisy, I do declare it!', a description so ludicrously inaccurate that Alice was reduced to tears of laughter and Francis warmed to his friend. David hovered about, looking mildly disgusted and obviously wanting Reece to get to some pre-planned professional activity they must have discussed between them.

'Oh, yes,' Reece began, eventually, after the elaborate series of greetings and exchanged had begun to subside. 'We do have a series of pictures in mind, Howells all, Mr Francis, Miss Alice, I must mention, before David bursts apart with anticipation. We are trying to introduce rather more animation and – what shall we call it? – being natural, let's say, into our portraiture. Of course, there will always be those for whom a portrait cannot really be a portrait unless they are sitting bolt upright and frowning at the camera, in stuffed shirts and collars around their ears, but the exposure time no longer requires long stretches of statuesque immobility, thank goodness; it's time enough to hold even a quite active pose, and where the pioneers and fashion setters go, it behoves us mortals and imitators to follow, so how would you feel about such a thing, Howells all? Something a little less formal, not quite so forbidding, to enter the family album? My gift, of course, on this occasion, a chance for me to celebrate the triumphant recovery of the lovely Alice in my own special way?'

Francis found a little authority through his smile.

'Of course, Reece. But my sister and I have been so remiss and so enmeshed in our discussions that we've neglected to eat and are now both ravenous. On such an extraordinary day, I suggest we all take an early tea in the garden, if I can grovel to Armstrong and the long-suffering kitchen staff convincingly enough, and when we have slaked our hunger and thirst, you will have your pictures to your heart's content, Reece.'

So Armstrong allowed himself to be amiably persuaded and tables and chairs were set up on the lawns at the back of the Grange. David, to his initial little twists of indignation, quickly curbed by glares from both Reece and Armstrong, was given the duties of bringing and setting up the equipment, with occasional conciliatory sandwiches and cakes from a serving maid, and the three friends enjoyed the sun and each other's company.

When they'd finished eating, Reece was telling a particularly risqué and outrageous tale about the Classical Greek session which Francis had interrupted, and he became so absorbed in it that he succeeded in tripping over his camera legs and almost dragging the entire thing over, to David's screech of despair. Reece was sitting on the ground looking up and said, 'That, Howells all, is truly beautiful. Hold that, please, now, hold that just as you are.'

So Francis and Alice, feeling a little foolish but determined on cooperation, did, and the best of the ensuing four photographs was framed and hung, a celebration forever afterwards of the day in September 1866 when two foot soldiers of Satan took their well-earned and overdue leave.